'We accompany Fandorin on a breathless gallop through duels, evil temptresses, doublecrossing agents, ghostly visitations, and several attempts on the hero's life which are foiled, happily, by his habit of wearing the "Lord Byron corset" . . . [Akunin's] clever interweaving of literary allusions and jokey elaborations on 19th-century literary themes give his novels a broader set of references than most crime writing'   Charlotte Hobson, *Daily Telegraph*

'It is all written with splendid style, panache, inventiveness, humour and self-awareness, and it is no wonder that Akunin's novels, featuring this hero, have been a huge success in Russia. They are perfect examples of escapist literature'

Allan Massie, *Scotsman*

'The novels can be read as a course in late 19th century Russian history . . . they are extraordinarily readable, full of incident and excitement, swift-moving and told with a sparkling light-heartedness which is impossible to resist'

T. J. Binyon, *Evening Standard*

'. . . a sparkling romp of a story . . . [with a] witty and beautifully constructed plot . . . *The Winter Queen* has echoes of the plots of the nineteenth-century classics all Russians know: duels, reckless gambling, superfluous men and mysterious beauties whose salons are full of despairing admirers'   Vanora Bennett, *TLS*

'He's [Fandorin] . . . an engaging personality – conscientious, honourable, and pleasingly naive. Hence one feels the instant appeal of this gentle mystery, and appreciates the extraordinary Russian success of Boris Akunin . . . It's a parable about the death of hope and innocence, as well as an effectively concocted story'

Lesley Chamberlain, *Independent*

'Boris Akunin has written a series of novels set in Tsarist Russia in the 1870s and featuring Erast Fandorin, a naive young police investigator . . . the story propels the idealistic Fandorin into the company of enigmatic and beautiful women, devious conspirators and a most unlikely Svengali intent on world domination . . . This may not be what we expect from Russian fiction, but it's all very fast-moving and enjoyable'   Nick Rennison, *Crime Time*

'The mixture of the grisly and the lighthearted is characteristic of Boris Akunin, who in Russia is roughly the counterpart of John Grisham . . . *The Winter Queen* is as delicate and elegant as a Fabergé egg'   Lev Grossman, *Time magazine*

Boris Akunin is the pseudonym of Grigory Chkhartishvili. He has been compared to Gogol, Tolstoy and Arthur Conan Doyle, and his Erast Fandorin books have sold over eight million copies in Russia alone. He lives in Moscow.

By Boris Akunin

The Winter Queen
Turkish Gambit
Leviathan
The Death of Achilles

The Winter Queen

BORIS AKUNIN

Translated by Andrew Bromfield

PHOENIX

A PHOENIX PAPERBACK

First published in Great Britain in 2003
by Weidenfeld & Nicolson
This paperback edition published in 2004
by Phoenix,
an imprint of Orion Books Ltd,
Orion House, 5 Upper St Martin's Lane,
London WC2H 9EA

First published in the Russia as *Azazel* in 1998
by I. Zakharov

3 5 7 9 10 8 6 4 2

This translation published by arrangement
with Random House Trade Publishing,
a division of Random House Inc.

ISBN 0 75381 759 4

Printed and bound in Great Britain by
Clays Ltd, St Ives plc

www.orionbooks.co.uk

In 19th-century Russia authority and privilege were formally structured in a hierarchy of equivalent military and civil ranks and titles generally known as 'The Table of Ranks', which was introduced by the Emperor Peter the Great in January 1722 in order to correlate status and identify seniority between different branches of service. As first published the Table included columns for military, civil and court ranks and fourteen levels or classes. A simplified version of the table is shown below in order to indicate the significance of the titles used in *The Winter Queen*.

The Table of Ranks

CIVIL HIERARCHY	MILITARY HIERARCHY	TITLE
1. Imperial Chancellor	Field-Marshal/ General-Admiral	Your (Supreme) Excellency
2. Full Privy Counsellor	General of Infantry General of Cavalry General of Artillery Admiral	
3. Privy Counsellor	Lieutenent-General Vice Admiral	Your Excellency
4. Full State Counsellor	Major-General Rear Admiral	
5. State Counsellor	Brigadier-General Commander	Your Worship
6. Collegiate Counsellor	Colonel Captain First Grade	Your (High) Honour
7. Court Counsellor	Lieutenant-Colonel Captain Second Grade	
8. Collegiate Assessor	Major Lieutenant-Captain	
9. Titular Counsellor	Captain of Infantry or Cavalry Lieutenant (navy)	Your Honour
10. Collegiate Secretary	Staff Captain of Infantry or Cavalry	
11. Naval Secretary		
12. Provincial Secretary	Lieutenant (army) Midshipman	
13. Senate/Synod/Cabinet Registrar	Second Lieutenant	
14. Collegiate Registrar	Ensign or cornet	

Chapter One

On Monday the thirteenth of May in the year 1876, between the hours of two and three in the afternoon, on a day which combined the freshness of spring with the warmth of summer, numerous individuals in Moscow's Alexander Gardens unexpectedly found themselves eyewitnesses to the perpetration of an outrage which flagrantly transgressed the bounds of common decency.

The public strolling the alleyways between blossoming lilac bushes and flower-beds ablaze with the flaming-scarlet blooms of tulips was smartly decked out: ladies holding aloft lace-work parasols (to avert the threat of freckles), nannies minding children in neat little sailor suits and young men affecting an air of boredom in fashionable cheviot frock coats or jackets cut in the short English fashion. With nothing apparently portending any disagreeable turn of events, a lazy satisfaction and gratifying tedium suffused the atmosphere, mingling with the scents of a mature and confident spring season. The rays of the sun beat down in real earnest, and every last one of the benches which happened to stand in the shade was occupied.

Seated on one of these benches located not far from the Grotto and facing the railings so as to afford a view of the beginning of Neglinnaya Street and the yellow wall of the

I

Manège, were two ladies. One of them, a very young lady (indeed, not really a lady at all, more of a girl), was reading a small morocco-bound volume and glancing about her from time to time with an air of distracted curiosity. Her much older companion, wearing a good-quality dark-blue woollen dress and sensible lace-up ankle-boots, rotated her needles in a regular rhythm as she concentrated on knitting some item in a poisonous pink, yet still found time to turn her head to the right and the left with a rapid glance so keen that there was certainly no way anything in the least bit remarkable could possibly escape it.

The lady's attention was caught immediately by the young man in narrow check trousers, a frock coat casually buttoned over a white waistcoat and a round Swiss hat: he was walking along the alley in such a remarkably strange manner, stopping every now and again as he attempted to pick out somebody among the strollers, then taking a few abrupt steps before stopping yet again. Glancing suddenly in the direction of our ladies, this unbalanced individual seemed to resolve upon some course of action, and immediately set off towards them with broad, decisive strides. He halted in front of the bench and addressed the young girl, exclaiming in a clownish falsetto:

'My lady! Has no one ever told you that your beauty is beyond all endurance?'

The girl, who was indeed quite wonderfully pretty, gaped at the impudent fellow in startled amazement, her strawberry-red lips parted slightly in fright. Even her mature companion seemed dumbfounded at such unheard-of familiarity.

'I am vanquished at first sight,' said the stranger, continuing with his tomfoolery (he was, in fact, a young man of perfectly presentable appearance, with hair trimmed fashionably short at the temples, a high, pale forehead and brown eyes glinting in feverish excitement). 'Pray allow me to impress upon your innocent brow an even more innocent, purely fraternal kiss!'

'Sir, you are quite drunk!' said the lady with the knitting,

2

recovering her wits and revealing that she spoke Russian with a distinct German accent.

'I am drunk on nothing but love,' the insolent fellow assured her and in the same unnatural, whining voice he demanded: 'Just one little kiss, or I shall lay hands upon myself this instant!'

The girl cowered against the back of the bench and turned her pretty face towards her protectress who remained undismayed by the alarming nature of the situation and displayed perfect presence of mind:

'Get away from here this instant! You are crazy!' she cried, raising her voice and holding her knitting out in front of her with the needles protruding in bellicose fashion. 'I call the constable!'

Then something utterly fantastic happened.

'Ah! So I am rejected!' the young man squealed in counterfeit despair, covering his eyes theatrically with one hand and swiftly extracting from his inside pocket a small revolver of gleaming-black steel. 'What meaning has life for me after this? A single word from you and I live. A single word from you and I die where I stand!' he appealed to the young girl, who was sitting there herself more dead than alive. 'You say nothing? Then farewell!'

The sight of a gentleman gesticulating with a gun could not fail to attract the attention of the promenading public. Several of those who happened to be close at hand – a stout lady holding a fan, a pompous gentleman with a cross of the Order of St Anne hanging round his neck, two girls from boarding school in identical brown frocks with pelerines – froze on the spot and some student or other even halted on the pavement on the far side of the railings. In short, there was reason to hope that the scandalous incident would rapidly be brought to a close.

What followed, however, occurred too rapidly for anyone to intervene.

'Here's to luck!' cried the drunk (or, perhaps, the madman), then he raised the hand holding the revolver high above his head, spun the chambers and set the muzzle to his temple.

'You clown! You motley buffoon!' whispered the valiant German matron, demonstrating a quite respectable knowledge of colloquial Russian.

The young man's face, already pale, turned grey and green by turns, he bit his lower lip and squeezed his eyes tight shut. The girl closed her eyes too, just to be on the safe side.

It was as well she did so, for it spared her a horrendous sight: when the shot rang out, the suicide's head was instantly jerked to one side and a thin fountain of red and white matter spurted from the exit wound just below his left ear.

The ensuing scene defies description. The German matron gazed around her indignantly as though calling on everyone to witness this unimaginable outrage, and then set up a blood-curdling squealing, adding her voice to the screeching of the schoolgirls and the stout lady, who had been emitting piercing shrieks for several seconds. The young girl lay there in a dead swoon: she had half-opened her eyes for barely an instant before immediately going limp. People came running up from every side, but it was all too much for the delicate nerves of the student who had been standing beyond the railings, and he took to his heels, fleeing across the roadway in the direction of Mokhovaya Street.

*

Xavier Feofilaktovich Grushin, Detective Superintendent of the Criminal Investigation Department of the Moscow Chief of Police, sighed in relief as he set aside the summary report on the previous day's serious crimes, adding it to the 'out' pile on his left. During the previous twenty-four hours nothing of any note which required the intervention of the CID had occurred in any of the twenty-four police precincts in this city of six hundred thousand inhabitants: there was one murder resulting from a drunken brawl between factory-hands (the murderer was apprehended at the scene), two cab-drivers had been robbed (the local stations could take care of those), and seven thousand eight hundred and fifty-three roubles had gone missing from the till at the Russo-Asian Bank (that was a matter for Anton Semyonovich at the Commercial Fraud Department). Thank God they'd stopped sending Grushin's department all those petty incidents of pickpocketing and maids who hanged themselves and abandoned infants; nowadays those all went into the 'Police Municipal Incidents Report' that was distributed to the departments in the afternoons.

Xavier Grushin yawned comfortably and glanced over the top of his tortoiseshell pince-nez at Erast Petrovich Fandorin, clerk and civil servant fourteenth class, who was writing out the weekly report to His Excellency the Chief of Police for the third time. Never mind, thought Grushin, let him get into neat habits early on; he'll be grateful for it later. The very idea of it, scraping away with a steel nib on a report for the top brass. Oh, no, my friend, you just take your time and do it the good old-fashioned way, with a goose quill, with all the curlicues and flourishes. His Excellency was raised in Emperor Nicholas I's day; he knows all about good order and respect for superiors.

Xavier Grushin genuinely wished the boy well and felt a fatherly concern for him, for indeed there was no denying life had dealt hard with the novice clerk, leaving him an orphan at the tender age of nineteen years. He had known no mother since he was a young child, and his hothead of a father had squandered his entire estate on worthless projects and then given up the ghost. First he'd built up a fortune during the railway boom and then he'd ruined himself in the banking boom. As soon as the commercial banks began going under the previous year plenty of respectable people had found themselves out in the cold. The most reliable interest-bearing bonds were suddenly reduced to worthless trash, to nothing, and the retired lieutenant Fandorin, who promptly departed this life under the blow, had left his only son nothing but a bundle of promissory notes. The boy should have finished his studies at the gymnasium and gone on to university, but instead it was out of the parental halls and off into the streets with you to earn a crust of bread. Xavier Grushin snorted in commiseration. The orphan had passed the examination for collegiate registrar all right (that was no problem for such a well-brought-up lad), but what on earth could have made him want to join the police? He should have a post in the Office of Statistics, or perhaps in the Department of Justice. His head was full of romantic nonsense and dreams of catching mysterious Cadoudals. But we don't have any Cadoudals here, my dear chap (Xavier Grushin shook his head disapprovingly), we spend most of our time around here polishing the seats of our pants and writing reports about the shopkeeper Potbelly dispatching his lawful spouse and three little ones with an axe in a drunken fit.

The youthful Mr Fandorin was only serving his third week in the Criminal Investigation Department, but as an experienced sleuth and a real old hand, Xavier Grushin could tell for certain that the boy would never make a go of it. He was too soft, too delicately raised. Once, during the first week, Grushin had taken him along to the scene of a crime (when the merchant's wife Krupnova had her throat cut). Fandorin had taken one look at the dead woman, turned bright green and gone creeping back all the way along the wall out into the yard. True enough, the merchant's wife had not been a very appetising sight, with her throat ripped open from ear to ear and her tongue lolling out of her mouth and her eyes bulging out of her head, and then, of course, there was that pool of blood she was swimming in. Anyway, Xavier Grushin had been obliged to conduct the preliminary investigation and write the report himself. In all honesty, the case had proved simple enough. The caretaker Kuzykin's eyes had been darting about so crazily in his head that Xavier Grushin had immediately ordered the constable to take him by the collar and stick him in the lock-up. Kuzykin had been in there for two weeks now and he was still denying everything. But that was all right, he'd confess. There was no one else who could have slit the woman's throat: in the thirty years he'd been working here the superintendent had developed the nose of a bloodhound. And Fandorin would come in handy for the paperwork. He was conscientious, he wrote good Russian and knew foreign languages, he was quick on the uptake and pleasant company – unlike that wretched drunk Trofimov who'd been demoted last month from clerk to junior assistant police constable over at the Khitrovka slums. Let him do his drinking and talk back to his superiors down there.

Grushin drummed his fingers in annoyance on the dreary standard-issue baize covering of his desk, took his watch out of his waistcoat pocket – oh, there was still a fair old spell to lunch! – and decisively pulled across the latest *Moscow Gazette*.

'Well now, what surprises have they got for us today?' he asked aloud, and the young clerk eagerly set aside his hateful goose-quill pen, knowing that the boss would start reading out the headlines and other bits and pieces and commenting on what he read: it was a little habit that Xavier Feofilaktovich Grushin had.

'Take a look at that now, young Mr Fandorin, right up there on the front page, where you can't possibly miss it!

The latest American corset
"LORD BYRON"
constructed from the most durable of whalebone
for a truly manly figure.
An inch-thin waist and yard-wide shoulders!

And yard-high letters to suit. And way down here in tiny little print we have:

The Emperor departs for Ems

But of course, how could the person of the Emperor possibly rival the importance of "Lord Byron"!'

Xavier Grushin's entirely good-natured grousing produced a quite remarkable effect on his clerk. For some reason he became embarrassed, his cheeks flushed bright red and his long, girlish eyelashes fluttered guiltily. While we are on the subject of eyelashes, it would seem appropriate at this point to describe Erast Fandorin's appearance in somewhat greater detail, since he is destined to play a pivotal role in the astounding and terrible events which will shortly unfold. He was a most comely youth with black hair (in which he took a secret pride) and blue eyes (ah, if only they had also been black!), rather tall, with a pale complexion and a confounded, ineradicable ruddy bloom on his cheeks. We can also reveal the reason for the young collegiate registrar's sudden discomfiture. The fact was that only two days previously he had expended a third of his first monthly salary on the very corset described in such vivid and glowing terms and was actually wearing his 'Lord Byron' for the second day, enduring exquisite suffering in the name of beauty, and now he suspected (entirely without justification) that the perspicacious Xavier Grushin had divined the origin of his subordinate's Herculean bearing and wished to make him an object of fun.

The superintendent, however, was already continuing with his reading:

'Turkish Bashi-Bazouk atrocities in Bulgaria

Well, that's not for reading just before lunch . . .

Explosion in Ligovsky

Our St Petersburg correspondent informs us that yesterday at six-thirty in the morning a thunderous explosion occurred at the rental apartment house of Commercial Counsellor Vartanov on Znamenskaya Street, completely devastating the apartment on the fourth floor. Upon arrival at the scene the police discovered the remains of a young man, mutilated beyond recognition. The apartment was rented by a certain Mr P., a private lecturer at the university, and it was apparently his body which was discovered. To judge from the appearance of the lodgings, something in the nature of a secret chemical laboratory had been installed there. The officer in charge of the investigation, Counsellor of State Brilling, conjectures that the flat was being used to manufacture infernal devices for an organisation of nihilist terrorists. The investigation is continuing.

Well, now, thanks be to God our Moscow's not Peter!'

Judging from the gleam in his eyes, the youthful Mr Fandorin would have begged to differ on that score. Indeed, every aspect of his appearance was eloquently expressive of the idea that in the real capital people have serious work to do, tracking down terrorist bombers, not writing out ten times over papers which, if truth were told, contain nothing of the slightest interest in any case.

'Right then,' said Xavier Grushin, rustling his newspaper, 'let's see what we have on the city page.

First Moscow Astair-House

The well-known English philanthropist Baroness Astair, through whose zealous and unremitting efforts the model refuges for boy orphans known as Astair-Houses have been established in various countries of the world, has notified our correspondent that the first institution of such a type has now opened its doors in our own golden-domed city. Lady Astair, having commenced her activities in Russia only last year, and having already opened an Astair-House in St Petersburg, has decided to extend her support and assistance to the orphans of Moscow . . .

Mmmm . . .

The heartfelt gratitude of all Muscovites . . . Where are our own Russian Owens and Astairs?

All right, enough of that. God bless all the orphans . . . Now what have we here?

A cynical escapade

Hmm, this is curious:

Yesterday the Alexander Gardens were the scene of a sad incident only too distinctly typical of the cynical outlook and manners of modern youth, when Mr N., a handsome young fellow of twenty-three, a student at Moscow University and the sole heir to a fortune of millions, shot himself dead in full view of the promenading public.

According to the testimony of eyewitnesses, before committing this reckless act N. swaggered and boasted to the onlookers, brandishing a revolver in the air. The eyewitnesses at first took his behaviour for mere drunken bravado. N., however, was in earnest and he proceeded to shoot himself through the head, expiring on the spot. From a note of outrageously atheistic import which was discovered in the pocket of the suicide, it is apparent that N.'s action was not merely the outcome of some momentary impulse or a consequence of *delirium tremens*. It would appear that the fashionable epidemic of pointless suicides, which had thus far remained the scourge of Petropolis, has finally spread to the walls of Old Mother Moscow. *O tempora, O mores!* To what depths of unbelief and nihilism have our gilded youth descended if they would make a vulgar spectacle even of their own death? If our home-grown Brutuses adopt such an attitude to their own lives, then how can we be surprised if they care not a brass farthing for the lives of other, incomparably more worthy individuals? How apropos in this connection are the words of that most venerable of authors, Fyodor Mikhailovich

Dostoevsky, in his new book published in May, *A Writer's Journal*: "Dear, good, honest people (for all of this is within you!), what realm is this into which you are withdrawing, what has made the dark silence of the grave so dear to you? Look, the spring sun is bright in the sky, the trees have spread their leaves, but you are weary before your life has even begun." '

Xavier Grushin sniffed with feeling and cast a strict sideways glance at his young assistant in case he might have noticed, then continued speaking in a distinctly cooler voice.

'Well, and so on and so forth. But the times really don't have anything at all to do with it. There's nothing new to all of this. We've had a saying for these types in the land of Rus since ancient times: "Just don't know when they're well off." A fortune of millions? Now who might that be? And see what scoundrels our precinct chiefs are – they put all sorts of rubbish in their reports, but they haven't bothered to include this. So much for their summary of municipal incidents! But then I suppose it's an open-and-shut case, he shot himself in front of witnesses . . . All the same, though, it's a curious business. The Alexander Gardens. That'll be the City Precinct, second station. I'll tell you what, young Mr Fandorin, as a personal favour to me, you get yourself smartly across there to Mokhovaya Street. Tell them it's for purposes of observation and what have you. Find out who this N. was. And most important of all, my dear young fellow, be sure to make a copy of that farewell note. I'll show it to my Yevdokia Andreevna this evening. She has a fondness for such sentimental stuff. And don't you keep me waiting either – you get yourself back here as quick as you can.'

Xavier Grushin's final words were already addressed to the back of the young collegiate registrar, who was in such great haste to forsake his dreary oil-cloth-covered desk that he very nearly forgot his peaked cap.

At the station the young functionary from the Criminal Investigation Department was shown through to the superintendent. However, on seeing what an insignificant and lowly individual had been dispatched on this errand, the superintendent decided not to waste any time on explanations and summoned his assistant.

'Be so kind as to follow Ivan Prokofievich here,' the superintendent said to the boy in a kindly voice (he might be only a small fry, but he was still from the Department). 'He'll show you everything and tell you all about it. And he was the very one who went to the dead man's apartment yesterday. My humble regards to Superintendent Grushin.'

They seated Erast Fandorin at a high desk and brought him the slim case file. He read the heading . . .

CASE
of the suicide
of hereditary honorary citizen Pyotr Alexandrov KO-KORIN, 23 years, a student of the Faculty of Law at the Imperial University of Moscow. Commenced on the 13th day of the month of May in the year 1876. Concluded on the . . . day of the month of . . . in the year 18 . . .

. . . and unfastened the knotted tapes with fingers trembling in anticipation.

'Alexander Artamonovich Kokorin's son,' explained Ivan Prokofievich, a scrawny, lanky veteran with a crumpled face that looked as though a cow had been chewing on it. 'Immensely rich man, he was. Factory owner. Passed away three years ago now, left the lot to his son. Now why couldn't he just enjoy being a student and make the most of life? Just what is it these people want? I can't make it out at all.'

Erast Fandorin simply nodded, not quite knowing what reply to make to that, and became absorbed in reading the statements of the witnesses. The number of reports was rather large, about a dozen in all, the most detailed of them drawn up from the testimony of the daughter of a Full Privy Counsellor, Elizaveta von Evert-Kolokoltseva, aged seventeen, and her governess, the spinster Emma Pfühl, aged forty-eight, with whom the suicide had been in conversation immediately prior to the shooting. However, Erast Fandorin failed to extract from the reports any information beyond that which is already known to the reader, for all of the witnesses repeated more or less the same thing, differing from each other only in their degree of perspicacity: some affirmed that the young man's appearance had instantly filled them with alarm and foreboding ('The moment I looked into his crazy eyes, I went cold all over,' stated Titular Counsellor's wife Khokhryakova, who went on, however, to testify that she had only seen the young man from the back); other witnesses spoke, on the contrary, of lightning from out of a clear blue sky.

The final item lying in the file was a crumpled note written on light-blue monogrammed paper. Erast Fandorin fastened his eyes greedily on the irregular lines (due, no doubt, to emotional distress):

Gentlemen living after me!

Since you are reading this little letter of mine, I have already departed from you and gone on to learn the secret of death, which remains concealed from your eyes behind seven seals. I am free, while you must carry on living in torment and fear. However, I wager that in the place where I now am and from where, as the Prince of Denmark expressed it, no traveller has yet returned, there is absolutely nothing at all. If anyone should not be in agreement, I respectfully suggest that they investigate for themselves. In any case, I care nothing at all for any of you, and I am writing this note so that you should not take it into your heads that I laid hands on myself out of some sentimental nonsense or other. Your world nauseates me, and that, truly, is quite reason enough. That I am not an absolute swine may be seen from the leather blotter.

Pyotr Kokorin

The first thought to strike Erast Fandorin was that the letter did not appear to have been written in a state of emotional distress.

'What does this mean about the blotter?' he asked.

The superintendent's assistant shrugged:

'He didn't have any blotter on him. But what could you expect, the state he was in? Maybe he was meaning to do something or other, but he forgot. It seems clear enough he was a pretty unstable sort of gentleman. Did you read how he twirled the cylinder on that revolver? And by the way, only one of the chambers had a bullet in it. It's my opinion, for instance, that he didn't really mean to shoot himself at all, just wanted to give his nerves a bit of a thrill, put a keener edge on his feeling for life, so to speak. So afterwards his food would have more savour and his sprees would seem sweeter.'

'Only one bullet out of six? That really was bad luck,' said Erast Fandorin, aggrieved for the dead man. But the idea of the leather blotter was still nagging at him.

'Where does he live? That is, where did he . . . ?'

'An eight-room apartment in a new building on Osto-zhenka Street, and very swish too' – Ivan Prokofievich was keen to share his impressions. 'Inherited his own house in the Zamoskvorechie district from his father, an entire estate, outhouses and all, but he didn't want to live there, moved as far away from the merchantry as he could.'

'Well then, was no leather blotter found there?'

The superintendent's assistant was astonished at the idea.

'Why, do you think we should have searched the place? I tell you, I'd be afraid to let the agents loose around the rooms of an apartment like that, they might get tempted off the straight and narrow. What's the point, anyway? Egor Nikifor-ich, the investigator from the district public prosecutor's office, gave the dead man's valet a quarter of an hour to pack up his things, and had the local constable keep an eye on him to make sure he didn't filch any of his master's belongings, and then ordered me to seal up the door. Until the heirs come forward.'

'And who are the heirs?' Erast Fandorin asked inquisitively.

'Now there's the catch. The butler says Kokorin has no brothers or sisters. There are some kind of second cousins, but he wouldn't let them inside the door. So who's going to end up with all that loot?' Ivan Prokofievich sighed enviously. 'Frightening just to think of it . . . Ah, but it's no concern of ours. The lawyer or the executors will turn up tomorrow or the next day. Not even a day's gone by yet, we've still got the body lying in the ice-house. But Egor Nikiforovich could close the case tomorrow, then things will start moving all right.'

'But even so it is odd,' the young clerk observed, wrinkling his brow. 'If someone makes special mention of some blotter or other in the last letter he ever writes, there must be something to it. And that bit about "an absolute swine" is none too clear either. What if there is something important in that blotter? It's up to you, of course, but I would definitely search the apartment for it. It seems to me that blotter is the very reason the note was written. There's some mystery here, mark my words.'

Erast Fandorin blushed, afraid that his impetuous suggestion of a mystery might appear too puerile, but the superintendent's assistant failed to notice anything strange about the notion.

'You're right there, we should at least have looked through the papers in the study,' he admitted. 'Egor Nikiforich is always in a hurry. There's eight of them in the family, so he always tries to sneak off home as quick as he can from inspections and investigations. He's an old man, only a year to go to his pension, so what else can you expect . . . ? I'll tell you what, Mr Fandorin. What would you say to going round there yourself? We could take a look together. And then I'll put up a new seal, that's easy enough. Egor Nikiforich won't take it amiss. Not in the least, he'll only thank us for not bothering him one more time. I'll tell him there was a request from the CID, eh?'

It seemed to Erast Fandorin that the superintendent's skinny assistant simply wished to examine the 'swish' apartment a bit more closely, and the idea of 'putting up' a new seal had not sounded too convincing either, but the temptation was simply too great. There truly was an air of mystery about this business . . .

*

Erast Fandorin was not greatly impressed by the décor of the deceased Pyotr Kokorin's residence (the *piano nobile* of a rich apartment building beside the Prechistenkie Gates), since he himself had lived in mansions that were its equal during the period of his father's precipitately acquired wealth. The collegiate registrar did not, therefore, linger in the marble entrance-hall with the Venetian mirror three *arshins* in height and the gilded moulding on the ceiling, but strode straight through into the drawing room, a lavish interior with a row of six windows along the wall, decorated in the super-fashionable Russian Style, with brightly painted wooden trunks, carved oak on the walls and a smart tiled stove.

'Didn't I say he had a taste for stylish living?' Fandorin's guide said to the back of his head, for some reason speaking in a whisper.

At this point in the proceedings Fandorin bore a remarkable resemblance to a year-old setter allowed out into the forest for the first time, who is crazed by the pungent and alluring scent of nearby game. Turning his head to the right and the left, he unerringly identified his target:

'That door over there, is that the study?'

'It is indeed, sir.'

'Then what are we waiting for?'

The leather blotter was not long in the seeking. It was

lying in the centre of a massive writing-desk, between a malachite inkstand and a mother-of-pearl shell that served as an ashtray. But before Fandorin could lay his impatient hands on the squeaky brown leather, his gaze fell on a portrait photograph set in a silver frame that was standing in the most conspicuous position on the desk. The face in the portrait was so remarkable that it completely drove all thought of the blotter from Fandorin's mind: gazing out at him in semi-profile was a veritable Cleopatra with a dense mane of hair and immense matt-black eyes, her long neck set in a haughty curve and a slight hint of cruelty evident in the wilful line of her mouth. Above all the collegiate registrar was bewitched by her expression of calm and confident authority, so unexpected on a girl's face (for some reason Fandorin very decidedly wanted her to be a girl, and not a married lady).

'She's a looker,' said Ivan Prokofievich with a whistle, popping up beside him. 'Wonder who she is? If you'll pardon me . . .'

And without the slightest trembling of those sacrilegious fingers he extracted the enchanting face from its frame and turned the photograph over. Inscribed on it in a broad, slanting hand were the words:

To Pyotr K.
And Peter went forth and wept bitterly. Once having given your love, never forswear it!
A.B.

'So she compares him with the apostle Peter, and herself with Jesus, does she? A little arrogant perhaps!' snorted the superintendent's assistant. 'Maybe this creature was the reason our student did away with himself, eh? Aha, and there's the blotter. So our journey wasn't wasted.'

Ivan Prokofievich opened the leather cover and extracted the single solitary sheet of writing on the light-blue note-paper with which Erast Fandorin was already familiar, but this time with a notary's seal and several signatures at the bottom.

'Excellent,' said the policeman, nodding in satisfaction. 'So we've found the will and testament too. Now I wonder what it says.'

It took him no more than a minute to run his eyes over the document, but that minute seemed an eternity to Fandorin, and he regarded it as beneath his dignity to peep over someone else's shoulder.

'That's a fine St George's Day present for you, Granny! And a fine little present for the third cousins!' Ivan Prokofievich exclaimed in a voice filled with incomprehensible gloating. 'Well done, Kokorin, he's shown them all what's what. That's the way to do it, the Russian way! Only it does seem a bit unpatriotic somehow. Anyway, that explains the bit about the "absolute swine".'

Finally abandoning in his impatience all notion of common decorum and respect for rank, Erast Fandorin grabbed the sheet of paper out of his senior officer's hand and read as follows:

Last Will and Testament

I, the undersigned Pyotr Alexandrovich Kokorin, being of sound mind and perfect memory, do hereby declare in the presence of the witnesses named hereunder my will concerning the property belonging to me.

All of my saleable property, of which a full inventory is held by my solicitor, Semyon Efimovich Berenson, I bequeath to the Baroness Margaret Astair, a British citizen, so that all of these resources may be used entirely as she shall deem fit for purposes of the education and upbringing of orphans. I am sure that Madam Astair will put these funds to more sensible and honest use than our own Russian captains of philanthropy.

This is my final and definitive will and testament, it is valid in law and supersedes my previous will and testament.

I name as my executors the solicitor Semyon Efimovich Berenson and the student of Moscow University Nikolai Stepanovich Akhtyrtsev.

This will and testament has been drawn up in two copies, of which I am retaining one and the other is to be delivered for safekeeping to the solicitor's office of Mr Berenson.

Moscow, 12th May 1876.

Pyotr Kokorin

Chapter Two

'Say what you will, Mr Grushin, but it's still odd!' Fandorin repeated vehemently. 'There's some kind of mystery here, I swear there is!' He said it again with stubborn emphasis, 'Yes, that's it precisely, a mystery! Judge for yourself. In the first place, the way he shot himself is absurd somehow, by pure chance, with the only bullet in the cylinder, as though he didn't really intend to shoot himself at all. What kind of infernal bad luck is that? And then there's the tone of the suicide note, you must admit that's a bit queer – as if it had just been dashed off in some odd moment, and yet it throws up an extremely important problem. The very devil of a problem.' The strength of Fandorin's feelings lent his voice a new resonance. 'But I'll tell you about the problem later. Meanwhile, what about the will? Surely that's suspicious?'

'And just what exactly do you find so suspicious about it, my dear young fellow?' Xavier Grushin purred as he glanced listlessly through the 'Police Municipal Incidents Report' for the last twenty-four hours. This not entirely uninformative reading matter usually arrived during the afternoon, since matters of great importance were not included in the document – for the most part it was a hotch-potch of trivial incident and absolute nonsense – but just occasionally something curious might turn up in it. In this edition there was a report on the previous day's suicide in the Alexander Gardens, but as the highly experienced Xavier Grushin had anticipated, it provided no details and, of course, it did not give the text of the suicide note.

'I'll tell you what! Although it looks as though Kokorin didn't really mean to shoot himself, the will, for all its defiant tone, is drawn up in full and proper order – notarised, signed by witnesses, with the executors named,' said Fandorin, bending down a finger as he made each point. 'And I should think so, it's an immense fortune. I made inquiries – two mills, three industrial plants, houses in various towns, shipyards in Libava, half a million alone in interest-bearing securities in the State Bank!'

'Half a million!' gasped Xavier Grushin, glancing up sharply from his papers. 'The Englishwoman's a very lucky lady, very lucky.'

'And by the way, can you explain to me how Lady Astair is involved in all of this? Why has everything been left to her and not to anyone else? Just what is the connection between her and Kokorin? That's what we need to find out!'

'He wrote himself that he doesn't trust our own Russian embezzlers of public funds, and the newspapers have been singing the Englishwoman's praises for months now. No, my dear chap, why don't you explain to me why it is that your generation holds life so cheap? The slightest excuse and – bang! And all with such pomp, such pathos, such contempt for the entire world. And just how have you earned the right to show such contempt?' Grushin asked, growing angry as he remembered how impudently and disrespectfully he had been addressed the evening before by his beloved daughter Sasha, a sixteen-year-old schoolgirl. The question, however, was largely rhetorical, since a young clerk's opinion on the matter was of little interest to the venerable superintendent, and he immediately stuck his nose back into the summary report.

In response Erast Fandorin became even more animated:

'Ah, that is the very problem I specially wanted to

mention. Take a man like Kokorin. Life gives him everything – riches and freedom and education and good looks.' (Fandorin threw in good looks simply to make up the phrase, although he had not the slightest idea of the deceased's appearance.) 'But he dices with death and eventually kills himself. Do you want to know why? Living in your world makes us young people feel sick – Kokorin wrote that in so many words, only he didn't expand on it. Your ideals – a career, money, public honours – for many of us they mean absolutely nothing. That's not the kind of thing we dream about now. Do you think there's nothing behind what they write about an epidemic of suicides? The very best of the educated young people are simply giving up on life, they're suffocated by a lack of spiritual oxygen, and you, the elders of society, fail completely to draw the appropriate conclusions!'

The entire emotional force of this denunciation was apparently directed against Xavier Feofilaktovich Grushin in person, since there were no other 'elders of society' to be observed in the vicinity, but not only did Grushin not take offence, he actually nodded his head in evident satisfaction.

'Ah yes,' he said with a derisive chuckle as glanced into the text of the report. 'Here's something concerning the lack of spiritual oxygen: "*The body of the cobbler Ivan Eremeev Buldygin, twenty-seven years of age, who had hanged himself, was discovered in Chikhachevsky Lane in the third district of the Meshchanskaya Precinct at ten o'clock in the morning. According to the testimony of the yard-keeper Pyotr Silin, the reason for the suicide was lack of funds for drink to relieve a hangover.*" That's the way all the best ones will leave us. There'll be no one but us old fools left soon.'

'You may mock,' Erast Fandorin said bitterly, 'but in Petersburg and Warsaw not a day goes by without university students, and even high-school students, poisoning or shooting or drowning themselves. You think it's funny . . .'

Repent, Mr Xavier Grushin, before it's too late, he thought vengefully to himself, although until that moment the idea of suicide had never even entered his head – he was a young man of far too vivacious a character. Silence ensued: while Fandorin pictured to himself a modest little grave without a cross outside the fence of the churchyard, Grushin carried on running his finger along the lines of print and turning the rustling pages.

'But really, this is dreadful nonsense,' he muttered. 'Have they all lost their minds, or what? Look here, two reports, one from the third district of the Myasnitskaya Precinct, on page eight, another from the first district of the Rogozhskaya Precinct, on page nine. Listen: *"At 35 minutes past 12 police inspector Fedoruk was summoned from his station to the building of the Moscow Fire Insurance Company on Podko-lokolny Lane at the request of the Kaluga landowner's wife Avdotya Filippovna Spitsyna (temporarily resident at the Boyar Hotel). Mrs Spitsyna testified that beside the entrance to the bookshop a certain respectably dressed gentleman who appeared to be about twenty-five years of age had attempted to shoot himself – he set a pistol to his temple, but apparently it misfired and the failed suicide fled the scene. Mrs Spitsyna demanded that the police find the young man and hand him over to the spiritual authorities for the imposition of a religious penance. No search was undertaken because no crime had been committed."'*

'There you are, isn't that just what I was saying!' Erast Fandorin cried triumphantly, feeling himself totally vindicated.

'Wait a moment, young man, that's not all,' the superintendent interrupted. 'Listen to what comes next. Page nine. *"Report of police constable Semenov* (he's from the Rogozhskaya Precinct). *Between 10 and 11 he was summoned by the petty bourgeois Nikolai Kukin, the shopkeeper at the grocery store Brykin and Sons, opposite the Malaya Yauza Bridge. Kukin informed him that a few minutes earlier a student had climbed on to one of the stone bollards of the bridge and set a pistol to his head, clearly intending to shoot himself. Kukin heard a metallic click, but there was no shot. After the click the student jumped down on to the road and walked away quickly in the direction of Yauza Street. No other eyewitnesses have been found. Kukin is petitioning for a police post to be set up on the bridge, since last year a girl of loose morals drowned herself there and this is damaging his trade." '*

'I don't understand it at all,' Fandorin said with a shrug. 'What strange kind of ritual is this? Could it be some secret society of suicides?'

'No . . . what society?' Xavier Grushin said slowly, then he began speaking faster and faster as he gradually became more animated. 'There is no society, my fine young gentleman, it's all much simpler than that. And all that business with the cylinder is clear now, it just never occurred to me before. It's this student of ours, Kokorin, who's been playing pranks. Look here.' He got up and strode quickly over to the map hanging on the wall beside the door. 'Here's the Malaya Yauza Bridge. From there he went along Yauza Street, idled away the time for an hour or so until he ended up on Podkolokolny Lane beside the insurance company, gave landowner's wife Spitsyna a good fright and then carried on towards the Kremlin. Some time after two he reached the Alexander Gardens, and there, as we know only too well, his journey came to an end.'

'But why? And what does it all mean?' Fandorin asked, gazing hard at the map.

'What it means is not for me to judge. But I have a good idea how things happened. Our well-heeled and pampered gilded youth decided to bid the world farewell. But before he died he wanted to give his nerves a bit of a thrill. I read somewhere that it's called "American roulette". It was invented in America, in the goldfields. You put a single shot in the cylinder, give it a twirl, and then – bang! If you're lucky you break the bank, if not, then it's goodbye and farewell. So our student deliberately set out on his voyage round Moscow in order to tempt fate. It's quite possible that he tried to shoot himself more than three times, but then not every eyewitness will bother to call the police. That landowner's wife who likes to save souls and Kukin with his private interest were vigilant enough, but God only knows how many attempts Kokorin made altogether. Or perhaps he struck a bargain with himself – I'll dice with death so many times, and then that's it. If I live, then so be it. But then, that's just me fantasising. That was no stroke of infernal bad luck in the Alexander Gardens. By two o'clock our student had simply run out of chances.'

'Mr Grushin, you have a genuine analytical talent,' said Erast Fandorin with sincere admiration. 'I can just see it all happening in front of my eyes.'

Grushin always enjoyed well-earned praise, even from a young whippersnapper.

'True enough. So there is something to be learned from the old duffers after all.' He said in a didactic tone, 'You should have served on investigations as long as I have, not just in these highly cultured times of ours, but back in Tsar Nicholas' days. Then it was nobody's concern what was detective work and what wasn't. Our department didn't even exist in Moscow then, there wasn't even an investigations office. One day you were looking for murderers, the next you were down at the market, reading folks the riot act, the day after that you were doing the rounds of the taverns, rounding up people without passports. But it all developed your powers of observation and knowledge of people, and helped you grow a thick skin – and there's no way you can manage without that in our police work,' the superintendent concluded with a broad hint, only to realise that the clerk was no longer listening to him, but frowning instead at some thought of his own that appeared to present him with some difficulty.

'Right then, what's that you're puzzling over? Out with it.'

'There's something I can't quite work out . . .' said Fandorin with a nervous twitch of his handsome half-moon eyebrows. 'This Kukin says it was a student on the bridge . . .'

'Of course a student, who else?'

'But how could Kukin know that Kokorin was a student? He was wearing a frock coat and a hat, and no one in the Alexander Gardens recognised him as a student . . . All the reports say "a young man" or "the gentleman". It *is* a puzzle.'

'You've got puzzles on the brain,' said Grushin with a wave of his hand. 'This Kukin of yours is a fool, and that's all there is to it. He saw a young gentleman in civilian clothes and just imagined he was a student. Or maybe our shopkeeper has a practised eye and he was able to recognise a student – after all, he deals with customers all day long from morning till night.'

'Kukin's never laid eyes on the likes of Kokorin in his dirty little shop,' Erast Fandorin objected quite reasonably.

'So what do you make of that?'

'I think it would be a good idea to question the landowner's wife Spitsyna and the shopkeeper Kukin a bit more thoroughly. Of course, Mr Grushin, it would be inappropriate for you to deal with such trifles, but if you will permit me, I could do it . . .' Erast Fandorin was already halfway out of his chair, so badly did he want Xavier Grushin's permission.

Xavier Grushin was on the point of taking a strict line, but he thought better of it. Why not let the boy get a whiff of real, live action and learn how to talk to witnesses? Perhaps he might just amount to something after all.

'I don't forbid it,' he declared imposingly, then quickly forestalled the exclamation of joy that was about to burst from the collegiate registrar's lips. 'But first, if you don't mind, finish the report for His Excellency. And I tell you what, my dear fellow. It's after three already. I think I'll be on my way home. You can tell me tomorrow where our shopkeeper got his student from.'

Chapter Three

From Miasnitskaya Street, where the Criminal Investigation Department had its office, to the Boyar Hotel, where, according to the report, the landowner's wife Spitsyna had her 'temporary residence', was a walk of only twenty minutes, and despite the impatience that was consuming him, Fandorin decided to stroll down there on foot. His tormentor, 'Lord Byron', who constricted the clerk's sides so mercilessly, had forced such a substantial breach in his budget that the expense of a cab could well have reflected in a drastic fashion on the adequacy of his diet. Chewing as he walked along on a fish-gristle pie bought at the corner of Gusiatnikov Lane (let us not forget that in the flurry of investigative excitement Erast Fandorin had been left without any lunch), he stepped out along Chistoprudny Boulevard, where antediluvian old women in ancient coats and caps were scattering crumbs for the fat, impudent pigeons. Horse-drawn cabs and phaetons dashed by along the cobbled roadway at a pace Erast Fandorin could not possibly match, redirecting his thoughts to his offended feelings – the very idea of a detective without a carriage and trotters was simply impossible as a matter of principle. Thank goodness the Boyar Hotel was on Pokrovka Street, but trudging on from there to the shopkeeper Kukin's place on the Yauza would take half an hour for certain. Any procrastination now could well be fatal, Erast Fandorin tormented himself (with some degree of exaggeration, it must be said), but His Lordship the Superintendent had begrudged him fifteen kopecks from the state purse. No doubt the Department allocated him eighty roubles every month for his own regular cabby. Those were the bosses' privileges for you: one of them rode home in his personal cab, while the other plodded the streets on official business.

But now at last on Erast Fandorin's left the bell-tower of Holy Trinity Church, which stood beside the Boyar Hotel, hove into view above the roof of Souchet's coffee house, and Fandorin quickened his stride in anticipation of important discoveries.

Half an hour later he was wandering with a weary and dejected stride down Pokrovsky Boulevard, where the pigeons – every bit as plump and impudent as those on Chistoprudny Boulevard – were fed not by old noblewomen, but by merchants' wives.

His conversation with the witness had proved disappointing. Erast Fandorin had caught the landowner's wife at the very last moment – she was on the point of getting into her droshky, piled high with various trunks and bundles, in order to take her leave of Russia's first capital city and set out for the province of Kaluga. Out of considerations of economy Spitsyna still travelled in the old-fashioned manner, not by railway but with her own horses.

This was undoubtedly a stroke of good fortune for Fandorin, since had the landowner's wife been hurrying to reach the railway station, no conversation at all would have taken place. But no matter which approach Erast Fandorin adopted in the discussion with his garrulous witness, its essential content remained entirely unaltered: Xavier Grushin was right, it was Kokorin that Spitsyna had seen – she had mentioned his frock coat and his round hat, and even his patent-leather gaiters with buttons, which had not been mentioned by the witnesses from the Alexander Gardens.

His only hope now was Kukin, and Grushin was very probably right about him as well. The shopkeeper had simply blurted out the first thing that came into his mind, and now he had Fandorin trudging all the way across Moscow and making a laughing-stock of himself in front of the super-intendent.

The glass door bearing the image of a sugar-loaf at the grocery store Brykin and Sons faced directly out on to the embankment, offering a clear view of the bridge – Fandorin noted that immediately. He also noted the fact that the windows of the shop were flung wide open (evidently because of the sweltering heat), so that Kukin might well have been able to hear a 'metallic click', since the distance to the nearest stone bollard of the bridge was certainly only fifteen paces at the most. A man of about forty wearing a red shirt, a black, woollen-weave waistcoat, velveteen trousers and bottle-shaped boots peeped round the door with an intrigued expression.

'Can I be of any help, Your Honour?' he asked. 'Perhaps you've managed to lose your way?'

'Kukin?' Erast Fandorin inquired in a strict voice, not ex-pecting to derive any consolation from the imminent explanations.

'Indeed, sir,' the shopkeeper replied cautiously, knitting his bushy eyebrows, but then immediately guessing the truth. 'Ah, you must be from the police, Your Honour? I'm most humbly grateful to you. I didn't expect you would be attending to me so soon. The local officer said his superiors would consider the matter, but I didn't really expect anything sir, not really, sir. But why are we standing out here on the doorstep? Please, come into the shop. I'm most grateful to you, sir, most grateful.'

He even bowed and opened the door and made a gesture of invitation as much as to say 'After you', but Fandorin did not budge. He said portentously, 'Kukin, I am not from the local station, I am from the Criminal Investigation Department. I have instructions to find the stu . . . the person you reported to the local inspector of police.'

'The skewdint, you mean?' the shopkeeper prompted him readily. 'Of course, sir, I remember his looks most precisely. A terrible thing, may God forgive him. As soon as I saw he'd clambered up on that post and put that gun to his head, I just froze, I did. That's it, I thought, it'll be just like it was last year, there'll be no tempting anyone into this shop, not even for a fancy loaf. And what fault is it of ours? What is it draws them here like bees to honey to do away with themselves? Stroll on down that way to the Moscow river, it's deeper there, and the bridge is higher, and . . .'

'Be quiet, Kukin,' Erast Fandorin interrupted him. 'You'd do better to describe the student. What he was wearing, what he looked like and why you decided he was a student in the first place.'

'Why, he was a skewdint right enough, he was, a real proper skewdint, Your Honour,' the shopkeeper said in surprise. 'Uniform coat and buttons, and little glasses perched on his nose.'

'A uniform coat, you say?' Fandorin exclaimed abruptly. 'He was wearing a student coat, then?'

'Why, what else, sir?' asked Kukin, with a pitying glance at the dim-witted functionary. 'If not for that, how was I to tell as he's a skewdint or he isn't? I reckon I can tell a skewdint from a clerk by his coat, so I do.'

Erast Fandorin could not really make any response to that just remark, so he took a neat little notepad with a pencil out of his pocket in order to record the witness's testimony. The notepad, which Fandorin had bought just before entering service with the Criminal Investigation Department, had lain idle for three weeks, and today was the first time he'd had any use for it – in the course of the morning the collegiate registrar had already covered several of its small pages with fine writing.

'Tell me what this man looked like.'

'Just an ordinary sort of person, really. Nothing much to look at, a bit pimply round the face, like. And them little glasses . . .'

'What kind of glasses, spectacles or a pince-nez?'

'You know, the kind on a ribbon.'

'A pince-nez, then,' said Fandorin, scribbling away with his pencil. 'Any other distinctive features?'

'He had this terrible slouch, with his shoulders almost up over the top of his head . . . A real skewdint, like I told you . . .'

Kukin gazed in perplexity at the 'clerk', who said nothing for a long time, frowning, rubbing his lips together and rustling his little notepad. Obviously he was thinking about something.

In the notepad it said: 'Uniform coat, pimples, pince-nez, bad slouch.' Well, a few pimples didn't mean much. The inventory of Kokorin's possesssions didn't say a word about any pince-nez. Perhaps he had dropped it? It was possible. The witnesses had not said anything about a pince-nez either, but they had not really been questioned much about the suicide's appearance – what would have been the point? A slouch? Hm. As he recalled, the *Moscow Gazette* had described 'a handsome young fellow', but the reporter had not been present at the incident. He had not seen Kokorin, and so he could easily have stuck in the 'handsome young fellow' simply for the sake of effect. That only left the student uniform coat, and that was something which could not be discounted. If it had been Kokorin on the bridge, it meant that during the interval between shortly after ten and half past twelve for some reason he had changed into a frock coat. But where, though? From the Yauza to Ostozhenka Street and then back to the Moscow Fire Insurance Company was a long way. You couldn't possibly cover the distance in an hour and a half.

Fandorin realised with a hollow, sinking feeling that only one alternative remained open to him: to take the shopkeeper Kukin by the collar and drag him down to the station on

Mokhovaya Street, where the suicide's body was still lying in the mortuary, packed in ice, and arrange an identification. Erast Fandorin imagined the gaping skull with the crust of dried blood and brains, and an entirely natural association brought back the memory of the merchant's wife Krupnova with her throat cut, who still continued to visit him in his nightmares. No, he definitely did not wish to make the trip to the 'cold room'. But there was some connection between the student from the Malaya Yauza Bridge and the suicide from the Alexander Gardens, which absolutely had to be cleared up. Who could possibly tell him whether Kokorin had pimples and a slouch, and whether he wore a pince-nez?

Well, firstly, there was the landowner's wife Spitsyna, but she was probably driving up to the Kaluga Gate by now. Secondly, there was the deceased's valet – what was it his name was, now? Not that it mattered in any case; the investigator had thrown him out of the apartment. Trying to find him now would just be a waste of time. That left the witnesses from the Alexander Gardens, and above all the two ladies with whom Kokorin had been in conversation during the final minute of his life. They at least must have got a good look at the details of his appearance. Here it was written in his notepad: '*Daughter of Full Privy Counsellor Eliz. Alexandrovna Evert-Kolokoltseva, 17, spinster Emma Gottliebovna Pfühl, 48, Malaya Nikitskaya Street, private residence.*'

He would be obliged to go to the expense of a cab after all.

*

The day was turning out to be a long one. The cheerful sun of May, still by no means weary of illuminating the golden-domed city, was reluctantly slipping down the sky towards the line of the roofs when Erast Fandorin, now two twenty-kopeck coins the poorer, descended from his cab in front of the smart mansion-house with the Doric columns, moulded-stucco facade and marble porch. Seeing his fare halt in hesitation, the cabman said, 'That's the one, all right, the general's house, don't you worry about that. This ain't my first year driving round Moscow.'

What if they won't let me in? – Erast Fandorin thought with a sudden twinge of fear at the possible humiliation. He took a firm grasp of the gleaming brass hammer and knocked twice. The massive door with bronze lion masks immediately swung open and a doorman dressed in rich livery with gold braid stuck his head out.

'To see the baron? From the office?' he asked briskly. 'Reporting or just delivering some document? Come on in, do.'

Finding himself in a spacious entrance hall, brightly illuminated by both a chandelier and gas burners, the visitor was deserted by his final shred of courage.

'Actually, I'm here to see Elizaveta Alexandrovna,' he explained. 'Erast Petrovich Fandorin, from the Criminal Investigation Department. On an urgent matter.'

'The Criminal Investigation Department,' the guardian of the portal repeated with a frown of disdain. 'Would that be in connection with yesterday's events? Out of the question. The young lady spent very nearly half the day in tears and she slept badly last night as well. I won't admit you and I won't announce you. His Excellency has already threatened your people from the precinct with dire consequences for tormenting Elizaveta Alexandrovna with their interrogations yesterday. Outside with you, if you please, outside.' And the scoundrel actually began nudging Fandorin towards the exit with his fat belly.

'But what about the spinster Pfühl?' Erast Fandorin cried out despairingly. 'Emma Gottliebovna, forty-eight years of age? I would like at least to have a few words with her. This is important state business!'

The doorman smacked his lips pompously.

'Very well, I will admit you to her. Go through that way, under the stairs. Third door on the right along the corridor. That is where the madam governess resides.'

The door was opened in response to Fandorin's knock by a gaunt individual who stared, unspeaking, at her visitor out of round brown eyes.

'I am from the police, my name is Fandorin. Are you Miss Pfühl?' Erast Fandorin inquired uncertainly, then repeated the question in German just to be sure: '*Polizeiamt. Sind Sie Fräulein Pfühl? Guten abend.*'

'Good evening,' the gaunt individual replied severely in heavily accented Russian. 'Yes, I am Emma Pfühl. Come in. Sit down there on that chair.'

Fandorin sat where he had been ordered to sit, on a Viennese chair with a curved back standing beside a writing desk on which some textbooks and stacks of writing paper were laid out in an extremely tidy fashion. It was a pleasant room with good light, but extremely boring, lacking in life somehow. The only spot of bright colour throughout its entire extent was provided by a trio of exuberant geraniums standing in pots on the window sill.

'Are you here about that stupid young man who shot himself?' Miss Pfühl inquired. 'I answered all of the policeman's questions yesterday, but if you wish to ask again, you may ask. I understand what the work of the police is, it is very important. My uncle Günter served as an Ober-wachtmeister in the Saxon Police.'

'I am a collegiate registrar,' Erast Fandorin explained, not wishing himself to be taken for a sergeant major, 'a civil servant, fourteenth class.'

'Yes, I know how to understand rank,' the German woman said with a nod, pointing to the lapel of his uniform jacket. 'So, mister collegiate registrar, I am listening.'

At that moment the door swung open without a knock and a fair-haired young lady with an enchanting flush on her cheeks came dashing into the room.

'*Fräulein Pfühl! Morgen fahren wir nach Kuntsevo!*[1] Honestly. Papa has given his permission!' she babbled rapidly

---

[1] Tomorrow we're going to Kuntsevo!

from the doorway, then noticing the stranger, she stopped short and lapsed into a confused silence, but the gaze of her grey eyes nonetheless remained fixed on the young official in an expression of the most lively curiosity.

'Well-brought-up young baronesses do not run, they walk,' her governess told her with feigned strictness. 'Especially when they are all of seventeen years old. If you do not run, but walk, then you have time to notice a stranger and greet him properly.'

'Good day, sir,' the miraculous vision whispered.

Fandorin leapt to his feet and bowed, his nerves appalling. The poor clerk was so overwhelmed by the girl's appearance that he was afraid he might fall in love with her at first sight, and that was something he simply could not do. Even in his dear papa's more prosperous days, a princess like this would have been well beyond his reach, and now the idea was even more ridiculous.

'How do you do,' he said very drily with a grave frown, thinking to himself: Cast me in the role of a pitiful supplicant, would you – A mere Titular Counsellor he, and a general's daughter she . . . – Oh no you don't, my dear lady! I still have a long way to go before I even reach Titular Counsellor.

'Collegiate registrar Erast Petrovich Fandorin, of the Criminal Investigation Department,' he said, introducing himself in an official tone. 'I am pursuing an investigation into yesterday's unfortunate incident in the Alexander Gardens. The need has arisen to ask a few more questions. But if you find it unpleasant – I quite understand how upset you must have been – it will be enough for me to have a word with Miss Pfühl alone.'

'Yes, it was quite horrible.' The young lady's eyes, already very large, widened still further. 'To be honest, I squeezed my eyes tight shut and saw almost nothing at all, and afterwards I fainted . . . But it is all so fascinating! Fräulein Pfühl, may I stay for a while too? Oh please! You know, I am really just as much a witness as you are!'

'For my part, in the interests of the investigation, I would also prefer it if the baroness were present,' said Fandorin, like a coward.

'Order is order,' said Emma Pfühl with a nod. 'I have told you over and over again, Lischen: *Ordnung müss sein*.[1] The law must be obeyed. You may stay.'

Lizanka (the affectionate name by which Fandorin, now hopelessly lost, was already thinking of Elizaveta Evert-Kolokoltseva) seated herself eagerly on the leather divan, gazing wide-eyed at our hero.

He took a grip on himself, turned to Fräulein Pfühl and asked:

'Can you please describe the gentleman's appearance for me?'

'The gentleman who shot himself?' she asked. '*Na ja*.[2] Brown eyes, rather tall, no moustache or beard, sideburns none either, a very young face, but not a very good one. Now the clothes . . .'

'We'll come to the clothes later,' Erast Fandorin interrupted her. 'You say it was not a good face? Why? Because of his pimples?'

'*Pickeln*,' Lizanka translated, blushing.

'*A ja*, the pimples,' the governess repeated the slightly unfamiliar word with relish. 'No, that gentleman did not have pimples. He had good, healthy skin. But his face was not very good.'

'Why?'

'It was nasty. He looked as though he did not wish to kill himself, but someone altogether different. Oh, it was a nightmare!' exclaimed Emma Pfühl, becoming excited at her recollection of events. 'Spring, such sunny weather, all the ladies and gentlemen out walking in the wonderful garden covered vith flowers!'

At these words Erast Fandorin cast a sidelong glance at

---

[1] There must be order.
[2] Well then.

Lizanka, but she had evidently long ago become quite accustomed to her companion's distinctive Germanic mode of speech and she was still gazing at him as trustingly and radiantly as ever.

'And did he have a pince-nez? Perhaps not on his nose, but protruding from a pocket? On a silk ribbon?' Fandorin threw out questions one after another. 'And did it not perhaps seem to you that he slouched? And another thing. I know he was wearing a frock coat, but was there not anything about him to suggest he was a student – uniform trousers, perhaps? Did you notice anything?'

'Always have I noticed everything,' the German woman replied with dignity. 'The trousers were check pantaloons of expensive wool. There was no pince-nez at all. No slouching either. That gentleman had good posture.' She began thinking and suddenly asked him: 'Slouching, pince-nez and a student? Why did you say that?'

'Why do you ask?' Erast Fandorin said cautiously.

'It is strange. There was one gentleman there. A student with a slouch wearing a pince-nez.'

'What? Where?' gasped Fandorin.

'I saw such a gentleman . . . *jenseits* . . . on the other side of the railings, in the street. He was standing there and looking at us. I even thought this student was going to help us get rid of that dreadful man. And he was slouching very badly. I saw that afterwards, after the other gentleman had already killed himself. The student turned and walked away quickly-quickly. And I saw that he had a bad slouch. That happens when children are not taught to sit correctly in childhood. Sitting correctly is very important. My wards always sit correctly. Look at the Fräulein baroness. See how she holds her back? It is very beautiful!'

At that Elizaveta Evert-Kolokoltseva blushed, and so prettily that for a moment Fandorin lost the thread of the conversation, although Fräulein Pfühl's statement was undoubtedly of the utmost importance.

Chapter Four

Shortly after ten o'clock in the morning the following day
Erast Fandorin, endowed not only with his chief's blessing,
but also with three roubles for exceptional expenses, arrived
at the yellow university building on Mokhovaya Street. His
mission was simple enough in principle, but would require a
certain degree of luck: to locate a rather ordinary-looking,
somewhat pimply student with a slouch and a pince-nez on
a silk ribbon. It was entirely possible that this suspicious
individual did not study at the premises on Mokhovaya
Street at all, but in the Higher Technical College or the
Forestry Academy or some other institute of learning, but
Xavier Grushin (regarding his young assistant with a mixture
of astonishment and joy) had concurred wholeheartedly in
Fandorin's surmise that in all probability the 'sloucher', like
the deceased Kokorin, pursued his studies at the university,
and there was a very good chance that he did so in the self-
same Faculty of Law.

Dressed in his civilian clothes, Fandorin dashed headlong
up the cast-iron steps of the front porch, rushed past the
bearded attendant in green livery and took up a convenient
position in the semi-circular window embrasure, a vantage
point which afforded an excellent view of the vestibule with
its cloakroom and the courtyard, and even the entrances to

both wings of the building. For the first time since his father had died and the young man's life had been diverted from the clear road straight ahead, Erast Fandorin beheld the venerable yellow walls of the university without an aching in his heart for what might have been but had not come to pass. Who could say which mode of existence was the more fascinating and more useful for society – the book-learning of a student or the gruelling life of a detective pursuing an investigation into an important and dangerous case? (Well, perhaps not dangerous exactly, but certainly crucially important and highly mysterious.)

Approximately one out of every four students who hove into this attentive observer's field of view was wearing a pince-nez, and in many cases it hung precisely on a silk ribbon. Approximately one student out of every five was sporting a certain quantity of pimples about his face. Nor was there any shortage of students with a slouch. However, all three of these features seemed stubbornly disinclined to combine together in the person of a single individual.

When it was already after one o'clock, Erast Fandorin extracted from his pocket a salami sandwich and fortified himself without leaving his post. By this time he had succeeded in establishing thoroughly amicable relations with the bearded doorkeeper, who told Fandorin to call him 'Mitrich' and had already imparted to the young man several extremely valuable pieces of advice concerning entry to the 'nuversity'. Fandorin, who had represented himself to the garrulous old man as a young provincial cherishing fond dreams of buttons adorned with the university crest, was already wondering whether or not he ought to change his story and interrogate Mitrich directly about the pimpled 'sloucher', when the doorman suddenly became animated, grabbing the peaked cap off his head and pulling open the door – this was Mitrich's regular procedure whenever one of the professors or rich students passed by, for which he would every now and again receive a kopeck, or perhaps even a five-kopeck piece. Glancing round, Erast Fandorin noticed a student approaching the exit, clad in a sumptuous velvet cloak newly retrieved from the cloakroom, with clasps in the form of lion's feet. Gleaming on the bridge of the fop's nose was a pince-nez, and adorning his forehead was a scattering of pink pimples. Fandorin strained hard in an attempt to diagnose the condition of this student's posture, but the confounded cape of his cloak and his raised collar thwarted his efforts.

'Good evening, Nikolai Stepanovich, would you like me to call you a cab?' the doorkeeper said with a bow.

'Tell me, Mitrich, has it stopped raining yet?' the pimply student inquired in a high-pitched voice. 'Then I'll take a stroll, I'm tired of sitting.' And he dropped a coin into the outstretched palm from between the finger and thumb of his white-gloved hand.

'Who's that?' Fandorin asked in a whisper, straining his eyes to follow the dandy's receding back. 'Doesn't he have a bit of a slouch?'

'Nikolai Stepanich Akhtyrtsev. Rich as they come, royal blood,' Mitrich declared reverentially. 'Doles out at least fifteen kopecks every time.'

Fandorin suddenly felt feverish. Akhtyrtsev! Surely he was the one who had been named as executor in the will!

Mitrich bowed respectfully to yet another teacher, the long-haired lecturer in physics, and on turning back discovered to his surprise that the respectable young provincial gentleman had vanished into thin air.

The black velvet cloak was easily visible from a distance and Fandorin had overhauled his suspect in a trice, but hesitated to hail him by name: what accusation could he actually put to him? Even supposing he were to be identified by the shopkeeper Kukin and the spinster Pfühl (at this point Erast Fandorin sighed heavily as he recalled Lizanka yet again for the umpteenth time), then what of that? Would it not be better to follow the guidance of the great Fouchet, that incomparable luminary of criminal investigation, and shadow the object of his interest?

No sooner said than done. Especially as shadowing the student proved to be quite easy: Akhtyrtsev was strolling at a leisurely pace in the direction of Tverskaya Street, without looking round, merely glancing after the pretty young milliners every now and then. Several times Erast Fandorin boldly stole up very close to the student and even heard him carelessly whistling Smith's serenade from *The Fair Maid of Perth*. The failed suicide (if, indeed, this were he) was clearly in the most cheerful of moods. The student halted outside Korf's tobacco shop and spent a long time surveying the boxes of cigars in the window, but he did not go in.

Fandorin was beginning to feel convinced that his 'mark' was idling away the time until some appointed hour. This conviction was reinforced when Akhtyrtsev took out a gold pocket watch and flicked open its lid, then increased his pace as he set off up the pavement, switching into a rendition of the more decisive 'Boys' Chorus' from the new-style opera *Carmen*.

Turning into Kamergersky Lane, the student stopped whistling and stepped out so briskly that Erast Fandorin was obliged to drop back a little, otherwise it would have looked too suspicious. Fortunately, before he reached Darzan's, the fashionable ladies' salon, the 'mark' slowed his pace and shortly thereafter came to a complete halt. Fandorin crossed over to the opposite side of the street and took up his post beside a bakery that breathed out the fragrant aromas of fancy pastries.

For about fifteen minutes, perhaps even twenty, Akhtyrtsev, displaying ever-more obvious signs of nervousness, strode to and fro in front of the decorative oak doors of the shop, into which from time to time busy-looking ladies would disappear, and from which deliverymen emerged bearing elegantly wrapped bundles and boxes. Waiting in a line along the pavement were several carriages, some even with coats-of-arms on their lacquered doors. At seventeen minutes past two (Erast Fandorin noted the time from a clock in the shop window) the student suddenly roused himself and dashed over to a slim, elegant lady wearing a short veil, who had emerged from the shop. Doffing his peaked cap, he began saying something, gesturing with his arms. Fandorin crossed the road with an expression of boredom on his face – after all, why should he not wish to drop into Darzan's?

'I have no time for you just at present,' he heard the lady declare in a clear voice – she was dressed in the latest Parisian fashion, in a dress of lilac watered silk with a train. 'Later. Come after seven, as usual, everything will be decided there.'

Paying no more attention to the agitated Akhtyrtsev, she walked off towards a two-seater phaeton with an open roof.

'But Amalia! Amalia Kazimirovna, by your leave!' the student called out after her. 'I was rather counting on a discussion in private.'

'Later, later!' the lady flung back at him. 'I'm in a hurry at the moment!'

A faint breath of wind lifted the light, gauzy veil from her face and Erast Fandorin froze in astonishment. He had seen those languid, night-black eyes, that Egyptian oval face, those capriciously curving lips before, and once seen such a face can never be forgotten. It was she, the mysterious A.B., who had bidden the unfortunate Kokorin never to forswear his love! Now the case was certainly assuming a completely different complexion.

Akhtyrtsev halted in dismay on the pavement, his head drawn back gracelessly into his shoulders (a slouch, a quite distinct slouch, Erast Fandorin noted conclusively), and meanwhile the phaeton unhurriedly bore the Egyptian queen away in the direction of Petrovka Street. Fandorin had to make a decision, and judging that the student would be easy enough to locate again, he abandoned him to his fate and set off at a run towards the corner of Bolshaya Dmitrovka Street, where a line of taxicabs was standing.

'Police,' he hissed at the drowsy Ivan in a peaked cap and padded kaftan. 'Quick, follow that carriage! And get a move on! Don't worry, you'll be paid the full fare.'

His Ivan drew himself up, pushed back his sleeves with exaggerated zeal, shook the reins, gave a bark, and his dappled nag set off, with its hoofs clip-clopping loudly against the cobbles of the road.

At the corner of Rozhdestvenka Street a dray carrying a load of planks swung out across the roadway, blocking it off completely. In extreme agitation Erast Fandorin leapt to his feet and even raised himself up on the tips of his toes, gazing after the phaeton, which had slipped through before the obstruction. He was fortunate enough to just catch a glimpse of it as it turned on to Bolshaya Lubyanka Street.

Never mind, God was merciful, they caught up with the phaeton at Sretenka Street, just as it plunged into a narrow and hunchbacked side street. The wheels of the cab began bouncing over potholes. Fandorin saw the phaeton halt and he prodded his cabby in the back to tell him to drive on and not give the game away. He deliberately turned to face the opposite direction, but out of the very corner of his eye he saw the lilac lady being greeted with a bow from some tall, liveried servant at the entrance to a neat little stone mansion. Round the first corner Erast Fandorin let his cab go and set off slowly in the direction from which he had come, as though he were out for a stroll. This time as he approached the neat little mansion he was able to survey it at his leisure: a mezzanine with a green roof, curtains covering the windows, a front porch with a projecting roof. But he was unable to discern any brass plaque on the door.

There was, however, a janitor in an apron and a battered peaked cap sitting in idle boredom on a bench by the wall. It was towards him that Erast Fandorin directed his steps.

'Tell me, my friend,' he began as he approached, extracting twenty kopecks of state funds from his pocket, 'whose house is this?'

'That's no secret,' the janitor replied vaguely, following the movement of Fandorin's fingers with interest.

'Take that. Who was that lady who arrived not long ago?'

The janitor took the money and replied gravely, 'The house belongs to General Maslov's wife, only she doesn't live here, she rents it out. And the lady is the tenant, Miss Bezhets-kaya, Amalia Kazimirovna Bezhetskaya.'

'And who is she?' Erast Fandorin pressed him. 'Has she been living here long? Does she have many visitors?'

The janitor stared at him in silence, chewing on his lips. Some incomprehensible process was working itself out in his brain.

'I'll tell you what, boss,' he said, rising to his feet and suddenly seizing tight hold of Fandorin's sleeve. 'You just hang on a moment.'

He dragged the vainly resisting Fandorin across to the porch and gave a tug on the clapper of a small bronze bell.

'What are you doing?' the horrified sleuth exclaimed, making futile attempts to free himself. 'I'll show you . . . Have you any idea who . . .?'

The door opened and the doorway was filled by a tall servant in livery with immense, sandy-coloured side-whis-kers and a clean-shaven chin – it was clear at a glance that he was no Russian.

'He's been snooping about asking questions about Amalia Kazimirovna,' the villainous janitor reported in a sugary voice. 'And offering money too, sir. I didn't take it, sir. So what I thought, John Karlich, was . . .'

The butler (for a butler is what he was, since he was an Englishman) ran the impassive gaze of his small, sharp eyes over the prisoner, handed the Judas a silver fifty-kopeck piece and moved aside slightly to make way.

'Really, this is all nothing but a misunderstanding!' said Fandorin, still struggling to collect his wits. He switched into English: 'It's ridiculous, a complete misunderstanding!'

'Oh no, please do go in, sir, please do,' the janitor droned from behind him, and to make quite sure he grabbed hold of Fandorin's other sleeve and shoved him in through the door.

Erast Fandorin found himself in a rather wide hallway opposite a stuffed bear holding a silver tray for receiving visiting cards. The shaggy beast's small glass eyes contemplated the collegiate registrar's predicament without the slightest trace of sympathy.

'Who? What for?' the butler asked succinctly in strongly accented Russian, entirely ignoring Fandorin's perfectly good English.

Erast Fandorin said nothing, under no circumstances wishing to reveal the secret of his identity.

'What's the matter, John?' Fandorin heard a clear voice that was already familiar to him ask in English. Standing on the carpeted stairs that must lead to the mezzanine was the mistress of the house, who had already removed her hat and veil.

'Aha, the young brunet!' she exclaimed in a mocking tone, turning towards Fandorin, who was devouring her with his eyes. 'I spotted you back there on Kamergersky Lane. One really should not glare at strange ladies in that way! Clever, though, I must say – you managed to follow me! Are you a student or just another idle ne'er-do-well?'

'Fandorin, Erast Petrovich,' he introduced himself, uncertain what else to add, but Cleopatra had apparently already found a satisfactory explanation for his appearance.

'I do like the bold ones,' she said with a laugh. 'Especially when they're so good-looking. But it's not nice to spy on people. If you find my person so very interesting, then come this evening – all sorts of people come visiting here. You will be quite able to satisfy your curiosity then. But wear tails. The manners in my house are free, but men who are not in the military must wear tails – that's the law.'

★

45

When evening arrived it found Erast Fandorin fully equipped. It was true, certainly, that his father's frock coat had proved to be a little broad for him in the shoulders, but the splendid Agafena Kondratievna, the provincial secretary's wife from whom Fandorin rented his little room, had pinned it in along the seams and it had really turned out quite respectable, especially if he did not button it. An extensive wardrobe, including an entire five pairs of white gloves, was the only property that the failed bank investor had bequeathed to his son. The items that looked best on him were the silk waistcoat from Burgess and the patent-leather shoes from Pironet. The almost-new top hat from Blanc was not too bad either, except that it tended to creep down over his eyes. But that was all right; hand it to the servant at the door and the problem was solved. Erast Fandorin decided not to take a cane, he felt that would be rather bad form. He gyrated in front of the chipped mirror in the dark hallway and was pleased by what he saw, above all by the waistline that was maintained so ideally by the strict 'Lord Byron'. In his waistcoat pocket lay a silver rouble, provided by Xavier Grushin for a bouquet ('a decent one, but nothing too fancy'). What kind of fancy bouquet would a rouble get you? Erast Fandorin sighed, and he decided to add fifty kopecks of his own – then he could afford Parma violets.

The bouquet meant that he had to go without a cab, and Erast Fandorin did not arrive at the palace of Cleopatra (the sobriquet which suited Amalia Kazimirovna Bezhetskaya best of all) until a quarter past eight.

The guests were already assembled. While he was still in the front hall after being admitted by the maid, the clerk heard the droning of a large number of men's voices, punctuated every now and again by *that* voice, with its magical, silver-and-crystal tones. Lingering for a second at the threshold, Erast Fandorin gathered his courage and strode in with a distinct nonchalance, hoping to produce the impression of an experienced man of the world. He need not have bothered – no one even turned to look at the new arrival.

Fandorin's gaze encountered a hall furnished with comfortable Moroccan-leather divans, velvet chairs and elegant little tables – it was all very stylish and modern. At the centre, her feet planted on a tiger-skin rug, stood the mistress of the house, dressed in Spanish costume – a scarlet dress with a corsage and a crimson camellia set in her hair. She looked so lovely that Fandorin caught his breath. He did not immediately examine the guests, merely registering the fact that they were all men, and that Akhtyrtsev was here, sitting somewhat apart from the others and looking terribly pale.

'Ah, here is the new admirer,' Bezhetskaya announced, glancing with an ironic smile in Fandorin's direction. 'That makes it a perfect baker's dozen. I shan't introduce everybody, it would take too long. You must tell us your name. I recall that you are a student, but I'm afraid I've forgotten your name.'

'Fandorin,' Erast Fandorin squeaked in a voice that trembled treacherously, then repeated the name, more firmly, 'Fandorin.'

Everybody glanced across at him, but only cursorily. It was evident that the newly arrived young fellow did not really interest them. It quite soon became clear that in this company there was only one centre of interest. The guests scarcely spoke to each other at all, addressing themselves predominantly to their hostess, and all of them, even a grave-looking old man wearing a diamond star, vied with each other to achieve a single goal – to attract her attention and eclipse the others, if only for an instant. There were only two who behaved differently – the taciturn Akhtyrtsev, who swigged incessantly from a bottle of champagne, and an officer of the hussars, a well-set-up young chap with a slight slant to his eyes and a smile that was all white teeth and black moustache. He gave the appearance of being rather bored and hardly even looked at Amalia Bezhetskaya, while contemplating the other guests with a wry grin of contempt. Cleopatra clearly favoured this rascal, calling him simply 'Hippolyte', and on a couple of occasions she cast him a glance that sent a melancholy pang through Erast Fandorin's heart.

Suddenly he roused himself. A certain plump gentleman with a white cross hanging round his neck had just taken advantage of a pause to interpose a word:

'Amalia Kazimirovna, you recently forbade us to gossip about Kokorin, but I have learned something rather curious.'

He stopped for a moment, pleased by the effect this had produced, and everyone turned to look at him.

'Don't be so tiresome, Anton Ivanovich. Tell us,' said a fat man with a tall forehead who looked like a prosperous lawyer.

'Yes, don't be tiresome,' the others took up the refrain.

'He didn't simply shoot himself, it was a case of "American roulette", or so the governor-general whispered to me today in the chancellery,' the plump gentleman informed them in a meaningful tone of voice. 'Do you know what that is?'

'It's common knowledge,' said Hippolyte, shrugging his shoulders. 'You take a revolver and put in one cartridge. It's stupid, but exciting. A shame the Americans thought of it before we did.'

'But what has that to do with roulette, Count?' the old man with the diamond star asked, mystified.

'Odds or evens, red or black, anything but zero!' Akhtyrt-sev cried out and burst into loud, unnatural laughter, gazing challengingly at Amalia Bezhetskaya (or, at least, so it seemed to Fandorin).

'I warned you that I would throw out anyone who mentions that,' said their hostess, now angry in earnest. 'And banish them from my house forever! A fine subject for gossip!'

An awkward silence fell.

'But you won't dare banish me from the house,' Akhtyrtsev declared in the same familiar tone. 'I would say I have earned the right to speak my mind freely.'

'And how exactly, may I inquire?' interjected a stocky captain in a guards uniform.

'By getting plastered, the snot-nosed pup,' said Hippolyte (whom the old man had addressed as 'Count'), deliberately attempting to provoke a scandal. 'With your permission, Amelie, I'll take him outside for a breath of fresh air.'

'When I require your intervention, Hippolyte Ivanovich, you may be sure that I shall request it,' Cleopatra replied, with a hint of malice, and the confrontation was nipped in the bud. 'I'll tell you what, gentlemen, since there is no interesting conversation to be got out of you, let's play a game of forfeits. Last time, when Frol Lukich lost, it was quite amusing to see him embroidering that flower and pricking his poor fingers so badly with the needle!'

Everyone laughed merrily, apart from one bearded gentleman with a bobbed haircut whose tailcoat sat on him slightly askew.

'Well, my dear Amalia Kazimirovna, you've had your fun at the old merchant's expense . . . Serves me right for being such a fool,' he said humbly, with a northern provincial accent. 'But honest traders always pay their debts. The other day we risked our dignity in front of you, so today why don't you take the risk?'

'Why, the commercial counsellor is quite right!' exclaimed the lawyer. 'A fine mind! Let Amalia Kazimirovna show some courage. Gentlemen, a proposal! Whichever one of us draws the forfeit will ask our radiant one to . . . well . . . to do something quite extraordinary.'

'Quite right! Bravo!' the cries came from all sides.

'Could this be rebellion? Pugachev's revolt?' their dazzling hostess laughed. 'What on earth do you want from me?'

'I know!' put in Akhtyrtsev. 'A candid answer to any question. No prevaricating, no playing cat-and-mouse. And it must be tête-à-tête.'

'Why tête-à-tête?' protested the captain. 'Everybody will be curious to hear.'

'If "everybody" is to hear, then it won't be candid,' said Bezhetskaya with a twinkle in her eye. 'Very well then, let us play at being candid, have it your way. But will the lucky winner not be afraid to hear the truth from me? The truth could prove rather unpalatable.'

Rolling his *r* like a true Parisian, the count interjected:

'*J'en ai le frisson d'y penser.*[1] To hell with the truth, gentlemen. Who needs it? Why don't we have a game of American roulette instead? Well, not tempted?'

'Hippolyte, I believe I warned you!' the goddess hurled her thunderbolt at him. 'I shall not say it again! Not a single word about *that!*'

Hippolyte instantly fell silent and even spread his arms wide, as if to show that his lips were sealed.

Meanwhile the adroit captain was already collecting forfeits in his cap. Erast Fandorin put in his father's cambric handkerchief with the monogrammed initials 'P.F.'

Plump Anton Ivanovich was entrusted with making the draw.

First of all he drew out of the cap the cigar which he himself had placed there and asked ingratiatingly, 'What am I bid for this fine thing?'

'The hole from a doughnut,' replied Cleopatra, with her face turned towards the wall, and everyone except the plump gentleman laughed in malicious delight.

'And for this?' Anton Ivanovich indifferently drew out the captain's silver pencil.

'Last year's snow.'

Then came a medallion watch ('a fish's ears'), a playing-card ('*mes condoléances*'), some phosphorous matches ('Kutuzov's right eye'), an amber cigarette-holder ('much ado about nothing', a hundred-rouble banknote ('three times nothing'), a tortoiseshell comb ('four times nothing'), a grape ('Orest Kirillovich's thick locks' – prolonged laughter at the expense of an absolutely bald gentleman wearing the order of St Vladimir in his buttonhole), a carnation ('to that one – never, not for anything'). Only two forfeits remained in the cap, Erast Fandorin's handkerchief and Akhtyrtsev's

---

[1] It makes me shiver just to think of it.

gold ring. When the ring gleamed and sparkled in the caller's fingers, the student leaned forward urgently, and Fandorin saw beads of sweat stand out on the pimply forehead.

'Shall I give it to this one, then?' drawled Amelia Bezhetskaya, who was clearly a little bored with amusing her public. Akhtyrtsev rose halfway to his feet, unable to believe his luck, and lifted the pince-nez off his nose. 'But no, I don't think so, not this one, the final one,' their tormentress concluded.

Everyone turned towards Erast Fandorin, paying serious attention to him for the first time. During the preceding minutes, as his chances had improved, his mind had been working ever more frantically to decide what he should do if he won. Now his doubts had been settled. It must be fate.

And then Akhtyrtsev jumped to his feet, came running over to him and whispered fervently:

'Let me have it, I implore you. What is it to you? . . . You're here for the first time, but my fate depends on it . . . Sell it to me, at least. How much? Do you want five hundred? A thousand? More?'

With a calm decisiveness that surprised even him, Erast Fandorin pushed the whispering student aside, walked over to their hostess and asked with a bow:

'Where shall we go?'

She looked at Fandorin with amused curiosity. Her stare set his head spinning.

'Over there will do, in the corner. I should be afraid to go somewhere alone with anyone as bold as you.'

Disregarding the mocking laughter of the others, Erast Fandorin followed her to the far corner of the hall and lowered himself on to a divan with a carved wooden back. Amalia Kazimirovna set a *pakhitosa* in a silver cigarette-holder, lit it from a candle and inhaled deliciously.

'Well, and how much did Nikolai Stepanich offer you for me? I could tell what he was whispering to you.'

'A thousand roubles,' Fandorin replied honestly. 'And then he offered more.'

Cleopatra's agate eyes glinted maliciously:

'Oho, how very impatient he is! So you must be a millionaire?'

'No, I'm not rich,' Erast Fandorin said modestly. 'But I consider it dishonourable to sell my luck.'

The other guests grew weary of trying to eavesdrop on their conversation – they could not hear anything anyway – and breaking up into small groups they struck up conversations of their own, although from time to time every one of them kept glancing over at the far corner.

Meanwhile Cleopatra surveyed her temporary lord and sovereign with frank derision.

'What do you wish to ask about?'

Erast Fandorin hesitated.

'Will the answer be honest?'

'Honesty is for the honest, and in our games there is but little honesty,' Bezhetskaya laughed with a barely perceptible hint of bitterness. 'I can promise candour, though. But please don't disappoint me by asking anything stupid. I regard you as an interesting specimen.'

Fandorin threw himself recklessly into the attack.

'What do you know about the death of Pyotr Alexandrovich Kokorin?'

His hostess was not frightened, she did not flinch, but Erast Fandorin imagined that he saw her eyes narrow for an instant.

'Why do you want to know that?'

'I will explain afterwards. First answer the question.'

'All right, I will. Kokorin was killed by a certain very cruel lady.' Bezhetskaya lowered her thick black lashes for a moment and darted a rapid, scorching glance at him from beneath them, like a rapier-thrust. 'And that lady goes by the name of "Love".'

'Love for you? Did he used to come here?'

'He did. And apart from me I believe there is no one here

with whom to fall in love. Except perhaps Orest Kirillovich.'
She laughed.

'And do you feel no pity at all for Kokorin?' asked Fandorin,
amazed at such callousness.

The queen of Egypt shrugged her shoulders indifferently.

'Everyone is master of his own fate. But is that not enough
questions for you?'

'No,' Erast Fandorin said hurriedly. 'How was Akhtyrtsev
involved? And what is the significance of the bequest to Lady
Astair?'

The buzz of voices suddenly grew louder, and Fandorin
glanced round in annoyance.

'You don't care for my tone?' Hippolyte asked in a thunderous voice, harassing the drunken Akhtyrtsev. 'Then how do
you care for this, old bean?' And he shoved the student's
forehead with the palm of his hand, apparently without any
great strength, but the miserable Akhtyrtsev went flying
back against an armchair, plumped down into it and remained sitting there, blinking his eyes in bewilderment.

'By your leave, Count, but this will not do!' said Erast
Fandorin, dashing across. 'You may be stronger, but that does
not give you any right . . .'

However, his faltering speech, at which the count had
scarcely even glanced around, was drowned out by the
resounding tones of the mistress of the house.

'Hippolyte! Get out! And do not dare set foot in here again
until you are sober!'

The count swore and stomped off towards the door. The
other guests gazed curiously at the wretchedly abject, limp
form of Akhtyrtsev, who was not making the slightest effort
to rise to his feet.

'You are the only one here who is anything like a man,'
Amalia Kazimirovna whispered to Fandorin, as she set off
towards the corridor. 'Take him away. And be sure to stay
with him.'

Almost immediately the lanky John appeared, having
exchanged his livery for a black frock coat and starched

shirtfront. He helped to get the student as far as the door and then rammed his top hat on to his head. Bezhetskaya did not come out to take her leave, and a glance at the butler's dour face told Erast Fandorin he had best be on his way.

Chapter Five

IN WHICH SERIOUS UNPLEASANTNESS
LIES IN WAIT FOR THE HERO

Out in the street, once he had taken a breath of fresh air, Akhtyrtsev appeared to revive somewhat. He was standing firmly on his own two feet without swaying, and Erast Fandorin decided that it was no longer necessary to support him by the elbow.

'Let's take a stroll as far as Sretenka Street,' he said, 'and I'll put you in a cab there. Do you have a long journey home?'

'Home?' In the flickering light of the kerosene street lamp the student's wan face appeared like a pale mask. 'Oh no, I'm not going home, not for the world! Let's take a drive somewhere, shall we? I feel in the mood for a talk. You saw . . . the way they treat me. What's your name? I remember, Fandorin. A funny name, that. And I'm Akhtyrtsev, Nikolai Akhtyrtsev.'

Erast Fandorin gave a gentle bow as he attempted to resolve a complex moral dilemma: would it offend against decency if he were to take advantage of Akhtyrtsev's weakened condition in order to worm out of him the information he required, since the 'sloucher' himself seemed rather inclined to a little candid conversation?

He decided that it would not. The investigative passion had indeed taken a powerful grip on him.

'The Crimea's not far from here,' Akhtyrtsev recalled. 'And

55

there's no need for a cab, we can walk. It's a filthy dive, of course, but they do have decent wines. Let's go, eh? I invite you.'

Fandorin raised no objections and they set off slowly (the student was just a little unsteady on his feet after all) along the side street towards the lights of Sretenka Street shining in the distance.

'Tell me, Fandorin, I suppose you think I'm a coward?' Akhtyrtsev asked, slurring his words slightly. 'For not calling the count out, for enduring the insult and pretending to be drunk? I'm no coward, and perhaps I'll tell you something that will convince you of that . . . He was deliberately trying to provoke me. I dare say she was the one who put him up to it, in order to be rid of me and not pay her debt . . . Oh, you've no idea what kind of a woman she is! . . . And for Zurov killing a man means no more than swatting a fly. He practises shooting with a pistol every morning for an hour. They say he can put a bullet into a five-kopeck piece at twenty paces. Call that a duel? There's absolutely no risk in it for him at all. It's simply murder called by a fancy name. And the main thing is, he won't pay for it, he'll squirm his way out of it somehow. He already has done more than once. Well, he might go travelling abroad for a while. But now I want to live, I've earned the right.'

They turned off Sretenka Street into another side street, rather seedy-looking, but even so it had not mere kerosene lamps, but gas lamps, and now ahead of them there loomed up a three-storey building with brightly lit windows. It had to be the Crimea, Erast Fandorin thought with a sinking heart – he had heard a great deal about this iniquitous establishment that was famous throughout Moscow.

No one met them at the tall porch with its bright lamps. Akhtyrtsev pushed against the tall, decoratively carved door with a habitual gesture and it yielded easily, breathing out warmth and a smell compounded of cooking and alcohol. There was a sudden din of voices and squeaking of violins.

After leaving their top hats in the cloakroom, the young

men fell into the clutches of an animated fellow in a scarlet shirt, who addressed Akhtyrtsev as 'Your Excellency' and promised him the very best table, that had been specially kept for him. The table proved to be by the wall and, thank God, it was a long way from the stage, where the gypsy choir was keening loudly and rattling its tambourines. Erast Fandorin, who found himself in a genuine den of debauchery for the first time, twisted his head first one way, then the other. The clientele here was extremely varied, but there did not appear to be a single sober individual among them. The tone was set by young merchants and stockbrokers with pomaded partings in their hair – everybody knew who had the money nowadays – but there were also gentlemen of a decidedly aristocratic appearance, and somewhere he even caught the golden gleam of monogrammed initials on an aide-de-camp's epaulette. The collegiate registrar's interest was aroused most strongly, however, by the girls who came to sit at the tables as soon as they were beckoned. Erast Fandorin blushed at the low-necked dresses they were wearing, and their skirts had slits through which round knees in net stockings protruded shamelessly.

'What, girls caught your eye, have they?' Akhtyrtsev laughed, ordering wine and a main course from a waiter. 'After Amalia I don't even think of them as creatures of the female sex. How old are you, Fandorin?'

'Twenty-one,' said Fandorin, adding a year to his age.

'Well, I'm twenty-three, and I've already seen a lot. Don't gawp at the whores, they're just a waste of time and money. And it leaves you feeling disgusted afterwards. If you must love, then love a queen! But then, why am I telling you that? You didn't end up at Amalia's by some fluke, after all. Has she bewitched you? She likes doing that, adding to her collection, and the exhibits have to be continually renewed. How does that song in the operetta go, *Elle ne pense qu'à exciter les hommes*[1] . . . But everything has its price, and I've

---

[1] She thinks only of turning men's heads.

already paid mine. Would you like me to tell you a story? Somehow I like you. You're remarkably good at keeping quiet. And it will be useful for you to know what kind of woman she is. Maybe you'll come to your senses, before you get swallowed up, like me. Or have you already been swallowed up, eh, Fandorin? What was that you were whispering to her over there?'

Erast Fandorin lowered his eyes.

'Then listen,' said Akhtyrtsev, launching into his story. 'Not long since you suspected me of cowardice, because I let Hippolyte off and didn't call him out to a duel. But I've fought a duel the like of which your Hippolyte has never even dreamed of. Did you hear the way she forbade us to talk about Kokorin? I should think so! His blood's on her conscience, on hers. And on mine, too, of course. Only I've redeemed my mortal sin by fear. Kokorin and I were in the same year at university, he used to go to Amalia's place too. We used to be friends once, but because of her we became enemies. Kokorin was a bit more free and easy than me, with a cute kind of face, but *entre nous*,[1] once a merchant always a merchant, a plebeian, even if you have studied at the university. Amalia had her fill of amusement out of us – first she would favour one of us, then the other. Called me Nicolas, and spoke to me familiarly, as though I were one of her favourites, and then for some stupid trifle or other she'd consign me to disgrace: she'd forbid me to show my face for a week, and then she was back to formal terms – Mr Akhtyrtsev, Nikolai Stepanych. Her policy is never ever to let anyone off the hook.'

'And what is this Hippolyte to her?' Fandorin asked cautiously.

'Count Zurov? I can't say exactly, but there's something special between them . . . Either he has some hold over her, or she has over him . . . But he's not jealous, he's not the problem. A woman like that would never allow anyone to be jealous of her. In a word, she's a queen!'

---

[1] between us.

He fell silent, because at the next table a company of tipsy businessmen had begun kicking up a racket – as they were getting ready to leave an argument had broken out about who was going to pay. In a trice the waiters had carried off the dirty tablecloth and spread out a new one, and a minute later the free table was already occupied by an extremely drunk functionary with whitish, almost transparent, eyes (no doubt the result of hard drinking). Flitting across to this reveller, a pudgy girl with brown hair put her arm round his shoulder and theatrically flung one of her legs over the other – Erast Fandorin gazed admiringly at a knee clad in tight red *fil de Perse*.

Meanwhile the student drained a full glass of Rhine wine, prodded at a bloody beefsteak with his fork and continued.

'D'you think, Fandorin, that it was the misery of love that made him lay hands on himself? Not a bit of it! I was the one who killed him.'

'What?' Fandorin could not believe his ears.

'You heard me,' Akhtyrtsev said with a nod, looking proud. 'I'll tell you all about it, just sit quietly and don't go interrupting me with questions.

'Yes, I killed him, and I don't regret it in the least. I killed him, fair and square in a duel. Yes, fair and square! Because no duel since time immemorial has ever been fairer than ours. When two men face up to each other, there's almost always some deception in it – one is a better shot and the other a worse, or else one is fat and makes an easier target, or else one spent a sleepless night and his hands are shaking. But Pierre and I did everything without any deception. She said – it was in Sokolniki, on the round alley, the three of us were out for a drive in the carriage – she said: "I'm fed up with the pair of you rich, spoiled little brats. Why don't you kill each other or something?" And Kokorin, the swine, said to her: "I will kill him too, if only it will earn me a reward from you." I said: "And for a reward I would kill. Such a reward as can't be divided between two. So it's a quick road to a damp grave for one of us if he doesn't back down." Things had already gone that far between Kokorin and me. "What, do you really love me so much, then?" she asked. "More than life itself," he said. And I said the same. "Very well," says she, "the only thing I value in people is courage, everything else can be counterfeited. Hear my will. If one of you really does kill the other he shall have a reward for his bravery, and you know what it shall be." And she laughs. "Only you are idle boasters," she says, "both of you. You won't kill anybody. The only interesting thing about you is your fathers' capital." I flew into a rage. "I cannot speak," I said, "for Kokorin, but for the sake of such a reward I will not begrudge either my own life or another man's." And she says, angry now, "I'll tell you what, I'm sick and tired of all your crowing. It's decided, you shall shoot at each other, but not in a duel, or else we shall never be rid of the scandal. And a duel is too uncertain. One of you will shoot a hole in the other's hand and turn up at my house as the victor. No, let it be death for one and love for the other. Let fate decide. Cast lots. And the one the lot falls to – let him shoot himself. And let him write a note so that no one will think that it might be because of me. Have you turned coward now? If you have turned coward, then at least out of shame you will stop visiting me – at least then some good will come of it." Pierre looked at me and said, "I don't know about Akhtyrtsev, but I won't funk it." And so we decided . . .'

The student fell silent and hung his head. Then he shook himself, filled his glass up to the brim and gulped it down. At the next table the girl in the red stockings broke into peals of laughter – the white-eyed fellow was whispering something into her ear.

'But what about the will?' Erast Fandorin asked, then bit his tongue, since he was not, after all, supposed to know anything about it. However, Akhtyrtsev, absorbed in his reminiscences, merely nodded listlessly:

'Ah, the will . . . She thought of that. "Didn't you want to buy me with money?" she said. "Very well, then, let there be money, only not the hundred thousand that Nikolai Stepanich promised." (It's true, I did make her an offer once – she almost threw me out.) "And not two hundred thousand. Let it be everything you have. Whichever one of you must die, let him go to the next world naked. Only I," she says, "have no need of your money, I can endow anyone you like myself. Let the money go to some good cause – a holy monastery or something of the sort. For prayers for forgiveness of the mortal sin. Well, Petrusha," she said, "your million should make a good thick candle, don't you think?" But Kokorin was an atheist, a militant. He was outraged: "Anybody but the priests," he said. "I'd rather leave it to all the fallen women, let each of them buy herself a sewing machine and change her trade. If there's not a single woman of the street left in all of Moscow, that'll be something to remember Pyotr Kokorin by." But then Amalia objected: "Once a woman's become debauched, you can never reform her. It should have been done earlier, when she was young and innocent." So Kokorin gave up on that and said, "Then let it go to children, to some orphans or other, to the Foundling Hospital." She lit up immediately at that. "For that, Petrusha, you would be forgiven a great deal. Come here and let me kiss you." I was furious. "They'll embezzle all your millions in the Foundling Hospital," I said. "Haven't you read what they write about the state orphanages in the newspapers? And anyway, it's way too much for them to have. Better give it all to the Englishwoman, Baroness Astair, she won't steal it." Amalia kissed me as well then. "Let's show our Russian patriots a thing or two," she said. That was on the eleventh, on Saturday. On Sunday Kokorin and I met and talked everything over. It was an odd kind of conversation. He kept blustering and swaggering and I mostly just kept quiet, and we didn't look into each other's eyes. I felt as though I was in some kind of daze . . . We called out an attorney and drew up our wills in due form, Pierre as my witness and executor, and I as his. We each gave the attorney five thousand to make him keep his mouth shut. It wouldn't have been worth his while to blab about it, anyway. And Pierre and I agreed on our arrangement – he was the one who suggested it. We meet at ten o'clock at my place in the Taganka district (I live on Goncharnaya Street). Each of us has a six-chamber revolver in his pocket with one round in the cylinder. We walk separately, but so that we can see each other. Whoever the dice choose goes first. Kokorin had read somewhere about American roulette and he liked the idea. He said, "Because of you and me, Kolya, they'll rename it Russian roulette, just you wait and see." And he said, "It's a bore to shoot yourself at home. Let's wind things up with a stroll and a few amusements." I agreed, it was all the same to me. I confess I'd lost heart, I thought I would lose. And it was hammering away in my brain – Monday the thirteenth, Monday the thirteenth. That night I didn't sleep at all, I felt like leaving the country, but when I thought of him left behind with her and laughing at me . . . Anyway, I stayed.

'And then in the morning Pierre turned up dressed like a dandy, in a white waistcoat, terribly cheerful. He was a lucky sort, and obviously he was hoping his luck would hold in this too. We threw the dice in my study. He got nine and I got three. I was prepared for that. "I'm not going anywhere," I said, "I'd rather die here." I spun the cylinder and put the barrel to my heart. "Stop!" he said to me. "Don't fire at your heart. If the bullet goes crooked you'll be in agony for ages. Shoot yourself in the temple or the mouth instead." "Thank you for your concern," I said, and at that moment I hated him so much I could easily have shot him without any duel. But I took his advice. I'll never forget that click, the very first one. It clanged so loudly right in my ear, like . . .'

Akhtyrstev shuddered convulsively and poured himself another glass. The singer, a fat gypsy woman in a shimmering golden shawl, began crooning some heart-rending melody in a low voice.

'I heard Pierre's voice say: "Right, now it's my turn. Let's go out into the air." Only then did I realise I was alive. We went to Shvivaya Hill, where there's a view over the city. Kokorin walking in front, with me about twenty paces behind. He stood for a while on the edge of the cliff, I couldn't see his face, then he raised the hand holding the pistol so that I could see it, spun the cylinder and quickly set it against his head – click. But I knew nothing would happen to him, I hadn't even been hoping it would. We threw the dice again. And I lost again. I went down to the Yauza, there wasn't a single soul around. I climbed up on a bollard by the bridge, in order to fall straight into the water . . . Again I was spared. We went off to one side and Pierre said to me: "This is becoming a bit of a bore. Let's give the Philistines a fright, shall we?" He was putting a brave face on it, I must give him that. We came out on to a side street and there were people there, and carriages driving along. I stood on the far side of the road. Kokorin doffed his hat, bowed to the right and the left, raised his hand, gave the cylinder a spin – and nothing. Well, we had to scoot out of there quickly. There was uproar and screaming and ladies squealing. We turned into a gateway, down on Maroseika Street already. We threw the dice, and what do you think? My turn again! He had two sixes, and I threw a two, I swear it. That's it, I thought, *Finito*,[1] nothing could be more symbolic than that. One gets everything, the other gets nothing. I tried to shoot myself for the third time outside the church of Kosma and Damian, that's where I was christened. I stood up on the porch, where the beggars are, gave them each a rouble, then took off my cap . . . When I opened my eyes I was alive. And one holy fool said to me: "If the soul itches – the Lord will forgive." If the soul itches – the Lord will forgive. I remembered that. Right, so we ran away from there. Kokorin chose a rather grander place, right beside the Galofteevsky Passage. He went into a confectioner's on Neglinny Lane and sat down, I stood outside the window. He said something to the lady at the next table and she smiled. He took out his revolver and pressed the trigger, I saw it. The lady laughed even more. He put the revolver away, chatted with her for a bit about something or other and had a cup of coffee. I was already in a daze, I couldn't feel a thing. There

---

[1] It's over.

63

was only one thought in my mind – now we have to throw the dice again.

'We threw them on Okhotny Ryad, beside the Hotel Loskutnaya, and this time the first turn fell to him. I threw seven and he threw six. Seven and six, only one point in the difference. We walked together as far as Gurov's inn, and there, where they're building the Historical Museum, we separated – he went into the Alexander Gardens, walking along the alley, and I walked along the pavement, outside the fence. The last thing he said to me was: "We're a pair of stupid fools, Kolya. If nothing happens this time, to hell with the whole damn business." I wanted to stop him, I swear to God, but I didn't. Why, I don't know myself. But that's a lie, I do know . . . I had a mean thought – let him twirl the cylinder one more time, and we'll see what happens. Maybe we'll be finished then . . . I'm only telling you this, Fandorin. This is like a confessional . . .'

Akhtyrtsev took another drink. Behind the pince-nez his eyes were dull and red. Fandorin waited with bated breath, even though the general course of subsequent events was already known to him. Akhtyrtsev took a cigar out of his pocket and struck a match with a trembling hand. The long, thick cigar looked remarkably out of place with his unattractive, puerile face. Wafting the cloud of smoke away from his eyes, Akhtyrtsev rose sharply to his feet.

'Waiter, our bill! I can't stay here any longer. Too noisy, too stuffy.' He tugged at the silk tie round his throat. 'Let's take a cab somewhere. Or just take a stroll.'

Out on the porch they halted. The lane was dismal and deserted. In all the buildings except the Crimea the windows were dark. The gas flame in the nearest street lamp fluttered and flickered.

'Or perhapsh I will go home,' Akhtyrtsev slurred, with the cigar clasped in his teeth. 'There should be cabsh jusht round the corner.'

The door opened and their recent neighbour, the white-eyed functionary, emerged on to the porch, with a peaked cap tilted over to one side of his head. Hiccuping loudly, he reached into the pocket of his uniform jacket and took out a cigar.

'Would you mind giving me a light?' he asked, moving closer to the young men. Fandorin detected a slight accent, possibly Baltic German, possibly Finnish.

Akhtyrtsev slapped first one pocket, then another, and there was a rattle of matches. Erast Fandorin waited patiently. Suddenly the appearance of the white-eyed man underwent an incomprehensible transformation. He seemed to become slightly shorter in height and slumped over slightly to one side. The next instant a broad, short blade seemed to appear out of nowhere in his left hand, and with an economical, elastic movement the functionary thrust the blade into Akhtyrtsev's right side.

Subsequent events moved very quickly, taking no more than two or three seconds, but to Erast Fandorin time seemed to be standing still. He had time to notice many things, time to think about many things, but he was quite unable to move, as though the glint of light on steel had hypnotised him.

Erast Fandorin's first thought was, *He's stabbed him in the liver*, and from somewhere or other his memory cast up a sentence from the gymnasium textbook on biology – *Liver: an organ in the body of an animal that separates blood from bile*. Then he saw Akhtyrtsev die. Erast Fandorin had never seen anyone die before, but somehow he knew immediately that Akhtyrtsev had died. His eyes seemed to turn to glass, his lips distended spasmodically, and from between them there erupted a jet of dark, cherry-red blood. Very slowly – and even, it seemed to Fandorin, elegantly – the functionary pulled out the knife, which was no longer gleaming, and turned calmly and unhurriedly towards Erast Fandorin, and then his face was very close: luminous eyes with black dots for pupils, thin bloodless lips. The lips moved, distinctly articulating a word: 'Azazel'. And then time's expansion came to an end, time contracted like a spring, then straightened out and struck Erast Fandorin in the right side with a force so great that he fell backwards and banged the back of his head painfully against the edge of the porch's parapet. *What is this? What is this 'Azazel'?* – wondered Fandorin. *Am I asleep, then?* And he also thought, *His knife must have hit the 'Lord Byron'. Whalebone. An inch-thin waist.*

The doors burst open and a jolly company came tumbling out, laughing, on to the porch.

'Oho, gentlemen, we have an entire battle of Borodino here,' a drunken merchant's voice cried out merrily. 'Weren't up to it, poor chaps! Can't take their drink!'

Erast Fandorin raised himself up a little, pressing one hand against his hot, wet side, to take a look at the man with the white eyes.

But strange to tell, there was no man with white eyes. Akhtyrtsev was lying where he had fallen – face down across the steps – and his top hat lay where it had rolled a little further away, but the functionary had disappeared without trace, vanished into thin air. And there was not a single soul to be seen anywhere in the street. Nothing but the dull glow of the street lamps.

Then suddenly the street lamps did the oddest thing – they began turning, and then spinning round and round, faster and faster. First everything became very bright, and then it went absolutely dark.

Chapter Six

IN WHICH THE MAN OF THE FUTURE
MAKES HIS APPEARANCE

'Lie down, lie down, there's a good chap,' said Xavier Grushin from the doorway when the embarrassed Erast Fandorin lowered his legs from the hard divan. 'What did the doctor tell you to do? I know all about it, I made inquiries. Two weeks in bed after discharge, so that the cut can heal up properly and your concussed brain can settle back into place, and you haven't even been lying down for ten days yet.'

He sat down and mopped his crimson bald spot with a check handkerchief.

'O-oh, that sun's really warm today, really warm. Here, I've brought you some marzipan and fresh cherries, help yourself. Where shall I put them?'

The superintendent surveyed the dark, narrow box of a room in which the collegiate registrar lodged. There was nowhere to put his bundle of presents: the host was lying on the divan, Xavier Grushin himself was sitting on the chair, and the table was cluttered with heaps of books. The room contained no other furniture, not even a cupboard, and the numerous items of the tenant's wardrobe were hanging on nails hammered into the walls.

'Does it ache a bit?'

'Not at all,' Erast Fandorin said, not entirely truthfully. 'The stitches could come out tomorrow. It just scraped my ribs a bit, but otherwise it's fine. And my head is in perfectly good order.'

'You might as well be sick for a while anyway, your salary's going through.' Xavier Grushin gave a little frown of guilt. 'Don't be angry with me, my dear fellow, for not popping round to see you for so long. I dare say you were thinking badly of the old man – when he needed to get his report written he was round to the hospital in a flash, but since then he has no more use for me, doesn't even show his face. I sent someone to the doctor to inquire, but I just couldn't get away to see you myself. The things that are going on in our department, we're in there all day and all night too, and that's the honest truth.' The superintendent shook his head and lowered his voice confidentially. 'That Akhtyrtsev of yours wasn't just anybody, he was the grandson of His Highness Chancellor Korchakov, no less.'

'You don't say!' Fandorin gasped.

'His father's the ambassador in Holland, married for the second time, and your acquaintance here in Moscow used to live with his aunt, the Princess Korchakova, in a private palazzo on Goncharnaya Street. The Princess passed away last year and left her entire estate to him, and he already had plenty from his deceased mother. It's pandemonium down in the office now, let me tell you. First of all they demanded that the case should be personally supervised by the governor-general, Prince Dolgoruky himself. But there is no case, and no leads to make a start on. Apart from you, nobody saw the killer. As I told you last time, Bezhetskaya has just vanished into thin air. The house is empty. No servants and no papers. It's a wild goose chase. Who she is, is a mystery, where she came from no one knows. According to her passport she's a noblewoman from Vilnius. They sent an inquiry to Vilnius, and there's no such person registered there. All right. His Excellency called me in to see him a week ago. "Don't take this amiss, Xavier," he said, "I've known you for a long time and I respect you as a conscientious officer, but this affair is just too big for you to handle. There's a special investigator

coming from St Petersburg, a special assignments officer
attached to the chief of gendarmes and head of the Third
Section, his Excellency Adjutant-General Lavrentii Arkadievich Mizinov." You get the idea – a really big noise. One of
the new men, a man of the people, a man of the future. Does
everything scientifically. An expert in all sorts of clever
business, we're no match for him.' Xavier Grushin snorted
angrily. 'So he's a man of the future, and Grushin is a man of
the past. All right. He got here three days ago, in the morning.
That would make it Wednesday the twenty-second. He's
called Ivan Franzevich Brilling, a State Counsellor. At thirty
years of age! The whole office has been set on its ear! It's
Saturday today, and I was in from nine o'clock this morning.
And last night till eleven o'clock everyone was in meetings,
drawing charts. Remember the refreshment room, where we
used to drink tea? Well now, where the samovar used to
stand, there's a telegraph apparatus and a telegrapher on duty
round the clock. You can send a telegram to Vladivostok,
even to Berlin if you like, and the answer comes back straight
away. He's kicked out half the agents and brought down half
of his own from Peter, they only obey his orders. He questioned me meticulously about everything and listened to
what I said very carefully. I thought he would retire me, but
no, apparently Superintendent Grushin still has his uses.
Actually, my dear chap, that's the reason I came to see you,'
Xavier Feofilaktovich Grushin suddenly recalled. 'I wanted to
warn you. He was intending to come here himself today, he
wants to question you in person. Don't you be upset, there's
no blame attached to you. You were even wounded in the
course of carrying out your duty. But be sure not to put the
old man on the spot, will you? Who could have known that
the case would take a turn like this?'

Erast Fandorin cast a miserable glance around his wretched
abode. A fine impression the big man from St Petersburg
would get of him.

'Maybe I'd better come into the Department? Honestly, I'm
feeling perfectly all right now.'

'Don't you even think about it!' said the superintendent with a flurry of his arms. 'Do you want to give me away for coming to warn you? You lie down. He made a note of your address, he'll definitely be here today.'

The 'man of the future' arrived that evening after six o'clock, by which time Erast Fandorin had managed to make thorough preparations. He told Agrafena Kondratievna that a general would be coming, so Malashka should wash the floor in the hallway, remove the rotten old trunk and not even dare to think of boiling up any cabbage soup. In his own room the injured man carried out a major clean-up: he hung the clothes to greater advantage on the nails and hid the books away under the bed, leaving on the table only a French novel, the *Philosophical Essays* of David Hume in English and Jean Debret's *Memoirs of a Paris Detective*. Then he hid Debret away and replaced him with *Instructions for Correct Breathing from the True Indian Brahmin Chandra Johnson*, from which he took the fortifying respiratory gymnastics that he performed every morning. Let this master of clever business see that the man who lived here might be poor, but he had not allowed himself to go to seed. In order to emphasise the graveness of his injury, Erast Fandorin stood a bottle containing some mixture or other (he borrowed it from Agrafena Kondratievna) on the chair, then he lay down and wrapped a white scarf round his head. He thought it created the appropriate effect – manly courage in the face of affliction.

At long last, when he was already thoroughly tired of lying there, there came a short, sharp knock at the door and then immediately, without waiting for any reply, an energetic gentleman entered the room, wearing a light, comfortable jacket with light-coloured pantaloons and no hat at all. The precisely combed light-brown hair revealed a tall forehead, two sardonic creases lay at the corners of the strong-willed mouth and the clean-shaven, dimpled chin positively exuded self-confidence. The penetrating grey eyes surveyed the room in an instant and came to rest on Fandorin.

'I see there is no need to introduce myself,' the visitor said merrily. 'You already have the basic facts about me, but presented in a rather unflattering light. Did Grushin complain about the telegraph?'

Erast Fandorin fluttered his eyelids and said nothing in reply.

'It's the deductive method, my dear Fandorin. Building up the overall picture from a few small details. The main thing is not to rush things, not to jump to the wrong conclusion, if the available evidence allows for different interpretations. But we can talk about that later, we'll have plenty of time. And as far as Grushin is concerned, it's very simple. Your landlady bowed to me almost down to the floor and called me "Excellency" – that's one. As you can see, I do not even remotely resemble an "Excellency", nor am I one yet, since the level of my rank only merits "Your Worship" – that's two. Apart from Grushin I told no one that I was intending to visit you – that's three. It is perfectly clear that the only opinion the detective superintendent can express of my activities is an unflattering one – that's four. Well, and as for the telegraph, without which, you must admit, modern detective work is quite impossible, it produced a genuinely indelible impression on the whole of your department, and our drowsy Xavier Grushin simply could not have failed to mention it – that's five. Well, am I right?'

'Yes,' said the astounded Fandorin, ignominiously betraying the kind-hearted Xavier Feofilaktovich Grushin.

'What's this, have you got haemorrhoids already at your age?' the astute visitor asked, transferring the mixture to the table and taking a seat.

'No!' said Erast Fandorin, blushing furiously, and at the same time breaking faith with Agafena Kondratievna too. 'It's . . . it's . . . my landlady got things mixed up. She's always getting things mixed up, Your Honour. Such a stupid woman . . .'

'I see. Call me Ivan Franzevich, or even better, simply "Chief", since we're going to be working together. I read your report,' Brilling continued without making the slightest pause to mark the transition. 'Intelligent. Observant. Efficient. I'm pleasantly surprised by your intuition – that's the most valuable thing of all in our profession. When you don't yet know how a situation is likely to develop, but instinct prompts you to take precautionary measures. How did you guess that the visit to Bezhetskaya's might be dangerous? Why did you think it necessary to wear a protective corset? Bravo!'

Erast Fandorin turned an even darker shade of crimson.

'Yes, it was a splendid idea. It wouldn't save you from a bullet, of course, but against cold steel it serves pretty well. I'll give instructions for a batch of such corsets to be bought for agents assigned to dangerous missions. What make is it?'

Fandorin replied bashfully: 'Lord Byron.'

'Lord Byron,' Brilling repeated, making a note in a little leather-bound book. 'And now tell me, when could you come back to work? I have something special in mind for you.'

'Good Lord, tomorrow, if you like,' Fandorin exclaimed fervently, gazing lovingly at his new boss, or rather new 'chief'. 'I'll dash over to the doctor's in the morning, get the stitches taken out and then I'm at your disposal.'

'That's splendid. How would you characterise Bezhetskaya?'

Erast Fandorin became flustered, and he made a rather awkward start, supporting his words with lavish gesticulations:

'She's . . . She's an exceptional woman. A Cleopatra. A Carmen . . . Indescribably beautiful, but it's not even a matter of her beauty . . . Has a magnetic gaze . . . No, the gaze isn't the thing, either . . . The main thing is – you can sense an immense power in her. A power so strong that she seems to be toying with everyone. Playing a game with some incomprehensible rules, but a cruel game. That woman, in my view, is highly depraved, and at the same time . . . absolutely innocent. As though she was taught wrongly when she was a child. I don't know how to explain it . . .' Fandorin turned pink, realising that he was spouting nonsense, but he finished what he was saying nonetheless. 'It seems to me she is not as bad as she wishes to appear.'

The State Counsellor scrutinised the young man curiously and gave a mischievous whistle:

'So that's how it is . . . I thought as much. Now I can see that Amalia Bezhetskaya is a genuinely dangerous individual . . . especially for young romantics during the period of puberty.'

Pleased with the effect that this joke produced on Erast Fandorin, Ivan Brilling stood up and looked around again.

'How much do you pay for this kennel, ten roubles?'

'Twelve,' Erast Fandorin replied with dignity.

'The style of décor is familiar. I used to live like this myself at one time. When I attended the gymnasium in the splendid city of Kharkov. You see, like you, I lost my parents at an early age. Well, for building character it's actually quite beneficial. Is your salary thirty-five roubles, according to the official table?' asked the State Counsellor, once again switching subjects without the slightest pause.

'Plus a quarterly bonus for overtime.'

'I'll give instructions for you to be paid a bonus of five hundred out of the special fund. For devotion to duty in the face of danger. And so, until tomorrow. Come in, and we'll work on the various scenarios.'

And the door closed behind the astonishing visitor.

*

The Criminal Investigation Police Department really was quite unrecognisable. There were unfamiliar gentlemen with files under their arms trotting along the corridors, and even his old colleagues no longer waddled along, but walked smartly, with an upright bearing.

In the smoking room – miracle of miracles – there was not a soul to be seen. Out of curiosity Erast Fandorin glanced into the former refreshment room, and true enough, standing there on the table in place of the samovar and the cups was a

Baudot apparatus, and a telegrapher in a double-breasted uniform jacket glanced up at the intruder with a strict, interrogatory glance.

The investigation headquarters was located in the office of the head of department, for the superintendent had been relieved of his duties as of the previous day. Erast Fandorin, still rather pale after the painful procedure of removing the stitches, knocked on the door and glanced inside. The office had also changed: the comfortable leather armchairs had disappeared and their place had been taken by three rows of simple chairs, and standing against the wall were two school blackboards, completely covered with charts of some kind. It looked as though a meeting had only just ended – Brilling was wiping his chalk-stained hands with a rag, and the officers and agents, talking intently among themselves, were moving towards the exit.

'Come in, Fandorin, come in, don't hang about in the doorway,' the new occupant of the office said, hurrying along Erast Fandorin, who was suddenly overcome by timidity. 'All patched up? That's splendid. You'll be working directly with me. I'm not allocating you a desk, you'll have no time for sitting down anyway . . . It's a pity you arrived late, we've just had a most interesting discussion concerning the "Azazel" in your report.'

'So there is such a thing? I wasn't mistaken?' said Erast Fandorin, pricking up his ears. 'I was afraid it was my imagination.'

'It wasn't your imagination. Azazel is a fallen angel. What mark did you get for scripture studies? You remember about the scapegoats? Well then, in case you've forgotten, there were two of them. One was intended for God, for the expiation of sins, and the other was for Azazel, so that he wouldn't be angered. In the Jewish Book of Enoch Azazel teaches people all sorts of rotten stuff: he teaches the men to make war and make weapons and the women to paint their faces and abort their young. In a word, he's a rebellious demon, the spirit of exile.'

'But what can it mean?'

'One of your Moscow collegiate assessors expounded an entire detailed hypothesis. About a secret Judaic organisation . . . He told us all about the Jewish Sanhedrin and about the blood of Christian infants. He presented Bezhetskaya as a daughter of Israel, and Akhtyrtsev as a lamb slaughtered on the sacrificial altar of the Jewish God. Such a load of nonsense. I've heard enough of those anti-Semitic ravings already in St Petersburg. When disaster strikes and the causes are not clear, they immediately start talking about the Sanhedrin.'

'And what is your hypothesis . . . Chief?' Fandorin asked, pronouncing the unaccustomed form of address with a certain trepidation.

'If you'd be so kind as to look this way.' Brilling walked across to one of the blackboards. 'These four circles at the top are the four scenarios. The first circle, as you see, has a question mark. This is the least likely scenario: the killer acted alone and you and Akhtyrtsev were his random victims. Possibly some maniac obsessed with demoniacism. That leaves us in a dead-end until further similar crimes are committed. I've sent off requests by telegram to all the provinces, asking if there have been any similar murders. I doubt they will produce any result – if such a maniac had shown his hand earlier, I should have known about it. The second circle with the initials "A.B." is Amalia Bezhetskaya. She is undoubtedly suspect. You and Akhtyrtsev could easily have been followed from her home to the Crimea. And then she has fled. However, the motive for the killing is not clear.'

'If she has fled, it means she's involved,' Erast Fandorin said heatedly. 'And that means the white-eyed man is no solitary killer.'

'That's not a fact, not a fact by any means. We know that Bezhetskaya is an impostress and she was using a false passport. She is probably an adventuress. She was probably living at the expense of rich patrons. But as for murder, especially by the hand of such an adroit gentleman . . . Judging from your report, this was no dilettante, but an entirely professional killer. A blow like that to the liver is exquisitely precise work. I've been to the morgue, you know, and examined Akhtyrtsev. If not for the corset, you'd be lying there beside him, and the police would believe it was a robbery or a drunken brawl. But let's get back to Bezhetskaya. She could have learned about the incident from one of her menials – the Crimea is only a few minutes' walk away from her house. There was a lot of commotion – police, idle onlookers woken from their sleep. One of the servants or the yard-keeper, say, recognised the dead man as one of Bezhetskaya's guests and told her. She, being quite reasonably afraid of a police inquiry and inevitable exposure, immediately goes into hiding. She has more than enough time to do so – your good Mr Grushin only turned up with a warrant in the afternoon of the following day. I know, I know, you were concussed, you didn't recover consciousness immediately. It took time for you to dictate the report, for the boss to scratch his head . . . Anyway, I have placed Bezhetskaya on the wanted persons list. She's probably no longer in Moscow. I think she's not even in Russia – that wouldn't be too hard, after ten whole days. We're drawing up a list of those who used to visit her house, but for the most part they are highly respectable individuals and tact is required. Only one of them rouses any serious suspicion in me.'

Ivan Franzevich jabbed the pointer at the third circle, which contained the initials 'C.Z.'

'Count Zurov, Hippolyte Alexandrovich by name. Evidently Bezhetskaya's lover. A man entirely devoid of moral principles, a gambler, a rabid duellist and general madcap. A Tolstoy-the-American type. There is some circumstantial evidence. He left in a state of extreme annoyance after a quarrel with the dead man – that's one. He could have waited and shadowed you and sent the killer – that's two. The yard-keeper testified that Zurov only came home just before dawn – that's three. And there's a motive too, although it's a weak one: jealousy or morbid vindictiveness. Possibly there was something else. The main point of doubt is that Zurov is not the kind of man who would use someone else to kill for him. However, information from our agents indicates that he is constantly surrounded by all sorts of shady characters, so this scenario actually appears quite promising. And this is the one that you, Fandorin, will follow up. Zurov is being investigated by a whole group of agents, but you will operate alone – you do that well. We'll discuss the details of the assignment later, but now let's move on to the final circle. This is the one that I am following up.'

Erast Fandorin wrinkled up his brow as he struggled to imagine what the initials 'N.O.' might represent.

'Nihilist organisation,' his chief explained. 'There are certain signs of a conspiracy here, only not a Jewish one, something more serious than that. That's really the reason why I was sent in. That is, of course, Prince Korchakov asked me as well – as you are aware, Nikolai Akhtyrtsev was the son of his deceased daughter. But this whole business could turn out to be far from simple. Our Russian revolutionaries are on the verge of schism. The most determined and impatient of these Robespierres have grown weary of educating the peasant – a job so long and tedious that an entire lifetime is not long enough. The bomb, the dagger and the revolver are far more interesting. I am expecting large-scale bloodshed in the very near future. What we have seen so far is nothing compared with what is to come. The terror against the ruling class could assume mass proportions. For some time now in the Third Section I have been handling the cases of the most extreme and conspiratorial terrorist groups. My patron, Lavrenty Arkadievich Mizinov, who is head of the corps of gendarmes and the Third Section, instructed me to investigate this "Azazel" that has turned up in Moscow. A demon is an extremely revolutionary symbol. You see, Fandorin, the very fate of Russia hangs in the balance.' Not a trace was left of Brilling's usual sardonic humour and a note of fierce determination had appeared in his voice. 'If the tumour is not surgically removed in the embryonic stage, then these romantics will give us a *révolution* that will make the French guillotine seem no more than a charming piece of idle mischief. You and I will not be allowed to grow old in peace, mark my words. Have you read Mr Dostoevsky's novel *The Possessed*? You should. It's a most eloquent prognosis.'

'So are there only four scenarios?' Erast Fandorin asked hesitantly.

'Not enough? Are we overlooking something? Speak up, speak up! I recognise no differences of rank where work is concerned,' his chief encouraged him. 'And don't be afraid of appearing ridiculous – that's just because you are so young in years. Better to say something stupid than miss something important.'

Embarrassed at first, Fandorin spoke with increasing fervour:

'It seems to me, Your Worsh . . . that is, Chief, that you are wrong to leave Lady Astair out of the picture. She is, of course, a most venerable and respected individual, but . . . but, after all, the bequest is worth a million! Bezhetskaya gains nothing by it, neither does Count Zurov, or the nihilists – except perhaps in the sense of the good of society . . . I don't know how Lady Astair is involved, perhaps she has nothing at all to do with all this, but for form's sake she really ought to be . . . After all, the investigatory principle says "*cui prodest*" – "seek the one who benefits".'

'Thanks for the translation,' Ivan Franzevich said with a bow, making Fandorin feel embarrassed. 'A perfectly fair comment, except that in Akhtyrtsev's story, which is included in your report, everything is comprehensively explained. The baroness's name came up by chance. I have not included her in the list of subjects, firstly because time is precious, and secondly because I myself am slightly acquainted with the lady. I have had the honour of meeting her.' Brilling smiled amicably. 'However, Fandorin, formally speaking you are correct. I do not wish to impose my own conclusions on you. Always think for yourself and never take anybody's word for anything. Pay a visit to the baroness and question her on any subject you feel necessary. I am sure that apart from anything else you will find it a pleasure to make her acquaintance. The municipal duty office will inform you of Lady Astair's Moscow address. And another thing, before you go, call in to the costume section and have your measurements taken. Don't come to work in your uniform again. My greetings to the baroness, and when you come back a little wiser, we'll get down to work – that is, to dealing with Count Zurov.'

Chapter Seven

IN WHICH IT IS ASSERTED THAT PEDAGOGY
IS THE MOST IMPORTANT OF ALL THE SCIENCES

On arriving at the address he had been given by the duty officer, Erast Fandorin discovered a substantial three-storey building which at first glance appeared somewhat to resemble a barracks, but was surrounded by a garden, the gates of which were standing invitingly open. This was the English baroness's newly opened Astair-House. A servant in a smart light-blue frock coat emerged from his striped booth and gladly explained that her ladyship did not reside here, but in the wing, and the entrance was from the side street, around the corner to the right.

Fandorin saw a gaggle of young boys in blue uniforms come running out of the doors of the building and begin galloping about the lawn with wild cries in a game of tag. The servant did not even attempt to call the young scamps to order. Catching Fandorin's glance of surprise, he explained:

'It's not against the rules. During the break you can turn cartwheels and somersaults if you like, as long as you don't damage the property. That's the rule.'

Well, the orphans here certainly seemed happy and carefree, not like the pupils at the Provincial Gymnasium, among whose number our collegiate registrar was himself numbered until quite recently. Rejoicing at the poor souls' good fortune,

Erast Fandorin set off along the fence in the direction indicated to him.

Round the corner began one of those shady side streets of
which the Khamovniki district possesses such an immense
number: a dusty roadway, drowsy little mansions with little
front gardens, spreading poplars which would soon release
their downy white fluff into the air. The two-storey wing in
which Lady Astair was staying was connected with the main
building by a long gallery. Beside the marble plaque bearing
the inscription *'First Moscow Astair-House. Management'*, a
grave-looking doorkeeper with sleekly combed side-whiskers
was basking in the sunshine. Fandorin had never before seen
such an imposing doorkeeper in white stockings and a three-
cornered hat, not even in front of the governor-general's
residence.

'No visitors today,' said this janissary, extending his arm
like a boom to block the way. 'Come tomorrow. On official
business from ten to twelve, on personal matters from two to
four.'

No, Erast Fandorin's relations with the doorkeeping tribe
were definitely not going well. Either his appearance was not
impressive enough or something about his face was not quite
right.

'Detective police. To see Lady Astair, on urgent business,'
he muttered through clenched teeth, in vengeful anticipation
of seeing the dummy in the golden galloons bow.

But the dummy did not even bat an eyelid.

'There's no point even trying to see Her Excellency, I
won't let you in. If you wish, I can announce you to Mr
Cunningham.'

'I don't wish to see any Mr Cunningham,' Erast Fandorin
snapped. 'Announce me to the baroness immediately, or
you'll be spending the night in the police station! And tell
her I'm from the Criminal Investigation Department on
urgent state business!'

The doorkeeper sized up the irate functionary with a
glance full of doubt, but nonetheless disappeared inside the

door. The scoundrel did not, however, invite Erast Fandorin inside.

Having been made to wait for rather a long time, Fandorin was on the point of bursting in without being invited, when the dour face in the side-whiskers glanced out again from behind the door.

'Her Ladyship will receive you all right, but she doesn't have much Russian, and Mr Cunningham has no time to translate, he's too busy. Unless perhaps you can explain yourself in French . . .' It was clear from his voice that the doorkeeper had little faith in such a possibility.

'I can even explain myself in English,' Erast Fandorin threw out casually. 'Which way shall I go?'

'I'll show you. Follow me.'

Fandorin followed the janissary through a spotless entrance hall upholstered with damask and along a corridor flooded with sunlight from a row of tall Dutch windows to a white and gold door.

Erast Fandorin was not afraid of conversing in English. He had grown up in the charge of Nanny Lizbet (at moments of strictness Mrs Johnson), a genuine English nanny. She was a warm-hearted and considerate but extremely prim and proper old maid, who was nonetheless supposed to be addressed not as 'Miss' but as 'Mrs', out of respect for her venerable profession. Lizbet had taught her charge to rise at half past six in summer and half past seven in winter, to perform callisthenic exercises until he just broke sweat and then sponge himself down with cold water, to count to two hundred as he cleaned his teeth, never to eat his fill and all sorts of other things absolutely essential for a gentleman to know.

A gentle female voice responded to his knock at the door: 'Come in! *Entrez!*'

Erast Fandorin handed the doorkeeper his peaked cap and went in.

He found himself in a spacious, richly furnished study, in which pride of place was given over to an extremely wide mahogany desk. Seated behind the desk was a grey-haired lady with an appearance that was not merely pleasant, but extremely agreeable. Behind the gold pince-nez her light-blue eyes sparkled with lively intelligence and affability. Fandorin took an immediate liking to the mobile features of the plain face, the duck-bill nose and broad, smiling mouth.

He introduced himself in English but did not immediately mention the purpose of his visit.

'Your pronunciation is splendid, sir,' Lady Astair praised him in the same language. 'I trust our formidable Timoth . . . Timofei did not give you too bad a fright? I confess I am a little bit afraid of him myself, but officials often call to the office, and then Timofei is quite invaluable, better than an English manservant. But take a seat, young man. Better sit over there in the armchair, you'll be more comfortable. So you are in the criminal police? That must be very interesting work. And what does your father do?'

'He is dead.'

'I am very sorry to hear it, sir. And your mother?'

'Also dead,' Fandorin blurted out, unhappy with the direction the conversation had taken.

'My poor boy. I know how lonely you must be. For forty years I have been helping poor boys like you escape their loneliness and find their path.'

'Find their path, My Lady?' Erast Fandorin did not quite follow.

'Oh, yes,' said Lady Astair, becoming animated as she quite clearly mounted her pet hobbyhorse. 'Finding one's own path is the most important thing for anyone. I am profoundly convinced that every individual possesses a unique talent, everyone is endowed with a divine gift. The tragedy of mankind is that we do not seek to discover this gift in the child and nurture it – we do not know how. A genius is a rare event among us, even a miracle, but what is a genius? It is simply a person who has been lucky. Fate has decreed that the circumstances of life themselves nudge the individual towards the correct choice of path. The classic example is

Mozart. He was born into the family of a musician and from an early age he found himself in an environment that nurtured ideally the talent with which nature had endowed him. But just try to imagine, my dear sir, that Wolfgang Amadeus was born into the family of a peasant. He would have become a crude rustic herdsman, amusing his cows by the magic trilling of his reed flute. If he had been born into the family of a rough military man, he would have become a mediocre officer with a love of military marches. Believe me, young man, within every child, every single one without exception, there lies a hidden treasure. One simply needs to know how to reach that treasure! There is a very nice North American writer by the name of Mark Twain. I suggested to him the idea for a story, in which people are judged, not according to their actual achievements, but according to the potential and the talent with which nature has endowed them. And then it will turn out that the very greatest general of all time was some unknown tailor who never served in the army, and the very greatest artist of all never held a brush in his hand, because he worked as a cobbler all his life. The basis of my system of education is to ensure that the great general is certain to find his way into the army and the great artist will be provided with paints in good time. My teachers patiently and persistently probe the mental constitution of each of their wards, searching in him for the spark of God, and in nine cases out of ten they find it!'

'Aha, then it is not there in everyone!' said Fandorin, raising his finger in triumph.

'In everyone, my dear young man, in absolutely everyone, it is simply that we pedagogues are not sufficiently skilful, or else the child is endowed with a talent for which the modern world has no use. Perhaps this person was needed in primordial society, or his genius will be required in the distant future – in a sphere which we today cannot even imagine.'

'Concerning the future – all right, I cannot undertake to judge,' Fandorin prefaced his argument, enthralled by the conversation despite himself. 'But concerning primordial society the issue is not quite clear. Exactly what talents did you have in mind?'

'I don't know that myself, my boy,' said Lady Astair with a disarming smile. 'Well, let us suppose the gift of guessing where there is water under the ground. Or the gift of sensing game in the woods. Perhaps the ability to distinguish edible roots from non-edible ones. I know only one thing, that in those distant times precisely such people were the main genii, and Mr Darwin or Herr Schopenhauer, had they been born in a cave, would have found themselves relegated to the position of tribal idiots. As a matter of fact, those children who today are regarded as mentally backward also possess a gift. It is, of course, not a gift of a rational nature, but nonetheless precious for all that. In Sheffield I have a special Astair-House for those whom traditional pedagogy has rejected. My God, what miracles of genius those boys demonstrate! There is a child there, who at the age of thirteen has barely learned to talk, but he cures any migraine with the touch of his hand. Another, who is entirely incapable of verbal communication, but can hold his breath for an entire four and a half minutes. A third can heat a glass of water simply by looking at it, can you imagine?'

'Incredible! But why only boys? What about girls?'

Lady Astair sighed and spread her hands.

'You are right, my friend. Of course, one should work with girls as well. However, experience has taught me that the talents with which the female nature is endowed are often such that modern society is not yet ready to understand them appropriately. We live in the age of men, and we are obliged to take that into consideration. In a society where men are the bosses, an exceptionally talented woman arouses suspicion and hostility. I would not wish my foster-daughters to feel unhappy.'

'But then how is your system arranged? How is the sorting, so to speak, of the children accomplished?' Erast Fandorin asked with keen curiosity.

'Do you really find it interesting?' the baroness asked in

delight. 'Let us go to the teaching building and you will see for yourself.'

Rising to her feet with an agility quite amazing for her age, she was ready to take him there and show him immediately.

Fandorin bowed, and her ladyship led the young man at first along the corridor, and then through the long gallery to the main building.

Along the way she told him about her work.

'Our institution here is quite new, it is only three weeks since it opened, and the work is still in its very earliest stage. My people have taken from the orphanages, and sometimes directly from the street, a hundred and twenty orphan boys aged from four to twelve years. If a child is older than that, it is hard to do anything with him, his personality is already formed. To begin with the boys were divided into groups by age, each with its own teacher, a specialist in that particular age. The teacher's main responsibility is to observe the children closely and gradually begin setting them various simple assignments. These assignments are like a game, but by using them it is easy to determine the general tendency of a child's character. At the initial stage one has to divine where a particular child's greatest talent lies – in the body, the head or the intuition. After that the children will be divided into groups not according to age, but according to type: rationalists, artistes, craftsmen, leaders, sportsmen and so on. Gradually the profile of the type is narrowed more and more, and the oldest boys are quite often tutored individually. I have been working with children for forty years, and you cannot imagine how much my alumni have achieved, in the most varied of spheres.'

'Why, that is quite magnificent, My Lady,' Erast Fandorin exclaimed in delight. 'But where can one find so many expert teachers?'

'I pay my teachers very well, because pedagogy is the most important of all the sciences,' the baroness said with profound conviction. 'And apart from that, many of my former pupils express a desire to remain in the Astair-Houses as teachers. This is really quite natural – after all, the Astair-House is the only family they have ever known.'

They entered a wide recreation hall, on to which the doors of several classrooms opened.

'Now where should I take you?' Lady Astair pondered. 'I think at least to the physics laboratory. My splendid Dr Blank, an alumnus of the Zurich Astair-House and a physicist of genius, is giving a demonstration lesson there at the moment. I lured him here to Moscow by setting up a laboratory for his experiments with electricity. And while he is here he has to show the children all sorts of clever physics tricks in order to stimulate their interest in that science.'

The baroness knocked on one of the doors and they stepped into the classroom. Sitting at the desks were about fifteen boys aged eleven to twelve wearing blue uniforms with a golden letter 'A' on the jacket collar. All of them were watching with bated breath as a sullen young gentleman with immense side-whiskers, dressed in a rather untidy frock coat and a shirt that was none too fresh, spun some kind of glass wheel that was sputtering out bright blue sparks.

'*Ich bin sehr beschaftigt, milady!*' Dr Blank shouted angrily. '*Spater, spater!*'[1] Then he began speaking in broken Russian, addressing the children. 'Und now, gentlemen, you vill see a genuine little rainbow! Its name is Blank Regenborn, "Blank's Rainbow". I invent it when I was young as you are now.'

Suddenly a small, unusually bright rainbow arced across from the strange wheel to the table that was crammed with all sorts of physics apparatus, and the boys began buzzing with delight.

'Just a little bit crazy, but a genuine genius,' Lady Astair whispered to Fandorin.

At that moment a child screamed loudly in the next classroom.

---

[1] I'm very busy, Milady! Later, later!

'Good Lord!' said Her Ladyship, clutching at her heart. 'That's from the gymnastics room! Let's go, quickly!'

She ran out into the corridor with Fandorin following her. Together they burst into a spacious, bright hall in which the floor was laid with leather mats and various pieces of gymnastics equipment were set along the walls, including wallbars, rings, thick ropes and trampolines. Rapiers and fencing masks lay cheek by jowl with boxing gloves and dumb-bells. A small group of seven-to-eight-year-old boys was clustered around one of the mats. Pushing his way through the children, Erast Fandorin saw a boy writhing in pain and, bending over him, a young man about thirty years of age dressed in gymnast's tights. The man had fiery ginger curls, green eyes and a determined-looking face covered with freckles.

'All right, my dear chap,' he said in Russian with a slight accent. 'Show me your leg, don't be afraid. I'm not going to hurt you. Be a man and bear it. Fell from the rings, m'lady,' he explained to the baroness in English. 'Weak hands. I am afraid the ankle is broken. Would you please tell Mr Izyumov?'

Her Ladyship nodded without speaking, and gesturing to Erast Fandorin to follow her, walked quickly out of the hall.

'I'll go for the doctor, Mr Izyumov,' she told him, speaking rapidly. 'This kind of thing happens frequently. Boys will always be boys . . . That was Gerald Cunningham, my righthand man. An alumnus of the London Astair-House. A brilliant teacher. He is in charge of the entire Russian branch. In six months he has mastered your difficult language, which is quite beyond me. Last autumn Gerald opened the Astair-House in St Petersburg and now he is here temporarily, helping to get things going. Without him I am like a woman with no hands.'

She stopped in front of a door bearing the inscription 'Doctor'.

'I do beg your pardon, sir, but I shall have to cut short our conversation. Some other time, perhaps? Come tomorrow and we'll talk. You have some business to discuss with me?'

'Nothing of any importance, My Lady,' said Fandorin, blushing. 'Indeed, I really . . . some other time. I wish you success in your noble profession.'

Erast Fandorin bowed awkwardly and walked quickly away. He felt very ashamed.

*

'Well, did you catch the villainess redhanded?' Fandorin's chief greeted his shamefaced subordinate merrily, raising his head from some complicated diagrams or other. The curtains in the office were closed and the lamp on the desk was lit, for it had already begun to grow dark outside. 'Let me guess. Her Ladyship had never even heard of Mr Kokorin, let alone of Miss Bezhetskaya, and the news of the suicide's bequest upset her terribly. Is that right?'

Erast Fandorin merely sighed.

'I met the lady concerned in St Petersburg. We considered her request to be allowed to conduct teaching activities in Russia in the Third Section. Did she tell you about the morons who are geniuses? Right then, let's get to work. Take a seat at the desk,' said Fandorin's chief with a wave of his hand. 'You have a fascinating night ahead.'

Erast Fandorin felt a pleasant tingling sensation of anxious anticipation in his breast – such was the effect produced on him by his dealings with the state counsellor.

'Your target is Zurov. You have already seen him, so you have a certain notion of the man. Getting into the count's house is easy enough, no recommendations are required. He runs something in the nature of a gambling den in his home, none too well disguised. The accepted style is all Hussars-and-Guards, but all sorts of good-for-nothing riff-raff turn up as well. Zurov maintained a house of a precisely similar kind in St Petersburg, but after a visit from our police he moved to Moscow. He is entirely his own master, listed at his regiment as being on indefinite leave for more than two years now. Let me state your task. Try to get as close to him as possible and get a good look at his entourage. Perhaps you might come across your white-eyed acquaintance there? But no amateur heroics, you can't possibly deal with a type like that on your own. Anyway, he is hardly likely to be there. I do not exclude the possibility that the count may himself take an interest in you – after all, you did meet at Bezhetskaya's house, and he is evidently not indifferent to her. Act in accordance with the situation. But don't get carried away. This gentleman is not to be trifled with. He cheats at cards, or as they say in that company, he "fixes the odds", and if he is caught in the act he deliberately provokes a scandal. He has a dozen or so duels to his account, and there are others we know nothing about. And he can crack your skull open without the excuse of a duel. For instance, in seventy-two at the Nizhny Novgorod Fair he got into an argument over cards with the merchant Svyshchov and threw that bearded gentleman out of the window. From the second floor. The merchant was badly smashed up and couldn't speak for a month, he could only mumble. But nothing happened to the count, he squirmed his way out of it. He has influential relatives in high places. What are these?' asked Ivan Brilling, as usual without any transition, as he placed a deck of playing cards on the desk.

'Cards,' Fandorin answered in surprise.

'Do you play?'

'I don't play at all. Papa forbade me even to touch cards, he said he'd already played enough for himself and me, and for the next three generations of Fandorins.'

'A pity,' said Brilling, concerned. 'Without that you'll get nowhere at Zurov's. All right, take a piece of paper and make notes . . .'

A quarter of an hour later Erast Fandorin could already distinguish the suits without hesitation and he knew which card was higher and which was lower, except that he still confused the picture cards a little – he kept forgetting which was higher, the queen or the jack.

'You're hopeless,' his chief summed up. 'But that's nothing to worry about. At the count's house they don't play preference and other such intellectual games. The more primitive the better for them, they want as much money as possible as quickly as possible. Our agents report that Zurov prefers *stoss*, and the simplified version at that. I'll explain the rules. The one who deals the cards is called the banker. The other player is the punter. Each of them has his own deck of cards. The punter selects a card from his deck, let's say a nine. He puts it face down in front of him.'

'The face – is that the side with the numbers on?' Fandorin inquired.

'Yes. Now the punter places a bet – let's say, ten roubles. The banker begins dealing: he lays the top card from his deck face up to the right (that's called the 'forehead'), and the next card to the left (that's called the 'dreambook').

'Forehead – R., dreambook – L', Erast Fandorin noted down diligently in his notepad.

'Now the punter reveals his nine. If the "forehead" also happens to be a nine, no matter what the suit, then the banker takes the stake. That's called "killing the nine". Then the bank, that's the sum of money that is being played for, increases. If the "dreambook" turns out to be a nine, then that's a win for the punter, he's "found the nine".'

'What if there's no nine in the pair?'

'If there doesn't happen to be a nine in the first pair, the banker lays out the following pair of cards. And so on until a nine does show up. That's all there is to the game. Elementary, but you can lose your shirt on it, especially if you're the punter and you keep doubling up. So get it into your head, Fandorin, that you must only play as the banker. It's simple. You deal a card to the right, a card to the left; a card to the right, a card to the left. The banker will never lose more than the first stake. Don't play as the punter, and if you have to because you've drawn lots, then set a low stake. In *shtoss* you can't have more than five rounds, and then the remainder of the bank goes to the banker. Now you can go and collect 200 roubles from the cashier's office to cover your losses.'

'A whole two hundred?' gasped Fandorin.

'Not "a whole two hundred" but "a mere two hundred". Do your best to make that amount last you all night. If you lose everything quickly, you don't have to leave immediately, you can hang about for a while. But don't arouse any suspicion, is that clear? You'll be playing every evening until you come up with a result. Even if it becomes clear that Zurov is not involved – well, that's a result too. One scenario less.'

Erast Fandorin moved his lips as he stared at his crib.

'Hearts – are they the red ones?'

'Yes, sometimes they're called "cors", from *coeur*.[1] Get along to the costume section, they've made an outfit in your size, and by lunchtime tomorrow they'll run you up an entire wardrobe for every possible occasion. Quick march, Fandorin, I've got enough to do without talking to you. Come straight back here from Zurov's place. I'm spending the night in the Department today.'

And Brilling stuck his nose back into his papers.

---

[1] hearts.

Chapter Eight

IN WHICH THE JACK OF SPADES
MAKES AN INOPPORTUNE APPEARANCE

In the smoke-filled hall the players were seated at six green
card tables – in some places in compact groups, in others in
fours or twos. There were also observers loitering beside each
table: fewer around games where the stakes were low and
rather more where the excitement of the 'spiel' was spiralling
upwards. Wine and hors d'oeuvres were not served at the
count's establishment. Those who wished to could go into
the drawing room and send a servant out to a tavern, but the
gamblers only ever sent out for champagne to celebrate some
special run of luck. On every side there resounded abrupt
exclamations incomprehensible to the non-gambler:

'*Je coupe.*'[1]

'*Je passe.*'[2]

'Second deal.'

'*Retournez la carte.*'[3]

'Well gentlemen, the hands are dealt!' – and so forth.

The largest crowd was standing round the table where a
high-betting game was taking place, one against one. The
host himself was dealing and a sweaty gentleman in a

---

[1] I strike.

[2] I pass.

[3] Show the card.

fashionable, over-tight frock coat was punting. The punter's luck was clearly not running – he repeatedly bit his lips and became excited, while the count was the very image of composure, merely smiling sweetly from under his black moustaches as he drew in the smoke from a curving Turkish *chibouque*. The well-tended, strong fingers with their glittering rings dealt the cards adroitly – one to the right, one to the left.

Among the observers, standing demurely at the back, was a young man with black hair whose face bore no resemblance to that of a gambler. It was immediately obvious to a man of experience that the youth came from a good family, had wandered into a gaming hall for the first time and felt entirely out of place. Several times old stagers with brilliantined partings in their hair had proposed that he might like to 'turn a card', but they had been disappointed – the youth never staked more than five roubles and positively refused to be 'wound up'. The experienced cardmaster Gromov, a man known to the whole of gambling Moscow, even threw the boy some 'bait' by losing a hundred roubles to him, but the money was simply wasted. The rosy-cheeked youth's eyes did not light up and his hands did not begin to tremble. This was an unpromising mark, a genuine 'louser'.

And meanwhile Fandorin (for of course it was he) imagined that he had been slipping through the hall like an invisible shadow without attracting anyone's attention, but in all honesty, he had not yet done a great deal of this 'slipping'. Once he had noticed an extremely respectable-looking gentleman slyly appropriate a gold half-imperial from a table and walk off with a highly dignified air. Then there were the two young officers who had been arguing in loud whispers in the corridor, but Erast Fandorin had not understood a word of their conversation: the lieutenant of dragoons was heatedly asserting that he was not some 'top-spinner' or other and he did not 'play the Arab' with his friends, while the cornet of hussars was upbraiding him for being some kind of 'fixer'.

Zurov, beside whom Fandorin had found himself every

now and then, was clearly in his native element in this society, and by far the biggest fish in the pond. A single word from him was enough to nip a nascent scandal in the bud, and once, at a mere gesture from their master, two thuggish lackeys took hold of the elbows of a gentleman who refused to stop shouting, and carried him out of the door in a trice. The count definitely did not recognise Erast Fandorin, although Fandorin had caught his quick, hostile gaze on himself several times.

'Fifth round, sir,' Zurov declared, and for some reason this announcement drove the punter to a paroxysm of excitement.

'I mark the duck!' he shouted out in a trembling voice and bent over two corners on his card.

A low whisper ran through the watching crowd as the sweaty gentleman tossed back a lock of hair from his forehead and cast a whole bundle of rainbow-coloured bills on to the table.

'What is a "duck"?' Erast Fandorin inquired in a bashful whisper of a rednosed gentleman who seemed to him to be the most good-humoured.

'That signifies the quadrupling of the stake,' his neighbour gladly explained. 'The gentleman desires to take his revenge in full in the following deal.'

The count indifferently released a small cloud of smoke and exposed a king to the right and a six to the left.

The punter revealed the ace of hearts.

Zurov nodded and instantly tossed a black ace to the right and a red king to the left.

From somewhere Fandorin heard a whisper of admiration: 'Exquisitely done!'

The sweaty gentleman was a pitiful sight. He glanced after the heap of bank notes as it migrated to a position beside the count's elbow and inquired timidly:

'Would you perhaps care to continue against an IOU?'

'I would not,' Zurov replied lazily. 'Who else wishes to play, gentlemen?'

His gaze unexpectedly came to rest on Erast Fandorin.

'I believe we have met?' the host asked with an unpleasant smile. 'Mister Fedorin, if I am not mistaken?'

'Fandorin,' Erast Fandorin corrected him, blushing furiously.

'I beg your pardon. Why do you do nothing but stand and stare? This is not a theatre we have here. If you've come, then play. Please have a seat.' He pointed to the newly vacated chair.

'Choose the decks yourself,' the kind old gentleman hissed in Fandorin's ear.

Erast Fandorin sat down and, following instructions, he said in an extremely decisive manner:

'But if you don't mind, Your Excellency, I will keep the bank myself. A novice's privilege. And as for the decks, I would prefer . . . that one and that one there.' And so saying, he took the two bottom packs from the tray of unopened decks.

Zurov smiled still more unpleasantly.

'Very well, mister novice, your terms are accepted, but on one condition: if I break the bank, you must not run off. Afterwards you give me the chance to deal. Well, what's the pot to be?'

Fandorin faltered, his resolve evaporating as suddenly as it had descended on him.

'A hundred roubles?' he asked timidly.

'Are you joking? This is not one of your taverns.'

'Very well, three hundred.' And Erast Fandorin placed all of his money on the table, including the hundred he had won earlier.

'*Le jeu ne vaut pas la chandelle*,'[1] said the count with a shrug. 'But I suppose it will do for a start.'

He drew a card from his deck and carelessly tossed three hundred-rouble notes on to it.

'I'll go for the lot.'

---

[1] The game is not worth the candle.

The 'forehead' was to the right, Erast Fandorin remembered, and he carefully set down a lady with little red hearts to the right, and to the left the seven of spades.

Hippolyte Alexandrovich Zurov turned his card over with two fingers and gave a slight frown. It was the queen of diamonds.

'Well done, the novice,' someone said with a whistle. 'He set up that queen very handily.'

Fandorin clumsily shuffled his deck.

'For the whole pot,' the count said derisively, tossing six notes on to the table. 'Dammit, if you don't place it, you'll never ace it.'

What was the card on the left called? Erast Fandorin could not remember. This one was the 'forehead', but the second one . . . Damnation! It was embarrassing. What if Zurov asked something? It would look bad if he had to check his crib.

'Bravo!' called out the audience. 'Count, *c'est un jeu intéressant,*[1] do you not think so?'

Erast Fandorin saw that he had won again.

'Be so kind as not to Frenchify in that way. It really is a stupid habit to go sticking half of a French phrase into Russian speech,' Zurov said irritably, glancing round at the speaker, although he himself interpolated French expressions now and again. 'Deal, Fandorin, deal. A card's not a horse, waiting to take you home in the morning. For the lot.'

To the right – a jack, that's the 'forehead', to the left – an eight, that's . . .

Count Hippolyte Zurov turned over a ten. Fandorin killed it at the fourth twist.

People were now pressing round the table on all sides and Erast Fandorin's success was worthily acclaimed.

'Fandorin, Fandorin,' Zurov muttered absent-mindedly, drumming on the deck of cards with his fingers. Eventually he drew out a card and counted out two thousand four hundred roubles.

---

[1] it's an interesting game.

The six of spades went straight to the 'forehead' from the very first twist.

'What kind of name is that?' exclaimed the count, growing furious. 'Fandorin! From the Greeks is it? Fandorakis, Fandoropoulos!'

'Why the Greeks?' Erast Fandorin asked, taking offence. The memory of how his good-for-nothing classmates had mocked his ancient surname was still fresh in his mind (at the gymnasium Erast Fandorin's nickname had been Fanny). 'Our line, count, is as Russian as your own. The Fandorins served Tsar Alexei Mikhailovich.'

'Yes indeed, sir,' said the same recent red-nosed old gentleman, Erast Fandorin's well-wisher, suddenly coming to life. 'There was a Fandorin at the time of Catherine the Great who left the most fascinating memoirs.'

'Fascinating, fascinating, today is most exasperating,' Zurov rhymed gloomily, heaping up a whole mound of bank-notes. 'For the entire bank! Deal a card, devil take you!'

'*Le dernier coup, messieurs!*'[1] came a voice from the crowd.

Everyone stared greedily at the two equally huge piles of crumpled notes, one lying in front of the banker, the other in front of the punter.

In absolute silence Fandorin opened up two fresh decks of cards, still thinking about the same thing. Pocket book? Handbook?

An ace to the right, another ace to the left. Zurov has a king. A queen to the right, a ten to the left. A jack to the right, a queen to the left (which one was the higher card, after all, jack or queen?). A seven to the right, a six to the left.

'Don't snort down my neck!' the count roared furiously, and the crowd recoiled from him.

An eight to the right, a nine to the left. A king to the right, a ten to the left. A king!

---

[1] The final round, gentlemen!

The men standing around were howling with laughter. Count Hippolyte Zurov sat there as though turned to stone.

Dreambook! Erast Fandorin remembered and smiled in delight. The card to the left was the dreambook. What a strange name it was!

Zurov suddenly bent forwards across the table and pinched Fandorin's lips into a tube with fingers of steel.

'Don't you dare smirk! If you happen to have won a bundle, then have the decency to behave in a civil manner!' the count hissed furiously, moving very close. His bloodshot eyes were terrible. The next moment he pushed Fandorin's chin away, leaned back against his chair and folded his arms on his chest.

'Count, that really is going too far!' exclaimed one of the officers.

'I don't believe I am running away,' Zurov hissed, without taking his eyes off Fandorin. 'If anyone's feelings are offended, I am prepared to reciprocate.'

A genuinely deadly silence filled the room.

There was a terrible ringing in Erast Fandorin's ears and there was only one thing he was afraid of now – he must not turn coward. And in fact he was also afraid that his voice would betray him by trembling.

'You are a dishonourable scoundrel. You simply do not wish to pay,' said Fandorin, and his voice did tremble, but that no longer mattered. 'I challenge you.'

'Playing the hero for the audience?' sneered Zurov. 'We'll see how you sing looking down the barrel of a gun. At twenty paces, with barriers. Either party can fire when he wishes, but afterwards you must stand at the barrier. Are you not afraid?'

I am afraid, thought Erast Fandorin. Akhtyrtsev said he can hit a five-kopeck coin at twenty paces, let alone a forehead. Or even worse, a stomach. Fandorin shuddered. He had never even held a duelling pistol in his hand. Xavier Grushin had once taken him to the police shooting range to fire a 'Colt', but that was entirely different. Zurov would kill him, he would kill him over a worthless trifle. And he would get clean away with it. There would be no way to catch him out. There were plenty of witnesses. It was a quarrel over cards, a common enough business. The count would spend a month in the guardhouse and then be released. He had influential relatives, and Erast Fandorin had no one. They would lay the collegiate registrar in a rough plank coffin and bury him in the ground and no one would come to the funeral. Except perhaps Grushin and Agrafena Kondratievna. And Lizanka would read about it in the newspaper and think in passing: what a shame, he was such a well-mannered policeman, and so very young. But no, she would not read it – Emma probably did not give her the newspapers. And of course, his chief would say: I believed in him, the fool, and he got himself killed like some stupid greenhorn. Decided to fight a duel, dabble in idiotic gentry sentiment. And then he would spit.

'Why don't you say something?' Zurov asked with a cruel smile. 'Or have you changed your mind about going shooting?'

But just then Erast Fandorin had a positively life-saving idea. He would not have to fight the duel straight away, at the very earliest it would be the following morning. Of course, to go running to his chief to complain would be mean and despicable, but Ivan Brilling had said there were other agents working on Zurov. It was entirely possible that one of the chief's people was here in the hall right now. He could accept the challenge and maintain his honour, but if, for example, tomorrow at dawn the police were suddenly to raid the house and arrest Count Zurov for running a gambling den, then Fandorin would not be to blame for it. In fact, he would not know a thing about it. Ivan Brilling would know perfectly well how to act without consulting him.

His salvation, one might say, was as good as in the bag, but Erast Fandorin's voice suddenly acquired a life of its own, independent of its owner's will, and began uttering the most incredible nonsense and moreover, amazingly enough, it was no longer trembling:

'No, I haven't changed my mind. But why wait until

tomorrow? Let's do it right now. They tell me, Count, that you practise from morning till night with five-kopeck pieces, and at precisely twenty paces?' (Zurov turned crimson.) 'I think we ought to go about things differently, as long as you don't funk it.' Now hadn't Akhtyrtsev's story come in very handy! There was no need to invent a thing – it had all been invented already. 'Let us draw lots and the one who loses will go out in the yard and shoot himself, without any barriers. And afterwards there will be the very minimum of unpleasantness. A man lost and he put a bullet through his forehead – it's a common story. And the gentlemen will give their word of honour that everything will remain a secret. Will you not, gentlemen?'

The gentlemen began talking and their opinion proved to be divided: some expressed immediate willingness to give their word of honour, but others suggested forgetting the quarrel altogether and drinking the cup of peace. Then one major with luxuriant moustaches exclaimed, 'But the boy is putting up a good show,' and that fuelled Erast Fandorin's fervour.

'Well then, Count?' he exclaimed with desperate insolence, finally slipping his reins. 'Can it really be easier to hit a five-kopeck piece than your own forehead? Or are you afraid of missing?'

Zurov said nothing, staring curiously at the plucky youngster, and his expression suggested that he was figuring something out.

'Very well,' he said at last with exceptional coolness. 'The terms are accepted. Jean.'

A lackey promptly flew over to Zurov. The count said to him:

'A revolver, a fresh deck and a bottle of champagne.' And he whispered something else in his ear.

Two minutes later Jean returned with a tray. He had to squeeze his way through the crowd, for now every last one of the visitors to the salon had gathered round the table.

With a deft, lightning-swift movement Zurov swung out

the cylinder of the revolver to show that all the bullets were in place.

'Here's the deck.' His fingers split open the taut wrapper with a crisp crackling sound. 'Now it's my turn to deal.' He laughed, seeming to be in an excellent frame of mind. 'The rules are simple: the first to draw a card from a black suit is the one to put a bullet through his forehead. Agreed?'

Fandorin nodded without speaking, beginning to realise that he had been cheated, monstrously duped by his adversary, killed even more surely than at twenty paces. The cunning Hippolyte had outplayed him, outsmarted him finally and absolutely! A cardmaster like him would never fail to draw the card he needed – certainly not from his own deck! No doubt he had an entire stack of marked cards.

Meanwhile Zurov, after demonstratively crossing himself, dealt the top card. It was the queen of diamonds.

'That's Venus,' the count said with an insolent smile. 'She's always coming to my rescue. Your turn, Fandorin.'

To protest or haggle would be humiliating, it was too late now to demand another deck. And it was shameful to delay.

Erast Fandorin reached out his hand and turned over the jack of spades.

Chapter Nine

'And that's Momus, the fool,' Hippolyte explained, stretching luxuriously. 'But it's getting rather late. Will you take
some champagne for courage or go straight outside?'

Erast Fandorin sat there bright red. He was choking with
fury, but not at the count – at himself, for being such a total
idiot. There was no point in such an idiot staying alive.

'I'll do it right here,' he growled in his anger, deciding that
he could at least play one last dirty trick on his host. 'Your
artful dodger can wash the floor. And spare me the champagne – it gives me a headache.'

In the same angry fashion, trying not to think about anything, Fandorin grabbed the heavy revolver and cocked the
hammer, then after hesitating for a moment over where
to shoot himself and deciding that it made no difference, he
set the barrel in his mouth, started counting in his mind –
'three, two, one' – and pressed the trigger so hard that he
pinched his tongue painfully with the barrel. However, no
shot ensued – there was nothing but a dry click. Totally
bemused, Erast Fandorin squeezed the trigger again – there
was another click, and this time the metal rasped repulsively
against a tooth.

'That'll do, that'll do!' Zurov took the pistol away from
him and slapped him on the shoulder. 'Good fellow! Even

tried to shoot yourself without taking Dutch courage, without any hysterics. A fine younger generation we have growing up, eh, gentlemen? Jean, pour the champagne. Mr Fandorin and I will drink to *bruderschaft*.'

Erast Fandorin, overcome by a strange apathy, did as he was bid: he listlessly drained his glass of the bubbly beverage and listlessly exchanged kisses with the count, who ordered him henceforth to address him simply as Hippolyte. Everyone around was laughing loudly and making a racket, but when the sound of their voices reached Fandorin's ears it was strangely muffled. The champagne prickled his nose and tears welled up in his eyes.

'How do you like that Jean!' the count laughed. 'It only took him a minute to remove all the pins. Very adroit, Fandorin, you must admit!'

'Yes, adroit,' Erast Fandorin agreed indifferently.

'I'd say so. What's your first name?'

'Erast.'

'Come on then, Erastus of Rotterdam, let's go and sit in my study and drink a little brandy. I'm fed up of all these ugly mugs.'

'Erasmus,' Fandorin automatically corrected him.

'What?'

'Not Erastus, but Erasmus.'

'I beg your pardon, I misheard. Let's go, Erasmus.'

Fandorin obediently stood up and followed his host. They walked through a dark enfilade and found themselves in a round room where a quite remarkable disorder prevailed – *chibouques*, pipes and empty bottles were scattered around, a pair of silver spurs were flaunting themselves on the table and for some reason a stylish English saddle was lying in the corner. Why this chamber should be called a 'study', Erast Fandorin could not understand, since there were neither books nor writing instruments anywhere in sight.

'Splendid little saddle, what?' Zurov boasted. 'Won it yesterday for a bet.'

He poured some brown-coloured beverage into glasses from

a round-bellied bottle, seated himself beside Erast Fandorin and said very seriously, even soulfully:

'Forgive me for my joke, brute that I am. I am bored, Erasmus. Plenty of folk around, but no real people. I'm twenty-eight, Fandorin, but I feel sixty, especially in the morning, when I wake up. In the evening or at night it's not too bad – I kick up a rumpus, play the fool. Only it's disgusting. It used to be all right before, but nowadays somehow it just gets more and more disgusting. Would you believe that just now when we were drawing lots, I suddenly thought: why not really shoot myself? And you know, I felt tempted . . . Why don't you say anything? Come on now, Fandorin, don't be angry. I very much want you not to bear a grudge. Tell me, what can I do to make you forgive me, eh, Erasmus?'

And then Erast Fandorin said in a squeaky, but perfectly clear voice:

'Tell me about her. About Bezhetskaya.'

Zurov tossed an exuberant lock of hair back from his forehead.

'Ah yes, I forgot. You're from the train.'

'From where?'

'That's what I call it. Amalia, she's a queen after all, she needs a train, a train of men. The longer the better. Take a piece of well-meant advice. Put her out of your head, or you're done for. Forget about her.'

'I can't,' Erast Fandorin replied honestly.

'You're still a babe-in-arms, Amalia's bound to drag you down into the whirlpool, the way she's dragged so many down already. Maybe the reason she took a shine to me was because I wouldn't follow her into the whirlpool. I don't need to, I have a whirlpool of my own. Not as deep as hers, but still quite deep enough for me to drown in.'

'Do you love her?' Fandorin asked bluntly, claiming his privilege as the offended party.

'I'm afraid of her,' said Hippolyte with a dismal laugh. 'More afraid than in love. And anyway, it's not love at all. Have you ever tried smoking opium?'

Fandorin shook his head.

'Once you've tried it, you'll hanker after it for the rest of your life. That's what she's like. She won't set me free! I can see perfectly well that she despises me and thinks I'm not really worth a damn, but she's spotted something or other in me. Worse luck for me! You know, I'm glad she's gone away, honest to God. Sometimes I used to think of killing her, the witch, strangling her with my own hands to stop her tormenting me. And she could tell all right. Oh yes, brother, she's clever. She was fond of me because she could play with me like with fire – first she would fan the flames, then she would blow them out, but all the time she knew that the fire might flare up and spread, and then she wouldn't escape with her life. Otherwise what does she need me for?'

Erast Fandorin thought enviously that there was a great deal that might make a woman love the handsome Hippo-lyte, this devil-may-care hothead, without any need for flames. A handsome fellow like him was probably plagued by women. How was it that some people had such im-moderate good luck? However, these were considerations that had nothing to do with the job in hand. He should be asking about business.

'Who is she, where from?'

'I don't know. She doesn't like to talk about herself very much. All I know is that she grew up abroad somewhere. I think it was in Switzerland, in some boarding school or other.'

'And where is she now?' asked Erast Fandorin, without really expecting he would have any luck.

Zurov, moreover, was clearly taking his time to reply, and Fandorin's heart stood still.

'Why, are you that badly smitten?' the count inquired morosely, and a hostile grimace momentarily distorted his handsome, capricious features.

'Yes!'

'Ye-es, well it makes no difference, if a moth is drawn to a candle-flame it will be burnt up anyway . . .'

Hippolyte rummaged among the decks of cards, unironed handkerchiefs and shop bills on the table.

'Where is it, damn it! Ah, I remember.' He opened a Japanese lacquered box with a mother-of-pearl butterfly on the lid. 'There you are. It arrived by municipal post.'

Erast Fandorin took the narrow envelope with trembling fingers. Written on it in a slanting, impetuous hand was: '*To His Excellency Count Hippolyte Zurov, Yakovo-Apostolsky Lane, at his own house.*' According to the postmark, the letter had been sent on the sixteenth of May, the day that Bezhetskaya had disappeared.

Inside he discovered a short note in French, with no signature: '*I am obliged to leave without taking my leave. Write to me at: London, Gray Street, the Winter Queen Hotel, for the attention of Miss Olsen. I am waiting. And do not dare to forget me.*'

'But I shall dare,' Hippolyte threatened vehemently, but then he immediately wilted. 'At least, I shall try . . . take it, Erasmus. Do whatever you like with it . . . Where are you going?'

'I must be off now,' said Fandorin, tucking the envelope into his pocket. 'I have to hurry.'

'Well, well,' the count nodded pityingly. 'Off you go, fly into the flame. It's your life, not mine.'

Outside in the yard Erast Fandorin was overtaken by Jean carrying a bundle.

'Here you are, sir, you left this behind.'

'What is it?' Fandorin asked in annoyance, glancing round.

'Are you joking, sir? Your winnings. His Excellency ordered me to be sure to catch up with you and return them to you.'

*

Erast Fandorin had a most peculiar dream.

He was sitting at a desk in a classroom in his Provincial Gymnasium. He had dreams of this kind – usually alarming and unpleasant – quite frequently, in which he was once again a pupil at the gymnasium and had been called out to the front in a physics or algebra lesson, and his mind was blank. However, this dream was not just miserable, but genuinely terrifying. Fandorin simply could not comprehend the reason for this fear. He was not up at the blackboard, but at his desk, with his classmates sitting around him: Ivan Brilling, Akhtyrtsev, some fine, handsome young fellow with a high, pale forehead and insolent brown eyes (Erast Fandorin knew that this must be Kokorin), two female pupils in white uniform aprons and someone else sitting with his back turned towards him. Fandorin was afraid of the fellow with his back to him and tried not to look in his direction, but he kept straining his neck to get a look at the girls – one dark-haired and one light-haired. They were sitting at their desks with their slim hands studiously clasped together in front of them. One turned out to be Amalia, and the other Lizanka. The first shot him a searing glance from her huge black eyes and stuck her tongue out, while the second smiled bashfully and lowered her downy eyelashes. Then Fandorin noticed that Lady Astair was standing at the blackboard holding a pointer, and everything suddenly became clear to him: this was the latest English method of education, in which boys and girls were taught together. And very good too. As though she had heard his thoughts, Lady Astair smiled sadly and said: 'This is not simply coeducation, this is my class of orphans. You are all orphans, and I must set you on the path.' 'By your leave, My Lady,' Fandorin said, surprised, 'I happen to know for certain that Lizanka is not an orphan, but the daughter of a full privy counsellor.' 'Ah, my sweet boy,' said Her Ladyship, smiling even more sadly, 'she is an innocent victim, and that is the same thing as an orphan.' The terrifying fellow sitting in front of Fandorin slowly turned round, and staring straight at him with whitish, transparent eyes, whispered: 'I, Azazel, am also an orphan.' He winked conspiratorially and finally, casting aside all restraint, said in Ivan Brilling's voice, 'And therefore, my young friend, I shall be obliged to kill you, which I sincerely regret . . . Hey, Fandorin, don't just sit there like a dummy. Fandorin!'

'Fandorin!' Someone was shaking the collegiate registrar by the shoulder, rousing him from his terrifying nightmare. 'Wake up now, it's morning already.'

He shook himself awake and jumped to his feet, turning his head this way and that. Apparently he had been dozing in his chief's office, he had been overcome by sleep right there at the desk. The joyful light of morning was pouring in through the window between the open curtains, and Ivan Brilling was standing there beside him, for some reason dressed as a *petit bourgeois*, in a cap with a cloth peak, a pleated kaftan and mud-stained, concertina-creased boots.

'Dropped off, did you? Couldn't wait?' Fandorin's chief asked merrily. 'Pardon my fancy dress, I had to go out in the night on an urgent matter. Go and get a wash, will you, stop gawping like that. Quick march.'

While Fandorin was on his way to get washed, he recalled the events of the previous night, remembering how he had dashed away from Hippolyte's house at breakneck speed, how he had leapt into the cab with its somnolent driver and ordered him to drive hard to Myasnitskaya Street. He had been so very impatient to tell his chief about his success, but Brilling had not been at his desk. Erast Fandorin had first dealt with a certain urgent matter, then sat down in the office to wait, and he had fallen asleep without realising it.

When he got back to the office Ivan Brilling had already changed into a light two-piece suit and was drinking tea with lemon. There was a second steaming glass in a silver holder standing opposite him, and there were bagels and plain bread rolls lying on a tray.

'Let's have some breakfast,' the chief suggested, 'and we can talk at the same time. I already know the basic story of your night-time adventures, but I have a few questions.'

'How can you know?' asked Erast Fandorin, feeling aggrieved. He had been anticipating the pleasure of telling his story and – to be honest – had intended to omit certain details.

'One of my agents was at Zurov's. I got back about an hour ago, but it would have been a shame to wake you. I sat and read his report. Fascinating reading, I didn't even find time to get changed.'

He slapped his hand down on several sheets of paper covered with fine handwriting.

'He's a clever agent, but his prose is terribly flowery. He imagines he has literary talent and writes to the newspapers under the name of "Maximus Zorky", dreams of a career as a censor. Listen to this, you'll find it interesting. Where is it? . . . Ah yes: "*Description of the subject. Name – Erasmus von Dorn or von Doren (determined by ear). Age – not more than twenty. Verbal portrait: height – two arshins, eight vershoks; build – skinny; hair – black and straight; beard and moustache – none, and appears unlikely to shave; eyes – bright-blue, close-set, slightly slanting towards the corners; skin white and clear; nose narrow and straight; ears – set close to the head, small, with short lobes. Distinctive feature – his cheeks are always flushed. Personal impressions: typical representative of vicious and depraved gilded youth, shows quite exceptional promise as an incorrigible duellist. After the events described above he and the Gambler withdrew to the latter's study. They talked for twenty-two minutes. They spoke quietly, with pauses. Because of the door I could hear almost nothing, but I did clearly make out the word 'opium' and also something about fire. I felt it was necessary to shadow von Doren, but he evidently discovered my presence and escaped me most cleverly, leaving in a cab. I suggest . . .*" Well, the rest is not very interesting.' Erast Fandorin's chief looked at him with curiosity. 'So what was it you were discussing about opium? Don't keep me waiting, I'm burning up with curiosity.'

Fandorin gave a brief account of the conversation with Hippolyte and showed Brilling the letter. Brilling heard him out most attentively, asked for clarification of several points and then fell silent, gazing out of the window. The pause continued for a long time, about a minute. Erast Fandorin sat quietly, afraid of disturbing the thinking process, although he had his own thoughts too.

'I am very pleased with you, Fandorin,' his chief said, coming back to life. 'You have been quite brilliantly effective. In the first place, it is absolutely clear that Zurov is not involved in the murder and does not suspect the nature of your activity. Otherwise, would he have given you Amalia's address? That gets rid of scenario three for us. In the second place, you have made a lot of progress with the Bezhetskaya scenario. Now we know where to look for that lady. Bravo. I intend to set all of the agents who are now free, including yourself, on to scenario four, which seems to me to be the basic one.' He jabbed his finger towards the blackboard, where the fourth circle contained the white chalk letters 'N.O.'

'How do you mean?' Fandorin asked anxiously. 'But, by your leave, Chief . . .'

'Last night I came across a very promising kind of trail, which leads to a certain *dacha* outside Moscow,' Ivan Brilling declared with quite evident satisfaction (that accounted for the mud-spattered boots). 'Revolutionaries use it as a meeting-place, moreover extremely dangerous ones. There also appears to be a thread leading back to Akhtyrtsev. We shall work on it. I shall need everybody. And it seems to me that the Bezhetskaya scenario is a blind alley. In any case, it is not urgent. We'll forward a request to the English via diplomatic channels and ask them to detain this Miss Olsen until the matter is clarified, and that will be an end of that.'

'That's exactly what we must not do under any circumstances!' Fandorin cried out so vehemently that Ivan Brilling was quite taken aback.

'Why not?'

'Surely you can see that it all fits together perfectly!' Erast Fandorin began very quickly, afraid of being interrupted. 'I don't know about the nihilists, it's entirely possible, and I understand its importance, but this is also a matter of importance, state importance! Look at the picture we have taking shape, Ivan Franzevich. Bezhetskaya has gone into hiding in London – that's one (he did not even notice that he had adopted his chief's manner of expressing his thoughts). Her butler is English, and a very suspicious character, the kind that will slit your throat without batting an eyelid. That's two. The white-eyed man who killed Akhtyrtsev spoke with an accent and also looks like an Englishman – that's three. Now for number four: Lady Astair is, of course, a most noble creature, but she is also an Englishwoman and Kokorin's estate, say what you will, has gone to her. Surely it's obvious that Bezhetskaya deliberately prompted her admirers to draw up their wills in favour of the Englishwoman!'

'Stop, stop,' said Brilling with a frown. 'What exactly are you driving at? Espionage?'

'It's obvious, surely?' Erast Fandorin said with a flurry of his arms. 'English plots. You know yourself the state of relations with England at the moment. I don't wish to say anything untoward about Lady Astair, she probably doesn't know a thing, but her organisation can be used as a cover, as a Trojan horse for infiltrating Russia.'

'Oh yes,' said his chief with an ironical smile. 'Queen Victoria and Mr Disraeli are not satisfied with the gold of Africa and the diamonds of India, they want Petrusha Kokorin's fabric mill and Nikolenka Akhtyrtsev's three thousand desyatins of land.'

And then Fandorin played his trump card.

'Not the mill, and not even the money! Do you remember the inventory of their property? I didn't pay any attention to it at first either. Among his other companies Kokorin had a shipbuilding yard in Libava, and the armed forces place orders there – I made inquiries.'

'When did you find time for that?'

'While I was waiting for you. I sent an inquiry by telegraph to the Ministry of the Navy. They work a night shift there too.'

'I see. Well, well. What else?'

'The fact that apart from his land, houses and capital Akhtyrtsev also had an oil well in Baku, from his aunt. I read in the newspapers that the English are dreaming of getting their hands on Caspian oil. And here you have it – by perfectly legal means! And see how securely planned it is: either the shipyard in Libava or the oil, in either case the English come out of it with something! You act as you wish, Ivan Franzevich,' said Fandorin, becoming impassioned, 'but I won't leave it at this. I'll carry out all your assignments, but after work I'll go digging for clues myself. And I'll get to the bottom of this.'

His chief began gazing out of the window again, and this time he was silent for even longer than before. Erast Fandorin was a bundle of raw nerves, but his character stood the test.

Finally Brilling sighed and began speaking – slowly, hesitantly, still thinking something through as he went along.

'Most likely it's all nonsense. Edgar Allen Poe, Eugène Sue. Meaningless coincidences. However, you are right about one thing – we won't contact the English . . . We can't act through our agent at the London embassy either. If you are mistaken, and you are most certainly mistaken, we shall make total fools of ourselves. If we are to assume that you are correct, the embassy will not be able to do anything in any case – the English will hide Bezhetskaya or tell us some pack of lies . . . And the hands of our embassy staff are tied – they're too exposed . . . So it's decided!' Ivan Brilling swung his fist energetically through the air. 'Of course, Fandorin, you would have come in useful to me here, but as the common folk say, love won't be forced. I've read your file, I know you speak not only French, but also German and English. Have your own way, go to London to see your *femme fatale.* I won't impose any instructions on you – I believe in your intuition. I'll give you one man in the embassy, Pyzhov is his name. His post is that of a humble clerk, like your own, but he deals with other matters. At the

Ministry of Foreign Affairs he is listed as a provincial secretary, but in our line he holds a different rank, a higher one.
A gentleman of many and varied talents. When you get there,
go straight to him. He is extremely efficient. I remain convinced, however, that your journey will be wasted. But in the
final analysis you have earned the right to make a mistake.
You'll get a look at Europe, travel a bit at the state's expense.
Although I believe you now have means of your own?'
Fandorin's chief squinted at the bundle lying unattended on
a chair.

Erast Fandorin started, dumbfounded at these words.

'My apologies, those are my winnings. Nine thousand six
hundred roubles, I counted them. I wanted to hand them in at
the cashier's office, but it was closed.'

'Why, dammit?' said Brilling dismissively. 'Are you in
your right mind? What do you think the cashier would write
in the receipts ledger? "Revenue from collegiate registrar
Fandorin's game of *shtoss*?" . . . Hmm, wait a moment.
It's not really proper for a mere registrar to go on a foreign
assignment.'

He sat down at the desk, dipped a pen into the inkwell and
began writing, speaking the words aloud.

'Now then. "Urgent telegram. To Prince Mikhail Alexandrovich Korchakov, personally. Copy to Adjutant-General
Lavrentii Arkadievich Mizinov. Your Excellency, in the
interests of a matter of which you are aware, and also in
recognition of exceptional services rendered, I request you to
promote collegiate registrar Erast Petrovich Fandorin immediately and without taking into account his length of
service" – ah, all right then, straight up to titular – not such
a very big cheese, either, but even so – "to Titular Counsellor.
I also request you to list Fandorin temporarily in the department of the Ministry of Foreign Affairs in the post of
diplomatic courier, first class." That's so that you won't be
delayed at the border,' Brilling explained. 'Right. Date.
Signature. By the way, you really will deliver diplomatic
post along the way – to Berlin, Vienna and Paris. For the

sake of secrecy, in order not to arouse unnecessary suspicion. No objections?' Ivan Brilling's eyes glinted mischievously.

'None at all,' Erast Fandorin mumbled, his thoughts still lagging behind the pace of events.

'And from Paris, already under a false identity, you will make your way to London. What was the name of that hotel?'

'The Winter Queen.'

Chapter Ten

On the twenty-eighth of June in the Western style, or the sixteenth of June in the Russian style, a hired carriage pulled up in front the Winter Queen Hotel on Gray Street. The driver in his top hat and white gloves jumped down from his box, folded out the step and bowed as he opened the black lacquered door bearing the legend:

DUNSTER & DUNSTER
SINCE 1848
LONDON REGAL TOURS

The first item to emerge from the door was a morocco leather travelling boot studded with silver nails, which was followed by a prosperous-looking, youthful gentleman sporting bushy moustaches that suited his fresh-faced complexion remarkably badly, a Tyrolean hat with a feather and a broad Alpine cloak. The young man leapt down on to the pavement in sprightly fashion, glanced around him at the quiet, entirely unremarkable little street and fixed his agitated gaze on the building of the hotel, a rather unprepossessing four-storey detached structure in the Georgian style which had clearly seen better times.

After hesitating for a moment, the gentleman pronounced in Russian, 'Ah, all right then.'

He then followed this enigmatic phrase by walking up the steps and entering the vestibule.

Literally one second later someone in a black cloak emerged from the public house located across the road, pulled a tall cap with a shiny peak right down over his eyes and began striding to and fro in front of the doors of the hotel.

This remarkable circumstance, however, escaped the attention of the new arrival, who was already standing at the counter and surveying a bleary portrait of some medieval lady in a gorgeous jabot – no doubt the 'Winter Queen' herself. The porter who had been dozing behind the counter greeted the foreigner rather indifferently, but on observing him give the boy who had done no more than carry in his travelling bag an entire shilling for his trouble, he welcomed him again far more affably, this time addressing the new arrival not merely as 'sir', but 'Your Honour'.

The young man inquired as to whether there were any rooms available and demanded the very best, with hot water and newspapers, before entering himself in the hotel's register of guests as Erasmus von Dorn from Helsingfors, following which, for doing absolutely nothing at all, the porter received a half-sovereign and promptly began addressing this half-witted alien as 'Your Lordship'.

Meanwhile 'Mr von Dorn' found himself suffering rather grave doubts. It was hard to believe that the brilliant Amalia Kazmirovna Bezhetskaya could be staying at this third-rate hotel. Something here was clearly not right.

In his bewilderment and dismay, he even asked the zealously attentive porter, now bent almost double, whether there was not another hotel of the same name in London, and received in reply a sworn oath assuring him that indeed there was not, nor ever had been, if one did not take into account the Winter Queen Hotel which had stood on the very same site but had burned to ashes more than a hundred years previously.

Could it really all have been in vain – the twenty-day round trip of Europe, and the false moustaches, and the luxurious carriage hired at Waterloo station instead of an ordinary cab and, finally, the half-sovereign expended to no effect?

Well, you'll just have to earn your *baksheesh* from me, my dear chap, thought Erast Fandorin (for let us call him so, disregarding his false identity).

'Tell me, my good man, has there not been a guest staying here by the name of Miss Olsen?' he asked with poorly feigned casualness, leaning his elbows on the counter.

Entirely predictable as the reply was, it pierced Erast Fandorin to the heart.

'No, My Lord, no lady by that name is staying here, or ever has.'

Discerning the dismay in the guest's eyes, the porter paused for effect before declaring reticently:

'However, the name mentioned by Your Lordship is not entirely unfamiliar to me.'

Swaying slightly to one side, Erast Fandorin fished another gold coin out of his pocket.

'Go on.'

The porter leaned forward in a gust of cheap eau-de-Cologne and whispered:

'Post arrives here in the name of that individual. Every evening at ten o'clock a certain Mr Morbid arrives, apparently a servant or a butler, and collects the letters.'

'Immensely tall, with big, light-coloured side-whiskers, looking as though he has never smiled in all his life?' Erast Fandorin asked quickly.

'Yes, My Lord, that's him.'

'And do the letters come often?'

'Yes, My Lord, almost every day, and sometimes more than one. Today, for instance' – the porter cast a meaningful glance behind himself in the direction of the pigeonholes on the wall – 'there are actually three of them.'

The hint was immediately taken.

'I would quite like to take a glance at the envelopes, merely out of idle curiosity,' Fandorin remarked, tapping on the counter with the next half-sovereign.

The porter's eyes began glittering feverishly: something quite incredible was going on, something beyond the grasp of reason, but extremely pleasant.

'Generally speaking, that is most strictly forbidden, milord, but . . . If it's just a matter of glancing at the envelopes . . .'

Erast Fandorin seized the envelopes avidly, but there was a disappointment in store for him – the envelopes carried no return address. His third piece of gold had apparently been expended in vain. But then his chief had sanctioned all outlays 'within reason and in the interests of the case' . . . What did the postmarks say?

The postmarks gave Fandorin cause for reflection: one letter was from Stüttgart, another from Washington, and the third all the way from Rio de Janeiro. Well now!

'And has Miss Olsen been receiving correspondence here for long?' Erast Fandorin asked, calculating in his head how long it would take letters to cross the ocean. And the address here also had to be communicated to Brazil! That put a rather strange complexion on the whole business – Bezhetskaya could not possibly have arrived in England more than three weeks previously.

The reply was unexpected.

'For a long time, My Lord. When I started working here – and that's four years ago now – the letters were already arriving.'

'How's that? Are you not confusing things?'

'I assure you, My Lord. Mr Morbid, it is true, only began working for Miss Olsen recently, from the early summer, I believe. In any case, before him a Mr Mobius used to come to collect the correspondence, and before that a Mr . . . mm, I'm sorry, I've forgotten what his name was. He was such an inconspicuous gentleman and not very talkative.'

Erast Fandorin desperately wanted to take a look inside the envelopes. He cast a quizzical glance at his informer. He would probably hold out against a further proposition. At this point, however, our newly fledged titular counsellor and diplomatic courier, first class, had a rather better idea.

'You say this Mr Morbid comes every evening at ten?'

'Like clockwork, My Lord.'

Erast Fandorin laid a fourth half-sovereign on the counter, then leaned across and whispered something in the lucky porter's ear.

The time remaining until ten o'clock was employed in a most productive fashion.

First of all Erast Fandorin oiled and loaded his courier's 'Colt'. Then he retreated to the bathroom and by alternately pressing the hot water and cold water pedals, in fifteen minutes or so he had filled the bath. He luxuriated for half an hour, and by the time the water cooled, his plan of subsequent action was already fully formed.

After gluing his moustaches back into place and admiring himself briefly in the mirror, Fandorin attired himself as an inconspicuous Englishman, in black bowler hat, black trousers and black necktie. In Moscow he would probably have been taken for an undertaker, but in London he felt certain that he would pass for the invisible man. And it would be just the thing for the night: conceal the shirtfront with the lapels, pull down the cuffs, and dissolve into the embrace of darkness – and that was extremely important for his plan.

There still remained an hour and a half for a stroll to familiarise himself with the neighbourhood. Erast Fandorin turned off Gray Street on to a broad thoroughfare entirely filled with carriages and almost immediately found himself in front of the famous Old Vic Theatre, which was described in detail in the guide book. Walking on a little further, he spied – oh, wonder! – the familiar profile of Waterloo station, from which the carriage had taken a good forty minutes to transport him to the Winter Queen – that scoundrel of a driver had charged him five shillings! And then there hove into view the grey Thames, bleak and uninviting in the evening twilight.

Gazing at its dirty waters, Erast Fandorin shivered as he was inexplicably seized by some macabre presentiment. The fact was that he simply did not feel at ease in this strange city. The people he met looked straight past him, and not one of them so much as glanced at his face, which you must admit would have been quite inconceivable in Moscow. And yet, Fandorin was haunted by the strange feeling that some hostile gaze was trained on his back. Several times the young man glanced round, and once he even thought he noticed a figure in black recoil behind a tall, round theatre billboard. After that Erast Fandorin took a firm grip on himself, abused himself for being over-anxious, and did not look back over his shoulder again. Confound those nerves of his! He even began wondering whether he ought to delay putting his plan into action until the following evening. Then it would be possible to pay a visit to the embassy and meet the mysterious clerk Pyzhov who had been mentioned by his chief. But such a cowardly excess of caution was dishonourable, and he did not wish to lose any more time. Almost three weeks had been wasted on trifling matters already.

The journey around Europe had proved less pleasant than Fandorin had anticipated in his first access of elation. Beyond the border post of Verzhbolov he had been depressed by the quite striking dissimilarity of the locality to the unpretentious open spaces of his homeland. As he looked out of the window of his train, Erast Fandorin had kept expecting that the neat little villages and toy towns would come to an end and a *normal* landscape would begin, but the further the train travelled from the Russian border, the whiter the houses became and the more picturesque the towns. Fandorin's mood became grimmer and grimmer, but he refused to allow himself to be reduced to snivelling. In the final analysis, he told himself, all that glisters is not gold, but nonetheless at heart he still felt a little nauseous.

After a while he had grown used to it and it did not seem so bad, it even began to seem as though Moscow was not so very much dirtier than Berlin, and the Kremlin with its gold-domed churches was finer than anything that the Germans had ever dreamed of. It was something else that had really played on his nerves – the military agent at the Russian embassy, to whom Fandorin had transmitted a sealed package, had ordered him to travel no further and await the arrival of secret correspondence for delivery to Vienna. The waiting had stretched out into a week, and Erast Fandorin had grown weary of sauntering along the shady Unter-den-Linden, and weary of admiring the plump swans in the Berlin parks.

The same story was repeated in Vienna, only this time he had been obliged to wait five days for a package destined for the military agent in Paris. Erast Fandorin had fretted nervously, imagining that 'Miss Olsen', not having received any word from her Hippolyte, must have moved out of the hotel and now it would never be possible to find her again. To calm his nerves Fandorin had spent long periods sitting in the cafés, eating large numbers of sweet almond pastries and drinking cream soda by the litre.

When it came to Paris, he had taken matters into his own hands, calling into the Russian legation for just five minutes, handing the documents to the colonel from the embassy and declaring that he was on a special assignment and could not delay even for an hour. To punish himself for the fruitless waste of so much time he had not even looked round Paris, beyond taking a drive in a fiacre along the boulevards that had been so recently extended by Baron Haussman, and then going straight to the Gare du Nord. There would be time for all that afterwards, on his return journey.

At a quarter to ten Erast Fandorin was already seated in the foyer of the Winter Queen Hotel, having concealed himself behind a copy of *The Times* with a hole pierced in it for purposes of observation. Waiting outside was a cab prudently hired in advance. Following instructions received, the porter demonstratively avoided looking in the direction of the guest who was rather over-dressed for summer, even striving to turn his back on him completely.

At three minutes past ten the bell jangled, the door swung open and a giant of a man clad in grey livery entered. It was him, the butler 'John Karlovich'! Fandorin pressed his eye up against a page bearing a description of a ball given by the Prince of Wales.

The porter cast a furtive glance at Mr von Dorn, who had become so inopportunely engrossed in his reading, and the villain even began raising and lowering his shaggy eyebrows, but fortunately the object of study either failed to notice this or else he regarded it as beneath his dignity to look round.

The waiting cab proved most opportune, for it turned out that the butler had not arrived on foot but in an 'egotist', a single-seater carriage, to which a sturdy little black horse was harnessed. No less opportune was the persistent drizzle, which obliged 'John Karlovich' to raise the leather hood of his carriage, so that now, no matter how hard he might try, he would be unable to detect anyone shadowing him.

Evincing not the slightest sign of surprise at the order to follow the man in grey livery, the cabby cracked his long whip and phase one of the plan moved into action.

It grew dark. The street lamps were lit, but not knowing London, Erast Fandorin very quickly lost his bearings among the tangle of identical stone blocks in this alien, menacingly silent city. After a certain time the houses became less tall and less frequent and he thought he could see the indistinct outlines of trees drifting through the gloom, and after another fifteen minutes there were large detached houses surrounded by gardens. The 'egotist' halted at one of these and disgorged a giant silhouette, which opened the tall barred gates. Leaning out of the cab, Fandorin saw the small carriage drive inside the fence, following which the gates were closed again.

The quick-witted cabby stopped his horse himself, then looked round and asked:

'Should I report this journey to the police, sir?'

'Here's a crown for you, and decide that question for yourself,' replied Erast Fandorin, deciding that he would not ask the driver to wait – he was too smart by half. And

Fandorin had no idea when he would be going back. Ahead lay total uncertainty.

Slipping over the fence proved to be quite simple – in his schooldays at the gymnasium he had surmounted higher obstacles.

The garden menaced him with its shadows and poked him inhospitably in the face with its branches. Ahead through the trees he could make out the vague white form of a two-storey house surmounted by a hipped roof. Trying to crunch as quietly as possible, Fandorin stole as far as the final bushes (they smelled like lilac – probably it was some English kind of lilac) and surveyed the lie of the land. It was not just a house, rather more like a villa. There was a lantern over the door. The windows on the first floor were brightly lit, but it looked as though the services were located there. Far more interesting was a lighted window on the second floor (at this point he recalled that for some reason the English referred to it as the 'first floor'), but how could he get up to it? Fortunately there was a drainpipe running close beside it, and the wall was overgrown with some kind of climbing vegetation that appeared to have taken a solid grip. The skills of his recent childhood might prove useful once again.

Like a black shadow Erast Fandorin dashed across to the wall and gave the drainpipe a shake. It seemed secure and it didn't rattle. Since it was vitally important not to make any noise, the ascent proceeded more slowly than Erast Fandorin would have wished, but eventually his foot found the project-ing ledge that encircled the second floor of the house most conveniently and, taking a cautious grip on the ivy, wild vine, liana – whatever the hell these serpentine stems were called – he began edging his way in tiny steps towards the cherished goal of the window.

For one instant he was overwhelmed by bitter dis-appointment – there was no one in the room. A lamp with a pink shade illuminated an elegant writing-desk with some papers, and in the corner he thought he could see the white form of a bed. Erast Fandorin waited for about five minutes, but nothing happened, except that a fat moth settled on the lamp, its shaggy wings fluttering. Would he really have to climb back down again? Or should he take a risk and clamber inside? He gave the window-frame a gentle push and it swung open slightly. Fandorin hesitated, berating himself for his indecision and procrastination, but he proved to have been right to delay, for just then the door opened and two people, a man and a woman, entered the room.

At the sight of the woman Erast Fandorin very nearly gave a whoop of triumph – it was Bezhetskaya! With her smoothly combed black hair tied back in a red ribbon, wearing a lacy peignoir over which she had thrown a brightly coloured gypsy shawl, to his eyes she appeared blindingly beautiful. Oh, such a woman could be forgiven any transgressions!

Turning towards the man – his face remained in shadow, but to judge from his stature it was Morbid – Amalia Bezhetskaya spoke in impeccable English (a spy, most definitely a spy!):

'So it was definitely him?'

'Yes, ma'am. Absolutely no doubt about it.'

'How can you be so certain? Did you actually see him?'

'No, ma'am. Franz was keeping watch there today. He informed me that the boy arrived at seven o'clock. The description matched perfectly, even your guess about the moustache was correct.'

Bezhetskaya laughed her clear, musical laugh.

'Nevertheless we must not underestimate him, John. This boy is one of the lucky breed, and I know that kind of person very well – they are unpredictable and very dangerous.'

Erast Fandorin's heart sank. Surely they could not be talking about him? No, it was impossible.

'Nothing simpler, ma'am. You only have to say the word . . . Franz and I will go over there and finish him off. Room fifteen, on the second floor.'

They *were* talking about him! Erast Fandorin was staying in room number fifteen on the third floor (the second floor,

English-style). But how had they found out? From where? Fandorin tore off his ignominious, useless moustache, disregarding the pain.

Amalia Bezhetskaya, or whatever her real name might be, frowned, and a harsh metallic note appeared in her voice:

'Don't you dare! It's my fault, and I shall correct my own mistake. For once in my life I trusted a man . . . But I am surprised that we did not get word of his arrival from the embassy.'

Fandorin was all ears now. They had their own people in the Russian embassy! Well, well, well! And Ivan Brilling had been doubtful. Say who, say it!

But Bezhetskaya began talking of other matters.

'Are there any letters?'

'Three today, ma'am.' The butler handed over the envelopes with a bow.

'Good. You may go to bed, John. I shall not require you any further today.' She stifled a yawn.

When the door closed behind Mr Morbid, Amalia Bezhetskaya tossed the letters carelessly on to the bureau and walked over to the window. Fandorin shrank back behind the projecting masonry, his heart pounding furiously. Gazing out blankly into the murky drizzle with her huge black eyes, Bezhetskaya (if not for the glass, he could have reached out and touched her) muttered pensively in Russian:

'How deadly boring, God help me. Stuck in this miserable place . . .'

Then she began behaving very strangely: she went up to a frivolous wall lamp in the form of a Cupid and pressed the god of love's bronze navel. The engraving hanging beside it (it appeared to be a hunting scene of some kind) slid soundlessly to one side, revealing a small copper door with a round handle. Bezhetskaya freed a slim, naked hand from its gauzy sleeve, turned the handle this way and that way, and the door opened with a melodic thrumming sound. Erast Fandorin pressed his nose against the windowpane, afraid of missing the most important part of the action.

Amalia Bezhetskaya, looking more than ever like an Egyptian queen, reached gracefully into the safe, took something out of it and turned round. She was holding a light-blue velvet attaché case.

She sat down at the bureau, extracted a large yellow envelope from the attaché case, and from the envelope she extracted a sheet of paper covered in fine writing. She slit open the newly received letters with a knife and copied something from them on to the paper. It all took no longer than two minutes. Then, having replaced the letter and the sheet of paper in the attaché case, Bezhetskaya lit a *pakhitoska* and inhaled deeply several times, gazing pensively into space.

The hand with which Erast Fandorin was gripping the vegetation had gone numb, the handle of his 'Colt' was sticking painfully into his side and his feet had begun to ache from being so unnaturally splayed. He could not continue standing in that position for long.

Eventually Cleopatra extinguished her *pakhitoska*, stood up and withdrew into the dimly lit far corner of the room, where a low door opened then closed again, and then followed the sound of running water. Evidently that was where the bathroom was located.

The blue attaché case remained lying seductively on the writing-desk, and women, as everyone knows, take a long time over their evening toilette . . . Fandorin pushed against the window frame, set his knee on the window sill and in a trice he was inside the room. Glancing now and again in the direction of the bathroom, from where he could still hear the sound of running water, he set about relieving the attaché case of its contents.

It proved to contain a large bundle of letters and the envelope he had already seen. Written on the envelope was an address:

Mr Nicholas M. Croog, Poste restante, l'Hotel des Postes, S.-Petersbourg, Russie

This was already progress. Inside the envelope there were sheets of paper divided up into columns and squares containing English writing in the slanting hand now so familiar to Erast Fandorin. The first column contained some kind of number, the second the name of a country, the third a rank or title, the fourth a date and the fifth another date – different dates in June in ascending numerical order. For instance, the last three entries, which to judge from the ink had only just been made, appeared as follows:

No. 1053F	Brazil	head of the emperor's personal bodyguard	sent 30 May	received 28 June 1876
No. 825F	United States of America	deputy chairman of a senate committee	sent 10 June	received 28 June 1876
No. 354F	Germany	chairman of the district court	sent 25 June	received 28 June 1876

Wait! The letters that had arrived at the hotel for Miss Olsen today had been from Rio de Janeiro, Washington and Stuttgart. Erast Fandorin rummaged through the bundle of letters and found the one from Brazil. It contained a sheet of paper with no salutation or signature, nothing but a single line of writing:

30 May, head of the emperor's personal bodyguard, No. 1053F

So for some reason Bezhetskaya was copying the contents of the letters she received on to sheets of paper, which she then sent to a certain Nikolai Krug in St Petersburg, or rather Mr Nicholas Krug. To what end? And why to St Petersburg? What could it all mean?

The questions came thick and fast, jostling each other for space in his mind, but he had no time to deal with them – the water had stopped running in the bathroom. Fandorin hastily stuffed the papers back into the attaché case, but it was too late to retreat to the window. A slim white figure was standing motionless in the doorway.

Erast Fandorin tugged the revolver out of his belt and commanded in a whispered hiss:

'Miss Bezhetskaya, one sound and I'll shoot you! Come over here and sit down! Quickly now!'

She approached him without speaking, gazing spellbound at him with those unfathomable, gleaming eyes, and sat down beside the writing-desk.

'You weren't expecting me, I suppose?' Erast Fandorin inquired sarcastically. 'Took me for a stupid little fool?'

Amalia Bezhetskaya said nothing, her gaze seemed thoughtful and slightly surprised, as though she were seeing Fandorin for the first time.

'What is the meaning of these lists?' he demanded, brandishing his 'Colt'. 'What has Brazil got to do with all this? Who is concealed behind the numbers? Well, answer me!'

'You've matured,' Bezhetskaya said unexpectedly in a quiet, pensive voice. 'And you seem a bit braver too.'

She dropped her hand and the peignoir slipped from a rounded shoulder so white that Erast Fandorin swallowed hard.

'Brave, impetuous, little fool,' she went on in the same quiet voice, looking him straight in the eyes. 'And so very good-looking.'

'If you're thinking of seducing me, you're wasting your time,' Erast Fandorin mumbled, blushing. 'I am not such a little fool as you imagine.'

Amalia Bezhetskaya said sadly:

'You are a poor little boy who doesn't even understand what he has got mixed up in. A poor, handsome little boy. And now there is nothing I can do to save you . . .'

'You'd do better to think about saving yourself!' said Erast Fandorin, trying hard not to look at that accursed shoulder, which had become even more exposed. Could skin really be such a glowing, milky white?

Bezhetskaya rose abruptly to her feet and he started back, holding his gun out in front of him.

'Sit down.'

'Don't be afraid, silly boy. What rosy cheeks you have. May I touch them?'

She reached out a hand and gently brushed his cheek with her fingers.

'You're hot . . . What am I going to do with you?'

She set her other hand gently on his fingers clutching the revolver. The matt black, unblinking eyes were so close that Fandorin could see two little pink reflections of the lamp in them. A strange listlessness came over the young man and he remembered Hippolyte's warning about the moth, but the memory was strangely abstract, it had nothing to do with him.

Then events moved very rapidly. With her left hand Bezhetskaya pushed the 'Colt' aside, with her right hand she seized Erast Fandorin by the collar and jerked him towards her, simultaneously butting his nose with her forehead. Fandorin was blinded by the sharp pain, but he would not have been able to see anything in any case, because the lamp went crashing to the floor and the room was plunged into pitch darkness. At the next blow – a knee to the groin – the young man doubled up, his fingers contracted convulsively, the room was lit up by a bright flash and there was the deafening roar of a shot. Amalia drew in a convulsive breath, half-sobbed and half-screamed, and then there was no longer anyone beating Erast Fandorin, no one squeezing his wrist. He heard the sound of a falling body. There was a loud ringing in his ears, twin streams of blood were flowing down over his chin, tears were pouring from his eyes, and his lower belly ached so sickeningly that all he wanted to do was curl up into a ball and wait for the agony to pass, groan until the unbearable pain went away. But he had no time for bellowing – he could hear loud voices and the sound of heavy footsteps from downstairs.

Fandorin grabbed the attaché case off the desk and threw it out of the window, then climbed over the window sill and almost fell, because his hand was still clutching the pistol. Later he was unable to recall how he climbed down the pipe, terrified all the while of not being able to find the attaché case in the darkness, but in fact it was clearly visible on the white gravel. Erast Fandorin picked it up and set off at a run, fighting his way through the bushes and mumbling rapidly to himself: 'A fine diplomatic courier . . . Killed a woman . . . My God, what am I going to do, what am I going to do . . . It's her own fault . . . I didn't want to do it at all . . . Now where shall I go . . . the police will be looking . . . Or these . . . murderers . . . I can't go to the embassy . . . Must flee the country, quickly . . . Can't do that either . . . They'll be watching all the railway stations and ports . . . They'll stop at absolutely nothing to get back their attaché case . . . Have to go into hiding . . . My God, Mr Brilling, what shall I do, what shall I do?'

As he ran along Fandorin glanced round and saw something that made him stumble and almost fall. Standing motionless in the bushes was a black figure in a long cloak. The moon-light traced the features of a strangely familiar, motionless, white face. Count Zurov!

Totally demented by this final blow, Erast Fandorin squealed and scrambled over the fence, darted to the right, then to the left (which direction had the cab come from?), then finally decided that it made no difference and ran off to the right.

Chapter Eleven

On the Isle of Dogs, in the maze of narrow streets behind Millwall Docks, night falls rapidly. Before you can so much as glance over your shoulder the twilight has thickened from grey to brown and one in every two or three of the sparse street lamps is already glowing. It is dirty and dismal, the Thames ladens the air with damp, the rubbish tips adding the scent of putrid decay. The streets are deserted, with the only life, both disreputable and dangerous, teeming around the shady pubs and cheap furnished lodgings.

The rooms in the 'Ferry Road' guesthouse are home to decommissioned sailors, petty swindlers and ageing port trollops. Pay sixpence a day and a separate room with a bed is yours to do with as you will – no one will stick their nose into your business – but a condition of the agreement is that for damaging the furniture, brawling or yelling in the night your host Fat Hugh will fine you a shilling, and if anyone refuses to pay up, he will throw them out on their ear. From morning to night Fat Hugh is at his post behind the counter by the door, strategically positioned so that he can see anyone either arriving or leaving or bringing anything in or, on the contrary, attempting to take anything out. The clientele here is a mixed bunch and you never know what they might be getting up to.

Take, for instance, that French artist with the shaggy red hair who has just gone scurrying past his landlord and into the corner room. The frog-eater has money all right – he paid for a week in advance with no arguments – he doesn't drink, just sits there locked in his room and this is the first time he's been out at all. So naturally, Hugh took the opportunity to glance into his lodgings, and what do you think he found? Him an artist, but never a sign of any paints or canvases in the place! Maybe he's some murderer or other, who knows – otherwise why would he be hiding his eyes behind those dark glasses? And maybe the constable ought to be told – the money's been paid in advance anyway . . .

Meanwhile the red-headed artist, unaware of the dangerous line taken by Fat Hugh's train of thought, locked his door and began behaving in a manner that was indeed more than simply suspicious. First of all he pulled the curtains tightly closed. Then he placed his purchases – a loaf of bread, cheese and a bottle of porter – on the table, pulled a revolver out of his belt and hid it under his pillow. But the disarming of this peculiar Frenchman was not complete at that. From the top of his boot he extracted a 'Derringer' – a small, single-shot pistol such as is usually employed by ladies and political assassins – and set this toy-like firearm beside the bottle of porter. From his sleeve the lodger withdrew a short, narrow stiletto, which he stuck into the loaf of bread. Only after all this did he light the candle, remove his blue spectacles and rub his eyes with a weary hand. Finally, after a glance round at the window to make sure that the curtains were not parting, he lifted the red-haired wig off his head and was revealed as none other than Erast Petrovich Fandorin.

The meal was over and done with in five minutes – the titular counsellor and fugitive assassin clearly had more important matters to attend to. Brushing the crumbs from the table, Erast Fandorin wiped his hands on his long Bohemian blouse, went over to the tattered armchair standing in the corner, fumbled under its upholstery and took out a small blue attaché case. Fandorin was impatient to continue the work with which he had been occupied all day and which had already led him to an extremely important discovery.

Following the tragic events of the previous night Erast Fandorin had been obliged in spite of everything to pay a brief visit to his hotel in order to pick up at least his money and his passport. Now let his good friend Hippolyte – that villainous Judas – and his henchmen search the railway stations and seaports in vain for 'Erasmus von Dorn'. Who would pay any attention to a poor French artist who had taken up residence in the very foulest sink of the London slums? And though Fandorin may have been obliged to take his life in his hands and run the risk of going out to the post office, there had been a very good reason for that.

But what should he make of that Zurov? His part in the story was not entirely clear, but it was certainly unseemly at the very least. His Excellency was not simple, not simple at all. The gallant hussar and open-hearted soul performed the most devious of manoeuvres. How cleverly he had passed on that address, how well he had worked it all out! In a word, a true game-master! He knew that the stupid gudgeon would take the bait and swallow the hook as well. But no, His Excellency had used some other allegory, about a moth. The moth had flown into the flame all right, flown in exactly as expected. And it had almost burned its wings. Serve the fool right. After all, it was clear enough that Bezhetskaya and Hippolyte had some interest in common. Only a romantic blockhead such as a certain titular counsellor (who had, in fact, been promoted to that rank over the heads of other, more worthy individuals) could have seriously believed in a fatal passion in the Castilian style. And he had even tried to fill Ivan Franzevich Brilling's head with all that nonsense. For very shame! Ha-ha! How beautifully Count Hippolyte Zurov had expressed it: 'I love her and I fear her, the witch. I'll strangle her with my own hands!' No doubt he had enjoyed toying with the babe-in-arms! And how exquisitely he had pulled it off, every bit as good as the first time, with the duel. His moves had been calculated simply and unerringly: take up a position at the Winter Queen Hotel and wait there calmly until the stupid moth 'Erasmus' came flying to the candle. This was not Moscow, there was no detective police, no gendarmes, Erast Fandorin could be taken with the greatest of ease. And all the clues securely buried. Might not Zurov perhaps be that 'Franz' whom the butler had mentioned? Ugh, these hideous conspirators. But which one of them was the leader – Zurov or Bezhetskaya? It seemed more likely after all that she was . . . Erast Fandorin shivered as he recalled the events of the previous night and the plaintive shriek with which Amalia had collapsed when she was shot. Perhaps she had been wounded and not killed? But the dismal chill that enveloped his heart told him that she was dead, the beautiful queen was dead, and Fandorin would have to live with that terrible burden to the end of his days.

It was, of course, entirely possible that the end was already near. Zurov knew who had killed her, he had seen Fandorin. The hunt must already be on right across London, right across England, indeed. But why had Zurov let him go last night, why had he allowed him to escape? Had he been frightened off by the pistol in Fandorin's hand? It was a riddle . . .

There was, however, another, even more puzzling riddle – the contents of the attaché case. For a long time Fandorin had been quite unable to make any sense at all of the mysterious list. His check had revealed that the number of entries on the sheets of paper was exactly the same as the number of letters and all of the information matched, except that in addition to the date indicated in each letter, Bezhetskaya had also entered the date of its receipt.

There were forty-five entries in all. The very earliest of them was dated the 1st of June and the three latest had made their appearance even as Erast Fandorin watched. The ordinal numbers in the letters were all different; the lowest was No. 47F (the Kingdom of Belgium, director of a governmental department, received on the 15th of June) and the highest was No. 2347F (Italy, a lieutenant of dragoons, received on the 9th of June). The letters had been dispatched from a total of nine countries, of which the most frequently occurring were England and France. Russia only appeared once in the sequence (No. 994F, a full state counsellor, received on the 26th of June, with a St Petersburg stamp from the 7th of June on the envelope – ooph, he mustn't confuse the calendars! – the 7th of June would be the 19th in the European style, that meant it had taken just a week to arrive). For the most part the positions and ranks mentioned were high – generals, senior officers, one admiral, one senator, even one Portuguese government minister, but there were also small fry such as the lieutenant from Italy, a court investigator from France and a captain of the Austro-Hungarian border guards.

Taking everything together, Bezhetskaya appeared to be some kind of intermediary, a transmission link or living postbox whose duties involved registering incoming information and then forwarding it – evidently to Mr Nicholas Croog in St Petersburg. It was reasonable to assume that the lists were forwarded once a month. It was also clear that some other individual had played the role of 'Miss Olsen' before Bezhetskaya, a fact which the hotel porter had not suspected.

At that point the obvious came to an end and an urgent need arose to apply the deductive method. If only the chief were there, he would have instantly listed off all the possible scenarios and everything would have been tidied up and neatly sorted away. But the chief was far away, and the unavoidable conclusion was that Brilling had been right, a thousand times right. There obviously existed a widely ramified secret organisation with members in many countries – that was one. Queen Victoria and Disraeli had nothing to do with the case (otherwise why send the reports to St Petersburg?) – that was two. Erast Fandorin had made a fool of himself with his English spies, this affair very definitely smacked of nihilists – that was three. And all the threads led nowhere else but back to Russia, which possessed the most fearsome and ruthless nihilists of all – that was four. And they included that treacherous werewolf Zurov.

His chief may have been right, but even so Fandorin had not squandered his travel expenses in vain. Even in his worst nightmares Ivan Brilling could hardly have imagined the true might of the multi-headed hydra with which he was doing battle. These were no students and hysterical young ladies with little bombs and pistols, this was an entire secret order involving ministers of state, generals, court investigators and even a Full State Counsellor from St Petersburg!

That was when Erast Fandorin was struck by a sudden insight (by this time it was already after noon). A Full State Counsellor – and a nihilist? It simply didn't make sense. The head of the imperial guard in Brazil was not really a problem – Erast Fandorin had never been to Brazil in his life and he had no idea of the local mores – but his imagination absolutely refused to picture a Russian state general holding a bomb in his hand. Fandorin was acquainted quite closely with one Full State Counsellor, Fedor Trifonovich Sevriugin, the director of the Provincial Gymnasium which he had attended for almost seven years. Could he possibly be a terrorist? Nonsense!

Then suddenly Erast Fandorin's heart was wrung with pity. These were no terrorists, these were all decent and respectable individuals! These were the victims of terror! Nihilists from various countries, each of them concealed behind a coded number, were reporting to central revolutionary HQ about the terrorist acts they had committed!

And yet, he could not actually recall any ministers being killed in Portugal in June – all the newspapers would most certainly have reported it . . . Which meant that they must be prospective victims, that was it! The 'numbers' were requesting permission from HQ to commit acts of terror. And no names were given in order to maintain secrecy.

Now everything fell into place, now everything was clear.

Ivan Brilling had said something about a thread connecting Akhtyrtsev to some *dacha* outside Moscow, but Fandorin, all fired up with his own fantastic ravings about spies, had not bothered to listen.

But stop. What did they want with a lieutenant of dragoons? He really was very small fry. Very simple, was Erast Fandorin's immediate reply to his own question. The obscure Italian obviously must have got under their feet somehow. In the same way that a youthful collegiate registrar from the Moscow detective police had once got under the feet of a certain white-eyed killer.

What should he do? He was simply sitting things out here, while the threat of death hung over so many honourable people! Fandorin felt especially sorry for the unknown general in St Petersburg. No doubt he was a worthy man, already middle-aged and distinguished, with little children . . . And it appeared that these Carbonarists sent out their villainous communiqués every month. No wonder there was blood flowing right across Europe every day! And the threads led back nowhere else but to St Petersburg. Erast Fandorin recalled the words once spoken by his chief: 'The very fate of Russia is at stake.' Ah, Ivan Brilling, ah Mr State Counsellor, not just the fate of Russia – the fate of the entire civilised world!

He could inform the clerk Pyzhov. Secretly, so that the traitor in the embassy would not sniff anything out. But how? The traitor could be anyone at all, and it was dangerous for Fandorin to show his face near the embassy, even in the guise of a red-headed Frenchman in an artist's blouse . . . He would have to take a risk, send a letter by municipal post to provincial secretary Pyzhov and mark it 'to be delivered personally'. Nothing superfluous, just his address and greetings from Ivan Franzevich Brilling. He was a clever man, he would understand everything. And they said the municipal post here delivered a letter to its addressee in little more than two hours . . .

And that was what Fandorin had done, so that when

evening came it found him waiting to see if there would be a cautious knock at the door.

There was no knock, however. Everything turned out quite differently.

Later, when it was already after midnight, Erast Fandorin was sitting in the tattered armchair in which the attaché case was concealed and dozing in a semi-slumber. On the table the candle had almost burned itself out, in the corners of the room a hostile gloom had gathered and thickened, and outside the window an approaching storm occasionally rumbled alarmingly. The very air seemed oppressive and stifling, as though some invisible, corpulent individual had sat down on his chest and would not let him get his breath. Fandorin was teetering somewhere on the ill-defined boundary between wakefulness and sleep. Important thoughts of practical matters would suddenly be swamped by irrelevant drivel, and then the young man would rouse himself and shake his head in order to avoid being sucked down into the whirlpool of sleep.

During one of these lucid intervals something very peculiar happened. First there was a strange, shrill squeak. Then Erast Fandorin could scarcely believe his own eyes as he saw the key protruding from the keyhole begin to turn of its own accord. The door creaked sickeningly as it swung open into the room, and a bizarre vision appeared in the doorway: a puny little gentleman of indeterminate age with a round, clean-shaven face and narrow eyes nestling in beds of fine, radiating wrinkles.

Fandorin shuddered and grabbed the revolver from the table, but the vision smiled sweetly, nodded contentedly and cooed in extremely pleasant, honeyed tenor tones:

'Well, here I am, my dear lad. Porfirii Pyzhov, son of Martin, servant of God and provincial secretary. Come flying to you the very moment you chose to beckon. Like the wind at the summons of Aeolus.'

'How did you open the door?' Erast Fandorin whispered in fright. 'I distinctly remember turning the key twice.'

'With this, a magnetic picklock,' the long-awaited visitor readily explained, displaying some kind of elongated little bar, which, however, immediately disappeared back into his pocket. 'An extremely handy little item. I borrowed it from a certain local thief. In my line of business I am obliged to maintain relations with the most dreadful types, denizens of the very darkest depths of society. The most absolute *misérables*, I assure you. Such types as Monsieur Hugo never even saw in his dreams. But they too are human souls and it is possible to find ways to approach them. In fact I am very fond of the scum and I even collect them a little. As the poet put it: each amuses himself as he may, but all shall be brought low by death one day. Or as the Teut would have it: *jedes tierchen hat sein plesirchen* – every little beastling has its own plaything.'

It was quite evident that this strange man possessed the ability to rattle off nonsense on any subject whatsoever without the slightest difficulty, but his keen eyes were wasting no time – they had already thoroughly ransacked both Erast Fandorin's person and the furnishings of his squalid chamber.

'I am Erast Petrovich Fandorin. From Mr Brilling. On extremely important business,' said the young man, although the first and second facts had been stated in his letter, and Pyzhov himself must undoubtedly have guessed the third. 'Only he did not give me any password. Probably he forgot.'

Erast Fandorin looked anxiously at Pyzhov, on whom his salvation now depended, but the little man merely threw up his short-fingered hands.

'There is no need of any password. Sheer nonsense and games for children. Can a Russian fail to know another Russian? It is enough for me to gaze into your bright eyes (Porfirii Pyzhov moved close up against Fandorin) and I see everything as clearly as though it were laid out before me. A youth pure-hearted and bold, filled with noble aspirations and patriotic devotion to his fatherland. Why, of course – in our department we have no other kind.'

Fandorin frowned – it seemed to him that this provincial secretary was playing the fool, taking him for some idiot child. And therefore Erast Fandorin related his story briefly and drily, without any emotions. It transpired that Porfirii Pyzhov was capable of more than mere tongue-wagging, he could also be an extremely attentive listener – in fact he had a positive talent for it. Pyzhov sat down on the edge of the bed, folded his hands across his belly, squeezed the narrow slits of his eyes even tighter – and it was as though he had disappeared. That is, he was quite literally all attention. Not once did Pyzhov interrupt the speaker, not once did he even stir. However, at times, at the key moments of the narrative, a subtle spark glimmered beneath his hooded eyelids.

Erast Fandorin did not divulge his hypothesis concerning the letters – that he saved for Ivan Brilling – and in conclusion he said:

'And so, Mr Pyzhov, you see before you a fugitive and involuntary homicide. I urgently need to get across to the continent. I need to get to Moscow, to see Mr Brilling.'

Pyzhov chewed on his lips and waited to see whether anything else would be said, then he asked in a quiet voice:

'And what of the attaché case? Why not forward it with the diplomatic post? That would be more reliable. One never knows . . . From what you have told me, these gentlemen are serious individuals, they will be searching for you in Europe as well. Of course I shall get you across the Channel, my sweet angel, that is no great business. Provided you disdain not the fisherman's frail bark, you shall sail tomorrow, and God speed! Riding the howling gale beneath your sails.'

'All of his winds seem to be gales,' thought Erast Fandorin, who in all honesty desperately did not wish to part with the attaché case which it had cost him so dear to obtain. Porfirii Pyzhov, however, continued as though he had not noticed the young man's hesitation.

'I do not interfere in other people's business, for I am an

unassuming and incurious individual. However, I can see there are many things that you are not telling me. And quite right, my peachy darling, the word is silver, but silence is golden. Ivan Franzevich Brilling is a high-flying bird. A haughty eagle, one might say, among starlings, who would not entrust important business to just anyone. Is that not so?'

'In what sense?'

'Why, regarding the attaché case. I would daub it with sealing-wax on every side, give it to one of the more keen-witted couriers and it would be wafted across to Moscow in a trice, as on a three-horse sleigh with bells a-jingling. And for my part I would dispatch a coded telegram – Receive, O ruler of the heavenly realms, this priceless gift.'

God knows, Erast Fandorin did not crave honours, he did not desire decorations or even fame. He would have surrendered the attaché case to Pyzhov for the good of the cause, for, after all, a courier really would be more reliable. But in his imagination he had already rehearsed so many times the triumphant return to his chief, with the spectacular presentation of the precious attaché case and the thrilling account of all the adventures that had befallen him . . . And now was none of this ever to be?

Cravenly putting his own interest first, Fandorin said austerely:

'The attaché case is concealed in a secure hiding place. And I shall deliver it myself. I answer for it with my life. Please do not take offence, Mr Pyzhov.'

'Why, of course not, of course not.' Pyzhov made no attempt to insist. 'Just as you wish. It will be less trouble for me. The devil take other people's secrets, I have quite enough of my own. If it is in a secure place, so be it.' He got to his feet and ran his gaze over the bare walls of the tiny room. 'You take a rest for the time being, my young friend. Youth needs sleep. I am an old man, and I have insomnia in any case, so in the meanwhile I shall issue instructions concerning the boat. Tomorrow (actually it is already today) I shall be here at very first light. I shall deliver you to the shore of the sea, embrace and kiss you in farewell and make the sign of the cross over you. And I shall remain here, an orphan abandoned in an alien land. Oh, it frets poor Ivan's heart to be stuck in foreign parts.'

At this point even Porfirii Pyzhov himself clearly realised that he had poured on the syrup a little too thickly and he spread his arms in acknowledgement of his guilt:

'I repent, my tongue has run away with me. But you know, I have missed living Russian speech so badly, I do so yearn for elegant turns of phrase. Our embassy know-alls express themselves most of the time in French, and I have no one with whom I can share the inmost stirrings of my soul.'

The thunder rumbled again, this time more seriously, and it seemed to have started raining. Suddenly all business, Pyzhov began preparing to depart.

'I must be going. Ai-ai-ai, how passionately the inclement elements do rage.'

In the doorway he turned round to caress Fandorin with a farewell glance and then with a low bow he melted away into the gloom of the corridor.

Erast Fandorin locked and bolted the door and hunched up his shoulders in a chill shiver as a peal of thunder reverberated above the very roof.

It was dark and eerie in the wretched little room, with its single solitary window that overlooked the naked stone yard without a single blade of grass. Outside the weather was foul, windy and rainy, but the moon was slewing through the tattered clouds strewn across the black and grey sky. A ray of yellow light falling through the crack between the curtains cut the squalid lodging in half, slashing through it as far as the bed, where Fandorin, beset by nightmares, tossed about in a cold sweat. He was fully dressed, including his boots, and he was still armed, except that the revolver was once again under his pillow.

Overburdened by the guilt of the murder, poor Erast Fandorin's conscience visited upon him a strange vision.

Dead Amalia was leaning over his bed. Her eyes were half-closed, a drop of blood trickled from beneath her eyelid, in her bare hand she held a black rose.

'What did I do to you?' the dead woman groaned piteously. 'I was young and beautiful, I was unhappy and lonely. They snared me in their web, they deceived and depraved me. The only man I loved betrayed me. You have committed a terrible sin, Erast, you have killed beauty, and beauty is a miracle from God. You have trampled underfoot a miracle from God. And why, what for?'

The drop of blood fell from her cheek straight on to Erast Fandorin's forehead. He started at the cold sensation and opened his eyes. He saw that Amalia was not there, thank God. It was all a dream, nothing but a dream. But then another icy drop fell on to his forehead.

What was it, Erast Fandorin wondered, shuddering in horror and finally waking up completely. He heard the howling of the wind, the drumming of the rain, the hollow rumbling of the thunder. What were these drops? It was nothing supernatural, however – the ceiling was leaking. Be still, foolish heart, be calm.

Then came the low but distinct whispering from behind the door:

'Why, what for?'

And then again:

'Why, what for?'

It's my bad conscience, Fandorin told himself. My bad conscience is giving me hallucinations. But this common-sensical, rational thought failed to dispel the hideous, viscous terror that was oozing in at every pore of his body.

Everything seemed quiet. A flash of lightning lit up the naked grey walls and then it was dark again.

A minute later he heard a quiet knocking at the window. Tap-tap. Then again: tap-tap-tap.

Steady now! It's nothing but the wind. A tree. A branch scraping the window. A perfectly ordinary occurrence.

Tap-tap. Tap-tap-tap.

A tree? What tree? Fandorin suddenly jerked upright. There was no tree outside the window! There was nothing but an empty yard. My God, what was it?

The strip of yellow between the curtains faded and turned to grey – the moon must have gone behind a cloud – and an instant later something dark, mysterious and terrifying loomed into sight out there.

He could endure anything but lying there like that, feeling the hairs rising on the nape of his neck. Anything but feeling himself losing his mind.

Erast Fandorin stood up and set off towards the window on legs that scarcely obeyed him, keeping his eyes fixed on that terrible patch of darkness. At the very moment when he jerked back the curtains, the sky was lit up by a flash of lightning and there outside the windowpane, right in front of him, Fandorin saw a deadly pale face with black pits for eyes. A hand glimmering with unearthly light slid slowly across the glass, its fingers extended in bright rays, and Erast Fandorin acted stupidly, like a little child – he sobbed convulsively and staggered backwards, then dashed back to the bed, collapsed on to it face-down and covered his head with his hands.

He had to wake up! Wake up as soon as possible! Our Father, Who art in Heaven, hallowed be Thy name, Thy kingdom come, Thy . . .

The tapping at the window stopped. He lifted his face out of the pillow and squinted cautiously in the direction of the window, but saw nothing terrible – just the night and the rain and the rapid flashes of lightning. It was his imagination. Definitely his imagination.

Fortunately Erast Fandorin managed to recall the teachings of the Indian Brahmin Chandra Johnson, who taught the science of correct breathing and correct living. The book of wisdom read:

Correct breathing is the basis of correct living. It will support you in the difficult moments of life, and through it you will attain salvation, tranquillity and enlightenment. Breathing in the vital force of *prana*, do not hasten to breathe it out again, but hold it a while in your lungs. The longer and more regular your breath is, the more vital force there is within you. That man has achieved enlightenment who, after breathing in *prana* in the evening, does not breathe it out again until the dawn light.

Well, Erast Fandorin still had a long way to go to reach enlightenment, but thanks to his regular morning exercises he had already learned to hold his breath for up to a hundred seconds, and to this sure remedy he resorted now. He filled his chest with air and became still, he 'was transformed into wood, stone, grass'. It worked – the pounding of his heart steadied a little, the terror receded. At the count of a hundred Fandorin released his breath noisily, soothed and reassured by the victory of the enlightened spirit over superstition.

And then he heard a sound that set his teeth chattering loudly. Someone was scratching at the door.

'Let me in,' a voice whispered. 'Look at me. I'm cold. Let me in . . .'

This is just too much, thought Fandorin indignantly, summoning his final remnants of pride. I'm going to open the door and wake up. Or . . . or I shall see that this is no dream.

In two bounds he was at the door, pulled back the bolt and heaved the door towards himself.

Amalia was standing in the doorway. She was wearing a white lace peignoir like the last time, but her hair was wet and tangled from the rain and a bloody patch had spread across her breast. The most terrifying thing of all was the unearthly glimmering of her face, with its motionless, lifeless eyes. A white hand trailing sparks of light reached out towards Erast Fandorin's face and touched his cheek in exactly the same way as the day before, but this time the fingers radiated such an icy chill that the unfortunate Fandorin staggered backwards, his mind reeling into madness.

'Where is the attaché case?' the spectre asked in a hissing whisper. 'Where is my attaché case? I sold my soul for it.'

'I won't give it to you!' Erast Fandorin cried out through parched lips. He staggered backwards to the armchair in the depths of which the purloined attaché case lay concealed, plumped down heavily on to the seat and put his arms around it for safety's sake.

The ghost went over to the table. She struck a match, lit the candle and suddenly shouted loudly in English:

'Your turn now! He's all yours!'

Two men burst into the room – the lofty Morbid with his head almost brushing the ceiling and someone else small and sprightly.

His mind now totally befogged, Fandorin did not even stir a muscle when the butler set a knife to his throat and the other man frisked him, discovering the 'Derringer' in the top of his boot.

'Look for the revolver,' Morbid ordered in English and the sprightly little fellow made no mistake, instantly discovering the 'Colt' hidden under the pillow.

All this time Amalia was standing by the window, wiping her face and hands with a handkerchief.

'Is that all?' she asked impatiently. 'What foul muck this phosphorus is. And the entire masquerade was a total waste of time. He lacked the brains even to hide the case properly. John, look in the armchair.'

She did not even look at Fandorin, as though he had suddenly been transformed into an inanimate object.

Morbid easily tugged Fandorin out of the armchair, keeping the blade of the knife pressed to his throat the whole time, and the sprightly fellow thrust his hand into the seat and pulled out the blue attaché case.

'Give it here.' Bezhetskaya went over to the table and checked the contents of the case. 'It's all there. He didn't have time to send anything on. Thank God. Franz, bring my cape, I'm chilled through.'

'So it was all a show?' Fandorin asked in a quavering voice as his courage began to return. 'Bravo. You are a great actress. I am glad that my bullet missed you. Such a great talent would have been lost . . .'

'Don't forget the gag,' Amalia said to the butler and, tossing the cape brought by Franz across her shoulders, she left the room – without so much as a final glance at the disgraced Erast Fandorin.

The sprightly little fellow – so it was him who had been watching the hotel, not Zurov at all – took a ball of fine string out of his pocket and bound the captive's arms tightly against his sides. Then he grabbed Fandorin's nose between his forefinger and thumb, and when the young man opened his mouth, he thrust a rubber pear into it.

'All in order,' Franz declared with a slight German accent, pleased with the result of his handiwork. 'I'll bring the sack.'

He darted out into the corridor and quickly returned. The last thing that Erast Fandorin saw before the coarse sack was pulled over his shoulders and right down to his knees was the stony, totally impassive face of John Morbid. But though it was, of course, a pity that of all faces the world should choose to show Erast Fandorin this one in farewell, and not the visage that had enchanted him so, the dusty darkness of the sack proved to be even worse.

'Let me tie a bit more string round the outside,' Fandorin heard Franz say. 'We don't have far to go, but it'll be safer that way.'

'Where's he going to go?' Morbid's bass replied. 'The moment he twitches I'll stab him in the belly.'

'We'll tie him a bit tighter in any case,' Franz sang, and he bound the string around the sack so tightly that it became hard for Erast Fandorin to breathe.

'Get moving!' said the butler, prodding the captive, and Fandorin set off like a blind man, not really understanding why they could not simply slit his throat there in the room.

He stumbled twice, and almost fell in the doorway of the

guesthouse, but John's massive ham of a hand caught him by the shoulder in time.

He could smell rain and hear horses snorting gently.

'You two, as soon as you've dealt with him, come back here and tidy everything up,' he heard Bezhetskaya's voice say. 'We are going back to the house.'

'Don't you worry, ma'am,' the butler rumbled. 'You've done your job, now we'll do ours.'

Oh, how Erast Fandorin longed to say something remarkable to Amalia in parting, something really exceptional, so that she would not remember him as a stupid, frightened little boy, but as a valiant warrior who fell in an unequal struggle against a whole army of nihilists. But the accursed rubber pear deprived him of even that final satisfaction.

And then, just when it seemed that fate could torment him no more after what he had already endured, the poor youth was struck yet another shattering blow.

'My darling Amalia Kazimirovna,' said a familiar light tenor voice in Russian. 'Will you not permit an old man to take a spin in your carriage with you? We could chat about this and that, and I should be a bit drier. As you can see, I am absolutely drenched. Your Patrick can take the *droshky* and drive behind us. You don't object, do you, my sweetheart?'

'Get in,' Bezhetskaya replied drily. 'But remember, Pyzhov, I am no darling of yours, let alone your sweetheart.'

Erast Fandorin lowed mutely, for with the rubber pear in his mouth it was quite impossible to burst out sobbing. The entire world had take up arms against the poor youth. Where could he draw the strength required to overcome the odds in this battle with a host of villains? He was surrounded on all sides by noxious traitors, venomous vipers (pah, now he had been infected by Porfirii Pyzhov's odious verbiage!). Bezhetskaya and her cutthroats, and Zurov, and even Pyzhov, that fickle fair-weather friend – they were all his enemies. At that moment Erast Fandorin did not even wish to go on living, so overwhelmed was he by disgust and weariness.

But as things stood, no one seemed very keen to persuade

him to go on living. In fact his escorts appeared to have something quite different in mind. Strong hands hoisted the captive up and set him down on a seat. The heavyweight Morbid clambered up and sat on his left, the lightweight Franz sat on his right and cracked his whip, and Erast Fandorin was thrown backwards.

'Where to?' asked the butler.

'We were told to go to pier number six. It's deeper there and the current's stronger too. What do you reckon?'

'It makes no odds to me. Number six will do as well as any.'

And so Erast Fandorin's imminent fate was spelled out for him quite clearly enough. They would take him to some solitary quayside, tie a rock to him and dispatch him to the bottom of the Thames, to rot among the rusty anchor chains and bottle shards. Titular Counsellor Fandorin would disappear without trace, for it would transpire that after the military agent in Paris he had not been seen by a single living soul. Ivan Brilling would realise that his protégé must have missed his footing somewhere, but he would never learn the truth. And in Moscow and Peter they would still be unaware of the viper that lurked in the bosom of their secret service. If only he could be unmasked!

Well, and perhaps he still could.

Even bound and stuffed into a long, dusty sack, Erast Fandorin was feeling incomparably better than twenty minutes earlier, when the phosphorescent spectre was glaring in at his window and his reason was paralysed by fear.

For as a matter of fact there was indeed a chance of salvation for the captive. Franz was adroit, but he had not guessed to feel Fandorin's right sleeve. In that sleeve lay the stiletto, and in the stiletto lay hope. If only he could contrive somehow to reach the handle with his fingers . . . Oh, it's not so simple when your hand is tied to your hip. How long would it take them to reach this pier number six? Would he have time?

'Sit still,' said Morbid, poking his elbow into the side of the captive, who was wriggling about (no doubt from fear).

'Indeed, my friend, twist and turn as you may, it changes nothing,' Franz remarked philosophically.

The man in the sack carried on twitching for about a minute before eventually emitting a brief, muffled hoot and falling quiet, evidently finally reconciled to his fate (before it yielded and slid out, the accursed stiletto had dealt him a painful cut on the wrist).

'Here we are,' John announced and got to his feet, peering about in all directions. 'Nobody here.'

'And who would there be, out in the rain, in the middle of the night?' asked Franz with a shrug of his shoulders. 'Come on, will you, get a move on. We've still got to get back.'

'Take his legs.'

They picked up the bundle bound round with string and carried it to a rough wooden pier for row-boats that thrust out over the black water like an arrow.

Erast Fandorin heard the squeak of planks underfoot and the splashing of the river. Deliverance was near. The moment the waters of the Thames closed over his head he would slash the blade across his bonds, slice open the sackcloth and rise quietly to the surface under the pier. There he would bide his time until these two were gone, and then his nightmare would be over – salvation, life, freedom! It all seemed so plain and easy that an inner voice suddenly whispered to Fandorin: Erast, things never happen like that in real life, fate is sure to play some dirty trick and upset your entire marvellous plan.

Alas, the inner voice was an omen of the very disaster it predicted, for the dirty trick put in an appearance without further delay – and it came not from the direction of the nightmarish Mr Morbid, but on the initiative of the genial Franz.

'Wait a moment, John,' Franz said, when they halted at the very edge of the pier and set their burden down on the rough boards. 'This won't do, throwing a living man into the water like some kitten. Would you like to be in his place?'

'No,' replied John.

'Well then,' said Franz, delighted. 'You see what I mean. Choking on that filthy rotten swill – brrrr! I wouldn't wish that on anyone. Let's do right by him: slit his throat first, so he won't suffer. One quick swipe, and it's all over, eh?'

Such philanthropic sentimentality made Erast Fandorin feel quite poorly, but dear, wonderful Mr Morbid muttered discontentedly:

'Oh no, I'll get my knife all bloody. And splatter it on my sleeve. This young puppy's caused enough trouble already. Never mind, he'll croak anyway. If you're so kind-hearted, you strangle him with a piece of string, that's your speciality, and meanwhile I'll go and look for a lump of iron or something of the sort.'

His heavy footsteps receded, leaving Fandorin alone with the humanitarian Franz.

'I shouldn't have tied any string round the outside of the sack,' the latter mused thoughtfully. 'I used it all up.'

Erast Fandorin lowed in approval – never mind, don't worry about it, I'll manage somehow.

'Eh, poor soul,' sighed Franz. 'Listen to him groan, it fair breaks your heart. Okay, my lad, don't you be frightened. Uncle Franz won't begrudge you his belt.'

There was the sound of approaching steps.

'There you are, a piece of rail. The very thing,' boomed the butler. 'Stick it in under the string. He won't surface for a month at least.'

'Wait a moment. I'll just slip this noose round his neck.'

'Ah, to hell with all your mollycoddling! Time's wasting, it'll be dawn soon!'

'I'm sorry, son,' Franz said sympathetically. 'Obviously that's the way it's meant to be. *Das hast du dir selbst zu verdanken.*'[1]

They picked Erast Fandorin up again and began swinging him backwards and forwards.

'Azazel!' Franz cried out in a solemn, formal voice, and a

---

[1] You only have yourself to thank.

second later the swaddled body plunged with a splash into the putrid water.

Fandorin felt neither the cold nor the oily weight of the water pressing down on him as he hacked through the soaking string with the stiletto. The most awkward part was freeing his right hand, but once it was loose, the job went swimmingly: one stroke and his left hand began assisting his right; another, and the sack was slashed from top to bottom; a third, and the heavy length of rail went plunging into the soft silt.

Now he just had to make certain not to surface too soon. Erast Fandorin pushed off with his legs, thrust his hands out in front of him and groped about with them in the turbid water. Somewhere here, very close, there ought to be the supports that held up the pier. There, his fingers had come into contact with slippery, weed-covered timber. Quietly now, without hurrying, up along the pillar. So there would be no splash, not a sound.

Under the wooden decking of the pier it was pitch-dark. Suddenly a round, white blob was thrust up out of the black, watery depths. Within this white circle a smaller dark one immediately took shape as Titular Counsellor Fandorin greedily gulped in the air above the river. It smelled of decay and kerosene. It had the magical smell of life.

Meanwhile up above, on the pier, a leisurely conversation was in progress. Concealed below, Erast Fandorin could hear every word. He had sometimes reduced himself to sentimental tears by imagining the words with which friends and enemies would remember him, the hero who met an untimely end, by rehearsing the speeches that would be pronounced over the gaping pit of his grave. One might say that his entire youth had been spent in dreams of this kind. Imagine, then, the young man's indignation when he heard what trivia formed the subject of the prattle between those who believed themselves his murderers! Not a word about the man over whose head the sombre waters had only just closed! A man with a mind and a heart, with a noble soul and exalted aspirations!'

'Oh,' sighed Franz, 'I'll pay for this little stroll with an attack of rheumatism. Feel how damp the air is. Well, what are we standing here for? Let's go, eh?'

'It's too soon yet.'

'Listen, what with all this running about I didn't get any supper. What do you think, will they give us something to eat or think up some other job for us to do?'

'That's not for us to worry our heads about. We'll do whatever they tell us.'

'If I could just grab a nice piece of cold veal on the way. My stomach's rumbling . . . Are we really going to uproot ourselves from the old familiar homestead? I've just settled in, got used to the place. What for? Everything worked out all right in the end.'

'She knows what for. If she's given the order, there's a reason.'

'That's true enough. She doesn't make mistakes. There's nothing I wouldn't do for her – I'd even shop my own dear old dad. That is, if I had one, of course. No mother would ever have done as much for us as she has.'

'That goes without saying . . . Right, that's it. Let's go.'

Erast Fandorin waited until the footsteps died away in the distance, counted to three hundred just to make sure, and only then began moving towards the shoreline.

When, after falling back several times, he finally hauled himself out with a great struggle on to the low but almost vertical parapet of the waterfront, the darkness was already beginning to melt away before the advancing dawn. The man who had failed to drown shuddered and shivered, his teeth chattered and then he was seized by the hiccups as well – he must clearly have swallowed a lot of the putrid river water. But it was still wonderful to be alive. Erast Fandorin cast a loving glance across the wide expanse of the river (on the far side there were lights shining sweetly), smiled affectionately at the sheer solidity of a low, squat warehouse, gave his approval to the regular swaying of the tugboats and harbour launches lined up along the quayside. A blissful smile lit up the wet face of this man risen from the dead with a smear of fuel oil on his forehead. He stretched sweetly, and then froze motionless in that absurd pose – a low, agile silhouette had detached itself nimbly from the corner of the warehouse and begun scurrying towards him.

'What vile brutes they are, what villainous knaves,' the silhouette lamented in a thin voice clearly audible from a distance as it came towards him. 'They can't be trusted to do anything, you always have to keep an eye on them. Where would you all be without Pyzhov, tell me that! You'd be as helpless as blind little kittens, you'd be done for.'

Fandorin dashed forward, overwhelmed by righteous fury. The traitor appeared to imagine that his satanic apostasy had remained undiscovered.

However, a glimpse of the malevolent gleam of metal in the hand of the provincial secretary made Erast Fandorin first halt and then begin backing away.

'That's a wise decision, my sweet strawberry,' Pyzhov said approvingly, and Fandorin saw what a catlike spring there was in his step. 'You're a sensible lad, I saw that straight away. Do you know what it is I have here?' He waved his weapon in the air and Fandorin saw a twin-barrelled pistol of unusually large calibre. 'A terrible thing. In the local criminal argot it is known as a "smasher". Here, if you would care to take a look, is where you load the two little explosive bullets – the very ones forbidden by the St Petersburg Convention of 1868. But criminals are genuine villains, my little Erast. What do they care for some philanthropic convention? And the bullet is explosive. Once it strikes the flesh, it unfolds its petals like a flower. It reduces flesh and bone to a bloody mush. So just you take it easy, my little darling, don't get twitchy, if I'm startled I might just fire, then afterwards I wouldn't be able to live with what I've done, I'd feel so guilty. It really is excruciatingly painful if it hits you in the belly or anywhere else around that area.'

Still hiccuping – no longer from the cold, but from fear – Fandorin yelled out:

'Judas Iscariot! You sold your homeland for thirty pieces of silver!' And he backed further away from the menacing muzzle of the gun.

'In the words of the immortal Derzhavin, inconstancy is the lot of mortal kind. And you do me a grave injustice, my little friend. I was not enticed by thirty shekels, but by a far more substantial sum, transferred in the most immaculate fashion to a Swiss bank – for my old age, to ensure that I do not die in the gutter. And what did you think you were doing, you little fool? Who did you think you were yelping and yapping at? Shooting at stone is merely a waste of arrows. This is a truly mighty structure, the pyramid of Cheops. You cannot butt it down with your forehead.'

In the meantime Erast Fandorin had shuffled back to the very edge of the quayside and been obliged to halt on feeling the low kerb press against the back of his heels. All appearances indicated that this was exactly what Pyzhov had been trying to achieve.

'That's very good now, that's quite splendid,' he intoned mellifluously, halting ten paces away from his victim. 'It wouldn't have been easy for me to drag such a well-nourished youth to the water afterwards. Don't you be alarmed, my rubicund little chappie, Pyzhov knows what he's about. Bang – and it's all over. No more red little face, just gooey red mush. Even if they fish you out they won't identify you. And your soul will soar straight up to the angels. It hasn't had a chance to sin yet, it's such a young soul.'

With these words he raised his weapon, screwed up his left eye and smiled in sweet anticipation. He was in no hurry to fire, he was clearly savouring the moment. Fandorin cast a despairing glance at the deserted shoreline illuminated by the bleary light of dawn. There was no one, not a single soul. This time it really was the end. He thought he saw something stirring over by the warehouse, but he had no time to make it out – there was a thunderous shot, appallingly loud, louder than the loudest of thunder. Erast Fandorin swayed backwards, then with a blood-curdling howl he plunged down into the river out of which only a few minutes earlier he had clambered with such great difficulty.

Chapter Twelve

Consciousness did not, however, desert the executed man and, strangely enough, there was absolutely no pain at all. Totally bemused, Erast Fandorin began flailing at the water with his arms. What had happened? Was he alive or dead? If he was dead, then why was everything so wet?

Zurov's head appeared above the kerb at the edge of the quay. Fandorin was not surprised in the least: in the first place, it would have been hard to surprise him with anything just at that moment, and in the second place, in the next world (if that was where he was) far stranger things might occur.

'Erasmus! Are you alive? Did I nick you?' Zurov's head cried out in an anguished voice. 'Give me your hand.'

Erast Fandorin thrust his right hand out of the water and with one mighty heave he was dragged up on to *terra firma*. The first thing that he saw when he rose to his feet was a small figure lying face down on the ground with one hand extended forwards, clutching a hefty pistol. In among the thinning, skewbald hair on the back of the figure's head was a black hole, beneath which a dark puddle was slowly spreading.

'Are you wounded?' Zurov asked anxiously, turning the wet Erast Fandorin round and feeling him all over. 'I don't understand how it could have happened. A perfect *révolution dans la balistique*.[1] No, it's quite impossible.'

'Count Zurov, is that you?' Fandorin wheezed, finally grasping the fact that all this was not taking place in the next world, but in this one.

'Don't be so formal. Have you forgotten that we drank to *bruderschaft*?'

'But why did you do it?' Erast Fandorin began shaking and shuddering again. 'Are you absolutely determined to do away with me? Did that cursed Azazel of yours offer you a reward to do it? Shoot then, shoot, curse you! You make me feel sick, all of you, worse than cold semolina!'

How the cold semolina came to be mixed up in the matter was not clear – no doubt it was something from his childhood, long ago forgotten. Erast Fandorin was about to rip open the shirt on his chest – there you are, there's my breast, shoot! – but Zurov thumped him unceremoniously on the shoulder.

'Stop raving, Fandorin. What Azazel? What semolina? Let me bring you to your senses.' And thereupon he delivered two resounding slaps to the exhausted Erast Fandorin's face. 'It's me. Hippolyte Zurov. It's no wonder your brains have turned to jelly after such trying adventures. Prop yourself up against me.' He put his arm around the young man's shoulders. 'Now I'll take you back to the hotel. I've got a horse tethered close by and he' (Zurov prodded Pyzhov's motionless body with his foot) 'has a *droshky*. We'll fly back like the wind. You'll get warmed up, down a dose of grog and explain to me what kind of circus it is you're involved in here.'

Fandorin pushed the count away violently:

'Oh no, you explain to me! How did you (hic) come to be here? Why were you following me? Are you in collusion with them?'

Disconcerted, Zurov twirled a black moustache.

---

[1] revolution in ballistics.

'I can't tell you all that in a couple of words.'

'Never mind, I've got plenty (hic) of time. I won't budge from this spot.'

'Very well then, listen.'

And this is the story that Hippolyte told.

*

'Do you think I gave you Amalia's address just like that, without thinking about it? No, brother Fandorin, there was an entire psychology behind it. I took a liking to you, a terribly strong liking. There's something about you . . . I don't know, perhaps you're marked in some way. I have a nose for people like you. It's as though I can see a halo above a man's head, a kind of faint radiance. They're special people, the ones with that halo, fate watches over them, it protects them against all dangers. It never occurs to the man to think what fate is preserving him for. You must never fight a duel with a man like that – he'll kill you. Don't sit down to play cards with him – you'll be cleaned out, no matter what fancy tricks you pull out of your sleeve. I spotted your halo when you cleaned me out at *stoss*, and then forced me to draw lots to commit suicide. I don't meet people like you often. Back in our unit, when we were crossing the desert in Turkestan, there was a lieutenant by the name of Ulich. He went wading straight into the thickest fighting and nothing ever happened to him, he just kept on grinning. Would you believe that near Khiva with my own eyes I saw the khan's guardsmen fire a volley at him? Not a scratch. And then he drank some *kumis* that had turned sour and it finished him. We buried Ulich in the sand. Then why did the Lord watch over him in battle? It's a riddle! So, Erasmus, you are one of those people too, you can take my word for it. I've loved you since that moment when you put a pistol to your head without the slightest hesitation and pulled the trigger. But my love, brother Fandorin, is a subtle substance. I can't love anyone who is inferior to me and I envy those who are superior to me with a deadly envy. I envied you too. I felt jealous of your halo and your unnatural luck. Look at you, today you've come out of the water bone dry. Ha, ha, that is to say, you've come out wet, of course, but still alive, and without a single scratch. And to look at you're a mere boy, a young whelp, nothing to look at at all.'

Until this moment Erast Fandorin had been listening with lively interest, even blushing a gentle pink in his pleasure, and for the time being he had stopped shivering, but at the word 'whelp' he scowled and hiccuped twice angrily.

'Don't go taking offence, I mean it in friendship,' said Zurov, and slapped him on the shoulder. 'Anyway, what I thought was: fate has sent him to me. Amalia is bound to go for someone like him. She'll like the look of what she sees so much that she'll be hooked. And that will be the end of it, I'll be free of this satanic compulsion once and for all. She'll leave me in peace, stop tormenting me and leading me around on a chain like a bear at a fairground. Let her bait the boy with those Egyptian tortures of hers. So I gave you the end of the thread, I knew you wouldn't renounce your quest . . . Here, put this cloak over you and take a sip from this flask. You'll hiccup yourself to death.'

While Fandorin, with his teeth chattering all the while, gulped down the Jamaican rum that splashed around on the bottom of the large flat flask, Hippolyte threw his dandified cloak with the crimson satin lining over Fandorin's shoulders and then briskly rolled Pyzhov's corpse to the edge of the quay with his feet, tumbled it over the kerb and shoved it into the water. A single muffled splash, and all that remained of the iniquitous provincial secretary was a dark puddle on a flagstone.

'Lord, have mercy on the soul of Thy servant whoever-he-was,' Zurov prayed piously.

'Py-pyzhov,' said Erast Fandorin, hiccuping again, although thanks to the rum at least his teeth were no longer chattering. 'Porfirii Martynovich Pyzhov.'

'I won't remember it anyway,' said Hippolyte with a careless shrug of his shoulder. 'To hell with him. The half-pint was a rotten lot as far as I can see. Attacking an unarmed man with a pistol – pah! You know, he was going to kill you, Erasmus. As a matter of fact, I saved your life, do you realise that?'

'I realise, I realise. Carry on with your story.'

'Carry on I will, then. I gave you Amalia's address and the next day I was plunged into such depression – such a deep depression, as God forbid you should ever know. I drank, and I went to the girls, and I threw away fifty thousand at the card table – and still it wouldn't let go of me. I couldn't sleep, couldn't eat. I could drink all right, though. I kept seeing you lovey-doving with Amalia and both of you laughing at me. Or even worse, forgetting about me completely. I pined like that for ten whole days, I felt like I was losing my mind. You remember Jean, my manservant? He's in hospital now. He tried to remonstrate with me, shoved his nose in, and I put his nose out of joint and broke two of his ribs. I was ashamed, brother Fandorin. It was as though I was in a raging fever. On the eleventh day I couldn't take any more of it. I decided, that's it, I'll kill them both and afterwards I'll do away with myself. Nothing could be worse than this. So help me God, I can't remember how I travelled across Europe. I was drinking like a Kara-Kum camel. When we were travelling through Germany I even threw a couple of Prussians out of the carriage. But I can't actually remember it. Perhaps I imagined it. When I recovered my wits I was in London. The first thing I did was go to the hotel. Not a trace of her or of you. The hotel's a godforsaken hole, Amalia's never stayed in places like that in all her life. The sly rogue of a porter doesn't have a word of French, and the only English I know is "bottul viskey" and "moov yoor ass" – a midshipman I used to know taught me that. It means give me a bottle of the strong stuff and look sharp about it. I ask that porter, the English shrimp, about Miss Olsen, and he jabbers something in his own lingo and shakes his head and points somewhere backwards. As if to say she's gone, but he doesn't know where. Then I take a stab at you: "Fandorin, I say, Fandorin, moov

Boris Akunin

yoor ass." And then – mind you, don't take offence, now –
then he opened his eyes wide in amazement. Your name
obviously means something indecent in English. Anyway,
the flunky and I failed to reach a mutual understanding.
There was nothing else for it, so I moved into that fleapit
and stayed there. The schedule was, in the morning I go to
the porter and I ask: "Fandorin?" He bows and says "Moning,
sya" – telling me you haven't arrived yet. Then I go across the
street to the tavern where I have my observation post. What
hellish boredom, those miserable mugs all around me, it's a
good thing I at least have my "bottul viskey" and "moov yoor
ass" to help me out. At first the tavern-keeper just gawped at
me, then he got used to it and started greeting me like a
member of the family. His trade was livelier because of me:
people gathered to watch me swigging spirits by the glass-
ful. But they were afraid to come close, they watched from
a distance . . . I learned some new words: "djin" – that's
juniper vodka, "ram" – that's rum, "brendy" – that's a
wretched kind of cognac. Well anyway, I would have stayed
sitting at my observation post until I drank myself into a
stupor, but on the fourth day, Allah be praised, you arrived.
And you arrived looking like a real dandy, in a big shiny
carriage, with moustaches. By the way, it's a shame you
shaved them off, they make you look more of a sport. Fancy
that, I think, you cock of the walk, you've spread your fine
tail now. Only now instead of "Miss Olsen" you'll get short
shrift for your pains! But that hotel twerp sang a different
song for you, so I decided I'd lie low and wait until you put
me on the scent and then see how the cards lay. I crept round
the streets after you like some sleuth from the detective
police. Pshaw! I was at my wits' end. I saw you agree terms
with a cab-driver and so I took measures of my own. I took a
horse from the stable and wrapped its hooves in towels from
the hotel to stop them clattering too loudly. The Chechens
do that when they're preparing for a raid. Not that they use
hotel towels, I mean they use some other kind of rags, you
understand me?'

Erast Fandorin remembered the night before last. He had been so afraid of losing sight of Morbid that he had not given a thought to looking behind him, but now it appeared that the shadower had been shadowed.

'When you climbed in through her window, a volcano started bubbling up inside me,' Hippolyte continued. 'I bit my hand until it bled. Here, look.' He thrust his strong, well-proportioned hand under Fandorin's nose, and indeed, there between the thumb and the forefinger was the perfect half-moon mark of a bite. 'That's it, I say to myself, now three souls will go flying off at once – one to heaven (I meant you) and two straight to hell . . . You dithered a little bit by the window, until you summoned up enough impudence to climb in. My last hope then was that she might throw you out. She doesn't like being taken unawares like that, prefers to order everyone else around herself. I wait, and I'm shaking in my boots. Suddenly the light goes out, there's a shot and she screams! O, I think, Fandorin's shot her, the hothead. Landed himself in a fine mess, a fine pickle! And then suddenly, brother Fandorin, I felt so miserable, as though I was completely alone in the whole wide world and there was no point in going on living . . . I knew she would come to a bad end, I wanted to do away with her myself, but even so . . . You saw me, didn't you, when you went running past? But I was frozen, just as though I was paralysed, I didn't even call out to you. It was as though I was surrounded by a haze . . . Then very queer things started happening, and every one queerer than the last. First of all it became clear that Amalia was alive. You must have shot wide in the darkness. She was howling and cursing the servants so loudly that the walls shook. She was giving some orders or other in English, the lackeys were running around in circles, poking about in the garden. I hopped into the bushes and lay low. My head was full of the most terrible muddle. I feel like the dummy in a game of preference. Everybody's making their bids, and I'm just sitting there with the discards. Oh no, I think, you've got the wrong man. Zurov's never been anybody's duffer. There's a little boarded-up hut in the garden, about the size of two dog kennels. I rip a plank off it and hide inside, it's not the first time I've had to do that kind of thing. I observed events, kept a sharp eye out, pricked up my ears. A satyr lying in wait for Psyche. And meanwhile they're kicking up a real rumpus! Just like at corps HQ before an imperial inspection. The servants come dashing out of the house, then dash back in again. Amalia shouts something every now and then, there are postmen bringing telegrams. I can't make sense of it all – what kind of rumpus has my Erasmus started in there? He seems such a well-mannered young man, too. What did you do to her, eh? Did you spot a lily on her shoulder, or what? She hasn't got any lily, not on her shoulder or anywhere else. Well, tell me, don't tease.'

Erast Fandorin merely gave an impatient wave of his hand, as if to say, get on with it, I have no time for such nonsense.

'Well, anyway, you stirred up an anthill. Your dead man (Zurov nodded in the direction of the river where Porfirii Martynovich Pyzhov had found his final resting-place) came calling twice. The second time it was almost evening already.'

'You mean to say you sat there all night and all day?' Fandorin gasped. 'With no food or drink?'

'Well, I can go without food for a long time, just as long as there's drink. And there was.' Zurov slapped his hand against the flask. 'Of course, I had to introduce rationing. Two sips an hour. It's hard, but I put up with worse during the siege of Mahram – I'll tell you about that later. To stretch my legs I got out and went to check the horse a couple of times. I'd tied her to the fence in a nearby park. I pulled her some grass and spoke to her a bit so she wouldn't get too lonely, and then went back to the hut. Back at home people would have led off an unguarded filly like that in an instant, but the people here are a bit slow on the uptake. It never occurred to them. In the evening my dun filly came in very handy. When the dead man drove up (Zurov nodded in the direction of the river again) for the second time, your enemies began gathering to launch their campaign. Imagine the scene. Amalia at the head in her coach like a genuine Bonaparte, with two sturdy fellows on the box. The dead man following her in a *droshky*. Then a pair of servants in a carriage. And a little distance behind, concealed in the black of night, there am I on my dun filly, like Denis Davydov – just four towels moving backwards and forwards in the dark.' Hippolyte gave a short laugh and shot a brief glance at the red strip of dawn that already lay along the river. 'They drove into some dismal dump, just like the Ligovka slums: lousy little houses, warehouses and mud. The dead man climbed into Amalia's coach – obviously in order to hold a council of war. I tethered my filly in a gateway and watched to see what would happen next. The dead man went into a house with some kind of signboard and stayed there about half an hour. Then the climate began to deteriorate, cannonades in the sky, rain lashing down. I'm soaked, but I wait – I'm curious. The dead man appeared again and hopped up into Amalia's coach. They're probably holding another consultation. But the water's pouring down my neck and my flask's getting empty. I wanted to give them Christ appearing to the multitude, scatter the whole rotten gang of them and demand an explanation from Amalia, but suddenly the door of the coach opened and I saw such an ungodly sight . . .'

'A ghost?' asked Fandorin. 'Glowing.'

'Precisely. Brrr. It made me shiver. I didn't realise straight away that it was Amalia. That made me feel curious again. She behaved strangely. First she went into the same door, then she disappeared in the next gateway, then she flitted back in the door again. Her servant followed her. A little while after that they led out a sack walking on legs. It was only later that I realised they'd nabbed you, at the time I was puzzled. After that their army divided up: Amalia and the dead man got into the coach, the *droshky* followed them, and the servants with the sack – with you, that is – drove off in the opposite direction. All right, I think, the sack's no business of mine. I have to save Amalia, she's got herself mixed up in some dirty business or other. I ride after the carriage and the *droshky*, my hooves making a gentle clippety-clop, clippety-clop. They hadn't gone very far before they stopped. I dismounted and held the dun by the muzzle, so she wouldn't whinny. The dead man climbed out of the coach and said (it was a quiet night, you could hear things from a long way off): "Oh no, my sweetheart, I'd better go and check. I have an uneasy feeling somehow. This youth of ours is a bit too sharp altogether. If you should need me you know where to find me." At first I felt indignant: what kind of "sweetheart" is she to you, you dratted old rogue? And then it dawned on me. Could they possibly be talking about Erasmus?' Hippolyte shook his head, clearly proud of his own shrewdness. 'Well, after that it's simple. The driver from the *droshky* moved across to the box of the coach. I followed the dead man. I was standing way over there behind that corner, trying to understand what you'd done to rile him. But the two of you were talking so quietly I couldn't hear a damned thing. I hadn't been thinking of shooting, and it was a bit dark for a good shot, but he would have killed you for sure – I could see that from his back. I have a good eye for such things, brother. What a shot! Now tell me Zurov wastes his time making holes in five-kopeck pieces! From forty paces straight into the back of the head, and you have to take the poor light into account.'

'Let us assume it wasn't forty,' Erast Fandorin said absent-mindedly, thinking of something else.

'How so not forty?' Hippolyte said, growing excited. 'You try counting it!' And he actually started pacing out the distance (the paces were perhaps a little on the short side), but Fandorin stopped him.

'Where are you going to go now?'

Zurov was amazed:

'How d' you mean, where? I'll get you back into decent shape, you'll explain to me properly what all this hullabaloo of yours is about, we'll have some breakfast, and then I'm going to see Amalia. I'll shoot the slippery serpent, to hell with her. Or I'll carry her off somewhere. Just you tell me, are we two allies or rivals?'

'I'll tell you how things are,' said Erast Fandorin, rubbing his eyes wearily. 'There's no need to help me – that's one. I'm not going to explain anything to you – that's two. Shooting Amalia is a good idea, but just make sure they don't shoot you instead – that's three. And I am no rival of yours, she turns my stomach – that's four.'

'I expect it would be best to shoot her after all,' Zurov said thoughtfully in reply to that. 'Goodbye, Erasmus. God willing, we'll meet again.'

*

After the shocks and upheavals of the night, for all its intensity Erast Fandorin's day turned out strangely disjointed, as though it were composed of separate fragments poorly connected with each other. It seemed as though Fandorin was thinking and taking meaningful decisions, even putting them into action, and yet all of this was taking place in isolation, outside of the general scenario. The last day of June was preserved in our hero's memory as a sequence of vivid pictures suspended in isolation from each other against an empty void.

Morning on the banks of the Thames in the dockland district. The weather is calm and sunny, the air is fresh after the thunderstorm. Erast Fandorin sits on the tin roof of a squat warehouse, clad only in his undergarments. Laid out beside him are his wet clothes and his boots (the top of one of the boots is torn). His open passport and banknotes are drying in the sun. His thoughts of his escape from a watery grave grow confused and wander, but always return to the main channel.

They think that I'm dead, but I'm alive – that's one. They think that nobody else knows about them, but I know – that's two. The attaché case is lost – that's three. Nobody will believe me – that's four. They'll put me in a madhouse – that's five . . .

No, from the beginning. They don't know that I am alive – that's one. They're no longer looking for me – that's two. It will take time for them to miss Pyzhov – that's three. Now I can pay a visit to the embassy and send a coded message to the chief – that's four . . .

No, I can't go to the embassy. What if Pyzhov is not the only Judas there? Amalia will find out and then everything will start all over again. I must not tell anyone at all about this whole business. Except the chief. And a telegram is no good for that. He'll think Fandorin's impressions of Europe have driven him crazy. Shall I send a letter to Moscow? I could do that, but it will get there too late.

What shall I do? What shall I do?

Today is the last day of June by the local calendar. Today Amalia will draw a line under the book-keeping for June and the envelope will go off to Nicholas Croog in St Petersburg. The first to die will be the Full State Counsellor, a distinguished man, with children. He is there somewhere in St Petersburg, they will find him and dispose of him in a moment. It is rather stupid of them to write from St Petersburg to London in order to get an answer back to St Petersburg. One of the penalties of conspiratorial secrecy. Obviously the branches of the secret organisation do not know where the headquarters is located. Or perhaps the headquarters shifts from country to country? Today it is in St Petersburg, but in a month's time it will be somewhere else. Or perhaps there is no HQ, just a single individual? Who, Croog? That would be too simple, but Croog has to be arrested with the envelope.

How can I stop that envelope?

I can't. It's impossible.

Stop! I can't stop it, but I can overtake it! How many days does the post take to reach St Petersburg?

The next act is played out a few hours later, in the office of the East Central Postal District of the City of London. The director is feeling flattered – Fandorin has introduced himself as a Russian prince – and he calls his visitor 'Prince' and 'Your Highness', enunciating the title with undisguised relish. Erast Fandorin is wearing an elegant morning coat and carrying a cane, an accessory without which any real prince is quite inconceivable.

'I very much regret, Prince, that your wager will be lost,' the postal director explains for the third time to the slow-witted Russian. 'Your country is a member of the International Postal Union, which was founded the year before last, uniting twenty-two states with a total population of more than three hundred and fifty million. Standard regulations and rates are in effect across this entire area. If the letter was sent from London today, the thirtieth of June, for urgent delivery, then you cannot overtake it – in exactly six days' time, on the morning of the sixth of July, it will arrive at the post office in St Petersburg. Well, not on the sixth, of course, but whatever the date would be by your calendar.'

'Why will it be there, but I won't?' the 'prince' asks, failing entirely to grasp the situation.

The director explains with an air of grave seriousness:

'You see, Your Highness, packages with an "urgent" stamp are delivered without a single minute of delay. Let us suppose that you board the same train at Waterloo station on which an urgent letter has been dispatched. You board the same ferry at Dover. And you also arrive at the Gare du Nord in Paris at the same time.'

'Then what is the problem?'

'The problem,' the director says triumphantly, 'is that there is nothing faster than the urgent post! You have arrived in Paris, and you have to change to a train going to Berlin. You have to buy a ticket – since, after all, you have not booked one in advance. You have to find a cab and travel all the way across the city centre to a different station. You have to wait for the Berlin train, which departs once a day. Now, let us return to our urgent letter. From the Gare du Nord it travels by special postal handcar around the circular railway line and is delivered to the first train travelling in an easterly direction. It may not even be a passenger train, but a goods train with a postal wagon.'

'But then I can do the very same!' Erast Fandorin exclaims excitedly.

The reply of the patriot of the postal service is strict:

'Perhaps in Russia such a thing might be feasible, but not in Europe. Hmm, let us suppose it is possible to suborn a Frenchman, but at your change of trains in Berlin all your efforts will come to nothing – the postal and railway workers in Germany are famous for their incorruptibility.'

'Can everything really be lost?' the despairing Erast Fandorin exclaims in Russian.

'I beg your pardon?'

'So you believe that I have lost my wager?' the 'prince' asks dejectedly, switching back into English.

'At what time was the letter sent? But it really doesn't matter. Even if you dash straight to the station from here, it is already too late.'

The Englishman's words produce a quite magical effect on the Russian aristocrat.

'At what time? Why, of course! Today is still June! Morbid will not collect the letters until ten o'clock. While she is copying them out . . . And encoding them! She can't send them just like that, in plain Russian! She will definitely encode them – but of course! And that means that the envelope will only go off tomorrow! And it will arrive not on the sixth, but on the seventh! On the twenty-fifth of June by our calendar!'

'I'm afraid I don't understand a thing, Prince,' says the director, gesturing helplessly with his hands, but Fandorin is no longer in the office – the door has just closed behind him.

A plaintive voice calls after him:

'Your Highness, your cane! . . . Oh my, these Russian boyars!'

*

And finally, the evening of this arduous day that seems to have been shrouded in fog, but has seen such important developments. The waters of the English Channel. The final sunset of June flaunting its outrageous colours above the sea. The ferry *The Duke of Gloucester* holding course for Dunkirk, with Fandorin posed at the prow like a true Briton, in a cloth cap, a checked suit and a Scottish cape. He gazes fixedly ahead, towards the shore of France that is approaching with such agonising slowness. Not once does Erast Fandorin glance back towards the white cliffs of Dover.

His lips whisper:

'Only let her wait until tomorrow to send it. Only let her wait . . .'

Chapter Thirteen

The lush sunshine of summer painted golden squares on the floor of the operations hall of the Central Post Office in St Petersburg. As evening drew near one of them, elongated by this time into an irregular oblong, reached the 'poste restante' window and instantly warmed the counter. The atmosphere became stifling and soporific, a fly droned drowsily, and the attendant sitting at the window was overcome by sudden fatigue – thank goodness his stream of customers was gradually drying up already. Another half-hour and the doors of the post office would be closed, then all he would have to do was hand in his register and he could go home. The attendant – but let us give him his own name, he was Kondratii Kondratievich Shtukin, who in seventeen years of service in the postal department had risen from simple postman to the glorious heights of a formal state rank – Kondratii Shtukin handed over a package from Revel to an elderly Finnish woman with the amusing name of Pyrvu and looked to see whether the Englishman was still sitting there.

The Englishman was still sitting there, he had not gone away. There was an obstinate nation for you, now. The Englishman had appeared early in the morning, when the post office had barely even opened, and having seated himself beside the partition with his newspaper, had sat there the whole day long, without eating or drinking or even, begging your pardon, leaving his post to do the necessary. As though he was rooted to the spot. Clearly someone must have made an appointment to meet him and failed to keep it – that happens often enough round here, but for a Briton it would be incomprehensible, they're such a disciplined people, so punctual. Whenever anyone, especially anyone of a foreign appearance, approached the window, the Englishman would draw himself up in eager anticipation and even shift his blue spectacles to the very tip of his nose. But so far none of them had been the one he was expecting. A Russian, now, would have given way to indignation long ago, thrown his hands up in the air and begun complaining loudly to everyone in earshot, but this fellow just stuck his nose into his *Times* and carried on sitting there.

Or perhaps the fellow had nowhere to go. Came here straight from the railway station – look at that checked travelling suit he had on, and the travelling bag – thinking he would be met, but he hadn't been. What else could he do? When he came back from lunch, Kondratii Shtukin had taken pity on the son of Albion and sent the doorman Trifon across to ask whether there was anything he needed, but the gentleman in checks had only shaken his head irritably and handed Trifon twenty kopecks, as much as to say: leave me alone. Well, have it your own way.

A little shrimp of a man who had the look of a cab-driver appeared at the window and pushed across a crumpled passport.

'Take a look would you, dear chap, see if there's anything for Nikolai Mitrofanich Krug.'

'Where are you expecting it from?' Kondratii Shtukin asked strictly, taking the passport.

The reply was unexpected:

'From England, from London.'

The remarkable thing was that a letter from London was found, only not under the Russian letter 'K', but the Latin letter 'C'. 'Look at that now, "Mr Nicholas M. Croog", if you don't mind! The things you do see at the poste restante counter!'

'But is that definitely you?' Shtukin asked, more out of curiosity than suspicion.

'Not a doubt about it,' the cab-driver replied rather rudely, thrusting his claw-like hand in through the window and snatching up the yellow envelope with the 'urgent' stamp.

Kondratii Shtukin handed him the register.

'Are you able to sign for it?'

'As well as anyone else.' And the boor entered some kind of scrawl in the 'received' column.

Shtukin followed the departure of this unpleasant customer with a wrathful eye, then cast his now customary sideways glance at the Englishman, but he had disappeared. He must have finally despaired of his appointment.

Erast Fandorin waited outside for the cab-driver with a sinking heart. So that was 'Nicholas Krug'! The further he pursued it, the more confusing this whole business became. But the most important thing was that his six-day tactical forced march across Europe had not been in vain! He had overtaken the letter and intercepted it. Now he would have something of substance to present to his chief. But he must not let this Krug get away from him!

The cabby hired by Fandorin for the entire day was dawdling away the time beside a stone post. He was feeling dazed by the imposed idleness and tormented by the thought that he had asked the strange gentleman for only five roubles – for this kind of excruciating torture he should have taken six. When his fare finally appeared in sight again, the cabby drew himself up straight and tightened his reins, but Erast Fandorin did not even glance in his direction.

The target appeared. He walked down the steps, donned a blue peaked cap and set off towards a carriage standing nearby. Fandorin unhurriedly set off in pursuit. The target halted by the carriage, doffed his cap once again and bowed, then held out the yellow envelope. A man's hand in a white glove emerged from the window and took the envelope.

Fandorin increased his pace in an attempt to catch a glimpse of the unknown man's face. He succeeded.

Sitting in the carriage and inspecting the wax seals against the light was a ginger-haired gentleman with piercing green eyes and a pale face with a profuse scattering of freckles. Fandorin recognised him immediately – of course, Mr Gerald Cunningham as large as life, the brilliant pedagogue, friend of orphans and right-hand man of Lady Astair.

The cabby's sufferings proved to have been all in vain – it would not be difficult to ascertain Mr Cunningham's address. In the meantime there were more urgent business that required attention.

Kondratii Shtukin was in for a surprise: the Englishman came back, and now he was in a terrible hurry. He ran over to the telegram reception counter, stuck his head right in through the window and began dictating something very urgent to Mikhal Nikolaich. And Mikhal Nikolaich began fussing and bustling about and actually hurrying, which was really not like him at all.

Shtukin was stung by curiosity. He got to his feet (fortunately there were no customers waiting) and as though he were simply taking a stroll, he set out in the direction of the telegraph apparatus at the far side of the hall. Halting beside Mikhal Nikolaich, who was working away intently with his key, he bent over a little and read the hastily scribbled message:

To the Criminal Investigation Department, Moscow Police, State Counsellor Mr Brilling. I have returned. Please contact me urgently. I await your reply by the apparatus. Fandorin

So that was it, now he understood. Shtukin glanced at the 'Englishman' with different eyes. A detective, are we? Hunting down bandits. Well, well.

The agent strode agitatedly around the hall for about ten minutes, no longer, before Mikhal Nikolaich, who had remained by the apparatus, gestured to him and held out the ribbon with the return telegram.

Kondratii Kondatievich Shtukin was on the spot in a flash and he read the message on the ribbon:

TO MR FANDORIN STOP MR BRILLING IS IN SPB STOP ADDRESS KATENINSKAYA ST SIVERS HOUSE STOP DUTY OFFICER LOMEIKO

For some reason this reply delighted the gentleman in checks quite remarkably. He even clapped his hands and inquired of Shtukin, who was observing him with interest:

'Where is Kateninskaya Street? Is it far?'

'Not at all,' Kondatii Shtukin replied courteously. 'It's very handy from here. Take the public coach, get out at the corner of Nevsky Prospect and Liteiny Prospect, and then . . .'

'Never mind, I have a cab,' the agent interrupted, and with a flourish of his travelling bag, he set off for the door at a run.

Erast Fandorin liked the look of Kateninskaya Street. It looked in fact exactly like the most respectable streets of Berlin or Vienna: asphalt, brand-new electric street lamps and substantial houses of several storeys. In a word – Europe.

Sivers' House, with the stone knights on the pediment and the entrance-way brightly illuminated even though the evening was still light, was especially fine. But then, where else would a man like Ivan Franzevich Brilling live? It was quite impossible to imagine him residing in some dilapidated old mansion house with a dusty yard and an orchard of apple trees.

The obliging doorkeeper reassured Erast Fandorin by informing him that Mr Brilling was home: 'Got in just five minutes ago, sir.' Today everything was going right for Fandorin, today he could do nothing wrong.

Taking the steps two at a time, he flew up to the second floor and rang the electric bell that was polished to a golden gleam.

Ivan Brilling opened the door himself. He had not yet had time to change and had only removed his frock coat – the bright enamel colours of a brand-new Cross of St Vladimir glittered where it hung below his starched collar.

'Chief, it's me,' Fandorin announced gleefully, savouring the effect produced by his words.

The effect certainly did exceed all expectations.

Ivan Franzevich Brilling stood there dumbfounded and waved his hands about as though he was trying to say: 'Holy Spirit preserve us! Get thee behind me, Satan!'

Erast Fandorin laughed.

'Well, weren't you expecting to see me?'

'Fandorin! Where have you sprung from? I'd given up hope of ever seeing you alive again.'

'But why?' the traveller inquired, not without a trace of coquettishness.

'Why, naturally! You disappeared without a trace. The last time you were seen was in Paris on the twenty-sixth. You never arrived in London. I asked Pyzhov and he told me you had disappeared without trace, the police were looking for you!'

'I sent you a detailed letter from London to the address of the Moscow detective office. All about Pyzhov and everything else. I expect it will arrive today or tomorrow. I didn't know that you were in St Petersburg.'

His chief frowned anxiously.

'You look quite awful. Have you fallen ill?'

'To be perfectly honest, I am desperately hungry. I spent the whole day on guard duty at the post office and I haven't had a single bite.'

'Guard duty at the post office? No, no, don't tell me about it. I'll tell you what we'll do. First of all I will give you some tea and pastries. My Semyon, the scoundrel, has been drinking heavily for the last two days, so I'm keeping house for myself. I mostly live on sweetmeats and fancy cakes from Filippov's. You do like sweet things, don't you?'

'Very much,' Erast Fandorin confirmed enthusiastically.

'So do I. It's a relic of my orphan childhood. You don't object if we eat in the kitchen, bachelor-fashion?'

As they walked down the corridor Fandorin had time to observe that Brilling's flat, although it was not very large, was furnished in a most practical and precise fashion – everything that was necessary, but nothing superfluous. The young man's interest was particularly attracted by a lac-quered box with two black metal horns or tubes hanging on the wall.

'That is a genuine miracle of modern science,' Ivan Franze-vich explained. 'It is called "Bell's apparatus". It has only just arrived from America, from an agent of ours. There is an inventor of genius there, a certain Mr Bell, thanks to whom it is now possible to conduct a conversation at a considerable distance, even a distance of several *vyersts*. The sound is transmitted along wires like telegraph wires. This is an experimental model, the apparatus is not yet in production. In the whole of Europe there are only two lines: one has been laid from my apartment to the secretariat of the head of the Third Section, the other has been installed in Berlin between the Kaiser's study and Bismarck's chancellery. So we are keeping well abreast of progress.'

'Magnificent!' Erast Fandorin exclaimed in admiration. 'How is it, can you hear clearly?'

'Not very, but you can make it out. Sometimes there is a loud crackling in the tube . . . Would you be happy with orangeade instead of tea? I somehow can't quite get the hang of the samovar.'

'I should say so,' Erast Fandorin reassured his chief, and like a good sorcerer Brilling set a bottle of orangeade on the table before him, together with a large dish covered with éclairs, cream puffs, light, fluffy marzipans and flaky almond cones.

'Tuck in,' said Ivan Brilling, 'and in the meantime I will

bring you up to date with our business. Afterwards it will be your turn for confession.'

Fandorin nodded, his mouth stuffed full and his chin lightly powdered with icing sugar.

'So,' his chief began, 'as far as I recall, you set out to St Petersburg to collect the diplomatic post on the twenty-seventh of May? Immediately after that events took an interesting turn here and I regretted having let you go – we needed every last man. I discovered through agents in the field that some time ago a small but extremely active cell of radical revolutionaries, absolute madmen, had been established in Moscow. Whereas ordinary terrorists set themselves the goal of exterminating those who "stain their hands with blood", meaning the highest officials of the state, these people had decided to set about those who "exult and prate idle nonsense".'

'With whom?' asked Fandorin, puzzled, and himself absorbed in dealing with a most delicate éclair.

'You know, the poem by Nekrasov: "From the exultant crowd of idle boasters Who stain their hands with other's crimson blood, Lead me into the camp of love's promoters Who perish for the greater cause of good." Well then, our "perishers for the greater cause of good" have demarcated their areas of responsibility. The leading organisation has been allocated those who "stain their hands" – the ministers, governors and generals. And our Moscow faction has decided to deal with "the exultant", those very same individuals who are "bloated and gorged". As we managed to learn through an agent infiltrated into the group, the faction has taken the name of "Azazel" – as a token of their daredevil opposition to the will of God. A whole series of murders was planned among the gilded youth, the "parasites" and the "high livers". Bezhetskaya was also a member of "Azazel". From what we know, she must be the emissary of an international anarchist organisation. The suicide – effectively the murder – of Pyotr Kokorin, which she organised, was Azazel's first operation. But I suppose you will be telling me all about Bezhetskaya.

The next victim was Akhtyrtsev, who was of even greater interest to the conspirators because he was the grandson of the chancellor Prince Korchakov. You see, my young friend, the terrorists' plan was insane, but at the same time devilishly cunning. They calculated that it is far easier to reach the offspring of important individuals than those individuals themselves, but that the blow struck against the hierarchy of the state is no less powerful. Prince Korchakov, by the way, is so crushed by the death of his grandson that he has almost given up working and is seriously contemplating retirement. And he is an extremely distinguished man, who has been responsible in many respects for shaping modern Russia.'

'What dark villainy!' Erast Fandorin cried in outrage, even setting aside an unfinished marzipan.

'But when I discovered that Azazel's ultimate goal was the assassination of the tsarevich . . .'

'It can't be true!'

'I'm afraid it is. Well then, when that was discovered, I was ordered to take decisive action. I was obliged to comply, although I would have preferred to piece together the whole picture first, but you understand, with the life of His Imperial Highness himself at risk . . . We carried out an operation, but it didn't go entirely smoothly. On the first of June the terrorists were planning to hold a gathering at the *dacha* in Kuzminki. You remember, I told you about that? At that time, of course, you were keen to pursue your own ideas. How did it go, by the way? Did you come up with anything?'

Erast Fandorin began lowing with his mouth full and swallowed an unchewed piece of cream cone, but Brilling relented:

'All right, all right, later. Eat. And so, we surrounded the *dacha* on all sides. I could only use my own agents from St Petersburg, without involving the Moscow gendarmerie and police – at all costs I had to avoid publicity.' Ivan Brilling sighed angrily. 'That was my fault, I was over-cautious. Basically, because we didn't have enough men, we failed to spread our net wide enough. There was an exchange of fire.

Two agents were wounded and one was killed. I'll never forgive myself . . . We didn't manage to take anyone alive, all we got were four corpses. The description of one of them was rather like your white-eyed fellow. Although he didn't have any eyes left as such – he blew half of his skull away with his last bullet. In the basement we found a laboratory for producing infernal devices and some papers, but as I said, there is a great deal about the plans and connections of Azazel that remains a mystery. An unsolvable one, I'm afraid . . . Even so, the sovereign, the chancellor and the head of the corps of gendarmes were very pleased with our operation. I told General Mizinov about you. Of course, you weren't in at the finish, but you helped us a great deal in the course of the investigation. If you have no objection, we can carry on working together in future. I take your fate into my own hands . . . Are you feeling stronger now? Right, now you tell me everything. What happened over in London? Did you manage to pick up Bezhetskaya's trail? What's all this hellish business with Pyzhov? Is he dead? All in the right order, starting at the beginning, don't miss anything out.'

The nearer his chief's story had drawn to its end, the brighter the envy had glowed in Erast Fandorin's eyes, and his own adventures, which he had been so proud of only recently, seemed to pale and fade in significance. An attempt on the life of the tsarevich! An exchange of fire! An infernal device! Fate had mocked Fandorin cruelly, tempted him with glory and led him off the main highway on to a miserable country track . . .

However, he gave Ivan Brilling a detailed account of his epic quest – except that he related the circumstances under which he was deprived of the blue attaché case rather vaguely and even blushed a little, a fact which apparently did not escape the attention of Brilling, who listened to the narrative in gloomy silence. When he reached the denouement, Erast Fandorin took heart again and he brightened up, unable to resist the temptation of dramatic effect.

'And I did see the man!' he exclaimed when he came to the

scene outside the St Petersburg Post Office. 'I know who holds in his hands the contents of the attaché case and all the threads of the organisation! "Azazel" is still alive, Ivan Franzevich, but it is in our hands!'

'Tell me then, devil take it!' his chief exclaimed. 'Enough of this puerile posturing! Who is this man? Where is he?'

'Here, in St Petersburg,' said Fandorin, savouring his revenge. 'A certain Gerald Cunningham, senior assistant to the same Lady Astair whom I have more than once drawn to your attention.' At this point Erast Fandorin cleared his throat tactfully. 'So the business with Kokorin's will is explained. And now it is clear why Bezhetskaya directed her admirers to the Astair-Houses. And note how cunningly that red-haired gentleman chose his lair. What a cover, eh? Orphans, branches all over the world, an altruistic patroness to whom all doors are open. All very clever, you must admit.'

'Cunningham?' Fandorin's chief queried. 'Gerald Cunningham? But I know the gentleman very well. We are members of the same club.' He spread his arms in amazement. 'An extremely industrious individual, but I find it impossible to imagine him being involved with nihilists and assassinating full state counsellors.'

'But he didn't kill them, he didn't!' exclaimed Erast Fandorin. 'I thought at first that the lists contained the names of victims. I told you that in order to convey my train of thought. When you're in a rush you can't work everything out at once. But afterwards, while I was jolting all the way across Europe in the train, it suddenly struck me! If it was a list of future victims, then why were the dates entered in it? Dates that were already past! That doesn't fit! No, Mr Brilling, we have something else here!'

Fandorin even leapt to his feet, his thoughts agitated him so powerfully.

'Something else? But what?' asked Brilling, screwing up his bright eyes.

'I think it is a list of members of a powerful international organisation. And your Moscow terrorists are only a small link, the very tiniest.' At the expression that these words brought to his chief's face, Erast Fandorin felt himself beginning to gloat – and was immediately ashamed of such an unworthy feeling. 'The central figure in the organisation, the main purpose of which remains as yet unknown to us, is Gerald Cunningham. You and I have both seen him, he is a most exceptional gentleman. "Miss Olsen", whose role has been played by Amalia Bezhetskaya since the month of June, is the organisation's registration centre, something like the personnel department. It receives information from all over the world concerning changes in the status of members of the society. Regularly, once a month, "Miss Olsen" forwards the new information to Cunningham, who has been based in St Petersburg since last year. I told you that Bezhetskaya has a secret safe in her bedroom. She probably keeps a full list of the members of this "Azazel" in it – it does seem as though that actually is the organisation's name. Or else it's their password, something rather like an incantation. I have heard the word spoken twice, and on both occasions it was when a murder was about to be committed. In general it is rather like a Masonic society, except that it is not clear why the fallen angel is involved. But it seems to be on a bigger scale than the Masons. Just imagine – forty-five letters in one month! And the people involved – a senator, a minister, generals!'

Erast Fandorin's chief gazed patiently at the young man, for the latter had clearly not yet concluded his narrative – he had wrinkled up his forehead and was thinking intensely about something.

'Mr Brilling, I was just thinking about Cunningham . . . He is a British subject, after all, so I suppose we couldn't simply turn up and search his house?'

'I suppose not,' Fandorin's chief agreed. 'Go on.'

'And before you can obtain sanction, he will hide the envelope so securely that we won't find anything and won't be able to prove anything. We still don't know what connections he has in high places and who will intercede for him. Special caution would seem to be recommended here. It would be best first to get a grip on his Russian operation and haul in the chain link by link, wouldn't it?'

'And how can we do that?' Brilling asked with lively interest. 'By means of secret surveillance? Logical.'

'We could use surveillance, but I think there is a more certain method.'

Ivan Brilling thought for a moment and then shrugged, as though surrendering. Flattered, Fandorin dropped a tactful hint.

'What about the full state counsellor who was created on the seventh of June?'

'Check the emperor's decrees on new titles?' Brilling slapped a hand against his forehead. 'Say, for the first ten days of June? Bravo, Fandorin, bravo!'

'Of course, Chief. Not even for the first ten days, just from Monday to Saturday, from the third to the eighth. The new general would hardly be likely to delay the happy announcement any longer than that. Just how many new full state counsellors appear in the empire in the course of a week?'

'Two or three perhaps, if there happens to be a bumper crop. I have never actually inquired.'

'Well then, we put all of them under observation, check their statements of service, their circles of acquaintances and so forth. We'll winkle out our "Azazalean" in no time at all.'

'Right, now tell me, has all the information you gathered been forwarded by post to the Moscow CID?' Brilling asked, following his usual habit of skipping without warning from one subject to another.

'Yes, Chief. The letter will arrive either today or tomorrow. Why, do you suspect someone in the ranks of the Moscow police? In order to emphasise its importance I wrote on the envelope: "*To be delivered to His Honour State Counsellor Brilling in person, or in his absence to His Excellency the Chief of Police*". So no one will dare to open it. And if he reads it the Chief of Police will certainly contact you.'

'That's logical,' Ivan Brilling said approvingly, and then fell silent for a long while, staring at the wall while his expression became gloomier and gloomier.

Erast Fandorin sat there with bated breath, knowing that his chief was weighing up all that he had heard and would now tell him what he had decided – to judge from his expression it was a difficult decision.

Brilling gave a loud sigh, followed by an oddly bitter laugh.

'Very well, Fandorin, I'll take all the responsibility on myself. There are certain ailments which can only be cured by surgery. That is what we will do. This is a matter of great importance, of state importance, and in such cases I have the right to dispense with the formalities. We will take Cunningham. And immediately, in order to catch him red-handed with the envelope. Do you believe the message is in code?'

'Undoubtedly. The information is too important. And after all, it was sent by ordinary post, even though it was for urgent delivery. It could have fallen into the wrong hands or been lost. No, Mr Brilling, these people do not like to take unnecessary risks.'

'All the more reason, then. That means Cunningham decodes it, reads it and writes it out again for his card index. He must have a card index! I am afraid that in her accompanying letter Bezhetskaya may inform him of your adventures, and Cunningham is a clever man – he will realise in an instant that you might have sent a report to Russia. No, he has to be taken now, without delay! And it would be interesting to read that accompanying letter. The business with Pyzhov bothers me. What if he is not the only one they suborned? We will talk things over with the English embassy later. They'll be thankful to us. You do claim that the list included subjects of Queen Victoria?'

'Yes, almost a dozen of them,' Erast Fandorin said with a nod, gazing at his chief adoringly. 'Of course, taking Cunningham now is the very best thing to do, but . . . What if we get there and we don't find anything? I would never forgive myself if because of me you had . . . That is, I am prepared in all instances . . .'

'Don't talk nonsense,' said Brilling, twitching his jaw in irritation. 'Do you really think that if things turn out badly I would hide behind a boy? I have faith in you, Fandorin. And that is enough.'

'Thank you,' said Erast Fandorin in a quiet voice.

Ivan Brilling bowed sarcastically.

'No need for gratitude. Right then, enough of these idle compliments. Let's get to work. I know Cunningham's address, he lives on Aptekarsky Island, in the wing of the St Petersburg Astair-House. Do you have a gun?'

'Yes, in London I bought a "Smith and Wesson". It's in my travel bag.'

'Show me.'

Fandorin quickly brought in from the hallway the heavy revolver that he liked so much for its weight and solidity.

'Rubbish!' his chief said peremptorily, after weighing the pistol on his palm. 'This is for American cowboys and their drunken shoot-outs in the saloon. It's no use to a serious agent. I'm taking it away from you, and I'll give you something better in exchange.'

He left the room for a short while and came back with a small, flat revolver, which fitted almost completely into the palm of his hand.

'There you are, a seven-round Belgian "Herstal". It's a new model, a special order. You wear it behind your back in a little holster under your coat. Quite indispensable in our line of work. It's light and it doesn't shoot very far or very accurately, but it's self-cocking, and that guarantees a rapid shot. After all, we don't need to hit a squirrel in the eye, do we? And the agent who stays alive is usually the one who fires first and more than once. Instead of a hammer to cock there is a safety catch – this little button here. It's rather stiff, to avoid accidental firing. Click it like that and then fire off all seven rounds if you like. Is that clear?'

'Yes,' said Erast Fandorin, gazing in fascination at the handsome toy.

'You can admire it later, there's no time just now,' said Brilling, pushing him in the direction of the door.

'Are we both going to arrest him together?' Fandorin asked excitedly.

'Don't talk nonsense.'

Ivan Brilling stopped beside the 'Bell's apparatus', took hold of a horn-shaped tube and pressed it to his ear, then cranked some kind of lever. The apparatus grunted and something inside it clanged. Brilling set his ear to the other horn protruding from the lacquered box and the horn gave out a squeaky sound. Fandorin thought he could just make out a faint, funny little voice pronouncing the words 'Duty adjutant' and then 'chancellery'.

'Is that you, Novgorodtsev?' Brilling bellowed into the tube. 'Is His Excellency in his office? No? I can't hear! No, no, don't worry. Don't worry, I say!' He drew as much air as he could into his lungs and began shouting even louder. 'An urgent detachment for an arrest! Send them immediatley to Aptekarsky Island. Ap-te-kar-sky! Yes! the wing of the Astair-House! As-tair-House! It doesn't matter what it means, they'll find it. And have a search group sent out! What? Yes, I will, in person. And hurry, major, hurry.'

He returned the tube to its resting-place and wiped his forehead.

'I hope that Mr Bell will improve his design, or soon all my neighbours will know everything about the Third Section's secret operations.'

Erast Fandorin was still entranced by the sorcery that had just been worked before his very eyes.

'Why, it's like something from *The Thousand and One Nights*! A genuine miracle! And there are still people who condemn progress!'

'We can talk about progress on our way. Unfortunately I have already dismissed my carriage, so we will have to look for a cab. Will you put down that damned travel-bag! Come on, quick march!'

*

The conversation about progress, however, never took place, for they rode to Aptekarsky Island in total silence. Erast Fandorin was trembling with excitement, and he made several attempts to draw his chief into conversation, but all in vain. Brilling was in a foul mood – he was clearly taking a great risk, after all, in launching an operation on his own authority.

The pale northern evening glimmered above the watery expanse of the Neva. It occurred to Fandorin that the bright summer night was most opportune – he would not be getting any sleep today in any case. And last night in the train he had not slept a wink either, he had been so worried that he might miss the envelope . . . The driver urged on his chestnut filly, earning his promised rouble honestly, and they reached their destination quickly.

The St Petersburg Astair-House, a beautiful yellow building that had previously belonged to the army engineers' corps, was smaller in size than its Moscow equivalent, but it was drowning in greenery. It was a heavenly spot, surrounded on all sides by gardens and rich *dachas*.

'Ah, what will happen to the children?' Fandorin sighed.

'Nothing will happen to them,' Ivan Brilling replied aggressively. 'Her Ladyship will appoint another director and that will be the end of the matter.'

The wing of the Astair-House proved to be an imposing Catherine-style mansion overlooking an agreeable, tree-shaded street. Erast Fandorin saw an elm tree charred black by lightning reaching out its dead branches towards the lighted windows of the tall second storey. The house was quiet.

'Splendid, the gendarmes have not yet arrived,' said the chief. 'We won't wait for them, the most important thing for us is not to put Cunningham on his guard. And to be prepared for all sorts of surprises.'

Erast Fandorin thrust his hand under the back flap of his jacket and felt the reassuring chill of his 'Herstal'. He felt his chest tighten – not out of fear, for with Ivan Franzevich

Brilling there was nothing to fear, but out of impatience. Now at last everything would finally be settled!

Brilling shook the little brass bell vigorously, producing a melodious trill. A head crowned with red hair glanced out of an open window on the *bel-étage*.

'Open up, Cunningham,' Fandorin's chief said in a loud voice. 'I have an urgent matter to discuss with you.'

'Is that you, Brilling?' the Englishman asked in surprise. 'What's the matter?'

'An emergency at the club. I must warn you about it.'

'Just a moment, I'll come down. It's my manservant's day off.' And the head disappeared.

'Aha,' whispered Fandorin. 'He got rid of his servant deliberately. He's probably sitting there with the papers!'

Brilling nervously rapped on the door with his knuckles. Cunningham seemed to be taking his time.

'Will he not make a run for it?' Erast Fandorin asked in panic. 'Through the rear door, eh? Perhaps I should run round the house and stand on that side?'

Just then, however, they heard the sound of steps from inside and the door opened.

Cunningham stood in the doorway in a long dressing-gown. His piercing green eyes rested for a moment on Fandorin's face, and his eyelids trembled almost imperceptibly. He had recognised him!

'What's happening?' the Englishman asked guardedly in his own language.

'Let's go into the study,' Brilling answered in Russian. 'It's very important.'

Cunningham hesitated for a second, then gestured for them to follow him.

After climbing an oak staircase, the host and his uninvited guests found themselves in a room that was furnished richly, but clearly not for leisure. The walls were covered from end to end with shelves holding books and some kind of files. Over by the window, beside an immense writing-desk of

Karelian birch, there was a rack holding drawers, each of which was adorned with a gold label.

However, Erast Fandorin's interest was not drawn to the drawers (Cunningham would not store secret documents in open view), but by the papers lying on the desk, where they had been hastily covered by a fresh copy of the *Stock Exchange Gazette.*

Ivan Brilling was evidently thinking along the same lines – he crossed the study and positioned himself beside the desk, standing with his back to the open window with the low sill. The evening breeze gently ruffled the lace curtain.

Grasping the significance of his chief's manoeuvre, Fandorin remained standing by the door. Now there was nowhere for Cunningham to go.

The Englishman seemed to suspect that something was wrong.

'You are behaving rather oddly, Brilling,' he said in faultless Russian. 'And why is this person here? I've seen him before, he's a policeman.'

Ivan Franzevich Brilling glared sullenly at Cunningham, keeping his hands in the pockets of his wide frock coat.

'Yes, he is a policeman. And in a minute or two there will be a lot of policemen here, and so I have no time for explanations.'

The young detective saw his chief's right hand come darting out of his pocket holding Fandorin's 'Smith and Wesson', but he had no time to register surprise. He pulled out his own revolver – things were beginning to move now!

'Don't!' the Englishman cried out, throwing his hands up in the air, and that very instant there was a thunderous shot.

Cunningham was thrown over backwards. Erast Fandorin gazed in amazement at the green eyes staring as though they were still alive and the neat dark hole in the middle of the forehead.

'My God, Chief, why?'

He turned towards the window. The black mouth of the barrel was staring straight at him.

'You killed him,' Brilling stated in a strange, unnatural voice. 'You're too good a detective. And therefore, my young friend, I shall be obliged to kill you, which I sincerely regret.'

Chapter Fourteen

Totally bemused, poor Erast Fandorin took a few steps forward.

'Stop!' his chief barked out furiously. 'And stop waving that pistol around, it isn't loaded. You might at least have taken the trouble to glance into the cylinder! Why must you be so trusting, damn you! You can never trust anyone but yourself!'

Brilling took an identical 'Herstal' out of his left pocket and dropped the smoking 'Smith and Wesson' on the floor at Fandorin's feet.

'My revolver here is fully loaded, as you will learn soon enough,' Ivan Brilling babbled feverishly, becoming more and more agitated with every word. 'I shall place it in the hand of the unfortunate Cunningham here, and it will be obvious that you killed each other in an exchange of fire. You will be guaranteed an honourable funeral with heartfelt speeches of farewell. I know that means a lot to you. And stop looking at me like that, you damned greenhorn!'

Fandorin realised with horror that his chief was absolutely crazy and in a desperate attempt to awaken Brilling's suddenly clouded reason he shouted:

'Chief, it's me, Fandorin! Ivan Franzevich Brilling! State Counsellor!'

'*Full* State Counsellor,' said Brilling with a crooked smile. 'You're behind the times, Fandorin. The emperor's decree was promulgated on the seventh of June. For a successful operation to disarm the terrorist organisation "Azazel". So you may address me as "Your Excellency".'

Brilling's dark silhouette against the window looked as though it had been cut out with scissors and pasted on grey paper. Behind his back the dead branches of a dry elm radiated in all directions, forming a sinister spider's web. A line from a childish jingle ran through Fandorin's head: ' "Won't you step into my parlour?" said the spider to the fly.'

Brilling's face suddenly contorted agonisingly, and Fandorin realised that his chief had hardened his heart sufficiently and now he could fire at any moment. Out of nowhere a thought suddenly came to him, shattering instantly into a string of brief thought-particles: the safety catch had to be off, otherwise you couldn't fire it, that meant half a second or a quarter of a second, not enough time, not nearly enough . . .

Erast Fandorin squeezed his eyes tight shut and with a blood-curdling howl he flung himself forward, aiming his head at his chief's chin. They were no more than five paces apart. Fandorin did not hear the click of the safety catch, but the shot thundered past him into the ceiling, as Brilling and Fandorin went flying over the window sill together and tumbled out of the window.

Fandorin's chest collided with the trunk of the dry elm and he went crashing downwards, breaking off branches and scraping his face as he fell. The stunning impact when he struck the ground almost made him lose consciousness, but his keen instinct for survival would not allow it. Erast Fandorin raised himself up on all fours, glaring around him like a madman.

His chief was nowhere to be seen, but the small black 'Herstal' was lying over beside the wall. Fandorin, still on all fours, pounced like a cat, grabbed the gun and began turning his head in all directions.

But Brilling had disappeared.

Fandorin only thought to look upwards when he heard the strained wheezing sound.

Ivan Franzevich Brilling was dangling in the air in an awkward and unnatural position. His polished gaiters were twitching a little above Fandorin's head. Protruding from just below his Cross of St Vladimir, where a crimson stain was creeping across his starched white shirt, was the sharp stump of a broken branch that had pierced the newly created general right through. The most terrible thing of all was that the lucid gaze of his eyes was fixed on Erast Fandorin.

'Disgusting,' his chief pronounced distinctly, wincing either in pain or revulsion. 'Disgusting . . .' And then in a hoarse, unrecognisable voice he gasped out: 'A-za-zel . . .'

An icy tremor ran through Fandorin's body, but Brilling continued gasping for about half a minute before finally falling silent.

As though this were some agreed signal, there was a clattering of hooves and clanging of wheels from round the corner. The gendarmes had arrived in their *droshkies*.

*

Adjutant-General Lavrenty Arkadievich Mizinov, head of the Third Section and chief of the corps of gendarmes, rubbed his eyes, which were red with fatigue. The golden aiguillettes on his dress uniform jingled dully. During the last twenty-four hours he had had no chance to change his clothes, let alone to get any sleep. The previous evening a special messenger had dragged General Mizinov away from the ball in honour of the Grand Duke Sergei Alexandrovich's name-day. And then it had all begun . . .

The general cast an unfriendly glance at the boy with the dishevelled hair and badly scratched nose who was sitting beside him and poring over some papers. He hadn't slept for two nights and he was still as fresh as a Yaroslavl cucumber. And he acted as though he had been sitting around in high-level offices all his life. Very well, let him work his sorcery. But this Brilling business! It simply defied comprehension!

'Well, Fandorin, will you be long? Or have you been distracted by yet another of your "ideas"?' the general asked strictly, feeling that after a sleepless night and an exhausting day he was unlikely to be having any more ideas himself.

'Just a moment, Your Excellency, just a moment,' the young whipper-snapper mumbled. 'There are just five entries left. I did warn you that the list might be in code. See what a cunning code it is, they haven't been able to identify half the letters, and I don't remember everyone who was in it myself . . . Aha, this is the postmaster from Denmark, that's who he is. Right, then, what's this? The first letter's not decoded, there's a cross, and a cross for the second one too, and the third and the fourth – two Ms, then another cross, then an N, then a D with a question mark, and the last two are missing. That gives us ++MM+ND(?)++.'

'Such gibberish,' sighed General Mizinov. 'Brilling would have guessed it in a moment. Are you quite sure it wasn't just a fit of temporary insanity? It's impossible even to imagine that . . .'

'Absolutely sure, Your Excellency,' Erast Fandorin repeated for the umpteenth time. 'And I quite distinctly heard him say "Azazel". Wait! I've remembered! Bezhetskaya had some *commander* or other on her list. We must assume this is him.'

'*Commander* is a rank in the British and American fleets,' the general explained. 'It corresponds to our captain second class.' He strode angrily across the room. 'Azazel, Azazel, what is this Azazel that has come to plague us? So far we clearly don't know a single thing about it! Brilling's Moscow investigation is totally worthless! We must assume it's all nonsense, invention, lies – including all those terrorists and that attempt on the tsarevich's life! He's bound to have tucked away all the loose ends! Palmed us off with a few corpses. Or did he really hand us some stupid nihilist idiots? That would be just like him – he was a very, very capable man . . . Curses, where can the results of that search have got to? They've been rummaging in there for days now!'

The door opened quietly and a glum, skinny face in gold-rimmed spectacles was thrust in through the crack.

'Captain Belozerov, Your Excellency.'

'At last! Talk of the devil! Send him in.'

A middle-aged officer of the gendarmes, whom Fandorin had seen the previous day at Cunningham's house, walked into the office, squinting and screwing up his weary eyes.

'We have it, Your Excellency,' he reported in a low voice. 'We divided the entire house and the garden into squares and turned everything upside-down and went through it all with a fine-toothed comb – not a thing. Then agent Ailenson, a detective with an excellent nose for a lead, thought of sounding out the walls in the basement of the Astair-House. And what do you think, General? We discovered a secret niche containing twenty boxes with about two hundred cards in each. The cypher was strange, some kind of hieroglyphs, quite different from the one in the letter. I gave instructions for the boxes to be brought here. I've set the entire cryptography section on to it and they're about to start work.'

'Well done, Belozerov, well done,' said the general, in a more generous mood now. 'And that man with the nose, recommend him for a decoration. Well then, let us pay a visit to the cypher room. Come along, Fandorin, it will be interesting for you too. You can finish up later, there's no great hurry now.'

They went up two floors and set off quickly along an endless corridor. As they turned a corner they saw an official running towards them, waving his hands in the air.

'Disaster, Your Excellency, disaster! The ink is fading before our very eyes, we can't understand it!'

Mizinov set off at a trot, which did not at all suit his corpulent figure: the gold tassels on his epaulettes fluttered like the wings of a moth. Belozerov and Fandorin disrespectfully overtook their high-ranking superior and were the first to burst in through the tall white doors.

The large room completely filled with tables was in absolute turmoil. About a dozen officials were dashing about, fussing over stacks of neat white cards set out across the tables. Erast Fandorin snatched one up, and caught a brief glimpse of barely discernible figures resembling Chinese hieroglyphs. Before his very eyes the hieroglyphs disappeared and the card was left absolutely blank.

'What devil's work is this?' exclaimed the general, panting heavily. 'Some kind of invisible ink?'

'I'm afraid it is far worse than that, Your Excellency,' said a gentleman with the appearance of a professor, examining a card against the light. 'Captain, didn't you say the card-file was kept in something like a photographic booth?'

'Precisely so, sir,' Belozerov confirmed.

'And can you recall what kind of lighting it had? Perhaps a red lamp?'

'Absolutely right. It was a red electrical lamp.'

'Just as I thought. Alas, General Mizinov, the card archive has been lost to us and cannot be restored.'

'How's that?' the general exclaimed furiously. 'Not good enough, Mr Collegiate Counsellor, you must think of something. You're a master of your trade, a leading light . . .'

'But not a magician, Your Excellency. The cards were obviously treated with a special solution and it is only possible to work with them in red light. Now the layer to which the characters were applied has been exposed to daylight. Very clever, you must admit. It's the first time I've come across anything of the sort.'

The general knitted his shaggy eyebrows and began snorting menacingly. The room fell silent, with the silence that comes before a storm. But the peal of thunder never came.

'Let's go, Fandorin,' the head of the Third Section said in a dejected tone of voice, 'you have work to finish.'

The final two encoded entries remained undeciphered – they contained information that had arrived on the final day, the thirtieth of June, and Fandorin was unable to identify them. The time had come to sum up the situation.

Striding to and fro across his office, the weary General Mizinov reasoned out loud.

'So, let us draw together the little that we do have. There exists a certain international organisation with the provisional name of "Azazel". To judge from the number of cards, which we shall now never be able to read, it has three thousand eight hundred and fifty-four members. We know something at least about forty-seven of them, or rather forty-five, since two of the entries remain undeciphered. However, that something amounts to no more than their nationality and the positions that they occupy. No name, no age, no address . . . What else do we know? The names of two dead Azazeleans, Cunningham and Brilling. And in addition, there is Amalia Bezhetskaya in England – if this Zurov of yours has not killed her, if she is still in England, and if that really is her name . . . "Azazel" acts aggressively, killing without hesitation. There is clearly some global purpose involved. But what is it? They are not Masons, because I myself am a member of a Masonic lodge, and no ordinary one either. Hmm . . . Remember, Fandorin, you didn't hear that.'

Erast Fandorin lowered his eyes meekly.

'It is not the Socialist International,' Mizinov continued, 'because the gentlemen communists don't have the stomach for this kind of business. And Brilling couldn't possibly have been a revolutionary, it's out of the question. Whatever he might have got up to in secret, my dear deputy hunted down nihilists with a will, and very successfully. What then does "Azazel" want? That, after all, is the most important thing! And we have not a single thing to go on. Cunningham is dead. Brilling is dead. Nikolai Krug is a mere functionary, a pawn. That scoundrel Pyzhov is dead. All the leads have been lopped off . . .' General Mizinov spread his arms in a gesture of indignation. 'No, I don't understand a single thing! I knew Brilling for more than ten years. I was the one who made his career! I discovered him myself. Judge for yourself, Fandorin. When I was governor-general of Kharkov I used to hold all kinds of competitions for school pupils and students in order to encourage patriotic feelings and the desire for useful reform in the younger generation. I was introduced to a skinny, awkward youth, a final-year gymnasium student who had written a very sensible and passionate composition on the subject "The Future of Russia". Believe me, he had the spirit and the background of a genuine Lomonosov – an orphan with no family or relatives at all, who had financed his own studies on mere coppers and then passed the examinations for the seventh form at the grammar school at the first attempt. A genuine natural diamond! I became his patron, sent him to St Petersburg University, then I gave him a place in my department – and never had cause to regret it. He was my finest assistant, my trusted deputy! He had made a brilliant career, all roads were open to him! Such a powerful, paradoxical mind, so resourceful, so assiduous! My God, I was even planning to marry my daughter to him!' said the general, clutching his forehead in his hands.

Out of respect for the feelings of his high-ranking superior, Erast Fandorin paused tactfully before clearing his throat.

'Your Excellency, I was just thinking . . . Of course, we don't have many leads, but still we do have something.'

The general shook his head as though he was dispelling his unwelcome memories, and sat down at the desk.

'I'm listening. Tell me what's on your mind, Fandorin. No one knows this whole business better than you.'

'Well, what I actually wanted to say was . . .' Erast Fandorin looked at the list, underlining something with a pencil. 'There are forty-four men here – two we were unable to figure out, and the Full State Counsellor – that is, Ivan Brilling – is no longer in the reckoning. At least eight of them can be identified without too much difficulty. Well, just think about it, Your Excellency. How many heads of the Emperor of Brazil's bodyguard can there be? Or number 47F, the head of a government department in Belgium, sent on the eleventh of June, received on the fifteenth. It will be easy enough to determine who he is. That's two already. The third is number 549F, a vice-admiral in the French fleet, sent on the fifteenth of June, received on the seventeenth. The fourth is number 1007F, a newly created English baronet, sent on the ninth of June, received on the tenth. The fifth is number 694F, a Portuguese government minister, sent on the twenty-ninth of May, received on the seventh of July.'

'That one's a dud,' said the general, who had been listening with great interest. 'The Portuguese government changed in May, so all the ministers in the cabinet are new.'

'Are they?' Erast Fandorin asked in dismay. 'Oh well, that means we'll have seven instead of eight. Then the fifth is an American, the deputy chairman of a Senate committee, sent on the tenth of June, received on the twenty-eighth, in my own presence. The sixth is number 1042F, Turkey, personal secretary to Prince Abdul-Hamid, sent on the first of June, received on the twentieth.'

General Mizinov found this information particularly interesting.

'Really? Oh, that is very important. And actually on the first of June? Well, well. On the thirtieth of May in Turkey there was a *coup*, Sultan Abdul-Aziz was overthrown and the new ruler, Midhat-Pasha, set Murad V on the throne. And then the very next day he appointed a new secretary for Abdul-Hamid, Murad's younger brother. What great haste, to be sure. This is extremely important news. Could Midhat-Pasha be planning to get rid of Murad and set Abdul-Hamid on the throne? Aha . . . Never mind, Fandorin, that's all way over your head. We'll have the secretary identified in a couple of shakes. I'll get on the telegraph today to Nikolai Pavlovich Gnatiev, our ambassador in Constantinople, we're old friends. Carry on.'

'And the last, the seventh: number 1508F, Switzerland, a prefect of cantonal police, sent on the twenty-fifth of May, received on the first of June. Identifying the rest will be a lot harder, and some of them will be impossible. But if we can at least identify these seven and put them under secret surveillance . . .'

'Give me the list,' said the general, holding out his hand. 'I'll give orders immediately for coded messages to be sent to the embassies concerned. We shall clearly have to collaborate with the special services of these countries. Apart from Turkey, where we have an excellent network of our own . . . You know, Mr Fandorin, I was abrupt with you, but don't take offence. I do value your contribution very highly and so on and so forth . . . It's just that it was painful for me . . . because of Brilling . . . Well, you understand.'

'I understand, Your Excellency. I myself, in a sense, was no less . . .'

'Very well, excellent. You'll be working with me. Investigating "Azazel". I'll set up a special group and appoint the most experienced people. We must untangle this whole sorry mess.'

'Your Excellency, I really ought to take a trip to Moscow . . .'

'What for?'

'I'd like to have a little talk with Lady Astair. She herself, being more a creature of the heavens than the earth' (at this point Fandorin smiled) 'was surely not aware of the true nature of Cunningham's activity, but she had known the gentleman since he was a child and might well be able to tell us something useful. It would be best not to talk to her formally, through the gendarmerie, surely? I am fortunate enough to be slightly acquainted with Her Ladyship, and I speak English. What if another lead of some kind were to come to light? Perhaps we might pick up something from Cunningham's past?'

'It sounds to the point. Go. But only for one day, no more. And now go and get some sleep. My adjutant will assign you your quarters. Tomorrow you'll take the evening train to Moscow. If we're lucky, by that time the first coded messages from the embassies will have arrived. On the morning of the twenty-eighth you'll be in Moscow, and in the evening I want you back here, and come immediately to me to report. At any time, is that clear?'

'Yes, Your Excellency.'

*

In the corridor of the first-class carriage on the St Petersburg—Moscow express, a very grand elderly gentleman sporting an enviable set of moustaches and whiskers and a diamond pin in his necktie smoked a cigar as he glanced with undisguised curiosity at the locked door of compartment number one.

'Hey there, be so kind,' he said, beckoning with a fat finger to a conductor who had made an opportune appearance.

The conductor dashed over to the stately passenger in a flash and bowed:

'What can I do for you, sir?'

The gentleman took hold of the conductor's collar between his finger and thumb and asked in a deep bass whisper:

'The young man travelling in the first compartment – who is he exactly? Do you know? He is quite remarkably young.'

'I was surprised at that too,' the conductor declared in a whisper. 'Everyone knows the first compartment is reserved for VIPs, they won't let just any old general in. Only someone on urgent and responsible state business.'

'I know.' The gentleman released a stream of smoke. 'Travelled in it myself once, on a secret inspection to Novorossia. But this individual is a mere boy. Perhaps he's someone's favourite son? One of our gilded youth?'

'Nothing of the kind, sir. They don't put favourite sons in number one, they're very strict about that. Except perhaps for one of the grand dukes. But I felt a bit curious about this one, so I took a quick glance at the train manager's passenger list.' The attendant lowered his voice still further.

'Well then?' the intrigued gentleman urged him impatiently.

Anticipating a generous tip, the conductor put his finger to his lips:

'From the Third Section. Specially important cases investigator.'

'I can understand the "specially". They wouldn't put anyone who was merely "important" in the first compartment.' The gentleman paused significantly. 'And what is he up to?'

'He locked himself in the compartment and hasn't been out since, sir. Twice I offered him tea, but he wasn't interested. Just sits there with his nose stuck in his papers, without even lifting his head. We were detained for twenty-five minutes leaving Petersburg, remember? Due to him, that was, sir. We were waiting for him to arrive.'

'Oho!' gasped the passenger. 'But that's quite unheard of!'

'It does happen, but only very rarely, sir.'

'And does the passenger list give his name?'

'Indeed no, sir. No name and no rank.'

The longer Erast Fandorin continued his study of the niggardly lines of the dispatches, tousling his hair as he did so, the higher he felt the mystical terror mounting towards his throat.

Just as he was about to set out for the station, Mizinov's adjutant had turned up at the state apartment where Fandorin had slept like a log for almost twenty-four hours and told him to wait – the first three telegrams had arrived from the embassies, they would be deciphered immediately and brought to him. The wait had lasted for almost an hour, and Erast Fandorin had been afraid he would miss the train, but the adjutant had reassured him on that score.

Fandorin was no sooner inside the immense compartment upholstered in green velvet, with a writing-desk, a soft divan and two walnut chairs with their legs bolted to the floor, than he opened the package and immersed himself in reading.

Three telegrams had arrived – from Washington, Paris and Constantinople. The heading on all of them was identical: 'Urgent. To His Excellency Lavrenty Arkadievich Mizinov in reply to your ref. No. 13476-8zh of 26th June 1876.' The reports were signed by the ambassadors themselves, but that was as far as the similarity went. The texts were as follows:

27th June (9th July) 1876. 12.15. Washington.

The person in whom you are interested is John Pratt Dodds, who on 9th June this year was elected vice-chairman of the Senate Budget Committee. A man very well known in America, a millionaire of the sort who are known here as 'self-made men'. Age 44. His early life, place of birth and background are unknown. He is assumed to have become rich during the California gold rush. He is regarded as an entrepreneur of genius. During the civil war between the North and the South he was President Lincoln's adviser on financial matters. It is believed by some that it was Dodds' diligence and not the valour of the federal generals that was responsible for the capitalist North's victory over the conservative South. In 1872 he was elected senator for the State of Pennsylvania. Well-informed sources tell us that Dodds is tipped to become secretary of the treasury.

9th July (27th) 1876. 16.45. Paris.

Thanks to the agent Coco, who is known to you, it has been possible to ascertain via the Ministry of War that on the 15th of June Rear-Admiral Jean Intrépide, who had recently been appointed to command the Siamese Squadron, was promoted to the rank of vice-admiral. He is one of the French fleet's most legendary personalities. Twenty years ago a French frigate off the coast of Tortuga came across a boat adrift in the open sea, carrying a boy who had obviously survived a shipwreck. As a result of the shock the boy had completely lost his memory and could not give his own name or even his nationality. Taken on as a cabin-boy and named after the frigate that found him, he has made a brilliant career. He has taken part in numerous expeditions and colonial wars. He especially distinguished himself in the Mexican War. Last year Jean Intrépide caused a genuine sensation in Paris when he married the eldest daughter of the Duc de Rohan. I will forward details of the service record of the individual in whom you are interested in the next report.

27th June 1876. Two o'clock in the afternoon. Constantinople.

Dear Lavrenty, your request quite flabbergasted me, the point being that this Anwar-Effendi, in whom you have expressed such pressing interest, has for some time now been the object of my own close scrutiny. According to information in my possession this individual, who is an intimate of Midhat-Pasha and Abdul-Hamid, is one of the central figures in a conspiracy that is presently coming to a head in the palace. We must soon expect the overthrow of the present sultan and the reign of Abdul-Hamid. Then Anwar-Effendi will most certainly become a figure of quite exceptional influence. He is highly intelligent, with a European education, and knows a countless number of Oriental and Western languages. Unfortunately we do not possess any detailed biographical information on this interesting gentleman. We do know that he is no more than 25 years old and was born in either Serbia or Bosnia. His origins are obscure and he has no relatives, which promises to be a great boon for Turkey if Anwar ever should become vizier. Just imagine it – a vizier without a horde of avaricious relatives! Such things are simply unheard of here. Anwar is by way of being Midhat-Pasha's *éminence grise*, an active member of the 'New Osman' party. Have I satisfied your curiosity? Now please satisfy mine. What do you want with my Anwar-Effendi? What do you know about him? Let me know immediately, it might prove to be important.

Erast Fandorin read the telegrams through once again and in the first one he underlined the words: 'His early life, place of birth and background are unknown'; in the second one the words: 'could not give his own name or even his nationality' and in the third the words: 'His origins are obscure and he has no relatives'. He was beginning to feel frightened. All three of them just seemed to have appeared out of nowhere! At some moment they had simply emerged out of the void and immediately set about clambering upwards with genuinely superhuman persistence. What were they, members of some secret sect? And what if they were not people at all, but aliens from another world, emissaries, say, from the planet Mars? Or worse than that, some kind of infernal demons? Fandorin squirmed as he recalled his nocturnal encounter with 'Amalia's ghost'. Bezhetskaya herself was yet another creature of unknown origin. And then there was that satanic invocation, 'Azazel'. Oh, there was definitely a sulphurous smell about this business . . .

There was a stealthy knock at the door. Erast Fandorin shuddered, reached rapidly behind his back for the secret holster and fingered the grooved handle of his 'Herstal'.

The conductor's obsequious face appeared in the crack of the door.

'Your Excellency, we're coming into a station. Perhaps you'd like to stretch your legs? There's a buffet there too.'

At the word 'Excellency' Erast Fandorin assumed a dignified air and cast a stealthy sidelong glance at himself in the mirror. Could he really be taken for a general? Well anyway, 'stretching his legs' sounded like a good idea, and it was easier to think as he walked. There was some vague idea swirling round in his head, but it kept eluding him, so far he couldn't quite get a grip on it, but it seemed to be encouraging him – keep digging, keep digging!

'I think I will. How long is our stop?'

'Twenty minutes. But you've no need to concern yourself about that, just take your time.' The conductor tittered. 'They won't leave without you.'

Erast Fandorin leapt down from the step on to a platform flooded with light by the lamps of the station. Here and there the lights were no longer burning in the windows of some compartments – evidently some of the passengers had already

retired for the night. Fandorin stretched sweetly, folded his
hands behind his back and prepared himself for a stroll that
would stimulate his mental faculties to more effective activity. However, at that very moment there emerged from the
same carriage a portly, moustachioed gentleman wearing a
top hat, who cast a glance of intense curiosity in the young
man's direction and proffered an arm to his youthful female
companion. At the sight of her charming, fresh face Erast
Fandorin froze on the spot, while the young lady beamed and
exclaimed in a clear, ringing voice:

'Papa it's him, that gentleman from the police! I told you
about him, remember? You know, the one who *interrogated*
Fräulein Pfühl and me!'

The word 'interrogated' was pronounced with quite evident pleasure, and the clear grey eyes gazed at Fandorin with
unconcealed interest. It must be admitted that the dizzying
pace of events during the preceding weeks had somewhat
dulled Erast Fandorin's memories of her whom, in his own
mind, he thought of exclusively as 'Lizanka' and sometimes,
in moments of particularly fanciful reverie, even as his
'tender angel'. However, at the sight of this lovely creature
the flame that had singed the heart of the poor collegiate
registrar instantly flared up with renewed heat and scorched
his lungs with sparks of fire.

'I'm not actually from the police,' Fandorin mumbled,
blushing. 'Fandorin, special assignments officer at the . . .'

'I know all about that, *je vous le dis tout cru*,'[1] the moustachioed gentleman said with a mysterious expression, and
the diamond in his necktie glinted. 'Affairs of state, no need
to go into details. *Entre nous soit dit*,[2] I've had some involve-
ment with that kind of business myself on more than
one occasion, so I understand everything perfectly.' He
raised his top hat. 'However, allow me to introduce myself.

---

[1] I tell you quite bluntly.
[2] Just between ourselves.

Full Privy Counsellor Alexander Apollodorovich Evert-Kolokoltsev, chairman of the Moscow Province Appellate Court. My daughter Liza.'

'But do call me "Lizzie", I don't like "Liza", it sounds like "geezer",' the young lady requested and then confessed naively, 'I've often thought about you. Emma liked you. And I remember that you are called Erast Petrovich. Erast is a lovely name.'

Fandorin felt as though he had fallen asleep and was having a wonderful dream. The most important thing was not to move a muscle, in case – God forbid! – he might wake up.

Chapter Fifteen

Erast Fandorin found that in Lizanka's company (somehow he could not really take to 'Lizzie') he felt equally content to speak or to remain silent.

The railway carriage swayed rhythmically across the points as the train, with an occasional low snarl of its whistle, hurtled at breakneck speed through the drowsy forests of the low Valdai Hills, wreathed in pre-dawn mist, and Lizanka and Erast Fandorin sat on the soft chairs in the first compartment and said nothing. For the most part they gazed out of the window, but they also glanced at each other from time to time, and if their glances happened by chance to cross they did not feel in the least bit shamefaced, but quite the opposite, it gave them a pleasant and happy feeling. Fandorin had begun deliberately trying to turn away from the window as smartly as possible, and every time that he succeeded in catching her glancing back at him, Lizanka would burst into quiet laughter.

There was also good reason for not speaking because they might wake the baron, who was dozing peacefully on the divan. Not so very long before Alexander Apollodorovich had been engaged in animated discussion of the situation in the Balkans with Fandorin and then abruptly, almost in mid-word, he had given a sudden snore and his head had slumped forward on to his chest, where it was now swaying comfortably in time to the rattling rhythm of the wheels of the carriage: da-dam, da-dam (this way and that, this way and that) da-dam, da-dam (this way and that, this way and that).

Lizanka laughed quietly at some thoughts of her own, and when Fandorin cast an inquiring glance at her, she explained:

'You know, you're so very clever. You explained to Papa all about Midhat-Pasha and Abdul-Hamid. And I'm so stupid, you can't even imagine.'

'You can't possibly be stupid,' Fandorin whispered with profound conviction.

'There's something I'd like to tell you, only I'm ashamed . . . But I'll tell you anyway. Somehow I have the feeling that you won't laugh at me. That is, you will laugh when you're here with me, but not without me, will you? Am I right?'

'Of course you are!' Erast Fandorin exclaimed loudly, but the baron twitched his eyebrows in his sleep, and the young man slipped back into a whisper. 'I shall never laugh at you.'

'Don't forget then, you promised. After that time you came to our house I imagined all sorts of things . . . And it was all so beautiful. Only very, very sad and always with a tragic ending. It's all because of Karamzin's *Poor Liza*. You remember, don't you, Liza and Erast? I imagined myself lying there in my coffin all pale and beautiful, with white roses all around me. Perhaps I drowned, or perhaps I died of consumption, and you are there sobbing and Papa and Mama are sobbing and Emma is there, blowing her nose. It's funny, isn't it?'

'Yes, it is,' Fandorin agreed.

'It's really such a miracle that we met like that at the station. We'd been staying with *ma tante* and we were supposed to have gone home yesterday, but Papa was detained on business in the ministry and we changed the tickets. That really is a miracle, isn't it?'

'There's nothing miraculous about it!' said Erast Fandorin in astonishment. 'It is the finger of fate.'

The sky outside the window looked strange – entirely

black, with a thin border of scarlet along the horizon. The official messages lying forgotten on the table were a dismal white.

*

The coachman drove Fandorin right across early-morning Moscow from the Nikolaevsky Station to Khamovniki. It was a bright and joyful day, and Lizanka's parting words were still ringing in Erast Fandorin's ears:

'You absolutely must come today! Do you promise?'

The timing fitted perfectly. Now he would go to the Astair-House, to see Her Ladyship. It would be best to go to the gendarmerie department later to have a word with the commanding officer, and – if he had managed to elicit anything important from Lady Astair – to send a telegram to General Mizinov. On the other hand, the remaining dispatches might have arrived from the embassies . . . Fandorin took a *papyrosa* out of his new silver cigarette-case and lit it rather clumsily. Should he not perhaps go to the gendarmerie first? But his horse was already trotting down Ostozhenka Street, and it would be stupid to turn back. So, first to Her Ladyship, then to the Department, then home to collect his things and move into a decent hotel, then change his clothes, buy some flowers and be at the Evert-Kolokoltsevs' house on Malaya Nikitskaya Street for six o'clock. Erast Fandorin smiled blissfully and broke into song: 'A mere Titular Counsellor he, and a General's daughter she . . .'

And now there was the familiar building with the wrought-iron gates and the manservant in the blue uniform beside the striped sentry box.

'Where can I find Lady Astair?' Fandorin cried, leaning down from his seat. 'In the Astair-House or in her rooms?'

'About this time Her Ladyship's usually in her rooms,' the gatekeeper replied with a jaunty salute, and the carriage rumbled on into the quiet side-street.

At the two-storey administration wing Fandorin ordered

the coachman to wait, and warned him that he might be waiting for some time.

The same self-important doorman whom Her Ladyship called 'Timofei' was idling about beside the door. However, unlike the previous occasion, he was not warming himself in the sunshine, but had moved into the shade, for the June sun beat down with a heat considerably greater than in March.

On this occasion Timofei also behaved quite differently, demonstrating a remarkable psychological talent – he doffed his peaked cap, bowed and asked in an obsequious voice how he should announce the visitor. Evidently something had changed in Erast Fandorin's appearance in the course of the previous month, and he no longer aroused in the door-keeping tribe an instinctive urge to seize hold of him and deny him admittance.

'No need to announce me. I'll go straight through.'

Timofei bent himself double and flung open the doors without a murmur, admitting the visitor into the damask-upholstered entrance hall, from where Erast Fandorin followed the bright sunlit corridor to the familiar white and gold door. It opened to greet him and a lanky individual wearing the same light-blue livery and white stockings as Timofei fixed the new arrival with an inquisitive eye.

'Fandorin, officer of the Third Section, on urgent business,' Erast Fandorin announced austerely. However, the lackey's equine features remained quite impassive and he was obliged to explain in English:

'State police, Inspector Fandorin, on urgent official business.'

Again not a single muscle trembled in the stony face, although the meaning of what was said had been understood – the footman inclined his head primly and disappeared behind the door, closing the two leaves tightly behind him.

Half a minute later they opened again. Standing in the doorway was Lady Astair herself. On seeing her old acquaintance she gave a happy smile:

'Oh, it's you, my dear boy. Andrew said it was some important gentleman from the secret police. Come in. How are you? Why do you look so tired?'

'I've come straight from the Petersburg train, My Lady,' Fandorin began to explain as he walked through into the study. 'Straight from the station to see you. The matter is very urgent indeed.'

'Oh yes,' the baroness said, nodding sadly, as she seated herself in an armchair and gestured for her guest to take a seat facing her. 'Of course, you wish to talk to me about dear Gerald Cunningham. It's all like some terrible dream, I can't understand it at all . . . Andrew, take the gentleman's hat . . . This is an old and trusted servant of mine, who has just arrived from England. My splendid Andrew, I missed him very badly. Leave us, Andrew, go my friend, you are not needed for the moment.'

The skeletal Andrew, who appeared anything but splendid to Erast Fandorin, bowed and withdrew, and Fandorin squirmed in the hard armchair, trying to make himself more comfortable – the conversation promised to be long and drawn out.

'My Lady, I am greatly saddened by what has happened. However, Mr Cunningham, your closest deputy of many years, has proved to be involved in an extremely serious criminal plot.'

'And now you will close down my Russian Astair-Houses?' Her Ladyship asked in a quiet voice. 'My God, what will become of the children . . . They have barely even begun to grow accustomed to a normal life. And there are so many talented individuals among them! I shall appeal to the emperor himself – perhaps I may be permitted to take my wards abroad.'

'Pray do not alarm yourself unnecessarily,' said Erast Fandorin in a gentle voice. 'Nothing will happen to your Astair-Houses. After all, that would simply be criminal. All I wish to do is to ask you some questions about Cunningham.'

'But of course! Anything at all. Poor Gerald . . . You know, he came from a very good family, the grandson of a baronet, but his parents were drowned on their way back from India and the boy was left an orphan at the age of eleven. In England we have very stringent laws of inheritance, everything goes to the eldest son – the title and the fortune – and the younger children often don't have a penny to their name. Gerald was the youngest son of a youngest son, without any means or any house, his relatives took no interest in him . . . I was just writing to send my condolences to his uncle, an absolutely worthless gentleman, who showed not the slightest concern for Gerald. But what can one do? We English place such importance on the formalities.' Lady Astair showed him a sheet of paper covered with large, old-fashioned handwriting with curlicues and intricate flourishes. 'In short, I took the child in. Gerald was discovered to have exceptional mathematical abilities and I thought he would become a professor, but a quick wit and ambition are not the best foundation for a scientific career. I soon noticed that the boy was respected by other children, that he enjoyed being in charge. He possessed an innate talent for leadership: uncommon will-power and discipline, the ability to discern unerringly the strong and weak sides of another person's character. He was elected head boy at the Manchester Astair-House. I had expected that Gerald would choose to enter the state service or take up politics – he would have made an excellent colonial official and in time, perhaps, even a governor-general. You can imagine my surprise when he expressed the desire to remain with me and make education his field.'

'But of course,' Fandorin said with a nod. 'In that way he was able to impose his influence on the immature minds of children and afterwards maintain contact with his ex-pupils . . .' Erast Fandorin stopped in mid-sentence, struck by a sudden realisation. God, how simple it all was! How amazing that he hadn't seen it before!

'Very soon Gerald became my irreplaceable lieutenant,' Her Ladyship continued, not noticing the change in Fandorin's expression. 'What a devoted, tireless worker! And a rare linguistic talent – without him I would have found it quite impossible to keep track of the work of our branches in so many countries. I know that his enemy was always vaulting ambition. It was a childhood psychological trauma, a desire to prove to his relatives that he would achieve everything without their help. I could sense it, I could sense the strange disparity – with all his ability and ambition he ought not to have been content with the humble role of a teacher, even one with a very decent salary.'

Erast Fandorin, however, was no longer listening. It was as though an electric lamp had been switched on in his head, illuminating everything that had previously been submerged in darkness. Everything fitted into place! Senator Dobbs appearing out of nowhere, the French admiral who had 'lost his memory', the Turkish effendi of unknown origin, and the deceased Brilling as well – yes, yes, him too! Aliens? Martians? Visitants from beyond the grave? Nothing of the sort! They were all ex-pupils of Astair-Houses, that was who they were! They were foundlings, only they had not been abandoned at the door of an orphanage, but quite the reverse, the orphanage had planted them in society. Each one of them had been given appropriate training, each one of them possessed an ingeniously identified and painstakingly nurtured talent! It was no accident that Jean Intrépide had been abandoned in the very path of a French frigate – evidently the youth was an exceptionally gifted sailor. For some reason, though, it had been necessary to conceal where the talented youth had come from. But then the reason was clear enough! If the world were to discover how many men making brilliant careers had been bred in Lady Astair's nursery, it would inevitably have been alerted. But in this way everything appeared to happen quite naturally. With a nudge in the right direction, the talent was certain to manifest itself. That was why every one of the cohort of 'orphans' had achieved such astounding success in his profession. That was why it was so important for them to report to Cunningham about their advancement in their careers – in that way they were validating their own worth, the correctness of the choice that had been made! And it was entirely natural that the only genuine loyalty any of these genii knew was to their own community – it was their only family, the family that had protected them against a cruel world, raised and developed the inimitable individual personality of each one of them. What a family it was – almost four thousand genii scattered throughout the world! Well done indeed to Cunningham and his 'talent for leadership'! But stop . . .

'My Lady, how old was Cunningham?' Fandorin asked with a frown.

'Thirty-three,' Lady Astair replied readily. 'He would have been thirty-four on the sixteenth of October. Gerald always held a party for the children on his birthday, and they did not give him presents – it was he who gave something to everyone. I think it consumed almost his entire salary . . .'

'No, it doesn't fit!' Fandorin cried out despairingly.

'What doesn't fit, my boy?' Her Ladyship asked in surprise.

'Intrépide was found at sea twenty years ago! Cunningham was only thirteen then. Dobbs got rich a quarter of a century ago, Cunningham was not even an orphan then! No, he's not the one!'

'What on earth are you trying to say?' the Englishwoman asked, blinking her clear blue eyes in bewilderment as she tried to fathom his thought.

Erast Fandorin stared back unblinkingly at her in silence, stunned by his hideous realisation.

'So it wasn't Cunningham . . .' he whispered. 'It was you all the time . . . You! You were there twenty years ago and twenty-five years ago, and forty! But of course, who else! And Cunningham really was no more than your right hand! Four thousand of your disciples, in essence your children. And for every one of them you were like a mother! It was you Morbid and Franz were talking about, not Amalia at all! You gave each of them a goal in life, you set each of them "on the path"! But it's appalling, appalling!' Erast Fandorin groaned as though he were in pain. 'From the very beginning you intended to use your pedagogical theory to establish a world-wide conspiracy.'

'No, not from the very beginning,' Lady Astair objected calmly. Some intangible but perfectly evident change had taken place in her. She no longer seemed to be a tranquil, agreeable old woman. A spark of intelligence, authority and indomitable strength had appeared in her eyes. 'At first I simply wanted to save mankind's poor, destitute children. I wanted to make them happy – as many of them as I could, whether it was a hundred or a thousand. But my efforts were a grain of sand in the desert. While I was saving one child the bloodthirsty Moloch of society was pulverising a thousand, a million young souls, in every one of which there burned the primordial spark of God. And I realised that my efforts were in vain. The sea cannot be emptied with a spoon.' Lady Astair's voice grew more forceful and her stooped shoulders grew straight. 'And I also realised that God had given me the strength to do more than save a handful of orphans. I could save mankind. Not in my own lifetime, perhaps, but twenty or thirty or fifty years after my death. It is my vocation, my mission. Every one of my children is a precious jewel, the crown of creation, a knight of the new humanity. Each of them will work incalculable good and change the world for the better with his life. They will write wise laws, unlock the secrets of nature, create masterpieces of art. And year by year there are more of them. In time they will transform this vile, unjust, criminal world!'

'What secrets of nature, what masterpieces of art?' Fandorin asked bitterly. 'You are interested in nothing but power. I've seen them – you have nothing but generals and future ministers out there.'

Her Ladyship smiled condescendingly:

'My friend, Cunningham was only in charge of my category "F", a very important category, but by no means the only one. "F" stands for Force, that is, everything related to the mechanisms of direct power: politics, the state apparatus, the armed forces, the police and so on. There is also a category "S" for Science, a category "A" for Art, and a category "B" for Business. And there are others as well. In forty years of work as an educator I have set sixteen thousand, eight hundred and ninety-three people on their way. Surely you can see how rapidly science, technology, art, legislation and industry have developed in recent decades? Surely you can see that since the middle of this nineteenth century of ours the world has become a kinder, wiser, more beautiful place? A genuine world revolution is taking place. And it is absolutely essential, otherwise the unjust order of society will produce a different, bloody revolution, which will set mankind back by several centuries. My children save the world every day. And just wait and see what will happen in the years to come. By the way, I recall you asking me why I do not take girls. On that occasion, I must confess, I lied to you. I do take girls. Only very few, but I take them. I have a special Astair-House in Switzerland where my dear daughters are educated. They are absolutely special material, perhaps even more precious than my sons. I believe you are acquainted with one of my foster-daughters.' Her Ladyship smiled slyly. 'For the moment, to be sure, she is behaving irrationally and has forgotten her duty. That happens with young women. But she will certainly return to the fold, I know my girls.'

From these words Fandorin realised that Hippolyte had not killed Amalia after all, but had evidently carried her off somewhere. However, the reminder of Bezhetskaya opened old wounds and weakened somewhat the impression (which must be admitted to be quite considerable) that the baroness's reasoning had made on the young man.

'A noble goal is a great thing, no doubt!' he exclaimed vehemently, 'but what about the means? For you killing a man means no more than swatting a mosquito.'

'That is untrue!' Her Ladyship objected heatedly. 'I genuinely regret every life that has been lost. But one cannot clean out the Augean stables without soiling one's hands. One man's life saves thousands, millions of other people.'

'And who did Kokorin save?' Erast Fandorin inquired sarcastically.

'I shall use the money of that worthless bon viveur to raise thousands of brilliant minds for Russia and the world. It cannot be helped, my boy, it was not I who arranged this cruel world so that there is a price to be paid for everything. It seems to me that in this case the price is quite reasonable.'

'Well, and what of Akhtyrtsev's death?'

'Firstly, he talked too much. Secondly, he plagued Amalia to excess. And thirdly – you yourself mentioned it to Ivan Brilling – the Baku oil. No one will be able to contest the will that Akhtyrtsev wrote, it remains valid.'

'And what of the risk of a police investigation?'

'A trifling matter,' said Her Ladyship with a shrug. 'I knew that my dear Ivan would arrange everything. Even as a child he was distinguished by a brilliant analytical mind and great organisational talent. What a tragedy that he is no longer with us! Brilling would have arranged everything quite perfectly if not for a certain extremely persistent young gentleman. We have all been very, very unlucky.'

'Wait a moment, My Lady,' said Erast Fandorin, finally realising the need for caution. 'Why are you being so frank with me? Surely you do not hope to win me over to your camp? If not for the blood that has been spilt, I would be wholeheartedly on your side, but your methods . . .'

Lady Astair interrupted him with a serene smile:

'No, my friend, I am not hoping to win you over with propaganda. Unfortunately we became acquainted too late – your mind, your character and system of moral values were already formed and now it is almost impossible to change them. There are three reasons why I am being so frank with you. Firstly, you are a very bright young man and I find you genuinely likeable. I do not wish you to believe I am a monster. Secondly, you committed a serious blunder by coming straight here from the station without informing your superiors. And thirdly, it was not by accident that I induced you to sit in that extremely uncomfortable armchair with such a strangely curved back.'

She made some elusive movement with her hand and two steel bands slid out of the high arm-rests, pinning Fandorin tightly against the armchair. Still not fully aware of what had happened, he tried to leap to his feet with a jerk, but he could not even really move, and the legs of the armchair seemed to be rooted to the floor.

Her Ladyship rang a bell and Andrew instantly entered the room, as though he had been eavesdropping outside the door.

'My splendid Andrew, please bring Professor Blank here as quickly as you can. Oh, and tell him to bring the chloroform. And tell Timofei to deal with the coachman.' She sighed sadly. 'There is nothing to be done about it . . .'

Andrew bowed without speaking and left the room. Silence hung heavy in the study. Erast Fandorin puffed and panted as he floundered in the steel trap, attempting to twist himself round in order to reach the life-saving 'Herstal' behind his back, but the confounded hoops had clamped him so tightly that he had to abandon the idea. Her Ladyship observed the young man's movements with a sympathetic eye, occasionally shaking her head.

Soon there was the sound of rapid steps in the corridor and two people entered the room: the genius of physics Professor Blank and the mute Andrew.

Casting a quick glance at the prisoner, the professor asked in English:

'Is this serious, My Lady?'

'Yes, it is rather,' she sighed. 'But rectifiable. Of course, it will cost us a little fuss and bother. I do not wish to resort to extreme measures unless it is absolutely necessary. I remembered, my boy, that you had been dreaming for a long time of experimenting on human material. It would appear that an opportunity has arisen.'

'But I am not yet entirely ready to work with a human brain,' said Blank uncertainly, scrutinising Fandorin, who was now calm. 'On the other hand, it would be a shame to squander such an opportunity . . .'

'In any case, he has to be put to sleep,' remarked the baroness. 'Did you bring the chloroform?'

'Yes, yes, just a moment.' The professor extracted a small bottle from a capacious pocket and splashed its contents generously on to a handkerchief. Erast Fandorin caught the sharp medicinal smell and was about to protest, but in two swift bounds Andrew was standing by the armchair and pressing his arm across the prisoner's throat with incredible strength.

'Goodbye, my poor boy,' Her Ladyship said, turning her face away.

Blank took a gold watch out of his waistcoat pocket, glanced at it over the top of his spectacles and pressed the odorous white rag firmly over Fandorin's face. And that was when Erast Fandorin was able to put the life-saving teachings of the incomparable Chandra Johnson to good use! The young man did not breathe in the treacherous fumes, which obviously contained no *prana*. The moment had come to practise the exercise of holding his breath.

'One minute will be more than adequate,' the scientist declared, pressing the handkerchief firmly over the mouth and nose of the doomed man.

'A-and-eight, a-and-nine, a-and-ten,' Erast Fandorin counted mentally, not forgetting to open and close his mouth spasmodically, roll his eyes and mimic convulsions. As a matter of fact, even if he had wished to breathe in, it would not have been easy, since Andrew was pressing down on his throat with a grip of iron.

Fandorin's count had exceeded eighty, his lungs were almost exhausted in their struggle with the desire to breathe in air, and still the moisture of that foul rag continued to chill his flaming face. Eighty-five, eighty-six, eighty-seven – he began counting with dishonest rapidity, attempting to fool that unbearably slow-moving second-hand with his last ounce of strength. Suddenly he realised that he should have stopped twitching and lost consciousness long ago, and he went limp and still, allowing his lower jaw to drop in order to make the trick look more convincing. On the count of ninety Blank removed his hand.

'Well, well,' he said, 'what remarkable resistance. Almost seventy-five seconds.'

The 'insensible' prisoner allowed his head to loll to one side and pretended to be breathing smoothly and deeply, although he desperately wanted to gulp in air with a mouth that was hungry for oxygen.

'Ready now, My Lady,' the professor announced. 'We can commence the experiment.'

Chapter Sixteen

IN WHICH A GREAT FUTURE IS PREDICTED FOR ELECTRICITY

'Take him to the laboratory,' said Her Ladyship. 'But you must hurry. In twenty minutes the break will begin. The children must not see this.'

There was a knock at the door.

'Timofei, is that you?' the baroness asked in accented Russian, before switching into English. 'Come in!'

Erast Fandorin did not dare to peep, not even through his eyelashes – if anyone were to notice he would be done for. He heard the doorkeeper's heavy footsteps and his voice speaking loudly, as though the people he was addressing were deaf:

'So everything's in the very best order, Your Excellency. All right' – he put in this last phrase in English. 'I offered the driver a drink of tea. Tea! You drink!' – again in English. 'He turned out to be a tough old devil all right. Keeps on drinking away, and still fresh as a daisy. Drink, drink – nossing! But then it was all right, he dozed off. And I drove his cab round the back of the house. It can stand there for a bit, I'll deal with it later, you don't need concern yourself about it, madam.'

Blank translated what he had said to the baroness.

'Fine,' she responded in English and then added in an undertone, 'Andrew, just make sure that he doesn't try to make a profit selling the horse and the carriage.'

Fandorin did not catch any reply – no doubt the taciturn Andrew had merely nodded.

'Get on with it, you reptiles, unfasten me,' thought Erast Fandorin, mentally urging his malefactors on. 'Your school-break's starting soon. I'll show you an experiment. Just as long as I don't forget about the safety catch.'

However, there was a serious disappointment in store for Fandorin – no one began to unfasten him. Someone breathed loudly right into his ear and he caught a whiff of onions (Timofei, the captive guessed with unerring perspicacity), then there was a low rasping sound, which was repeated a second time, then a third, and a fourth.

'That's it. I've unscrewed it,' the doorkeeper announced. 'Catch hold, Andriukha, and away we go.'

They lifted up Erast Fandorin together with the armchair and bore him away. Opening his eyes very slightly, he glimpsed the gallery and the Dutch windows illuminated by the sun. Everything was clear now, they were taking him to the main building, to the laboratory.

When his bearers stepped carefully into the recreation hall, trying to avoid making any noise, Fandorin thought seriously about whether he should suddenly come to and disrupt the educational process with blood-curdling screams. Let the little children see the kind of business their kind ladyship was involved in. But the sounds coming from the classrooms conveyed such a feeling of peace and comfort – the measured bass of the teacher's voice, a peal of boyish laughter, a phrase of music from a choir – that Fandorin did not have the heart to do it. Never mind, in any case it was still too early to show his hand, he thought in justification of his own spinelessness.

Then it was too late and the classroom hubbub had been left far behind. Erast Fandorin took a peep and saw that they were carrying him up some staircase. A door creaked and a key turned in a lock.

Even through his closed eyelids he saw the bright flash of the electric light. He surveyed his surroundings rapidly through a single squinting eye, managing to distinguish some porcelain utensils, wires and metal coils. He disliked the look of it all very much. In the distance there was the muffled ringing of a bell – evidently the lesson was over – and almost immediately he heard the clear sound of voices.

'I do hope everything will work out well,' sighed Lady Astair. 'I should regret it if the young man were to die.'

'I hope so too, My Lady,' the professor replied, clearly nervous, and began clanking some object made of iron. 'But alas, there is no such thing as science without sacrifices. A heavy price must be paid for every new step forward in knowledge. Fine feelings won't get you very far. But if this young man means so much to you, that bear of yours ought not to have poisoned the coachman, but simply slipped him a sleeping draught. Then I would have started with the coachman and left the young man for later. That would have improved his chances.'

'You are right, my friend. Absolutely right. That was an unforgivable mistake.' Her Ladyship's voice was filled with sincere regret. 'But do the best you can. Explain to me again, what exactly is it that you intend to do?'

Erast Fandorin pricked up his ears – this was a question that he also found extremely interesting.

'You are familiar with my general concept,' Blank proclaimed in a fervent voice, even ceasing his metallic clanking. 'It is my belief that taming the force of electricity is the key to the coming century. Yes, indeed, My Lady! There are still twenty-four years remaining until the twentieth century, but that is not so very long. In the new century the world will be transformed beyond all recognition, and this great transformation will be brought about precisely thanks to electricity. Electricity is not just a source of light, as the ignorant masses suppose. It is capable of working miracles, great and small. Imagine a horseless carriage that runs on an electric motor! Imagine a train without a steam engine – fast, clean, silent! And mighty cannon striking down the enemy with a controlled bolt of lightning! Or an omnibus with no horse required to pull it.'

'You have told me all of this many times before,' the baroness gently interrupted the enthusiast. 'Please explain to me the medical application of electricity.'

'Oh, that is the most interesting part,' said the professor, growing even more excited. 'That is the very sphere of electrical science to which I intend to devote my life. Macro-electricity – turbines, motors, powerful dynamos – these will change the outside world, but microelectricity will change man himself, correcting the imperfections in nature's design for *Homo sapiens*. It is electrophysiology and electrotherapy that will save mankind, not your clever know-alls who spend their time playing the great politician or, even more funny, daubing pictures.'

'You are mistaken, my boy. They are also performing very important and necessary work. But please continue.'

'I'll give you the means to make a man, any man, ideal, to rid him of his faults. All the defects that determine a person's behaviour are located here, in the sub-cortex of the brain.' A rigid finger tapped Erast Fandorin very painfully on the temple. 'To explain in simple terms, there are regions of the brain that control logic, pleasures, fear, cruelty, sexual feeling and so on and so forth. A man could be a harmonious personality if all of these regions functioned in balance, but that almost never happens. In one person the region responsible for the instinct of self-preservation is over-developed, and that person is a pathological coward. In another the zone of logic is insufficiently active, and that person is a complete and utter fool. The burden of my theory is that it is possible to use electrophoresis, that is, a specifically targeted and strictly dosed discharge of electrical current, to stimulate certain regions of the brain and suppress other, undersirable, regions.'

'That is very, interesting,' said the baroness. 'You know, my dear Gebhardt, I have never restricted you financially at all, but why are you so convinced that adjusting the psyche in this manner is possible in principle?'

'It is possible! Of that there is not the slightest doubt! Are you aware, My Lady, that in Incan burial sites skulls have been discovered with an identical opening just here?' The finger prodded twice again at Erast Fandorin's head. 'This is the location of the region that controls fear. The Incas knew that, and even with their primitive instruments they were able to gouge the cowardice out of boys of the warrior caste and render their soldiers fearless. And the mouse? Do you remember that?'

'Yes, your "fearless mouse" that flung itself at a cat made a great impression on me.'

'Ah, but that is merely the beginning. Imagine a society in which there are no criminals! When a vicious murderer, a maniac or a thief is arrested he is not executed or sentenced to hard labour – he is simply subjected to a small operation and the unfortunate man, freed forever of his morbid cruelty, excessive lust or inordinate greed, becomes a useful member of society! And just imagine if one of your boys, already so talented, were to undergo my electrophoresis, reinforcing his abilities still further!'

'I certainly will not give you any of my boys,' the baroness interrupted. 'An excess of talent leads to insanity. You had better experiment on criminals. And now tell me, what exactly is a "blank individual"?'

'It is a relatively simple operation. I think I am almost ready for it. It is possible to deliver a shock to the region where memory is accumulated so that a person's brain becomes a blank page, as though you had wiped it clean with an eraser. All of the intellectual abilities will be retained, but the acquired skills and knowledge will disappear. What you have is a person as blank as a new-born baby. Do you recall the experiment with the frog? After the operation it had forgotten how to hop, but its motor reflexes were intact. It had forgotten how to catch midges, but its swallowing reflex remained. Theoretically it would have been possible to teach it all of this again. Now let us take our patient here . . . What are you two doing standing there gawping? Take him and put him on the table. *Macht schnell!*[1]

This was the moment at last! Fandorin readied himself. But the base, dastardly Andrew gripped him so firmly by the shoulders that it was quite pointless even to attempt to reach for the revolver. Timofei clicked something and the steel hoops constricting the prisoner's chest fell away.

'One, two and up!' commanded Timofei, holding Erast Fandorin by the legs, and Andrew, maintaining his firm grip, lifted him with ease out of the chair.

They carried their guinea-pig over to the table and laid him out on his back, with Andrew still grasping him by the elbows and the doorman clutching his ankles. The bell could be heard ringing again – the break between classes was over.

'After I apply a synchronous electrical discharge to two regions of the brain, the patient will be completely purged of all previous experience of life and transformed, so to speak, into a little infant. He will have to be taught everything all over again – how to walk and to chew, how to use the toilet, and later how to read, write and so on. I expect that your teachers will find that interesting, especially as you already have some notion of the proclivities of this individual.'

'Yes, he has excellent reactions, he is courageous, with well-developed logical thinking and unique powers of intuition. I hope that is all capable of being restored.'

In different circumstances Erast Fandorin would have felt flattered by such a complimentary testimonial, but now it made him squirm in horror – he imagined himself lying in a pink cot with a dummy in his mouth, goo-gooing senselessly, with Lady Astair leaning over him and saying, 'Aren't we a naughty boy now, lying there all wet again!' No, death would be better than that!

'He's having convulsions, sir,' Andrew was the first to comment. 'I hope he won't come round.'

'Impossible,' retorted the professor. 'The anaesthetic will

---

[1] Quickly!

last for at least two hours. Slight convulsions are quite normal. There is only one danger, My Lady. I did not have sufficient time to calculate precisely the charge required. If I use more than necessary it will kill the patient or make him an idiot for life. If I do not use enough, the sub-cortex will retain vague residual images, which under the influence of external stimuli might one day fuse to form specific memories.'

The baroness was silent for a moment and then she said, with evident regret:

'We cannot take any risks. Make the charge on the strong side.'

There was a strange buzzing sound, followed by a crackling that made Fandorin's flesh creep.

'Andrew, cut away two circles of hair – here and here,' said Blank, touching the head of his subject. 'I need to attach the electrodes.'

'No, let Timofei do that,' Lady Astair declared firmly. 'I am leaving. I do not wish to see this – I shall not be able to sleep tonight if I do. Andrew, you will come with me. I shall write a few urgent telegrams and you will take them to the telegraph. We must take precautionary measures – after all, our friend here will soon be missed.'

'Yes, yes, My Lady, you will only be in my way here,' the professor replied absent-mindedly, absorbed in his preparations. 'I shall inform you immediately of the outcome.'

At long last the iron talons in which Erast Fandorin's elbows had been grasped released their grip.

No sooner had the footsteps beyond the door receded into silence than Fandorin opened his eyes, tore his legs free, flexed his knees and gave Timofei a kick in the chest that sent him flying into the corner. A moment later Erast Fandorin had already leapt down on to the floor and, still blinking in the light, pulled out his trusty 'Herstal' from under his coat-tails.

'Don't move or I'll kill you!' the resurrected victim hissed vengefully, and at that moment he really did want to shoot both of them – Timofei as he sat there stupidly batting his eyelids and the mad professor standing there frozen in amazement with two metal knitting needles in his hand. Thin wires led from the needles to some cunning apparatus with a number of small winking lamps. The laboratory was positively crammed full with all sorts of curious items, but now was clearly not the time to be studying them.

The doorkeeper made no attempt to get up off the floor and simply kept crossing himself with small, rapid movements, but Fandorin could see that the situation with Blank was less secure and the scientist was not scared in the least, merely infuriated at this unexpected obstacle, which could ruin his entire experiment. The thought ran through Fandorin's head: he's going to throw himself at me! And suddenly the desire to kill him shrivelled and melted away without trace.

'Don't do anything stupid! Stay where you are!' Fandorin shouted, his voice trembling slightly.

That very moment Blank roared: '*Mistkerl! Du hast alles verdorben!*'[1] – and made a dash at him, crashing into the edge of the table on the way.

Erast Fandorin pressed the trigger. Nothing happened. The safety catch! He clicked on the button. Then he pressed the trigger twice. Ba-bang! There was a double peal of thunder and the professor fell face-down, with his head at the very feet of the gunman.

Fearing an attack from behind, Fandorin swung round sharply, ready to fire again, but Timofei merely huddled back against the wall and began jabbering in a tearful voice:

'Don't kill me, Your Honour! Don't do it! In Christ's name! In God's name, Your Honour!'

'Get up, you scoundrel!' howled Erast Fandorin, half-deafened and crazed. 'That way! March!'

Prodding the doorkeeper in the back with the barrel of his gun, he drove him along the corridor and then down the

---

[1] Swine! You've ruined everything!

staircase. Timofei staggered along with short steps, gasping out loud every time the gun-barrel nudged against his spine.

They rushed quickly through the recreation hall, and Fandorin tried not to look at the teachers peering out from behind the open doors of the classrooms and the silent children in little blue uniforms peeping out from behind their backs.

'Police!' Erast Fandorin shouted into empty space. 'Teachers, keep the children in the classrooms! And stay there yourselves!'

Sweeping through the long gallery at the same half-walking, half-running pace, they came to the wing. When they reached the white and gold door Erast Fandorin shoved Timofei with all his might, and the doorkeeper rammed open the doors with his forehead, scarcely managing to stay on his feet. No one. The room was empty!

'Forward march! Open every door!' ordered Fandorin. 'And remember: one false move and I'll shoot you like a dog!'

The doorkeeper merely threw his arms up into the air and raced back into the corridor. In five minutes they examined all the rooms on the first floor. There was not a single soul, except in the kitchen, where the poor coachman, slumped heavily across the table with his dead face twisted to one side, was sleeping the sleep of eternity. Erast Fandorin cast a quick glance at the crumbs of sugar in his beard and the puddle of spilt tea, then ordered Timofei to move on.

On the second floor there were two bedrooms, a dressing-room and a library. The baroness and her servant were not there either. Where could they be? Had they heard the shots and hidden somewhere in the Astair-House? Or had they fled the scene altogether?

In his fury Erast Fandorin swung the hand holding the revolver through the air and suddenly a shot rang out. The bullet whined as it ricocheted off the wall and hit the window, printing a neat little star with radiating points on the glass. Damn, the safety catch was off, and the trigger was light, Fandorin remembered, and he shook his head to get rid of the ringing in his ears.

The shot produced a magical effect on Timofei. The doorkeeper sank to his knees and began whining:

'Your Hon . . . Your Worship . . . Don't take my life. The devil led me astray. I've got little children, and a sick wife! I'll show you! As sure as God's holy I will! They're down in the cellar, in the secret basement! I'll show you, but spare my soul!'

'In what basement?' Erast Fandorin asked menacingly, raising the pistol as though he really did intend to enact justice there and then.

'You follow me, follow me, Your Honour.'

The doorkeeper leapt to his feet and, glancing round at every moment, led Fandorin back to the first floor, into the baroness's study.

'I just happened to peep once, by chance . . . She wouldn't let me anywhere near it. She didn't trust me. Why should she – a Russian, Orthodox, none of their English blood in me.' Timofei crossed himself. 'Only that Andrew of hers was ever allowed in there, but not me, oh no!'

He darted round behind the desk, turned a handle on a cabinet, and the cabinet suddenly moved to one side, revealing a small copper door.

'Open it!' ordered Erast Fandorin.

Timofei crossed himself again three times and pushed the door. It opened without a sound, revealing a stairway that led down into darkness.

Prodding the doorkeeper in the back, Fandorin began cautiously descending the stairs. They ended in a blank wall, but there was a low corridor running off at a sharp angle to the right.

'Go on! Go on!' Erast Fandorin hissed at the reluctant Timofei.

They turned the corner into pitch-black darkness. I should have brought a candle, Fandorin thought, reaching into his pocket for matches with his left hand, but suddenly somewhere ahead of him there was a bright flash and a loud report. The doorkeeper gave a gasp and sank down on to the floor, but Erast Fandorin held out his 'Herstal' in front of him and pressed the trigger until the hammer began clicking against empty shell cases. A hollow silence fell. With trembling fingers Fandorin took out the matchbox and struck a match. Timofei was slumped against the wall in a formless, motionless heap. Taking a few steps forward, Erast Fandorin saw Andrew lying on his back on the ground. The trembling flame glimmered for a moment in the glassy eyes before it went out.

On finding oneself in the dark, the great Fouché teaches us, one should screw one's eyes tight shut and count to thirty to give the pupils time to contract, and then one's vision will be capable of discerning the most insignificant source of light. In order to be quite certain, Erast Fandorin counted to forty before opening his eyes, and indeed – there was a ray of light filtering through from somewhere. Extending ahead of him the hand clutching the now useless 'Herstal', he took a step forward, then another, then a third, and in front of him he saw a door standing slightly ajar, with a faint beam of light emerging from the gap. The baroness could only be in there. Fandorin stepped decisively towards the glowing beam and pushed the door hard.

His gaze fell on a small room with some kind of shelves covering the walls. In the middle of the room stood a desk on which a candle burning in a bronze candlestick illuminated the face of Lady Astair, tracing its lines in shadows.

'Come in, my boy,' she said calmly. 'I have been expecting you.'

Erast Fandorin stepped inside and the door suddenly slammed shut behind him. With a shudder he turned round and saw that the door had no hinge and no handle.

'Come a little closer,' Her Ladyship said in a quiet voice. 'I wish to take a closer look at your face, because it is the face of fate. You are a pebble that was lying on my road. The pebble over which I was fated to stumble.'

Stung by this comparison, Fandorin moved closer to the desk and noticed a smooth metal casket lying in front of the baroness.

'What's that?' he asked.

'We'll come to that shortly. What have you done with Gebhardt?'

'He's dead. It's his own fault – he shouldn't have argued with a bullet,' Fandorin replied rather coarsely, trying not to think about the fact that he had killed two people in a matter of minutes.

'That is a great loss for mankind. He was a strange man, obsessive, but a truly great scientist. So now there is one Azazel less.'

'What is Azazel?' Fandorin blurted out. 'And what has that demon got to do with your orphans?'

'Azazel is no demon, my boy. He is a great symbol of the saviour and enlightener of mankind. The Lord God created this world, created men and left them to their own devices. But men are so weak and so blind, they transformed God's world into hell. Mankind would have perished long ago if it were not for those outstanding individuals who have appeared among them from time to time. They are not demons and not gods, I call them *héros-civilisateurs*. Thanks to each of them mankind has taken a leap forward. Prometheus gave us fire. Moses gave us the concept of the law. Christ gave us a moral core. But the most precious of these heroes was the Judaic Azazel, who taught man a sense of his own dignity. It is said in *The Book of Enoch*: 'He was moved by love for man and revealed unto him secrets learned in the heavens.' He gave man a mirror, so that man could see behind himself – that is, so that he had a memory and could remember his past. Thanks to Azazel a man is able to practise arts and crafts and defend his home. Thanks to Azazel woman was transformed from a submissive bearer of children into an equal human being possessing the freedom to choose – whether to be ugly or beautiful, whether to be a mother or an Amazon, to live for the sake of her family or the whole of mankind. God merely dealt man his cards, but

Azazel teaches him how to play to win. Every one of my charges is an Azazel, although not all of them know it.'

'How do you mean, "not all of them"?' Fandorin interrupted.

'Only a few are initiated into the secret goal, only the most faithful and incorruptible,' Her Ladyship explained. 'It is they who undertake all the dirty work, so that the rest of my children might remain unsullied. "Azazel" is my advance guard, destined gradually, little by little, to lay hold of the wheel that steers the rudder of the world. Oh, how our planet will blossom when it is led by my Azazels! And it could have happened so soon – in a mere twenty years . . . The other alumni of the Astair-Houses, uninitiated into the secret of "Azazel", simply make their own way through life, bringing inestimable benefit to mankind. I merely follow their successes, rejoicing in their achievements, and I know that if the need should arise, not one of them will refuse to help their mother. Ah, what will become of them without me? What will become of the world? But no matter, "Azazel" lives on, he will carry my work to its conclusion.'

Erast Fandorin interjected indignantly:

'I've seen your Azazels, your "faithful and incorruptible" devotees! Morbid and Franz, Andrew and that other one with the eyes of a fish, who killed Akhtyrtsev! Are these your vanguard, My Lady? Are these the most worthy?'

'Not these alone. But these also. Do you not remember, my friend, I told you that not every one of my children is able to find his way in the modern world, because their gift has remained stranded in the distant past, or will only be required in the distant future? Well then, it is pupils such as these who make the most faithful and devoted executors. Some of my children are the brain, others are the hands. But the man who eliminated Akhtyrtsev is not one of my children. He is a temporary ally of ours.'

The baroness's fingers absent-mindedly caressed the polished surface of the casket, and as though by accident pressed in a small, round button.

'That is all, my dear young man. You and I have two minutes left. We shall depart this life together. Unfortunately, I cannot let you live. You would cause harm to my children.'

'What is that thing?' cried Erast Fandorin, seizing hold of the casket, which proved to be quite heavy. 'A bomb?'

'Yes,' said Lady Astair with a smile of commiseration. 'A clockwork mechanism. The invention of one of my talented boys. There are thirty-second boxes, two-hour boxes, even twelve-hour boxes. It is impossible to open the box and stop the mechanism. This bomb is set for one hundred and twenty seconds. I shall perish together with my archive. My life is over now, but what I have achieved is not so very little. My cause will be continued and people will yet remember me with a kind word.'

Erast Fandorin attempted to pick the button out with his nails, but it was useless. Then he rushed to the door and began feeling all over it with his fingers and hammering on it with his fists. The blood throbbed in his ears, counting out the pulse of time.

'Lizanka!' the doomed Fandorin groaned in his despair. 'My Lady! I do not wish to die! I am young! I am in love!'

Lady Astair gazed at him compassionately. Some kind of struggle was obviously taking place within her.

'Promise me that you will not make hunting down my children the goal of your life,' she said in a quiet voice, looking into Fandorin's eyes.

'I swear it!' he exclaimed, willing at that moment to promise anything.

After an agonising pause that lasted for an eternity, Her Ladyship gave a gentle, motherly smile.

'Very well, my boy. Have your life. But hurry, you have forty seconds.'

She reached under the desk and the copper door squeaked as it swung open into the room.

Casting a final glance at the figure of the grey-haired woman sitting motionless in the flickering candlelight,

Fandorin launched himself along the dark corridor in immense bounds. His momentum flung him hard against the wall, then he scrambled up the stairs on all fours, straightened up and crossed the study in two great leaps.

Ten seconds later the oak doors of the wing of the Astair-House were almost knocked off their hinges by a powerful impact and a young man with a face contorted by fear fell out and tumbled head over heels across the porch. He dashed along the quiet, shady street as far as the corner, where he stopped, panting heavily. He looked round and stood there motionless.

Seconds passed and nothing happened. The sun complacently gilded the crowns of the poplars, a ginger cat dozed on a bench, chickens clucked somewhere in a yard nearby.

Erast Fandorin clutched at his wildly pounding heart. She had deceived him! Tricked him like some little boy! And escaped through some rear entrance!

He broke into sobs of impotent rage, and as though in reply, the wing of the building responded with an identical sobbing. Its walls trembled, its roof swayed almost imperceptibly, and from somewhere under the ground he heard the hollow boom of the detonation.

The Final Chapter

IN WHICH OUR HERO
BIDS FAREWELL TO HIS YOUTH

Inquire of any inhabitant of Russia's first capital city concerning the best time to enter into lawful wedlock and naturally the reply one will receive is that a man who is thoroughly serious in his intentions and wishes to set his family life on a firm foundation from the very outset must certainly not marry at any other time than late September, for that is the month most ideally suited to embarking on a long and tranquil voyage across the waves of life's wide ocean. September in Moscow is sated and indolent, trimmed with gold brocade and ruddy-cheeked with the maple's crimson blush, like a merchant's wife from Zamoskvorechie decked out in her finest. If one marries on the final Sunday of the month the sky is certain to be a translucent azure and the sun will shine with a sedate delicacy, so that the groom will not perspire in his tight starched collar and close-bodied black tail-coat, nor will the bride freeze in that gauzy, ethereal, enchanting concoction for which no appropriate name even exists.

Choosing the church in which to celebrate the wedding is an entire science in itself. Thanks be to God, in golden-domed Moscow the choice is extensive indeed, but that merely increases the responsibility of the decision. The genuine old-time Muscovite knows it is good to get married on Sretenka Street, in the Church of the Assumption in Pechatniki, for then husband and wife will share a long life together and die on the same day. The church most auspicious for the generation of numerous offspring is St Nicholas of the Great Cross, which has extended across an entire city block in the Kitai-Gorod district. Those who prize quiet comfort and domesticity above all else should choose St Pimen the Great in Starye Vorotniki. If the groom is a military gentleman, who nonetheless does not wish to end his days on the battlefield, but close to the home hearth in the bosom of his family, then the wisest thing to do would be to take the marriage vows in the Church of St George on Vspolie Street. And of course, no loving mother would ever allow her daughter to marry on Varvarka Street, in the church of the holy martyr Varvara, which would doom the poor soul to a lifetime of torment and suffering.

However, individuals of high birth or rank do not really enjoy much freedom of choice, for their church must be both stately and spacious in order to accommodate a guest-list that represents the cream of Moscow society. And 'all of Moscow' had indeed gathered at the wedding ceremony that was drawing to its conclusion in the decorous and grandiose Zlatoustinskaya Church. The idle onlookers crowding round the entrance, where the long line of carriages was drawn up, kept pointing out the carriage of the governor-general, Prince Vladimir Andreevich Dolgoruky himself, a sure sign that the wedding celebration was definitely from the very top flight.

Admission to the church had been strictly by personal invitation, but even so the assembled guests numbered as many as two hundred. There were numerous glittering uniforms from the military and the state service, numerous ladies with naked shoulders, numerous tall coiffures, ribbons, decorations and diamonds. All of the chandeliers and candles were lit, the ceremony had been going on for a long time and the guests were tired. All the women, regardless of their age and marital status, were excited and emotional, but the men were clearly languishing as they exchanged remarks about other business in low voices – they had finished discussing the young couple ages ago. The whole of Moscow society knew the father of the bride, Full Privy Counsellor Alexander Apollodorovich von Evert-Kolokoltsev, and they had already seen the pretty Elizaveta Evert-Kolokoltseva at numerous balls, since she had come out the previous season, and so curiosity was focused for the main part on the groom, Erast Petrovich Fandorin. Not very much was known about him: a St Petersburg sort who made flying visits to Moscow on important business; a careerist with close connections to the inner sanctum of state power; not, as yet, of very high rank, but still very young and climbing the ladder very fast. There were not many people his age sporting the order of St Vladimir in their buttonholes. Privy Counsellor Evert-Kolokoltsev was clearly a prudent man with an eye to the future.

The women were more taken by the young couple's youth and beauty. The groom was very touchingly agitated, blushing and blanching by turns and stumbling over the words of his vow – in short, he was quite wonderful. And as for the bride, Lizanka Evert-Kolokoltseva, she seemed such a heavenly creature that it quite made one's heart flutter just to look at her. That frothy white dress, that weightless, floating veil and that wreath of Saxony roses – it was all absolutely perfect. When the bride and groom took a sip of red wine from the chalice and kissed each other, the bride was not overcome by embarrassment, on the contrary she smiled happily and whispered something to her groom that made him smile too.

This is what Lizanka whispered to Erast Fandorin:

'Poor Liza has decided not to drown herself and to get married instead.'

Fandorin had been suffering terribly all day long from the incessant attention and his state of total dependence on the people around him. A great number of old fellow-pupils from the gymnasium had turned up, as well as 'old friends' of his father (all of whom had vanished without trace during the final year of his life, only to resurface now). First Fandorin had been taken to a bachelor's breakfast at the Prague tavern on Arbat Street, where he had endured being nudged in the side, winked at and offered condolences on some mysterious misfortune. Then he had been taken back to the hotel, where the barber Pierre had arrived and tugged painfully on his hair as he curled it into a voluptuous quiff. He was not supposed to see Lizanka before the church, and that was also a torment to him. In the three days since the groom had arrived from St Petersburg, where he was now employed, he had hardly seen his bride at all – Liza had been busy all the time with important preparations for the wedding.

Then after the bachelor's breakfast Xavier Feofilaktovich Grushin, bright scarlet in his black tail-coat and white best-man's ribbon, had seated the groom in an open carriage and driven him to the church. As Erast Fandorin stood on the steps and waited for the bride, someone had shouted something to him from out of the crowd and one young lady threw a rose at him and scratched his cheek. Finally they brought Lizanka, who was almost completely invisible behind wave upon wave of transparent material. They stood side by side in front of the lectern, with the choir singing and the priest chanting, 'For great is God's mercy and love towards man' and then something else, they exchanged rings and stood on the carpet, and then Liza said that phrase about poor Liza, and Erast Fandorin suddenly relaxed, glanced around, saw the faces and the tall dome of the church, and everything felt good.

It had been good afterwards too, when everyone came up and congratulated them so warmly and sincerely. He had especially liked Governor-General Vladimir Andreevich Dolgoruky, plump and good-natured, with his round face and drooping moustaches. He said he had heard many complimentary things about Fandorin and wished him a happy marriage with all his heart.

Then they went out into the square and everyone there was shouting, but he could not see very much because the sun was shining so brightly.

He and Lizanka got into an open carriage, and suddenly he could smell flowers.

Lizanka removed her long white glove and squeezed Erast Fandorin's hand tightly in her own. He stealthily moved his face close to her veil and took a quick breath of the aroma of her hair, her perfume and her warm skin. At that very moment (they were driving past the Nikitskie Gates) Fandorin's glance happened to fall on the porch of the Church of the Ascension, and it was as though his heart were suddenly clutched by an icy hand.

Fandorin saw two boys about eight or nine years of age, wearing tattered blue uniforms. They were sitting there among the beggars, seeming lost and chanting plaintively in small, shrill voices. The little paupers twisted their necks in curiosity to watch as the glittering wedding procession drove by.

'What's wrong, my love?' Liza asked, frightened at the sudden pallor of her husband's face.

Fandorin did not answer.

A search of the secret basement in the wing of the Astair-House had failed to produce anything of interest. A bomb of unknown design had produced a powerful, compact explosion which caused hardly any damage to the building but entirely demolished the subterranean premises. Nothing remained of the archive, nor of Lady Astair herself – unless, that is, one counted a small scrap of silk material from a dress.

Deprived of its leader and source of finance, the international network of Astair-Houses had collapsed. In some countries the orphanages had been taken over by the state or by charitable societies, but for the most part the institutions had simply closed down. In Russia at least, both Astair-Houses had been closed on the orders of the Ministry of Public Education as hotbeds of godlessness and pernicious ideas. The teachers had all left and most of the children had simply wandered off.

From the list seized from Cunningham it had been possible to identify eighteen former wards of Astair-Houses, but that was of little use, since it was impossible to determine which of them were members of the organisation 'Azazel' and which were not. Nonetheless, five of them (including the Portuguese government minister) had retired, two had committed suicide and one (the Brazilian life-guardsman) had even been executed. An extensive intergovernmental investigation had identified numerous notable and highly respected individuals who were former pupils of Astair-Houses. Many of them made no effort to conceal the fact, actually priding themselves on the education they had received. Certainly, some of 'Lady Astair's children' had preferred to go into hiding in order to avoid the troublesome attentions of the police and secret services, but the majority remained in their positions, since there was no crime of which they could be accused. Henceforth, however, the path to the highest level of state service was barred to them, and when appointments were made to high positions it became customary once again, as in feudal times, to pay particular attention to an individual's origins and pedigree – God forbid that some 'foundling' (the style in which the competent circles referred to Lady Astair's wards) should ever worm his way up to the top! The general public, however, was not even aware that any purge had taken place, since a series of carefully co-ordinated precautions and safeguards was implemented by the governments concerned. For some time rumours circulated of a global conspiracy of either Masons or Jews, or else of both of them together, and Mr Disraeli's name was mentioned, but then it all seemed to die down, especially as the whole of Europe was agitated by the grave crisis that was brewing in the Balkans.

Fandorin had been obliged in the line of duty to participate in the investigation of the 'Azazel Affair', but had demonstrated so little diligence that General Mizinov thought it best to assign his capable young colleague to different work, to which Erast Fandorin applied himself with far greater energy. He felt that his conscience was not entirely clear in relation to the Azazel business and that he had played a somewhat ambiguous role. The oath sworn to the baroness (and broken against his own will) had substantially marred the happiness of the weeks preceding his wedding.

And now, on the very day of that wedding, what should happen but that Fandorin's gaze should fall upon the victims of his own 'self-sacrifice, valour and praiseworthy zeal' (as described in the imperial decree concerning his decoration).

Suddenly dejected, Fandorin hung his head morosely, and as soon as they arrived at her father's house on Malaya Nikitskaya Street, Lizanka acted decisively to take matters into her own hands: she withdrew with her gloomy husband into the cloakroom that was located beside the entrance hall and gave the strictest possible instructions that no one was to enter without permission – fortunately the servants had enough to do in dealing with the guests arriving at the house, who had to be kept occupied until the banquet. Heavenly odours wafted through from the kitchen, where the chefs specially hired from the Slaviansky Bazaar had been labouring indefatigably since the crack of dawn. Behind the firmly closed doors of the ballroom the orchestra was running through its final rehearsal of the Viennese waltzes, and in general everything was proceeding according to plan. All that remained to be done was to restore the spirits of the demoralised groom.

Reassured on having ascertained that the cause of this sudden melancholia was not some inopportune reminiscence of an absent rival, the bride set confidently to work. Erast Fandorin's only response to direct questions was to mumble incoherently and attempt to turn away from her, and Lizanka was obliged to change tactics. She stroked her husband's cheek, kissed him first on the forehead, then on the lips, and then on the eyes, and gradually he relented, thawed and became entirely manageable again. The newly-weds, however, were in no hurry to join their guests. The baron had already come out into the hall several times and approached the closed door, even cleared his throat tactfully, but he had not dared to knock.

Eventually he was obliged to do so.

'Erast!' Alexander Apollodorovich called (as of today he had begun to address his son-in-law in familiar fashion). 'Forgive me, my friend, but there is a special messenger here from St Petersburg to see you. On some urgent matter!'

The baron glanced round at the dashing young officer in the plumed helmet who was posed in absolute immobility beside the entrance. Under his arm the special messenger was holding a square parcel wrapped in government standard-issue grey paper, with sealing-wax eagles.

The bridegroom glanced out, red-faced, from behind the door.

'You wish to see me, Lieutenant?'

'Mr Fandorin? Erast Petrovich Fandorin?' the messenger inquired in a clear voice with a guards officer's lilt.

'Yes, I am he.'

'An urgent secret package from the Third Section. Where should I put it?'

'Why, in here if you like,' said Fandorin, making way for him. 'Excuse me, Baron.' (He was still unaccustomed to being on first-name terms with his father-in-law.)

'I understand. Business is business,' said his father-in-law, bowing his head and closing the door after the messenger, while he himself remained outside to make quite sure that no one would intrude.

The lieutenant placed the package on a chair and extracted a sheet of paper from behind the lapel of his uniform jacket.

'Please be so kind as to sign for receipt.'

'What is it?' Fandorin asked as he signed.

Lizanka stared curiously at the package, showing not the slightest inclination to leave her husband alone with the courier.

'I was not informed,' the officer replied with a shrug. 'It weighs about four pounds. I believe you are celebrating a happy event today? Could it perhaps be in that connection?

In any case, please accept my personal congratulations. There is a letter here which will probably make everything clear.'

He drew a small envelope without any address on it out of his cuff:

'Permission to leave?'

Erast Fandorin examined the seal on the envelope, then nodded.

The special messenger saluted, turned smartly on his heels and left the room.

The drawn shades made the room rather dark and Fandorin walked over to the window that looked directly out on to Malaya Nikitskaya Street, opening the envelope as he went.

Lizanka put her arms round her husband's shoulders and breathed in his ear.

'Well, what is it? Congratulations?' she asked impatiently and then, catching sight of the glossy piece of card with two golden rings, she exclaimed, 'Why, so it is! Oh, how lovely!'

That very second Fandorin's attention was caught by a rapid movement outside the window and he glanced up to see the courier behaving in a rather strange fashion. He went racing down the steps, launched himself at a run into a waiting cab and shouted to the coachman:

'Go! Nine! Eight! Seven!'

As the coachman swung his whip he glanced round for an instant. Just an ordinary coachman: a hat with a tall crown, a greying beard, nothing unusual about him but the colour of his eyes – extremely light, almost white.

'Stop!' Erast Fandorin shouted furiously, and without thinking what he was doing, he leapt over the window sill out into the street.

The coachman cracked his whip and his pair of blacks set off at a trot.

'Stop or I'll shoot!' Fandorin roared as he ran in pursuit, although he had nothing to shoot with – in honour of the wedding his trusty 'Herstal' had been left at the hotel.

'Erast! Where are you going?'

Fandorin glanced back as he raced along. Lizanka was

leaning out of the window with an expression of total bewilderment on her face. The next moment flames and smoke came bursting out of the window and Fandorin was hurled roughly to the ground.

For a while everything was quiet, dark and peaceful, then from the bright daylight that stung his eyes and the dull roaring in his ears he realised that he was alive. He could see the cobblestones of the roadway, but he could not understand why they were right there in front of his eyes. The sight of the grey stone was disgusting and he tried to turn away, but that only made things worse – he saw a pellet of horse dung lying beside something disagreeably white, with two small gold circles glittering on it. Erast Fandorin sat up with a jerk and read the line written in a large, old-fashioned hand, with curlicues and intricate flourishes:

'My Sweet Boy, This is a Truly Glorious Day!'

The meaning of the words failed to penetrate the fog in the concussed youth's mind, and in any case his attention was distracted by another object that was sparkling cheerfully where it lay in the very middle of the road.

Erast Fandorin did not realise what it was for a moment. The only thought that came to him was that the ground was definitely no place for *that*. Then he recognised it: a gold ring glittering on the third finger of a slim girl's arm severed at the elbow.

*

The foppishly dressed but terribly slovenly young man stumbled along Tverskoi Boulevard with rapid, erratic steps, paying no attention to anyone – expensive crumpled frock coat, dirty white tie, dusty white carnation in his buttonhole. The promenading public stepped aside to make way for this strange individual and gazed after him curiously. It was not at all a question of the dandy's deathly pallor – after all, there was no shortage of consumptives in Moscow – nor even that he was undoubtedly drunk as a lord (he was staggering uncertainly from side to side), there was nothing new in that. No, the attention of those he encountered, especially the ladies, was attracted by one particularly intriguing feature of his appearance: despite his obvious youth the bon viveur's temples were a stark white, as though they were thickly coated with hoar frost.

If you have enjoyed
The Winter Queen
don't miss

LEVIATHAN

Boris Akunin's next novel in the
Erast Fandorin series, available
from Weidenfeld & Nicolson

Price: £9.99
ISBN: 0 29764 552 8

An extract follows . . .

From Commissioner
Gauche's black file

Record of an examination of the scene of the crime carried out on the evening of 15 March 1878 in the mansion of Lord Littleby on the rue de Grenelle (7th arrondissement of the city of Paris) [A brief extract]

. . . For reasons unknown all the household staff were gathered in the pantry, which is located on the ground floor of the mansion to the left of the entrance hall (room 3 on diagram 1). The precise locations of the bodies are indicated on diagram 4, in which:

No. 1 is the body of the butler, Étienne Delarue, age 48 years

No. 2 is the body of the housekeeper, Laura Bernard, age 54 years

No. 3 is the body of the master's manservant, Marcel Prout, age 28 years

No. 4 is the body of the butler's son, Luc Delarue, age 11 years

No. 5 is the body of the maid, Arlette Foche, age 19 years

No. 6 is the body of the housekeeper's granddaughter, Anne-Marie Bernard, age 6 years

No. 7 is the position of the security guard Jean Lesage, age 42 years, who died in the St-Lazare hospital on the morning of 16 March without regaining consciousness

No. 8 is the body of the security guard Patrick Trois-Bras, age 29 years

No. 9 is the body of the porter, Jean Carpentier, age 40 years.

The bodies shown as Nos. 1–6 are in sitting positions around the large kitchen table. Nos. 1–3 are frozen with their heads lowered onto their crossed arms, No. 4 is resting his cheek on his hands, No. 5 is reclining against the back of the chair and No. 6 is in a kneeling position beside No. 2. The faces of Nos. 1–6 are calm, without any indication whatever of fear or suffering. On the other hand, Nos. 7–9, as the diagram shows, are lying at a distance from the table and No. 7 is holding a whistle in his hand. However, none of the neighbours heard the sound of a whistle yesterday evening. The faces of No. 8 and No. 9 are set in expressions of horror, or at the very least of extreme consternation (photographs will be provided tomorrow morning). There are no signs of a struggle. A rapid examination also failed to reveal any sign of injury to the bodies. The cause of death cannot be determined without a post-mortem. From the degree of rigor mortis the forensic medical specialist Maître Bernhem determined that death occurred at various times between ten o'clock in the evening (No. 6) and six o'clock in the morning, while No. 7, as stated above, died later in hospital. Anticipating the results of the medical examination, I venture to surmise that all of the victims were exposed to a potent and fast-acting poison inducing a narcotic effect, and the time at which their hearts stopped beating depended either on the dose of poison received or the physical strength of each of the victims.

The front door of the mansion was closed but not locked. However, the window of the conservatory (item 8 on diagram 1) bears clear indications of a forced entry: the glass is broken and on the narrow strip of loose cultivated soil below it there is the indistinct imprint of a man's shoe with a sole 26 centimetres in length, a pointed toe and a steel-shod heel (photographs will be provided). The felon probably gained entry to the house via the garden only after the servants had been poisoned and sank into slumber, otherwise they would certainly have heard the sound of breaking glass. It remains unclear, however, why, after the servants had been rendered harmless, the perpetrator found it necessary to enter the house through the garden, when he could quite easily have walked through into the house from the pantry. In any event, the perpetrator made his way from the conservatory up to the second floor, where Lord Littleby's personal apartments are located (see diagram 2). As the diagram shows, the left-hand section of the second floor consists of only two rooms: a hall, which houses a collection of Indian curios, and the master's bedroom, which communicates directly with the hall. Lord Littleby's body is indicated on diagram 2 as No. 10 (see also the outline drawing). His Lordship was dressed in a smoking jacket and woollen pantaloons and his right foot was heavily bandaged. An initial examination of the body indicates that death occurred as a result of an extraordinarily powerful blow to the parietal region of the skull with a heavy, oblong-shaped object. The blow was inflicted from the front. The carpet is spattered with blood and brain tissue to a distance of several metres from the body. Likewise spattered with blood is a broken glass display case which, according to its nameplate, previously contained a statuette of the Indian god Shiva (the inscription on the nameplate reads: 'Bangalore, 2nd half XVIII century, gold'). The missing sculpture was displayed against a background of painted Indian shawls, one of which is also missing.

From the report by Dr Bernhem on the results of pathological and anatomical examination of the bodies removed from the rue de Grenelle

. . . however, whereas the cause of Lord Littleby's death (body No. 10) is clear and the only aspect which may be regarded as unusual is the force of the blow, which shattered the cranium into seven fragments, in the case of Nos. 1–9 the picture was less obvious, requiring not only a post-mortem but in addition chemical analyses and laboratory investigation. The task was simplified to some extent by the fact that J. Lesage (No. 7) was still alive when he was initially examined and certain typical indications (pinhole pupils, suppressed breathing, cold clammy skin, rubefaction of the lips and the ear lobes) indicated a presumptive diagnosis of morphine poisoning. Unfortunately, during the initial examination at the scene of the crime we had proceeded on the apparently obvious assumption that the poison had been ingested orally, and therefore only the victims' oral cavities and glottises were subjected to detailed scrutiny. Since no pathological indications were discovered, the forensic examination was unable to provide any conclusive answers. It was only during examination in the morgue that each of the nine deceased was discovered to possess a barely visible injection puncture on the inner flexion of the left elbow. Although it lies outside my sphere of competence, I can venture with reasonable certainty the hypothesis that the injections were administered by a person with considerable experience in such procedures: 1) the injections were administered with great skill and precision, not one of the subjects bore any visible signs of haematoma; 2) since the normal interval before narcotic coma ensues is three minutes, all nine injections must have been administered within that period of time. Either there were several operatives involved (which is unlikely), or a single operative possessing truly remarkable skill – even if we are to assume that he had prepared a loaded syringe for each victim in advance. Indeed, it is hard to imagine that a person in full possession of his faculties would offer his arm for an injection if he had just witnessed someone else lose consciousness as a result of the procedure. Admittedly, my assistant Maître Jolie believes that all of these people could have been in a state of hypnotic trance, but in all my years in this line of work I have never encountered anything of the sort. Let me also draw the commissioner's attention to the fact that Nos. 7–9 were lying on the floor in poses clearly expressive of panic. I assume that these three were the last to receive the injection (or that they offered greater resistance to the narcotic) and that before they lost consciousness they realized that something suspicious was happening to their companions. Laboratory analysis has demonstrated that each of the victims received a dose of morphine approximately three times in excess of the lethal threshold. Judging from the condition of the body of the little girl (No. 6), who must have been the first to die, the injections were administered between nine and ten o'clock on the evening of 15 March.

TEN LIVES FOR A GOLDEN IDOL!

Nightmare crime in fashionable district

Today, 16 March, all of Paris is talking of nothing but the spine-chilling crime which has shattered the decorous tranquillity of the aristocratic rue de Grenelle. The Revue parisienne's correspondent was quick to arrive at the scene of the crime and is prepared to satisfy the legitimate curiosity of our readers.

And so, this morning as usual, shortly after seven o'clock, postman Jacques Le Chien rang the doorbell of the elegant two-storey mansion belonging to the well-known British collector Lord Littleby. M. Le Chien was surprised when the porter Carpentier, who always took in the post for his Lordship in person, failed to open up, and noticing that the entrance door was slightly ajar, he stepped into the hallway. A few moments later the 70-year-old veteran of the postal service ran back out onto the street, howling wildly. Upon being summoned to the house, the police discovered a scene from the kingdom of Hades – seven servants and two children (the 11-year-old son of the butler and the six-year-old granddaughter of the house-keeper) lay in the embrace of eternal slumber. The police ascended the stairs to the second floor and there they discovered the master of the house, Lord Littleby, lying in a pool of blood, murdered in the very repository which housed his celebrated collection of oriental rarities. The 55-year-old Englishman was well known in the highest social circles of our capital. Despite his reputation as an eccentric and unsociable individual, archaeological scholars and orientalists respected Lord Littleby as a genuine connoisseur of Indian history and culture. Repeated attempts by the directors of the Louvre to purchase items from the lord's diverse collection had been disdainfully rejected. The deceased prized especially highly a golden statuette of Shiva, the value of which is estimated by competent experts to be at least half a million francs. A deeply mistrustful man, Lord Littleby was very much afraid of thieves, and two armed guards were on duty in the repository by day and night.

It is not clear why the guards left their post and went down to the ground floor. Nor is it clear what mysterious power the malefactor was able to employ in order to subjugate all of the inhabitants of the house to his will without the slightest resistance (the police suspect that use was made of some quick-acting poison). It is clear, however, that he did not expect to find the master of the house himself at home, and his fiendish calculations were evidently thwarted. No doubt we should see in this the explanation for the bestial ferocity with which the venerable collector was slain. The murderer apparently fled the scene of the crime in panic, taking only the statuette and one of the painted shawls displayed in the same case. The shawl was evidently required to wrap the golden Shiva – otherwise the bright lustre of the sculpture might have attracted the attention of some late-night passer-by. Other valuables (of which the collection contains a goodly number) remained untouched. Your correspondent has ascertained that Lord Littleby was at home yesterday by chance, through a fatal confluence of circumstances. He had been due to depart that evening in order to take the waters, but a sudden attack of gout resulted in his trip being postponed – and condemned him to death.

The immense blasphemy and cynicism of the murders on the rue de Grenelle defy the imagination. What contempt for human life! What monstrous cruelty! And for what? For a golden idol which it is now impossible to sell! If melted down the Shiva will be transformed into an ordinary two kilogram ingot of gold. A mere 200 grams of yellow metal, such is the value placed by the criminal on each of the ten souls who have perished. Well may we exclaim after Cicero: *O tempora! O mores!*

There is, however, reason to believe that this supremely heinous crime will not go unpunished. That most experienced of detectives at the Paris préfecture, M. Gustave Gauche, to whom the investigation has been entrusted, has confidentially informed your correspondent that the police are in possession of a certain important piece of evidence. The commissioner is absolutely certain that retribution will be swift. When asked whether the crime was committed by a member of the professional fraternity of thieves, M. Gauche smiled slyly into his grey moustaches and enigmatically replied: 'Oh no, young man, the thread here leads into good society.' Your humble servant was unable to extract so much as another word from him.

J. du Roi

WHAT A CATCH!

The golden Shiva is found! Was the 'Crime of the Century' on the rue de Grenelle the work of a madman?

Yesterday, 17 March, between five o'clock and six o'clock in the afternoon, 13-year-old Pierre B. was fishing by the Pont des Invalides when his hook became snagged so firmly at the bottom of the river that he was obliged to wade into the cold water. ('I'm not so stupid as to just throw away a genuine English hook!' the young fisherman told our reporter.) Pierre's valour was richly rewarded: the hook had not caught on some common tree root but on a weighty object half buried in the silt. Once extracted from the water the object shone with an unearthly splendour, blinding the eyes of the astonished fisherman. Pierre's father, a retired sergeant and veteran of the Battle of Sedan, guessed that it must be the famous golden Shiva for which ten people had been killed only two days earlier, and he handed in the find at the préfecture.

What are we to make of this? For some reason a criminal who did not baulk at the cold-blooded and deliberate murder of so many people has chosen not to profit from the spoils of his monstrous initiative! Police investigators and public alike have been left guessing in the dark. The public appears inclined to believe that belated pangs of conscience must have led the murderer, aghast at the horror of his awful deed, to cast the golden idol into the river. Many go so far as to surmise that the miserable wretch also drowned himself somewhere close at hand. The police, however, are less romantically inclined and they discern clear indications of insanity in the inconsistency of the criminal's actions.

Shall we ever learn the true background to this nightmarish and unfathomable case?

A bevy of Parisian beauties

A series of 20 photocards forwarded cash on delivery for a price of 3 fr. 99 cent., including the cost of postage. A unique offer! Hurry – this is a limited edition!
Paris, rue Cuypel, 'Patoux et fils' printing house.

PART ONE
Port Said to Aden

Commissioner Gauche

At Port Said a new passenger had boarded the *Leviathan*, occupying stateroom No. 18, the last first-class cabin still vacant, and Gustave Gauche's humour had immediately improved. This newcomer looked highly promising: that self-assured and unhurried way of carrying himself, that inscrutable expression on the handsome face which at first glance appeared altogether young, until the subject removed his bowler hat, unexpectedly revealing hair greying at the temples. A curious specimen, the commissioner decided. It was clear straight away that he had character and what they call *a past*. All in all, definitely a potential client for papa Gauche.

The passenger walked up the gangway swinging his holdall while the porters sweated as they struggled under the weight of his ample baggage: expensive squeaky suitcases, high-class pigskin travelling bags, voluminous bundles of books and even a folding tricycle (one large wheel, two small ones and a bundle of gleaming metal tubes). Bringing up the rear came two poor devils lugging an imposing set of gymnastic weights.

Gauche's heart, the heart of an old sleuth (as the commissioner himself was fond of testifying), had thrilled to the lure of the hunt when this newcomer proved to have no golden badge – neither on the silk lapel of his dandified summer coat, nor on his jacket, nor on his watch chain. Warmer now, very warm, thought Gauche as he vigilantly scrutinized the fop from beneath his bushy brows and puffed on his favourite clay pipe. But of course, why had he, old dunderhead that he was, assumed that the murderer would definitely board the steamship at Southampton? The crime was committed on 15 March and today was already 1 April. It would have been perfectly easy to reach Port Said while the *Leviathan* was rounding the western contour of Europe. And there you had it, everything fitted: clearly the right kind of character for a client, plus a first-class ticket, plus the most important thing – no golden whale.

For some time now Gauche's dreams had been haunted by that accursed badge with the acronym for the steamship company of the Jasper–Artaud Partnership, and without exception his dreams had been uncommonly bad ones. Take the most recent case, for instance.

The commissioner was out boating with Mme Gauche in the Bois de Boulogne. The sun was shining high in the sky and the birds were twittering in the trees. Suddenly a gigantic golden face with inanely goggling eyes loomed up over the treetops, opened cavernous jaws that could have accommodated the Arc de Triomphe with ease, and began sucking in the pond. Gauche broke into a sweat and laid into the oars. Meanwhile it transpired that events were not taking place in the park at all, but in the middle of a boundless ocean. The oars buckled like straws, Mme Gauche was jabbing him painfully in the back with her umbrella, and an immense gleaming carcass blotted out the entire horizon. When it spouted a fountain that eclipsed half the sky, the commissioner woke up and began fumbling around on his bedside table with trembling fingers – where were his pipe and those matches?

Gauche had first laid eyes on the golden whale on the rue de Grenelle when he was examining Lord Littleby's mortal remains. The Englishman lay there with his open mouth frozen in a soundless scream – his false teeth had come halfway out and his forehead was crowned by a bloody soufflé. Gauche squatted down on his haunches: he thought he had spotted a glint of gold between the corpse's fingers. Taking a closer look, he chortled in delight. Here was a stroke of uncommonly good luck, the kind that only occurred in crime novels. The helpful corpse had literally handed the investigation an important clue – and not even on a plate, but on the palm of its hand. There you are, Gustave, take that. Now may you die of shame if you dare let the person who smashed my head open get away, you old blockhead!

The golden emblem (at first, of course, Gauche had not known that it was an emblem, he had thought it was a bracelet charm or a monogrammed hairpin) could only have belonged to the murderer. But naturally, just to be sure, the commissioner had shown the whale to the junior manservant (what a lucky lad he was – 15 March was his day off and that had saved his life!), but the manservant had never seen his Lordship with the trinket before.

After that the entire ponderous mechanism of the police system had whirred into action, flywheels twirling and pinions spinning, as the minister and the prefect threw their very finest forces into solving the 'Crime of the Century'. By the evening of the following day Gauche already knew that the three letters on the golden whale were not the initials of some high liver hopelessly mired in debt, but the insignia of a newly established Franco-British shipping consortium. The whale proved to be the emblem of the miracle-ship *Leviathan*, newly launched from the slipway at Bristol and currently being readied for its maiden voyage to India.

The newspapers had been trumpeting the praises of the gigantic steamship for more than a month. Now it transpired that on the eve of the *Leviathan*'s first sailing the London Mint had produced gold and silver commemorative badges: gold for the first-class passengers and senior officers of the ship, silver for second-class passengers and subalterns. Aboard this luxurious vessel, where the achievements of modern science were combined with an unprecedented degree of comfort, no provision at all was made for third class. The company guaranteed travellers a comprehensive service, making it unnecessary to take any servants along on the voyage. 'The shipping line's attentive valets and tactful maids are on hand to ensure that you feel entirely at home on the *Leviathan*,' promised the advertisement printed in newspapers right across Europe. Those fortunate individuals who had booked a cabin for the first cruise from Southampton to Calcutta received a gold or silver whale with their ticket, according to their class – and a ticket could be booked in any major European port from London to Constantinople.

Very well then, the emblem of the *Leviathan* was not as good as the initials of its owner, but this only complicated the problem slightly, the commissioner had reasoned. There was a strictly limited number of gold badges. All he had to do was to wait until 19 March (that was the day appointed for the triumphant first sailing), go to Southampton, board the steamer and look to see which of the first-class passengers had no golden whale. Or else (which was more likely), which of the passengers who had laid out the money to buy a ticket failed to turn up for boarding. He would be papa Gauche's client. Simple as potato soup.

Gauche thoroughly disliked travelling, but this time he couldn't resist. He badly wanted to solve the 'Crime of the Century' himself. Who could tell, they might just give him a division at long last. He only had three years left to retirement. A third-class pension was one thing, but a second-class pension was a different matter altogether. The difference was 1500 francs a year, and that kind of money didn't exactly grow on trees.

In any case, he had put himself forward. He thought he would just nip across to Southampton and then, at worst, sail as far as Le Havre (the first stop) where there would be gendarmes and reporters lined up on the quayside. A tall headline in the *Revue parisienne*: ' "Crime of the Century" solved: our police rise to the occasion.' Or better still: 'Old sleuth Gauche pulls it off!'

Ha! The first unpleasant surprise had been waiting for the commissioner at the shipping line office in Southampton, where he discovered that the infernally huge steamship had 100 first-class cabins and ten senior officers. The tickets had all been sold. All 132 of them. And a gold badge had been issued with each and every one. A total of 142 suspects, if you please! But then only one of them would have no badge, Gauche had reassured himself.

On the morning of 19 March the commissioner, wrapped up against the damp wind in a warm woolly muffler, had been standing close to the gangway beside the captain, Mr Josiah Cliff, and the first lieutenant, M. Charles Renier. They were greeting the passengers. The brass band played English and French marching tunes by turns, the crowd on the pier generated an excited hubbub and Gauche puffed away in a rising fury, biting down hard on his entirely blameless pipe. For alas, due to the cold weather all of the passengers were wearing raincoats, overcoats, greatcoats or capotes. Now just try figuring out who has a badge and who doesn't! That was unpleasant surprise number two.

Everyone who was due to board the steamship in Southampton had arrived, indicating that the criminal must have shown up for the sailing despite having lost the badge. Evidently he must think that policemen were total idiots. Or was he hoping to lose himself in such an immense crowd? Or perhaps he simply had no option?

In any case, one thing was clear: Gauche would have to go along as far as Le Havre. He had been allocated the cabin reserved for honoured guests of the shipping line.

Immediately after the ship had sailed a banquet was held in the first-class grand saloon, an event of which the commissioner had especially high hopes since the invitations bore the instruction: 'Admission on presentation of a gold badge or first-class ticket'. Why on earth would anyone bother to carry around a ticket, when it was so much simpler to pin on your little gold leviathan?

At the banquet Gauche let his imagination run wild as he mentally frisked everyone present. He was even obliged to stick his nose into some ladies' décolletés to check whether they had anything dangling in there on a gold chain, perhaps a whale, perhaps simply a pendant. He had to check, surely?

Everyone was drinking champagne, nibbling on various savoury delicacies from silver trays and dancing, but Gauche was hard at work, eliminating from his list those who had their badge in place. It was the men who caused him the greatest problems. Many of the swines had attached the whale to their watch chains or even stuck it in their waistcoat pockets, and the commissioner was obliged to inquire after the exact time on eleven occasions.

Surprise number three: all of the officers had their badges in place, but there were actually four passengers wearing no emblem, including two of the female sex! The blow that had cracked open Lord Littleby's skull like a nutshell was so powerful it could surely only have been struck by a man, and a man of exceptional strength at that. On the other hand, as a highly experienced specialist in criminal matters, the commissioner was well aware that in a fit of passion or hysterical excitement even the weakest of little ladies was capable of performing genuine miracles. He had no need to look far for examples. Why, only last year a milliner from Neuilly, a frail little chit of a thing, had taken her unfaithful lover, a well-nourished *rentier* twice as fat and half as tall again as herself and thrown him out of a fourth-floor window. So it would not do at all to eliminate women who happened to have no badge from the list of suspects. Although who had ever heard of a woman, especially from good society, mastering the knack of giving injections like that?

What with one thing and another, the investigation on board the *Leviathan* threatened to drag on, and so the commissioner had set about dealing with things in his customary thorough fashion. Captain Josiah Cliff was the only officer of the steamship who had been made privy to the secret investigation, and he had instructions from the management of the shipping company to afford the French guardian of the law every possible assistance. Gauche exploited this privilege quite unceremoniously by demanding that all the individuals of interest to him be assigned to the same saloon.

It should be explained at this point that out of considerations of privacy and comfort (after all, the ship's advertisement had boasted: 'On board you will discover the atmosphere of a fine old English country estate') those individuals travelling first class were not expected to take their meals in the vast dining hall together with the 600 bearers of democratic silver whales, but were assigned to their own comfortable 'saloons', each of which bore its own aristocratic title and in appearance resembled a high-society hotel, with crystal candelabra, fumed oak and mahogany, velvet-upholstered chairs, gleaming table silver, prim waiters and officious stewards. For his own purposes Commissioner Gauche had singled out the Windsor saloon. Located on the upper deck in the bow section, it had three walls of continuous windows affording a magnificent view, so that even when the day was overcast there was no need to switch on the lights. The velvet upholstery here was a fine shade of golden brown and the linen table napkins were adorned with the Windsor coat of arms.

Standing around the oval table with its legs bolted to the floor (a precaution against any likelihood of severe pitching and rolling) there were ten chairs, with their tall backs carved in designs incorporating a motley assortment of gothic knick-knacks. The commissioner liked the idea of everyone sitting around the same table and he had ordered the steward not to set out the name plates at random but with strategic intent: he had seated the four passengers without badges directly opposite himself so that he could keep a close eye on those particular pigeons. It had not proved possible to seat the captain himself at the head of the table, as Gauche had planned. Mr Josiah Cliff did not wish (as he himself had expressed it) 'to have any part in this charade', and had chosen to base himself in the York saloon where the new Viceroy of India was taking his meals with his wife and two generals of the Indian army. York was located in the prestigious stern, as far removed as possible from plague-stricken Windsor, where the head of the table was taken by first mate Charles Renier. The commissioner had taken an instant dislike to Renier, with that face bronzed by the sun and the wind, that honeyed way of speaking, that head of dark hair gleaming with brilliantine, that dyed moustache with its two spruce little curls. A buffoon, not a sailor.

In the course of the twelve days that had elapsed since they sailed, the commissioner had subjected his saloon-mates to close scrutiny, absorbed the rudiments of society manners (that is, he had learned not to smoke during a meal and not to mop up his gravy with a crust of bread), more or less mastered the complex geography of this floating city and grown accustomed to the ship's pitching, but he had still made no progress towards his goal.

The situation was now as follows:

Initially his list of suspects had been headed by Sir Reginald Milford-Stokes, an emaciated, ginger-haired gentleman with tousled sideburns. He looked about twenty-eight or thirty years old and behaved oddly, either gazing vaguely into the distance with those wide green eyes of his and not responding to questions, or suddenly becoming animated and prattling on about the island of Tahiti, coral reefs, emerald lagoons and huts with roofs made of palm leaves. Clearly some kind of mental case. Why else would a baronet, the scion of a wealthy family, go travelling to some God-forsaken Oceania at the other end of the world? What did he think he would find there? And note, too, that this blasted aristocrat had twice ignored a question about his missing badge. He stared straight through the commissioner, and when he did happen to glance at him he seemed to be scrutinizing some insignificant insect. A rotten snob. Back in Le Havre (where they had stood for four hours) Gauche had made a dash to the telegraph and sent off an inquiry about Milford-Stokes to Scotland Yard: who was he, did he have any record of violent behaviour, had he ever dabbled in the study of medicine? The reply that had arrived just before they sailed contained nothing of great interest, but it had explained away the strange mannerisms. Even so, he did not have a golden whale, which meant it was still too early for Gauche to remove the ginger gentleman from his list of potential clients.

The second suspect was M. Gintaro Aono, a 'Japanese noble-man' (or so it said in the register of passengers). He was a typical Oriental, short and skinny. He could be almost any age, with that thin moustache and those narrow, piercing eyes. He remained silent most of the time at table. When asked what he did, he mumbled in embarrassment: 'An officer of the Imperial Army.' When asked about his badge he became even more embarrassed, cast a glance of searing hatred at the commissioner, excused himself and left the room, without even finishing his soup. Decidedly suspicious! An absolute savage. He fanned himself in the saloon with a bright-coloured paper contraption, like some pederast from one of those dens of dubious delight behind the rue de Rivoli, and he strolled about the deck in his wooden slippers and cotton robe without any trousers at all. Of course, Gustave Gauche was all in favour of liberty, equality and fraternity, but a popinjay like that really ought not to have been allowed into first class.

And then there were the women.

Mme Renate Kleber. Young, barely twenty perhaps. The wife of an employee of a Swiss bank, travelling to join her husband in Calcutta. She could hardly be described as a beauty, with that pointy nose, but she was lively and talkative. She had informed him she was pregnant the very moment they were introduced. All her thoughts and feelings were governed by this single circumstance. A sweet and ingenuous woman, but absolutely insupportable. In twelve days she had succeeded in boring the commissioner to death by chattering about her precious health, embroidering nightcaps and other such nonsense. Nothing but a belly on legs, although she was not very far along yet and the belly was only just beginning to show. Gauche, naturally, had chosen his moment and asked where her emblem was. The Swiss lady had blinked her bright little eyes and complained that she was always losing things. Which seemed very likely to be true. For Renate Kleber the commissioner felt a mixture of irritation and protectiveness, but he did not take her seriously as a client.

When it came to the second lady, Miss Clarissa Stamp, the worldly-wise detective felt a far keener interest. There was something about her that seemed not quite right. She appeared to be a typical Englishwoman, nothing out of the ordinary. No longer young, with dull, colourless hair and rather sedate manners, but just occasionally those watery eyes would give a flash of devilment. He'd seen her type before. What was it the English said about still waters? There were a few other little details worthy of note. Mere trifles really, no one else would have paid any attention to that kind of thing, but nothing escaped Gauche, the sly old dog. Miss Stamp's dresses and her wardrobe in general were expensive and brand new, everything in the latest Parisian style. Her handbag was genuine tortoiseshell (he'd seen one like it in a shop window on the Champs-Elysées – three hundred and fifty francs), but the notebook she took out of it was old and made of cheap writing paper. On one occasion she had sat on the deck wearing a shawl (it was windy at the time), and it was exactly like one that Mme Gauche had, made of dog's hair. Warm, but not at all the thing for an English lady. And it was curious that absolutely all of Clarissa Stamp's new things were expensive but her old things were shoddy and of the very poorest quality. This was a clear discrepancy. One day just before five o'clock tea Gauche had asked her: 'Why is it, my dear lady, that you never put on your golden whale? Do you not like it? It seems to me a very stylish trinket.' And what was her response? She had blushed an even deeper colour than the 'Japanese nobleman' and said that she had worn it already but he simply hadn't noticed. It was a lie. Gauche would have noticed all right. The commissioner had a certain subtle ploy in mind, but he would have to choose exactly the right psychological moment. Then he would see how she would react, this Clarissa.

Since there were ten places at the table and he only had four passengers without their emblems, Gauche had decided to make up the numbers with other specimens who were also noteworthy in their own way, even though they had badges. It would widen his field of inquiry: the places were there in any case.

First of all he had demanded that the captain assign the ship's chief physician, M. Truffo, to Windsor. Josiah Cliff had muttered a little but eventually he had given way. The reason for Gauche's interest in the physician was clear enough – skilled in the art of giving injections, he was the only medic on board the *Leviathan* whose status entitled him to a golden whale. The doctor turned out to be a rather short, plump Italian with an olive complexion, a tall forehead and a bald patch with a few sparse strands of hair combed backwards across it. It was simply impossible to imagine this comical specimen in the role of a ruthless killer. In addition to the doctor, another place had to be allocated to his wife. Having married only two weeks previously, the physician had decided to combine duty and pleasure by making this voyage his honeymoon. The chair occupied by the new Mme Truffo was completely wasted. The dreary, unsmiling Englishwoman who had found favour with the shipboard Aesculapius appeared twice as old as her twenty years and inspired in Gauche a deadly ennui – as, indeed, did the majority of her female compatriots. He immediately dubbed her 'the sheep' for her white eyelashes and bleating voice. As it happened, she rarely opened her mouth, since she did not know French and for the most part conversations in the saloon were, thank God, conducted in that most noble of tongues. Mme Truffo had no badge of any kind, but that was only natural, since she was neither an officer nor a paying passenger.

The commissioner had also spotted in the register of passengers a certain specialist in Indian archaeology, Anthony F. Sweetchild by name, and decided that an Indologist might just come in handy. After all, the deceased Lord Littleby had also been something of the kind. Mr Sweetchild, a lanky beanpole with round-rimmed spectacles and a goatee, had himself struck up a conversation about India at the very first dinner. After the meal Gauche had taken the professor aside and cautiously steered the conversation round to the subject of Lord Littleby's collection. The Indian specialist had contemptuously dismissed his late lordship as a dilettante and his collection as a 'cabinet of curiosities' assembled without any scholarly framework. He claimed that the only item of genuine value in it was the golden Shiva and said it was a good thing the Shiva had turned up on its own, because everybody knew the French police were good for nothing but taking bribes. This grossly unjust remark set Gauche coughing furiously, but Sweetchild merely advised him to smoke less. The scholar went on to remark condescendingly that Littleby had, admittedly, acquired a fairly decent collection of decorative fabrics and shawls, which happened to include some extremely curious items, but that really had more to do with the native applied arts and crafts of India. The sixteenth-century sandalwood chest from Lahore with carvings on a theme from the *Mahabharata* was not too bad either – and then he had launched into a rigmarole that soon had the commissioner nodding off.

Gauche had selected his final saloon-mate by eye, as they say. Quite literally so. The commissioner had only recently finished reading a most diverting volume translated from the Italian. Cesare Lombroso, a professor of forensic medicine from the Italian city of Turin, had developed an entire theory of criminalistics according to which congenital criminals were not responsible for their antisocial behaviour. In accordance with Dr Darwin's theory of evolution, mankind passed through a series of distinct stages in its development, gradually approaching perfection. But a criminal was an evolutionary reject, a random throwback to a previous stage. It was therefore a very simple matter to identify the potential robber or murderer: he resembled the monkey from which we were all descended. The commissioner had pondered long and hard about what he had read. On the one hand, by no means every one of the motley crew of robbers and murderers with whom he had dealt in the course of thirty years of police work had resembled gorillas, some of them had been such sweet little angels that a single glance at them brought a tender tear to the eye. On the other hand, there had been plenty of anthropoid types too. And as a convinced anticlerical, old Gauche did not believe in Adam and Eve. Darwin's theory appeared rather more sound to him. And then he had come across a certain individual among the first-class passengers, a type who might have sat for a picture entitled 'The Typical Killer': low forehead, prominent ridges above little eyes, flat nose and crooked chin. And so the commissioner had requested that this Étienne Boileau, a tea trader, be assigned to the Windsor saloon. He had turned out to be an absolutely charming fellow – a ready wit, father of eleven children and confirmed philanthropist.

It had looked as though papa Gauche's voyage was unlikely to terminate even in Port Said, the next port of call after Le Havre. The investigation was dragging on. And, moreover, the keen intuition developed by the commissioner over the years was already hinting to him that he had drawn a blank and there was no serious candidate among the company he had assembled. He was beginning to glimpse the sickening prospect of cruising the entire confounded length of the route to Port Said and Aden and Bombay and Calcutta – and then hanging himself in Calcutta on the first palm tree. He couldn't go running back to Paris with his tail between his legs! His colleagues would make him a laughing stock, his bosses would start carping about the small matter of a first-class voyage at the treasury's expense. They might even kick him out on an early pension . . .

At Port Said, since the voyage was turning out to be a long one, with an aching heart Gauche bankrupted himself by buying some more shirts, stocked up on Egyptian tobacco and, for lack of anything else to fill his time, spent two francs on a cab ride along the famous waterfront. In fact, there was nothing exceptional about it. An enormous lighthouse, a couple of piers as long as your arm. The town itself produced a strange impression, neither Asia nor Europe. Take a look at the residence of the governor-general of the Suez Canal and it seemed like Europe. The streets in the centre were crowded with European faces, there were ladies strolling about with white parasols and wealthy gentlemen in panama hats and straw boaters plodding along, paunches to the fore. But once the carriage turned into the native quarter a fetid stench filled the air and everywhere there were flies, rotting refuse and grubby little Arab urchins pestering people for small change. Why did these rich idlers bother to go travelling? It was the same everywhere: some grew fat from gorging on delicacies while others had their bellies swollen by hunger.

Exhausted by these pessimistic observations and the heat, the commissioner had returned to the ship feeling dejected. But then he had a stroke of luck – a new client, and he looked like a promising one.